OVER THE EDGE

MARJA GRAHAM

To those who are scared to be seen,
but desperate to be known.

PLAYLIST

Just Like a Movie - Wallows

Homesick - Noah Kahan

All Falls Down - Lizzy McAlpine

mirrorball - Taylor Swift

My Funny Valentine - Frank Sinatra

Too Sweet - Hozier

Only Ones Who Know - Arctic Monkeys

Just like Heaven - The Cure

Let's Fall in Love for the Night - FINNEAS

Smoke Signals - Phoebe Bridgers

Tribulation - Stripped - Matt Maeson

He Could Be the One - Hannah Montana

Evangeline - Stephen Sanchez

Author's Note

Dear reader, thank you for picking up book 2 in the Fool's Gambit series. Garrett and Evelyn's story is a standalone, but there may be a few spoilers for book 1—On the Rocks. These characters and this book are so special to me. I learned so much from them and their resistance to letting themselves find the love that they deserve.

This story is a happy one, but also discusses sensitive topics. Your mental health matters, so please note that **Over the Edge** includes discussions and depictions of:

Financial exploitation

Alcohol use

Childhood neglect and an absent parent

Mentions of depression and anxiety

Mentions of cheating – not involving a main character

A character being admitted to a hospital

Sexually explicit content

1

Evelyn

I hadn't expected to end my night playing therapist to a werewolf in a jazz bar bathroom, but life hasn't been exactly going my way recently. And I'm not quite sure she's a werewolf. She could be a vampire. It's not like it matters, because whatever paranormal creature Elodie plays is about as realistic as the fact the show's producers are passing her off as fourteen years old. But isn't that the time-honored tradition? Hot people in their mid-to-late twenties playing freshman in high school is about as classic as the lie I've been repeating all night.

"No. I'm totally fine with being here," I comfort her.

I like parties, just not this party. But I couldn't exactly back out when Avery, my oldest friend and confidant, is about to leave for eight months to rehearse for, then co-headline a North American tour. I don't exactly want to celebrate her leaving, even if I should be excited for her.

"I'm sorry, I really didn't mean to bring down the mood. It's just so..." Her defined biceps shift as she leans back against the edge of the sticky bathroom sink. Werewolf, definitely werewolf. I think it's the skintight red leather dress that threw me off for a second. But her brown skin has been emphasized by a spray tan that gives her an extra glow no undead entity would have.

I offer her a soft smile. "Overwhelming?"

"Yeah. I mean, it's supposed to be the best night ever." She sags further.

Tonight's party is good, but that's not hard when you have live music and an open bar. Still, tomorrow there will be another party, documented for outsiders to experience through glimpses on social media, declared to be "the best night ever."

"And we're having so much fun we've run to hide in the bathroom," I say, cheerily. I can practically see her *Holy shit, I'm in New York!* dreams lose a bit of their shine.

"Am I bad at this?"

"Where are you from?"

"Nebraska," she says. "Is it that obvious?" Yes. More that she's new to the people and places like this, not that there's any Midwesternness about her that gives it away.

"Give yourself some time to get used to it, and you'll be just fine."

"Is that what happened to you?"

"Yes," I say, because that's far more relatable than the truth. It's not like being the younger sister to an internationally beloved member of the boy band Fool's Gambit is a typical bonding experience. Elodie seems nice enough, and if I can be a comforting stranger in a bathroom in some post-midnight hour, I'll gladly be that for her.

I grew up around this; by the time I was fourteen, my brother's face was on posters in my classmates' bedrooms. Everyone loved Fool's Gambit, treating whoever your favorite member as a crucial personality trait. The lead singer, and my long-term personal nemesis, Wesley, was the charmer, for those who wanted a lighthearted clown. My brother, Drew, was the drummer for the ones who wanted a broody, shy type. Jared is a sweetheart and was the rhythm guitarist with a heart of gold who's turned into a great dad. Then there's Garrett, the bassist who is currently on my shit list after backing out of helping me move to Manhattan a few months ago.

It was weird growing up like that, sure, but it was something that's become normal over the last fifteen years. Eventually, I was old enough to go to the parties, and by then I was desensitized to it. It was never new and exciting like it is for Elodie now. And because I'm friends with America's indie-pop sweetheart, Avery Sloane, the award shows and after parties never stopped, even when Drew's music career came to a crashing halt.

A desperate knock rattles the bathroom door, and I turn to Elodie. "Ready to face the music?"

"As I'll ever be," she says, putting on a brave face and rolling back her shoulders.

Music blasts as we push through the door, the bass so unrestrained I feel it in my skull. Blue and pink neon blankets the room, and the well-dressed attendees are scattered around the stage. Before the door has a chance to fully close, a girl in a velvet pantsuit rushes to grab it and locks herself in the bathroom. Elodie and I exchange a few more words before someone, maybe her co-star, whisks her away. It's for the best because Avery finds me soon after.

With fiery red hair and a mosaic of dark tattoos contrasting against her pale skin visible from the slit of her black dress, she's hard to miss. In heels, her height rivals even the tallest attendees of her party. As always, she's unapologetic about the space she takes up. That's how she's always been with her appearance, words, and music. She doesn't have time to care if it bothers anyone. It's a trait I used to wish would rub off on me, but after knowing her for fourteen years, I've started to give up hope.

I'm loud in my own right, but it's more that I word vomit in the hopes something I say is worth listening to. I like people and want them to like me right back, but sometimes I struggle with the whole having a filter thing. I dance like everyone's watching on purpose, so they'll be comfortable enough to dance with me. But in a room like this? Most people here barely spare me a passing glance.

If you were to rank people in the room by their status, at face value, I would occupy one of the lowest rungs. That's pretty much irrelevant because I met Avery when she was opening for Fool's Gambit and the both of us were mere mortals in comparison to the sensation my brother was a part of. There's a sort of kinship that can only come from being the only two young girls on a music tour. Years later, she keeps me along for the ride.

The cover band on stage transitions into a new song just as Avery reaches me. My brows arch into a *you can't be serious* look.

"This wasn't on the approved setlist. They must have gone rogue," she explains with a shrug. "It's not my fault that Lyla West has been hanging out in the Hot 100 for so long."

I don't hate the song. I mean, I liked it enough to write and record it. There's the simple fact that it's always a bit jarring to hear my own lyrics in someone else's voice, especially when they don't know Lyla West is in the room with them.

"I don't mind," I insist.

"It's my party. I can tell them to stop."

"Don't. People are dancing," I tell her, and she follows my gaze to the dance floor in front of the low stage. Bodies gyrating. Wide smiles. Drinks held high and spilling over onto sweat-drenched skin. Something like pride swells in my chest knowing I contributed to the collective euphoria.

"Just like they will when you finally release the next one. Any progress?" she asks in a voice loud enough to cut through the music, but low enough no one else can eavesdrop.

The feeling in my chest curdles, warping into the low-grade anxiety that has been my constant companion these last few months. "No."

"It'll come to you. It always does," she says with a confidence I wish I had.

"You're right," I say, not wanting to admit this album doesn't feel the same as my last three. I moved to Manhattan seven months ago to dedicate myself to working on it and ever since then I've barely managed to write more than a chorus before scrapping it. My manager, Vincent, is patient and has been so great with how I've wanted to manage my career, but I can tell he's getting anxious about my rapidly approaching deadline. "Having a good time tonight?"

"Enough. This is my funeral, and I intend to regret being alive in the morning." she says.

"Interesting sentiment from the hostess."

"Like you would want to take my place. I wore black for a reason."

"Different reason than every other day?"

"This particular shade is for Wesley," she says. Her voice is heavy with the years' long resentment she's carried for her ex-best friend turned co-headliner. I don't blame her; Wesley Hart's ego is reason enough to hate him, even if it weren't for Avery or the fact that he slept with my brother's girlfriends on multiple occasions. I like people, but Wesley? I make a special exception for him.

"Good to know it was made custom for the occasion," I play along.

Avery's face morphs into a plastic expression and I turn to find a man dressed in an overpriced white T-shirt and slacks coming our way. I offer to get drinks and leave them to talk. At the bar I grab our usual. Filthy martini for Avery and Aperol Spritz for me. The olives in the martini swish along the inside of the glass as I dodge elbows and party goers who have lost their spatial awareness. When I get back two more people have joined the conversation. Avery flashes me a *thank God, I need alcohol to get through this conversation* look as I hand over her glass. I don't have a chance to shoulder my way into the circle because my phone lights up in my purse. My brows pinch as I check the incoming call.

"Sorry, I should really get this," I yell in Avery's direction then falter. I blink, startled as I reexamine the caller ID.

There's not exactly a quiet corner in the bar, but I manage to put some distance between me and the loudest party goers before picking up.

"Hello?"

The silver beading of my dress digs into my arms as I hug myself to fight the chill of the hospital room. Even if I wasn't having the time of my life at Avery's party, I'd prefer it to the stark, unlit hospital room. Particularly because the man lying unconscious in the bed hooked up to an IV and heart monitor is the one who's been avoiding me since I moved from Nashville to Manhattan.

If he were awake, I would ask him about it. But I guess the whole reason I'm here is because he's out cold.

I'm halfway through what must be my hundredth time cycling between Instagram and my messages when there's a metallic clink. I look up to find a bleary-eyed Garrett examining the IV in his arm, yanking it toward him as he squints, which makes the IV stand bump the edge of his hospital bed.

Garrett has these classic features that would make him a believable lead in period dramas. A sweep of blond hair that's usually diligently styled but is currently disheveled, sticking up at odd angles, yet manages to look roguishly intentional. Sharp cheekbones and a long, narrow nose with a flat tip, like whatever master sculptor was diligently chiseling him accidentally chipped off the end. Maybe I'd be lured in by his looks, that is if I didn't know him.

"Good morning, or maybe night? I'm not sure since it's three a.m. and I'm supposed to be at home in bed." I uncross my legs and stand up from the chair shoved in the corner.

"Eve?" His voice cracks on the nickname. He's the only one who shortens my name that way, like he's making some point by doing it. Like I'm still his bandmate's little sister who hovered around with childish hopes of being included.

"Did you think you put someone else down to be called in a case like this? What a weird typo to make, but I guess that would make more sense than choosing me. You know, since you haven't talked to me in months," I say through a forced smile. I won't let him get to me. He does, usually, but I know I get to him, too. I get a certain pleasure in cracking his stony exterior.

I've known him for nineteen years, back when he wasn't a household name, and he was just one of the boys practicing music in my parents' garage every afternoon after school. Well, every afternoon until the world became obsessed with Fool's Gambit. No one could get enough of them. Even after the band broke up ten years ago, people have kept the boys tucked in the part of their hearts designed to store nostalgia.

But to me, they were just the guys in the garage. People who weren't mine, but a part of my life, nonetheless. Always have been, no matter how many sold out stadiums they had with tens of thousands of fans screaming their names.

We've grown up, grown complicated. My brother barely plays anymore. Wes has his solo career, but still makes sure his ego is everyone's problem. Jared has a family. And Garrett went and got his law degree.

"Nice dress." He nods. Somehow, he manages to look in control of the situation, like the hospital is exactly where he wanted to end up tonight.

"Thanks, I thought I'd dress up for the occasion. It's not like I was at a party or anything," I say.

"You didn't have to go through all that effort," he says dryly.

"It's not like you gave me much of a choice. You see, when a hospital calls asking you to come in for an emergency, it's kind of a dick move to not show up. Kinda like if you tell someone you're going to help them move but then stop talking to them."

Fine. I'm bitter and it's three in the morning. I'm supposed to be buried in my overpriced comforter right now, excuse me for being a bit annoyed.

"You can leave now that you've upheld social norms." He cocks his head toward the door, effectively dismissing me.

"I don't think you're in any position to make that call. I'm going to go get someone who can provide medical advice and then they can tell me whether or not I should leave you."

There's probably a button he could push, but I don't like fighting, I don't like blowing up, and this is a good enough excuse to walk away before I say something I'll regret. It's always hard with Garrett, though. There's this urge to push and get some reaction out of him.

I find a nurse then wait in the hall for the verdict. I'm not particularly fond of hospitals, though I doubt many people are. A hospital was where my family started to fray. Drew collapsed on stage during Fool's Gambit's last performance. It's weird seeing someone who you've always looked up to, someone strong and full of life, look so distant and small.

He was fine, but also not fine. Concussed. But that didn't do any lasting damage. After that day he stopped playing music. Stopped talking to our parents. Barely talked to me until our parents were getting on my case for the smallest things. He said it over and over again.

"I'm fine."

Depression and anxiety are a bitch, but we only started talking about that recently. He's doing better now that he's going to therapy and taking medication. He's happier than ever, living with his girlfriend Lacey and running his bar in Atlanta.

Still, I'm not the biggest fan of hospitals.

I collect his belongings and I'm given a bundle of wrinkled clothes, slightly bent glasses, wallet, watch, and keys. The doctor is leaving just as I get back and she holds the door open for me as I enter the room.

"I thought you might want to walk out of here in something that covers your ass," I say, then drop his belongings on the bed. It's a nice ass. I've looked a few times. You know, to see what all the fuss is about. The world won't suffer if he showed it off a bit.

"Thanks."

I leave the room again and a few minutes later he steps out in a rumpled designer suit. His glasses sit at an odd angle on his nose.

I fold my arms over my chest, still determined to stand my ground. "Care to explain why I'm here?"

"Wes isn't reliable," he says flatly.

"So you just skipped over any other viable options. Got it."

"I knew you'd show up," he explains simply. It's not like I can refute that, since I'm already here. I would show up for anyone, though. He's not special.

"How convenient for you. Because from what I remember, you didn't show up for me seven months ago."

"I sent movers."

"I remember," I snap, my voice rising. "It was so fun to open my door at eight in the morning expecting you and finding three huge strangers instead. Makes a girl feel really safe in a new city."

Up until now, I've lived in Nashville or its surrounding suburbs my entire life. I was a bit anxious about the process until Garrett agreed to help. It wasn't like I expected Garrett to become my best friend. But it hurt when he didn't show up and explained it away with an excuse about work. It made me feel small, the same way I do now. I'm just a convenient person to have around, not someone he cares about. Got it.

"I guess I should have told you they were coming." He shrugs, his voice bordering on disinterested, but something flickers across his face.

"You guess?"

"Um, are you ready for the discharge paperwork?" a nurse asks hesitantly, her eyes flicking between us. She's not the only one looking at us. When I glance around the room a few other staff members start to hurry along.

"Thank you." He takes the pen and clipboard then shoots me a sharp glance. "I'm ready for this to be over with."

Likewise.

2

Garrett

"It's a system error," I say, impatiently eying the guard at the front desk. "It was working yesterday and now…" I tap my credential badge to get through the gate the same way I have for the last seven years I've worked at Holt and Walker. The light blinks red and the security system emits a low, angry beep for the third time this morning. "This keeps happening."

I just want to get to work and move on with my day. I'm fucking tired after only getting a few hours of sleep, but that doesn't change the fact that the copyright case I was working on yesterday before my unfortunate incident is still waiting for me in my office. Taking time off would likely only trigger another one of the stress-induced migraines that caused me to faint last night. Well, that and a mix of exhaustion and dehydration, according to what the doctor told me yesterday.

"Let me check, again," the guard says as he taps away at the computer.

"Don't bother," says a familiar whiskey-smooth voice from behind me. "Nothing's broken."

I turn as a tall brunette in a gray pantsuit and dagger sharp stilettos strides toward me. "It's a wonder. You were in the hospital only what, five hours ago? And you still manage to come to work early. Wow. Really setting a high bar for all of us," Calista Holt muses, maintaining a neutral mask. But based on the fact that I'm locked out and she's one of a select few with the authority to block my entry to the building, I doubt her expression is concealing delight.

"Expected me to stay home?" I ask.

The guard stops typing next to me. Holt is one of those people authority rolls off of in waves. When she tells you not to bother, you don't.

"No, that's why I'm here earlier than I'd like to be to haul you and your Armani suit to breakfast. We should hurry, we have a reservation." She doesn't wait for an answer. Instead, she turns on a heel and heads back toward the bank of windows at the entrance. After I take a beat to register the massive pile of shit I've found myself in, I follow, closing the distance between us in time to catch the door.

Her driver is already holding a door open for the sleek Rolls Royce from the company she hires.

"You have to understand—" I start.

"Not a fucking word until I have another coffee," Holt says, holding up a manicured finger. "Or you will never see your office again."

I slam my mouth shut, knowing that given the chance, Holt will follow through on her threat.

It's another twenty minutes before we arrive at the breakfast spot Holt selected. Fern. A sun drenched restaurant draped in so many vines you'd think it was an upscale Rainforest Cafe. The host seats us along the wall of windows then promises our server will be with us shortly. Unable to wait much longer, I flag down a passing server with a carafe of coffee to fill Holt's cup.

"There's no reason I shouldn't be able to get back to work today." I jump right back into my defense from earlier. This breakfast is a waste of both of our time.

"You must have hit your head quite hard," she says as she pours cream into her coffee. "Remind me, whose name is on the wall the moment you walk out of the elevators?"

"Walker's."

"Funny, so glad you think it's the right time for jokes," she says. "My name is on that wall *first*. A name that means something in the world of entertainment labor law. So, imagine what would happen if it came out that one of my employees had worked himself to the point of collapse? Not any employee, either. One of my most public-facing senior associates."

In my late teens and early twenties, I was headlining international tours and writing platinum records. Now at thirty-three, I have a conventional career working as an entertainment lawyer and leveraging my old connections. But there are still eyes on me, reporters more than happy to make a paycheck from a whiff of gossip. I'm not just an employee who fainted on company time. Up until now, being a public figure has been an asset. But after last night, it's turned me into a liability.

"Okay, so I'll take a few days off." I shrug, trying not to show my distaste for the idea. Time off just means time to fall behind. It means I'll send myself back into a spiral with even more of the episodic migraines I've been apparently failing to manage.

"Two weeks minimum."

"No," I bark, immediately shutting down the idea. The longest I've ever been away from the office is a few days. Two weeks? Forget that.

"You fainted in my firm. At *my* firm." Iron strikes through her words. "If you had done so in the comfort of your own home, sure, you could avoid this. But that would imply you spend any time at home. You take two days of PTO every year around this time, and you have weeks you can use. So this is me approving your request for time off."

"I don't need it," I bite out. Tension starts to build behind my eyes. I can't have another migraine here. Not when I'm supposed to be proving I'm good to get back to work.

"You do, and your denial of it makes me think it's been long overdue."

"I take two weeks off and then I get to come back?" I ask.

"You take two weeks off, then I'll determine if you seem like you'll repeat the same mistake. *Then* we move on from there." For the first time this morning, Holt smiles and it has everything to do with the platters being carried toward us. She raises her mug to her ruby-painted lips and says,

"Now we're going to enjoy a meal celebrating the start of a well-earned vacation."

My best friend, Wes, is a dick, but that's common knowledge. Buying the security footage from my little accident at the office and playing it on my eighty-inch TV when I walk into my living room, is just an unwelcome reminder.

"I've watched it ten times already. Gotta get my money's worth," he says as he kicks his cowboy boot clad feet up on my coffee table, sending a dusting of dirt onto the glass tabletop. He loves those damn boots. Grew up on a ranch in rural Tennessee and brought them with him to boarding school in Nashville, pissing off our teachers with the blatant breach of dress code.

In addition to the boots, he's wearing a faded, cropped sweatshirt and jeans. His overgrown brown hair is tucked under a backward baseball cap.

"Do I want to know how much it cost you?" I glare at my TV where I'm met with the image of me at my desk tapping away at a keyboard.

"Less than it should have. I would have given the guy three grand but he settled for one. Your firm should invest in better security."

"You could watch this at your own place."

Wes shakes his head. "Too many paparazzi."

"Bullshit. You have four places to pick from in Manhattan alone," I say, knowing the reason Wes is here is because he's bored. The guy is rarely ever satiated by what's in front of him, and more often than not this becomes my problem.

"But your couch is more comfortable than mine," he whines. "Also, I'm getting a poster made of this frame. Do you want me to send you one too?" Wes pauses the video right before I hit the ground face down. Up until seeing the clip, I was happily living under the delusion that I was found at my desk. Watching myself stand up to reach for my bag before I hit the thinly carpeted flooring is something I could have lived without.

I shouldn't be looking at screens to begin with. The doctor told me I have a minor concussion from the fall. I'm actually surprised it wasn't worse now that I've been given this viewing experience.

God, then Evelyn was there. Of course she was, I didn't give her much of a choice in the matter since I was the one who put her name down as my emergency contact the moment she moved here.

Evelyn's one of those people who will do anything for anyone if they so much as ask. But that's not the reason why I chose her. If someone had to show up for me, I wanted it to be her. I just didn't expect it to ever happen. Or for her to show up in that tiny fucking dress that showed off those lethal legs of hers. Those damn legs. Any small amount of pleasure I got from her being there was shut down with the reminder I screwed up all those months ago.

She's been in my life forever. It was years after the band broke up when I started seeing her differently. It snuck up on me and I still can't shake it. When it came to her moving day, I wanted to help but being alone with her for hours on end? I just couldn't do it. I ran away at the last minute and fucked the whole thing up.

"At any point are you going to ask me how I'm doing, or should I go change and lock myself upstairs until you leave?" I ask as I take a step toward the doorway. I might as well get Holt's mandated vacation over with and start packing.

"I was under the assumption you would deflect if I did." Wes smirks. Fair. If he didn't show up, I'd have avoided talking to him about it. My guess is that Evelyn told Avery, who told Wes. Lovely.

"So, your response instead was bribing security guards so you could shove it in my face? Really warms my heart."

"Eh, you don't have one of those," he says, then pats the couch next to him. "Come tell me about your worries and woes."

I accept his weak invitation and slump onto the couch next to him. "I had another migraine."

"Shit, man." Wes sits upright and turns to me with the first hint of genuine concern. He knows about the migraines. They're episodic and only really triggered by stress or major life changes. Usually, if I can keep everything together then I don't have to worry. I rarely had them on tour, but once I started at Columbia Law School, they were a constant companion. A reminder that if I wasn't ahead of everyone else, I was falling behind.

"I'll be fine," I insist. "I'll make junior partner at the firm at the end of the year then I'll be fine." It's what I've been promising myself for months. It's been what I've been working for since I was fourteen and was sent off to get the best high school education I could. I'm so close I can practically taste it.

Wes's eyes narrow. "Is this the first one you've had recently?"

"Yes." No. They've gotten bad enough that I've been keeping medication with me. That's what I was reaching for in the video. "I'm taking a vacation, though. There's no need to worry about it." Wes doesn't need to know the vacation is against my will.

"Glad you're taking care of yourself this time. This way I won't have to worry about you in LA. I mean, you could come with me now that you have some time off. Be like the good old days when it was us on stage."

"And babysit you so you don't ditch rehearsal for a once in a lifetime party with a rooftop pool that is exactly like every other party we've gone to with rooftop pools?" I say to avoid a conversation I don't want to have.

I don't mind an award show after party or helping my clients, but two weeks around rehearsals for a tour I'm not a part of? I can't do that. Music was only part of my path, but it's a part I'm done with. I don't need to be distracted by that now.

"I'm turning over a new leaf. I'm a new man. I started meditating," he says.

"Since when?"

"This morning, but that's not the point," he explains too quickly for me to comment. "I'm going to try. It's going to be different this time."

I know he's not talking about trying for the tour or rehearsal, or even the endless interviews, he has an easy charm that the public hasn't stopped falling for since he was seventeen. No, Avery is who he's concerned about.

"Great. See you don't need me there. You're an adult, even if most fifth graders are better at communicating their feelings."

"It's not my fault these younger generations are all about mental health and self-advocacy. I'm repressed, as is my right as a millennial," he asserts.

"I already know where I'm headed," I remind him. "There's a porch railing I've been needing to fix, and I should work on my truck."

"You're going home for two weeks? The last time you did that was…" his cheeks puff as he lets out a long, contemplative breath. "Damn, we were in high school," he says referring to the times I would fly home from St. George's. It was the boarding school in Nashville where we and the other two members of the band, Drew and Jared, met.

"I guess I'm due for a longer visit then." I shrug, like I haven't been avoiding this since I was eighteen.

3

Evelyn

"The new Morgan Tuesday album is what Lyla West's last album was trying to be. The storytelling, instrumentals, and lyricism were exactly what we expected from Lyla in a break up album, but where she floundered, Morgan delivered," says Clement Meryl, one of the two hosts of *Get Out of My Head* podcast.

His co-host, Walt Parish, picks up on the train of thought, adding his own comment. "I think three solid albums was too much to ask from Lyla. But I think I'm going to say what's on everyone's mind. People don't care about Lyla West anymore. We liked the whole faceless celebrity with a hidden identity for the first few years, but after five years? It's tired and drawn out."

"Seriously, for all we know she's a serial killer."

"Honestly, that would be more interesting than what we know about her now," Walt says, fighting a chuckle at his own reply.

A chirping ringtone blares through my speakers, interrupting the podcast and my startled heart clatters in my chest. I reach frantically to answer the call while wrestling the wheel of my car.

"Ev, you're listening to that damn brain rot excuse for music journalism, weren't you?" Avery accuses the moment I accept her call, completely forgoing any greeting despite the fact it's been two weeks since I saw her at her going away party.

"I'm not," I say as convincingly as possible. Headlines and podcasts are a vice I can't shake. Being both Lyla West and Evelyn Mariano, I maintain most of my privacy. Still, I can't help but be drawn to the opinions of others, drinking them in and then being driven to deliver what the public wants.

This need to deliver is part of why I'm fleeing Manhattan. I'm not necessarily running from my problems. I'm relocating them somewhere more scenic. Mountains rise against the horizon and the Hudson River glimmers through copses of wind-swept trees. It's hard to imagine I'm only two hours out of the city.

"You absolutely were. I know you can't help yourself. The fact that you listen to men who should never have been given the right to access recording equipment is the one thing I hate about you," she huffs. There's a rolling cheer in the background. From the sporadic updates she's sent me, I think she's at a music festival in Washington, lounging in her trailer to avoid mingling as much as possible before she heads back to LA.

"I'm not listening to them. I'm talking to you. I do not have the auditory processing prowess to be able to do both," I relent on the technicality. It's not like she believed me in the first place.

"So, you were."

"Yes, I was."

"I need to figure out how to put a damn child's lock on your phone. You're a masochist for listening to that shit. It doesn't matter what they're saying about Lyla, you're only going to get in your head about the next album."

"Too late. I've been in my head since an article called unlucky album three 'dry, uninspired, and lacking direction,'" I remind her.

Really, I think it was the perfect description of how I was feeling during and after the album. I was coming off the worst break up of my life, drained from balancing music and my day job as one of the heads of the design department at a boutique PR firm. Most of all, I was trying not to show it, keep it all in, and not let it disrupt the careful balance I was struggling to maintain.

"So, your solution is a trip to a newly discovered circle of hell to find inspiration? It's not too late to come to join me in LA. Beaches, great food, parties, could be fun," she says, and I'm tempted, but I need to focus.

"This place is cute...didn't you get the pictures I sent?" I ask to distract her.

"Ev, the town literally counts the number of couples who get engaged there. I think it called me single in no less than forty languages," she says, referring to Hartsfall's welcome sign.

The sign not only displays the population, 3761, but also a running count of the engagements that have taken place over the last fifty-four years in the quaint town tucked in New York's Hudson Valley. From what I've read, and the various social media rabbit holes I've fallen down at midnight for the last few weeks to combat my anxiety induced insomnia, whenever there's a new engagement the bell rings in the clock tower so the entire town can cheer.

"What better place to write love songs than a town that has an entire economy based on it?" I ask.

I failed with my last album. I know it. The podcast bros know it. The millions of people who streamed it and supported me anyway know it. For weeks after, the public disappointment was crushing. I've always taken what people think of me to heart. It's just one point on the laundry list of reasons I've kept my identity from the public and all of the people closest to me, excluding Avery. I thought separating me as a person from my music would allow for me to take things less personally, art is subjective and all that, but it still cuts deep, the wounds still aching every time I look at them too closely.

"You know what I think? I think you need a muse," she purrs.

"I'm not having a torrid affair with an art student with a tragic backstory who thinks their life is an indie film."

"Okay, then just a one-night-stand."

"I tried. You remember how that ended!" I half yelp, half bite out the last word as I swerve to avoid hitting a rabbit that is close enough to the faded color of the asphalt that I didn't see it until almost too late. As someone who shouldn't have been given a driver's license in the first place, months in the city without any practice have me on edge. I readjust my grip on the steering wheel, my knuckles going white.

"Noah was good at trivia, his efforts to carry us through the sports category will be missed," she says forlornly.

Noah was my one and only failed attempt at a one-night-stand after I moved to New York. I was feeling the full brunt of my deadline, and Avery suggested I make use of her tried and true methodology. One night turned into breakfast and then weekly trivia with our small circle of friends that stretched for two months.

I would have let it go longer if it weren't for the, capital C, Conversation.

"I don't know, you just feel closed off. It's like I don't really know you," he had said.

We'd been watching TV and he asked how my job was going. I gave him the vague "it's fine, I'm just stuck on a project" response. He told me I could bounce ideas off of him, which, no, I couldn't. It spiraled into him asking to be let in more and me saying that I'm an open book, an outright lie but one I tell convincingly due to practice and living in a state of denial.

"You know me. We have great conversations," I'd said half-heartedly.

"Whenever I ask about certain things you just shut off. Like, it's simple stuff too. You know everything about me. It's so one sided." He'd looked at me like he'd opened a gift at Christmas expecting one thing then getting something different.

The worst part was he was right. I hate when men do that. Getting to know people has always come easily but letting them know me has never come as naturally. I've always been terrified of sharing the wrong thing, too much, being too much. Becoming Lyla has only made it worse.

But when it comes to meeting new people, I don't think there's such a thing as a boring person if you ask them the right questions. Usually, this gets me by for a while, especially with men. I'll redirect to their fantasy football league that they describe with the zealous vigor of someone detailing the politics in their favorite fantasy novel or shift to something philosophical and abstract. Aliens are always a good topic—everyone has an opinion on aliens even if they don't think they do. There's the added benefit that nothing about my personal life comes up when talking about aliens.

Noah and my relationship had a fairly standard life cycle. You'd think with a graveyard of exes I'd have something to write about. But no matter how much I like people, I don't love them.

The last person I loved, I left. My best friend. Quinn—the most important person in my life and I'm too much of a coward to tell her the truth.

There's a screech of microphone feedback that comes from Avery's side of the call that zips through my spine in a visceral, nails on a chalkboard way that flips my stomach.

"Fuck," she grits out then a door opens and slams closed. "But seriously, I think you should consider it. A small town could be a good place for some inspiration. Have a whirlwind romance and then go back to the city. There's a hard limit for when it has to end that will play off that anxious attachment style of yours."

"Not the worst idea, but I'll probably be one of five single people since this is a couples' trip destination," I say and take a moment to picture it.

If nothing else, it would be good album fodder. Track one would be loud and evocative of 2000s pop, the embodiment of a life in the city. Then two and three would slow down and be more stripped down, the travel and a meet-cute. It would sound bittersweet, falling in love and letting go.

The bones are there, but the execution…not so much. The ideas have never been an issue. Each of them gives me this rush of adrenaline, this push that makes me believe it's finally working. And then when I sit at my piano or write the lyrics, it's always flat, like a three-dimensional illusion you're convinced you can grab but you're only met with empty air and disappointment.

The best of my three albums was my second. I was riding the high of a relationship that was so easy to write down to the point that the deluxe edition had five extra songs. I couldn't contain all the feelings I had for Oliver, the one and only man I ever saw a potential future with. Replicating that now would be a fool's errand. Though, now in hindsight, I was more in love with the idea of being in love with him than anything.

We were friends in college and fell into a relationship after we graduated. It was steady. We had everything in common before the break up and managed to stay close friends after. Three years later, I'm still not sure if I regret it. There are so many what ifs clinging to the back of my mind, cobwebs I can see but never quite reach. I think we needed to try and fail or we'd always wonder *what if we just tried?*

"Ahh, yes, because the rest of the general population agrees with me about the location." There's a muffled voice then Avery talks, her voice is quieter as if she's holding the phone away from her face. "Yeah, I'll be there in a second." She pauses and it gives me a moment to process my surroundings.

The air feels lighter here already. It's likely some place-bo-like expectation that comes from the lack of bodies bustling through the streets and the expanse of green leaves on the cusp of turning shades of gold and copper.

I've always preferred living in a city. Even when I lived in the suburbs as a kid I always came up with excuses to drive into Nashville. Then I moved to the city during college while attending Vanderbilt. The sounds of people make me feel less lonely, the constant swell of traffic and ambient conversation is better than any white noise machine. But this gentle landscape is one I could relax into for a while.

"Sorry, I have to go to meet with the choreographers about some last minute changes before my set because some of the dancers got food poisoning. You better not put that podcast back on the moment I hang up," she warns. "And even if you don't want me getting my hands all over your songs, maybe it's time to consider talking to Drew."

"I'll think about it. Have fun shaking ass in front of thousands of people on questionable drugs. Love you."

"Love you," she says then hangs up.

It's not the worst idea to ask my brother for help, but that's easier said than done. I know he's seeing a therapist and addressing his complicated relationship with music, but I don't want to waltz in and disrupt any progress he's made by dragging him into my secret life. It's not like I could take it back. Secrets like mine are all or nothing.

It only takes a few more minutes to cross the county line. Instead of taking the turn off toward my rental, I continue down the main road. I know the moment I'm unpacked I'm supposed to get to work. Vincent is anxiously waiting for updates. I promised to call once I got settled. So naturally, I'm putting off getting settled as long as I can.

The speed limit slows to a crawl as I enter town. Squat redbrick shops are squished shoulder to shoulder lining a circular road that loops around a central grassy park with a gazebo at its heart. Sandwich board signs pepper the sidewalk, declaring specials and testing out bad but endearing puns to passersby. Pedestrians cross the streets without looking. Some are dressed in hiking gear setting off for the network of trails nearby, others look like they are ready to pose for a picnic stock photo.

I pull into the parking lot and turn off my car with a sigh of relief. Flipping down the sun visor, I examine my appearance in the mirror. I'm a fidgeter, without being able to get up and move for the last few hours my hands have been running through my hair causing my braid to puff up around the crown of my head. I free my thick, dark strands then run my fingers through the resulting waves.

A crisp breeze welcomes me as I crack open the door. The mild mid-September weather carries the promise of the turning season. Change is in the air and I hope it claims me along with the end of summer.

It's a quick walk to the center of town toward the park. The gazebo is bigger than anything you'd find in a backyard, large enough that it could be used as a stage in a pinch. Along the edge closest to me, there's a red painted wooden sign with carved, curling storybook letters, *Welcome to Hartsfall: Embrace the feeling of falling.*

I pull out my phone to take a picture to send to Avery, and just as I tap the camera icon on my phone, a man gets on one knee in the gazebo.

4

Evelyn

Gravel crunches under tires as I pull up the steep drive-way. The house I've rented is excessive for one person to spend four weeks in. But the moment I saw the listing with its wraparound porch and swing, I was a goner.

The road, Austen Dr.—yes, as in Jane Austen—is lined with about ten houses that fit the similar mold of Victorian style homes with bay windows and cute picket fences. At the edge of each property trees tower high to give a layer of privacy.

Four weeks.

That's how long I've been given to write thirteen songs good enough to convince the rest of the world and my label I'm worth keeping around. Reverb Records took a shot on me, letting me remain anonymous, and it's mostly paid off. With the end of my contract looming, I'm doing my best to stay optimistic they'll keep playing along with my little experiment.

Due to the fact that I'm already a hazard on the road, I've put off answering the texts from Mom, but if I don't answer soon she'll assume the worst and I won't hear the end of it at least until after the New Year. In the past, I've avoided telling her about trips because of her insistence on constant updates and her general paranoia. But she's been in the habit of sending me things *I might have lost in the move.* So, I needed to tell her about my trip so I don't return to a pile of packages, or I'd have to take a shot in the dark if she vaguely asks how I like the newest item without any context clues.

Mom

> Make sure to get gas before you hit quarter of a tank

> Someone got lost on this trail. DON'T GO!!!!

This is followed by the exact geographical coordinates of the trail.

Mom

> Tell me when you're there.

Evelyn

> Got to the house safe

I take a selfie, posing with a thumbs up and the house in the background for good measure.

Ever since I was eighteen and my brother started closing down lines of communication to us, they started getting into my business more and more. From what they've told me, back home in Italy mental health wasn't something they talked about openly like they have slowly come to do in the United States. They didn't know how to deal with his depressive episodes, so they started holding tighter to me as if trying to make sure they didn't lose me too.

So, I oblige the worried texts and how they voice their opinions about my life choices. If treating me like I'm a teenager who lives at home helps calm their worries, I can handle it.

I wait for Mom to like my message before I pop open the trunk of the car and drag out my two overstuffed suitcases. The wheels rattle and jerk as I drag them up the rest of the uneven drive. I have to do an awkward hugging dance to lug them up the three steps to the porch. When I crouch to catch my breath, my line of vision is directed to the medium sized package obscuring the looping cursive *Welcome* on the faded tan mat. The only thing I had delivered was my baby grand that is already in the house and doesn't exactly fit on a doorstep.

Leaning closer, I read the label.

To: Alina Nicolescu

Good to know I didn't order a mystery package in a wine and cheese induced fugue state. This should be an easy fix.

I've been in contact with Alina Nicolescu for the last month. She's the landlord of the property, but I didn't know she lived in the area. The primary reason for our communication was because I needed to see if she'd agree to having me deliver my piano a few days in advance. I could technically use a keyboard but I avoid them if I can. The feeling of the keys is different without the weight of the hammer striking a chord and I want to do everything I can to make the most out of this trip.

Opening the rental app, I navigate to the messaging feature.

I think I have one of your packages, can I bring it by?

As I wait, I open the lock box and add the key that falls out to the novelty *I Heart NYC* keychain. I bought it years ago before I moved there, and would regularly stay with Avery whenever I flew out to work with my production team. Using my hip, I bump open the door and roll my two large suitcases into the entryway.

The interior has the warmth of a hug. Natural light filters through small panes of stained glass that line the wall closest to the stairs, scattering the afternoon light against the walls. From the faded but intricate jewel toned runner on the staircase to what looks like the original iron light fixtures hanging in the entryway, this is a home that wants to be lived in.

My phone chimes just as I examine the cross stitch on the wall that is a rendition of the town welcome sign and gazebo.

Happens all the time.

I'm in the green house across the street. If you want to bring it over, my grandson should be around. I'll be back from town soon and would love to say hello. If you have time I'll make tea and I can show you the old photos.

I Googled Alina as part of my deep dive into everything Hartsfall and also because there was an odd sense of familiarity that came whenever I read her name. The thing is, I know her. Technically, I know of her. Growing up I never had the cool factor of listening to classic rock or niche underground artists because we were an opera and classical music household. To this day Mom has a stack of opera CDs she uses and refuses to transition to using a streaming service. But for the first time in my life, it's given me a glimmer of insider knowledge.

The reason Alina wasn't a name that came to mind outright was because Mom always favored Italian and Spanish operas. In her prime, Alina was known as a jewel of a mezzo who specialized in German and French, so though I've heard recordings, they weren't as frequent in the rotation as Cecillia Bartoli. Alina and I bonded over this connection and she was more than happy to help me get a piano into the rental as long as I promised to come over and accompany her at least once during my stay. She has her own piano, and has proudly told me she used to be able to accompany herself but arthritis has gotten in the way of that.

The houses are all up on slight inclines from the road. Alina has warned me to be wary of rainy days since the natural drainage works as well as the experimenting with natural deodorant in the middle of summer.

There's a pleasant stretch in my calves as I climb the opposite hill to Alina's. A faded blue Ford truck rests at the end of the driveway, parked with the front facing the road. Denim dressed legs poke out from under the body of the truck ending in a pair of scuffed leather work boots.

I clear my throat. "Excuse me, I'm renting the house across the street. I came to drop off a package that was supposed to be delivered here. Alina said it would be okay if I came by."

The gruff voice that rumbles from under the truck is muted. "Give me a minute."

As minutes pass, I shift the box from one side to the other as I wait with no sign he'll be finishing any time soon. Just as I start to consider saying I'll come back later, a red convertible glides up the drive.

The woman behind the wheel is wearing a floral scarf to secure the gray hair flowing down her back. A bright pop of maroon is painted onto a mouth lined with wrinkles. She's petite with a proud jut to her chin that tells me it would be a mistake to call her frail. Hers isn't a forced type of classic look that people try on, she wears it with enviable grace.

I give her my full attention and wave. "Hello! Good to finally meet you. I got to the house and it's just perfect. Thank you again for working with me on the whole piano situation."

"If you play for me, that's enough," she says, her voice laced with an Eastern European accent. "We always need more musicians. Art makes life tolerable."

"Well, I hope I live up to expectations," I say, caught in the familiar need to impress even strangers.

Alina looks over my shoulder and I turn to look back at the man standing behind me.

The white cloth of his shirt covers his face as he uses the fabric to wipe sweat from his brow. He tugs the shirt up further only to expose more of the toned topography of his body. It's like Avery bought a damn Etsy spell to conjure up the perfect local love interest to taunt me.

And maybe it's for the best, because damn. I'm practically drooling over the guy, and I haven't even seen his face. His sweep of blond hair remains perfectly styled, even though he was just under a truck. A breath catches in my lungs as my gaze snags on a familiar pair of browline glasses dangling from the grease-stained forefinger of one hand while he uses the other to wipe his face with the white fabric of his shirt.

Plenty of people have bent glasses with brown detailing. There's no reason my heart has started tumbling in my chest. It's not—

"Garrett, come get my bags. We're going inside," Alina calls.

5

Garrett

I glare at the traitorous box on Alina's mahogany coffee table. I know for a fact there wasn't a mix up between 2107 and 2108 Austen Dr. because I brought this exact box with the dented corner inside yesterday.

It's not like I should be surprised Alina is scheming again. I could live without it, though.

"Can I help you?" I ask as I direct my attention to where Evelyn is staring at me with those damn sage green eyes of hers. Evelyn is the type of person who takes up space. It's not just her body but also her voice and this presence that all but forces you to look at her. Of course, there's the fact that I do like looking at her… Who wouldn't?

She's all soft features and long, tan legs. Green eyes that shine so bright it's impossible to look away. Dark waves that beg you to run your fingers through them. It doesn't matter if she's my old bandmate's little sister, it's not like I'll do anything about this damn persistent attraction I have for her. I only see her three or four times a year for a handful of minutes each, so why shouldn't I drink her in when I have a chance?

"Did you know that you have an evil twin with the same name as you who lives in the city? The resemblance is eerie," Evelyn says as she tilts her head to inspect me, causing her mess of hair to drape to one side.

We're sitting on opposite sides of Alina's cluttered coffee table. Alina herself is humming in the kitchen preparing tea. It's a trap to get Evelyn and I alone in the same way her leaving a box on the doorstep of the rental to get Evelyn to come over was. If that woman didn't practically raise me, I'd leave.

"Be serious," I say.

"I am. I'm warning you that you might have a doppelganger out there. That could be terrible luck." She maintains her wide-eyed expression of awe as she continues. "If anything, I'm saving you from someone who says they'll help you move and then not follow through."

"I helped," I remind her.

"You hired movers."

"I thought we got this out of our systems two weeks ago." I grit my teeth, guilt surging in my gut.

"I didn't want to assume you remembered everything—hospital trip and all," she says. "If you want a recap, I got you coffee and you hired movers. But I assume you're okay, given your current circumstances."

I didn't know that. Shit. But the small detail of coffee shouldn't change anything. The fact she did that catches me off guard. I rarely expect much from people, so when they do show up for me, I don't know how to react to it. I was an ass at the hospital, but I shouldn't have been.

With her here now, I'm feeling the same way as when I bolted at the thought of being alone with her during her move. She's not strictly off limits. But there's a reason I'm known for only being good for a handful of nights before moving on to someone new. If I want to keep Evelyn in my life, then nothing can come from what I feel for her.

"I'm sorry, all right? Something came up with work," I say. "Can we move on from it?"

"Only if you tell me how you convinced this nice woman to call you her grandson. If this is a hostage situation, I will call the police." She pauses for a moment, brows creasing as she attempts to piece things together. "Wait. *Is* she your grandma?"

If anyone's a hostage here, it's me.

"Not technically." Though, if I remind Alina, all I'll get is a lecture about gratitude.

"Then what are you doing here?" she asks as she settles back against the couch.

"I'm from here."

"Prove it."

"Like most of the general population, I don't carry my birth certificate with me so you'll just have to take my word for it."

"Well, according to *Teen Vogue*, and pretty much any other media outlet, you're from Nashville," she says disbelievingly.

It's a false assumption I've fed into over the years. The stories always talked about how Fool's Gambit started in Nashville when we were in high school, which is true. I left Hartsfall when I was fourteen after I passed St. George's entrance exam, packed my bags, and stepped toward the future. It's not like there's much for me here, besides sour memories. The version of me I built in Nashville is the person I used to wish I was before I grew up and realized how diluted that fantasy was.

"I bet I know why *you're* here," I say. She's the exact type of person who would come to Hartsfall, like all the other optimists who don't take a moment to see through the alluring veneer.

"Vacation." She points an accusatory finger at my face. "And don't you dare give me one of those judgmental ass looks. Avery has already given me an entire lecture about my choice of location. I don't need shit from you too."

"I don't know what you're talking about," I lie.

"Your eyebrows do this thing that makes it look like your face is telling me I'm stupid." She waves at my face.

I try to correct whatever offensive expression I'm wearing. And maybe I am judging her, but only in the way that I judge all the other tourists. They come here with impossibly high expectations and this idea that the town will be a way of ignoring things that are irrevocably broken. If your relationship is doomed, a weekend here won't fix a damn thing.

"That's not my intention," I say. Being here brings out a version of me that I'm not sure if I'm comfortable with her seeing.

"Well, you should reign in your eyebrows then. Or maybe try shaving them off," she says, as if offering to be the one wielding the razor.

"*Cosmopolitan* put out an article a few years ago of celebrities without eyebrows, so I already know that's a bad idea."

"Oh yeah. You did look terrible in that." Her lips quirk into a smile then she sits upright and points again. "See, that's exactly what I'm talking about. It's like the entire top half of your face is shaming me for consuming popular media."

"Can we move past your impressive niche knowledge of my micro expressions? I'm not judging you. It's that the article came out six years ago, so don't blame me for wondering why you recalled it so easily." Seems like she reads plenty of articles about me. But it's not like she's doing it on purpose, if I'm mentioned, her brother often is too. It's better if it's nothing.

"Maybe I like looking at ugly pictures of you to make me feel better," she says.

"How exactly would that make you feel better?"

"I don't know, I'm bullshitting here. As if I spend my free time compiling photos of you in a folder on my phone." She shrugs, and for some reason the reality of her joke disappoints me.

"Oddly specific for something you're vehemently denying."

A light clinking of porcelain comes from the kitchen and I take it as my cue to escape and help Alina. In the kitchen, she's arranged a set of blue country rose teacups with gold inlays on saucers along with a matching tea pot on a polished silver tray.

"You'll only need two. I'm heading out," I tell her.

"You have nowhere to be but here. We have a guest. She's agreed to play and why would you miss out on that as a fellow musician?" She adds a little jar of sugar cubes to the tray. "You could join in."

I hesitate as a stone weighs down my stomach because the truth is, I miss playing music with people, being a part of something larger than myself. I miss it enough that it's a bad idea to do it again. There was a reunion for the band in January that only reminded me how good we were, despite our squabbling. I spent weeks after throwing myself even harder into work filling the hole in my chest, reminding myself of the life I have right now. The one I always planned on having where I didn't have to rely on anyone but myself. I promised a few years with the band to Wesley and that's what I gave him.

"Fine," I say, knowing because it's Alina that this isn't a fight I can win. "One song."

I gingerly grab the tray, making sure to not take out my frustrations on the China that's older than I am, and follow her out into the living room. Alina said she got the set from some prince or a Hollywood actor she had a tryst with back in the day. That's who she claims most of her prized possessions have come from. I've lost count of her affairs. It might be better to keep track of the celebrities and public figures she wasn't involved with.

Her home has always reminded me of a museum. Everything is from a time when things were built to last. Her walls are covered in old framed photographs. Some are of her from past performances. Others are from each of her three weddings. Scattered throughout are a few of her children and grandchildren who rarely visit. She's never cared for them because she thinks they're greedy and boring, and there's nothing worse to Alina than being boring.

One of the first things I realized coming here as a kid was any question about these pictures would be answered with a story. Once I learned that, I used it to my advantage to prolong my visits. The alternative was going home, seeing if my mom came back when night inevitably came. Thinking about those times is bittersweet, back then I thought of her as my mom and not Lana. Alina's has never been my home, but it's never felt empty, not even when I'm the only one here. It's too stuffed with old memories to let that happen.

That time talking about Alina's weddings, after telling every detail down to the flowers in each bouquet she'd simply said, "I loved them all. That's why." Some part of me believed if that were true, maybe she had enough love to spare for me. I'm grateful it turned out to be true.

The sound of the piano pulls me back to the moment, followed by Alina's voice. "Accompany her, dear boy?" she calls from where she's getting Evelyn settled at her parlor grand piano, which is roughly a foot larger than a baby grand and has a fuller, richer sound.

It's the first instrument I ever learned to play. I make sure to keep it tuned so I can accompany her during my visits, since Alina hasn't been able to play it since her arthritis has made it impossible, but she still loves to sing. My old cello rests on a stand beside it, one that was suited for me when I was fourteen and about five inches shorter.

"Give me a minute to tune." I move from the coffee table to retrieve my cello.

Evelyn nods in acknowledgement, already immersed in flipping through the age-yellowed sheet music of a German aria.

I rosin my bow, falling into muscle memory of the act. Everything is in good condition. I've played a few times since I arrived two weeks ago. Once ready, I pull out a stool and position the cello between my knees and bend my body to adjust to the size. Starting with the C and working my way through, adjusting the tension in the strings accordingly. In the background, Evelyn's fingers skim along the keys, stopping and reviewing any areas of the song giving her trouble in a flurry of sound.

Ready, I look toward Evelyn and her eyes lock with mine. Holding. We've heard each other play before, so many times over the years that the moments blended together. But never like this.

"Alina, we're ready for you," I say, breaking the spell.

Alina's teacup clinks as she places it on its saucer. She adjusts her silky shawl over her shoulders then takes her usual place in the hollow curve of the piano. A breath and a roll of her shoulders then Evelyn and I start, perfectly in sync.

We play three and a half measures before Alina's velvety voice fills the room. I've heard this song a thousand times and can play it from memory without a second thought, but with Evelyn at the piano it sounds startlingly new.

She has a musicality that animates the song, she breathes through the rests, giving life to the respite between notes. It's been years since I've heard her, but even back then she was talented. You couldn't walk into a room and not stop to listen.

I used to go get water from the kitchen during band practice and she'd be at the piano in the living room. I'd watch, but she never noticed. She never looked up when she was playing, the instrument capturing her full attention. I thought it was a shame she didn't turn it into more than a hobby. She's better than her brother ever was.

Playing together now has a natural give and take as we support Alina's voice. It's imperfect in parts. Evelyn plays a wrong note then I come in a beat too early. We've never played together. But when we weave together just right, it's like we're being carried together on the stream of sound.

The need to stay and the instinct to get up and leave crush against each other like I'm caught in a fault line. When I was in Fool's Gambit, I lived for this moment when everyone on stage or in rehearsal fit together. I belonged in those moments with those people. It was undeniable. For the same reason I turned down Wesley's invitation to go to LA, this moment with Evelyn makes me want to run.

I stay.

It's one song, even if it's sweet poison.

Evelyn catches me looking when I didn't even realize that I was and something foreign pinches in my stomach. Her lips have parted and her face is flushed. Our eyes remain locked for another heartbeat before she breaks away.

Alina draws out the visit another hour after we finish the song. She brings out an old photo album, poring over old costumes and cast pictures. Evelyn drinks up the experience, indulging Alina to talk about her favorite times in Vienna and Milan.

It's been an effort to urge them toward the door. I know if Evelyn stays any longer, Alina will invite her for dinner. We're nearly done with the night, I just need to get Evelyn the rest of the way off the porch and headed home.

"This was the perfect welcome to town," Evelyn says. "Thank you."

"You haven't seen the town. You've just been in this house humoring me. I stole your first night. Let me make it up to you," Alina insists. There's a dangerous glimmer in her eye that makes me certain generosity isn't on her mind. "Garrett, take her into town tomorrow."

"I can't—" I start.

"You can. You have no plans. You've spent the last two weeks fixing the house. There's no more to fix. If you wanted a new project, then I'd have to break something." She wields each sentiment like a blade slashing through any hope of escape.

I've spent the last two weeks working to that end. I couldn't stay still and have filled my hours with every project I could find. It's part of the reason I came here instead of a regular vacation spot. I knew I could be practical and effective with my time. Still, I spent three days that first week in a dark room fighting migraines that hit me full force the moment I remembered the cases I was falling behind on. But because of my work on the house, I'm fresh out of reasons to say no to Alina's proposal.

"Hasn't stopped you before," I mutter under my breath. There have been times in the past when I've let a month or two go by without visiting and a text will come through with a picture of a porch step that needs to be replaced or a gutter that's been torn from the siding. Every time there are signs of suspicious methods. There are only so many times the siding can come loose from the house before it stops being a coincidence.

"There's no better way to get to know a place than spending time with a *local*." Evelyn's voice is sweet but there's something akin to Alina's upturned scheming expression on her face.

"Ten a.m. I'll meet you by the gazebo," I say.

6

Evelyn

I sleep the same way I have for the last few months. An urgent need to do something I'm incapable of looms over me until I shut my eyes in the dark only to blink them open to a blaze of sunlight. It's the flavored seltzer water of sleep, in the sense that I did technically sleep but I barely get an aftertaste of rest.

I kill the time before meeting Garrett by covering the basics I neglected yesterday. Namely, I shove all my clothes in drawers then go to the grocery store to get my standard store brand "Blizzard Flakes" that has questionable nutritional value but at least gives me something sweet to look forward to in the mornings, as well as a month's worth of instant ramen.

Once back at the rental, lingering in the kitchen with my bowl of nothing more than sugary milk, I finally brave the trench of despair that is my email.

Vincent has taken to sending me links to articles and books on boosting creativity. I don't have the heart to tell him that yoga isn't the answer we're looking for. I know this because

I tried and the only result was being the sweatiest person in a very clinical looking red light enhanced studio with women who made the splits look far too easy. Try as I might, I can't self-help listicle my way into creativity. I've gone on walks wearing weighted wristbands I impulse bought, rearranged my apartment (swapped my side table and floor lamp), and downloaded a language learning app. None of that changed anything besides what side of the couch I have to sit on to get good lighting.

Today's book recommendation is on the healing power of nature by a middle-aged divorcee who hiked the Appalachian trail. I reply over email to not disrupt the text thread we have going about celebrities that look like their dogs.

Another email comes in as I'm drafting my explanation that backpacking is a sure-fire way to not get an album out of me because I will go missing or be eaten by a bear. Every muscle in my body locks.

Quinn.

The name on the email is one I'm familiar with but haven't seen in my inbox since I quit my PR job. One that I used to look forward to every day because I was working with my best friend.

In my surprise I forget my surroundings and my elbow knocks over my bowl, causing milk to slosh onto the counter and dribble on my leg. A few used paper towels later, I reopen my email and my pulse quickens.

> *Hi, Evelyn,*
>
> *Debra finally quit and they're hiring for her old position. I know you were aiming for it before you left, so I wanted to let you know. If New York isn't working out, I know that they'd love to have you back.*
>
> *Regards,*
> *Quinn*

Under her name is the standard company sign off for Henderson Creative, the boutique PR firm we both worked at for six years after we graduated. Before now, the longest we'd been apart had been for summer vacations. It's been seven months since I told her I didn't need her to drive me to the airport because I didn't want to be fighting tears through security. I cried in the airport bathroom, already missing her and questioning the choice I couldn't take back.

My heart clenches at the curt, formal email that is so completely her. From class projects to texts, she says exactly what she needs to and nothing more.

I met Quinn during the first week of classes. I had been rushing from my dorm after throwing on the first clothes I could find, and Quinn stopped to tell me that there was a pair of frothy bubble gum pink underwear tucked into the ankle of my jeans. I'd passed by at least a hundred people and she was the only one who took the time to point it out.

It was a time in my life when I was desperate for someone to just be honest with me. At that point, any time when I texted Drew I knew that the only response I'd get from him was "I'm fine," as he pretended that the world wasn't crashing in on him. My parents were the same. Quinn was the person I needed, someone I didn't have to be on edge around, trying to constantly anticipate what could buoy her mood. Shortly after, the addition of Oliver made us into an inseparable trio. Through the rest of college and the reality of adulthood, we stuck by each other in those small ways that mean the most. Picking up ginger tea for Quinn when she was on her period. The three of us going together to Oliver's dad's seventh, eighth, and ninth weddings. The two of them coming to dinner with my parents to act as buffers against their barrage of questions.

The distance between Quinn and I didn't start because of my move. It was before that when I became Lyla. I had planned on telling her, but then her parents pulled her into their long overdue divorce. After that there was always something that made me hesitate.

A promotion I didn't want to overshadow.

A trip we wanted to plan.

A break up.

My break up with Oliver.

My move brought it all to a roaring crescendo. I reached a point where half of what I was telling her was just lies. I would text about the new company I was working at, even though there wasn't one. Or I'd tell her I was having the best time and the adjustment wasn't so bad. So, I gave one word answers or made excuses not to call until she reciprocated my energy.

This email is the Quinn version of saying, "I miss you. Talk to me dammit," which is so rare that if I was home, I'd print it out and stick it to my fridge to memorialize it.

I anxiously tap between my text messages and my email. Texting is casual; it could start a much needed conversation. But I'm not sure if I'm ready for that, especially now that my brain is ever so conveniently failing me after I abandoned my actual job to pursue a dream. You know, really directing a spotlight onto the shit show I've made of my personal life. Email feels cold though, impersonal, which I hate even more than potential confrontation.

I look back to the email and genuinely consider it. With one simple yes, I can go back to the way things were. All I have to do is finish up this album and not sign the contract renewal from Reverb that I should be hearing about any day now. If I want, I can act like the last five years never happened. That sounds damn nice right about now, but with my recent string of questionable decisions, I should think about it a little longer.

Evelyn

I'll lyk. On vacation. Look at this place - you'd love it

I copy and paste a link to a travel blog post about Hartsfall that I know she'll appreciate more than Avery did.

Quinn

Cute

I'd demand to watch Netflix specials

I smile to myself, happy to share Hartsfall with her. The only flaw in Quinn's impeccable taste, and really I wouldn't consider it a flaw even if she definitely does, is her love of low budget small town romance movies. The predictable plots and cheesy dialogue were the white noise of our college years.

Of course

I wait for another text but after a few minutes nothing comes. I still have half an hour before I meet Garrett, so I go up and change out of my stained sweats and into jeans and a T-shirt. To my dismay, this only takes a few minutes and when I get back to the living room I'm faced with my piano. The stupid motherfucker. It's not its fault I'm struggling, but somehow it manages to look smug.

There's no getting around the fact that if I want to write the way I used to, I need to play. I go to the piano and pull out the black bench. As I sit, I'm greeted with a view of the deck out back that extends into a sprawling yard with a fire pit.

I guide the keyboard cover back so it slots into place with a light thud. My fingers hover over the spread of black and white. I welcome the familiar hum of possibility, of being in complete control of where I'll start.

Music is the voice I've relied on so many times when I couldn't find the right words to express how I feel. Playing the piano I can set free every emotion I keep to myself. All the things that contradict the illusion that I'm perfectly content. I can be the version of myself the people I care about need me to be if I have music. That matters far more than the album, but both are slipping away from me.

Simple. I'll start simple with something I don't have to put any effort into to get right. My hands drift down into position for an E major scale. After all this time, a thrill still rushes through me with how fast I can make my way up and down the octaves without stumbling.

The keys are cool to the touch.

E F# G#

The vibration of the hammers striking strings in the body of the piano.

A B C#

C# C# C#

It's like my brain's scratched against a Brillo pad, but I press the key again and again, drawing out the torment.

Out of tune.

It's out of tune. Fucking perfect.

Garrett has claimed one of the benches along the walking path weaving alongside the gazebo. Today he's wearing a button down and slacks, far closer to what I'm used to seeing him in. Still, I won't be unable to unsee the way he lifted his shirt. That has been filed in a very permanent folder in the back of my mind.

"Do you?" Garrett asks, tilting his head toward me, yet somehow managing to keep his eyes on his phone as he taps at the screen.

"Do I what?" I ask. Did he say something while I was remembering exactly how speechless a passing glimpse of his abs made me feel yesterday?

He sighs as if it's a burden to continue the conversation that he started. "Do you have a warrant out for your arrest as the rhinestones on your chest are declaring to the general populace?"

"Oh, this little thing?" I pick at the fabric of my white shirt emblazoned with ruby red rhinestone lettering. "I try to keep people guessing. Maybe I do and this is the best way to throw people off my trail."

"That line of logic is inherently flawed."

"Thank you for your freakish ability to make jokes less funny. I just like seeing what puts you on edge. Don't you worry, I have plenty more shirts that I'll save just for you." I packed a variety of clothes, but over the years I've thoroughly enjoyed seeing what can get a reaction out of him. When I was rifling through the dresser this morning, I couldn't help myself.

"Why? New York apartments are small enough without having to accommodate *novelty* T-shirts," he says, making the word novelty sound dirty, and not the fun type of dirty either.

His mention of my apartment has me bristling. Right, I'm supposed to be mad at him. It's not like I expected us to make each other friendship bracelets or anything when he agreed to help me move. But there's always been something about Garrett.

He gets all annoyed with me, and I just want to toy with him more. The only times I've seen him blush are when I feed him a stupid innuendo or three. It's like there's a secret part of himself he lets out around me. Sue me for wanting more of it. But work always comes first for Garrett, stupid to think he'd make an exception for me.

"Avery and I get them for each other every year," I explain. It's a bit of a compromise to the problem of *what do you get someone who can buy themself anything they might want?* The answer: shirts from the bowels of the internet. "If you're done with helping an oil company steal property from orphans, shall we go our merry little way?"

"Whatever you think I do, I promise stealing property from orphans has nothing to do with it." With this statement he finally rises from the bench. Once standing he brushes off his already immaculately clean slate gray slacks. "Let's get this over with then."

It quickly becomes apparent that Garrett's interpretation of a "tour" is to point at the buildings we pass and read off the signs. The bookstore, which who would have guessed, sells books! A salon that I can go to if I need a haircut. His enthusiasm is absolutely infectious.

When we walk by Love is Brewing, a coffee shop with a scalloped awning and a rich scent of pastries wafting out whenever someone opens the door, he says, "You can get okay coffee here and the Wi-Fi is terrible if more than two people are using it."

"If I were to order a coffee, what would you suggest?" I ask, attempting to start an actual conversation.

He stops in his tracks; two lines etch between his brows. "Are you trying to make me look like an ass?"

"What?" Startled by the accusation, I blink up at him.

"I know you don't drink coffee so why would you ask for a recommendation?" he asks, like I'm trying to catch him in a trick question.

I don't drink coffee, but it's not like I expect him to know that. It makes me jittery and my stomach queasy. I'm more of a tea or Diet Coke girl unless I'm in desperate need of a boost and I'll grab an energy drink that will inevitably mess up my sleep pattern for at least a week, as if it isn't already fucked.

"I'm not. I'm just trying to make conversation because you obviously would rather be working. Seriously, if you don't want to be here with me, just go. And it's not like I expect you to know my order."

"I've known you for the better part of two decades, it would take more effort to not know basic facts about you. I bet you can tell me my order," he counters.

Cappuccino with whole milk. So, yeah, maybe I do.

"I guess you have a point," I begrudgingly admit, a flush heating my cheeks.

"And as for leaving, I can't."

"Yes, you can. I promise I can handle myself," I say. I was planning on doing this by myself anyway. Teasing and flirting is one thing, but I don't particularly love the idea that he'd rather be anywhere else than with me.

He pulls off his glasses and rubs at his temples, making him appear older. Garrett always looked more grown up than anyone else his age when we were younger. It could have been attributed to his sharp bone structure, but even when youth softened his features there was an air about him. His clothes were always impeccably clean and put together in a way that stood out in contrast to the other boys' carelessness.

"Alina has this uncanny ability to know when I lie. If she asks how the tour went, she'll know. Also, we have at least ten pairs of eyes on us waiting for me to fail for the town betting pool." He replaces his glasses.

"There's a betting pool?" I perk up at the prospect.

"Unfortunately." He starts walking again with measured strides that have me rushing to keep pace. "This is Lost and Found, it's a wine bar." He points, actively ignoring my question.

I grab him by the arm and pull him out of the way of a couple in matching athletic wear that makes me wish I could look half as good in elastane and spandex. "You can't just mention a betting pool in casual conversation and not elaborate, especially when I'm involved in one of said bets."

"It's not really about you."

"If I wasn't walking, your sad excuse for a tour would have put me to sleep by now. You owe me," I tease.

"Fine," he says. "But you're not allowed to type anything. There are strict rules and I don't particularly want to have to skinny dip in September."

"Don't tempt me with a good time." I lift my eyebrows suggestively, which only causes him to avert his gaze as his lips pull into a tight line.

Instead of acknowledging my comment with a response, he pulls out his phone and scrolls for a moment before holding it in front of my face. When I reach for the phone he pulls it away. Apparently, my enthusiasm at the prospect of skinny dipping is enough for him to distrust me with the device.

Haven (Museum)

Odds of Garrett making it all the way through main street without giving up?

Fletcher (Pub/Garage)

I give him until the gazebo

Poppy (Pottery Studio/Inn)

All the way

There are a few other messages as well as a few sets of numbers that I assume are the bets.

Garrett has a whole life I had no clue about, one full of people and places he's never mentioned. The knowledge rocks through me, pushing me off balance.

"Why don't you talk about this place?" I ask.

"It never came up," he explains firmly as he starts to walk away from me and my question.

I match his stride and damn maybe I should have kept up with yoga if speed walking has me this winded. "And you conveniently made everyone you know believe you were from Tennessee. So, I don't see how I'd think to ask. Do you hate this place or something?"

"I don't hate Hartsfall. It's all this." He waves his hand around and as if to punctuate his point, the bell in the clock-tower rings out over the square marking another engagement somewhere within the town limits. The wince that contorts his features is lightning quick, but I catch it.

"You hate love. How original," I say.

"Though I don't particularly seek out romance, I don't hate love. But this isn't love." I can practically see him building up the walls to block me out as he talks. "This is a fantasy. Every issue you come here with? You'll walk right out with it too, but with this delusional idea that it's been fixed by a quick vacation. Relationships sure as hell aren't built on a foundation of tourist traps."

"Wow, tell me how you really feel. I bet you hate mall Santas too."

"I do. The entire practice is creepy," he agrees, regaining his usual impassive composure.

"Maybe you have a point about the mall Santas. But selling the fantasy of four guys singing love songs to predominantly female audiences, that's okay in your book? Isn't that the same thing?"

Millions of people have listened to him perform songs promising that there's someone for everyone out there, that everyone will have their happy ending. I know fantasy is a part of entertainment, but it really pisses me off that he's essentially writing off all the people that helped him earn millions.

"Of course it isn't," he says. "A proposal, that kind of shit is supposed to matter. Singing to thousands of people on stage isn't exactly undying commitment."

I catch myself running my thumb over my left ring finger then shove my hand deep into my pocket. I can't think too hard about it. If I think about it, it means it was real when I do my best to pretend it isn't.

"Who are you to determine if this place matters to them or not?" I demand, my voice coming out sharper than I intend, but I'm losing my will to care. He doesn't want to be here? Great. Let me give him a good reason to want to leave besides his superiority complex.

"Why are you worked up about this?" he asks. "It's not like you expect me to be some sort of undying romantic. You know I'm not."

That's true enough. From what I've seen over the years, the public's perception of him as an unattainable bachelor is spot on. He's no playboy, like Wes, but he's only ever spotted with this male model or that senator's daughter a handful of times until he seems to lose interest.

"These people, in love or not, are here to have a good time. You have no right to judge them. Learn how to keep that chip you have on your shoulder to yourself," I start. People like him get off on sucking the joy out of small things that bring others happiness. Sure, maybe I like to post pictures every time I get an overpriced Aperol Spritz with dinner, but it makes me happy, dammit. "And from how I see it right now, if I walk away from this tour, you're the only one who has something to lose."

Garrett's jaw works as he considers. "I'll put more effort into the rest of the tour."

"You're not getting off that easy. You still owe me for the move."

"If I put on my best impression of an underpaid college tour guide can we let it go."

"As if you could ever have that much pep," I counter.

"Okay, a very calm, semi-disinterested college tour guide," he corrects.

"That's a step up from what you're doing now." Out of the corner of my eye I spot a woman wriggling into an oversized sweater from one of the strategically placed tourist gift shops. "Let me add one more thing to those terms, then yes."

As we leave the gift shop, I hand Garrett my phone so he can take a picture of us in our new matching T-shirts that say *You never stop falling in Hartsfall*. I made sure to look over all the options to find the one that will be the best retribution. The vibrant pink on pink combo was obviously the best choice.

I step in front of Garrett while he takes a moment to adjust the settings on the phone then tests the angle of the camera with his outstretched arm. After the first picture, he checks then takes a few more. It's almost cute how much effort he's putting into something that makes him look constipated.

"I don't get the point of this," he says as he gives me back my phone, which is now loaded with pictures that might be considered blackmail worthy.

I give him a purposefully suggestive once over. "I have a thing for men in novelty tourist shirts. This is a big turn on for me."

"I'll make sure to never wear them around you so you don't get the wrong idea." He grimaces and looks past me but there's the slightest tinge of pink that reaches the tips of his ears. "So now that your overt attempt at public humiliation is underway, can we finish the tour?"

"Yes, but for my next stipulation. Show me something you can't find on a travel blog or a tourism page. If you dislike the tourist stuff so much, show me something you actually like." Who knows when I'll have another chance to learn more about Garrett, so I'm going to take this opportunity while I can.

"Fine. But you're not allowed to complain if you think it's boring," he says, his shoulders stiffening like he's preemptively bracing for my complaints, an interesting reaction from someone who was *just* complaining.

Garrett finally starts giving tidbits beyond what I can find in the audio walking tour that I found on the town's outdated, beige website. I learn that the owners of the two flower shops, Winnie and Sara are divorced, which has led to a long-standing rivalry.

"Whatever one you step into first is where you're pledging your loyalties. If you go to the other one after they'll upcharge you. One time I was getting Alina flowers and Sara had closed early, so I went to Winnie's and I'm still certain that whatever she put in the bouquet gave me a rash," he explains and absentmindedly scratches at his forearm.

He gives the same treatment to the pub where everything is good except for the Tuesday special, fish tacos. Then he points down an alley that leads to a trail where the high schoolers sneak off to.

Sure, I'd like to linger at some of the shop windows longer than his brisk pace allows, but I can do that later. I have weeks for that. Watching Garrett take more care in talking about his hometown feels like I've stumbled upon light flowing through a cracked door that's usually sealed shut. I doubt I'll ever actually know what he's thinking, but that makes this glimpse all that more enticing.

I'm still struggling to picture the version of him that grew up here. To me he's always been a city person, someone always pushing forward to the next best thing. It's hard to imagine him walking lazily around the square on a summer afternoon with nowhere to be.

"I guess I'll pretend not to know you in public then," I say once we reach the edge of the parking lot where our cars are waiting. From the looks of it, he has the cherry red convertible that Alina was driving the other day. The image of his timeless features conjures images of drive-in movies or being picked up to go to a school dance in a way that I've never experienced. Not that I'd want it with him, and not that he'd ever do anything close to it. He's made it clear he thinks those types of things are manufactured.

"No," he says, stopping my hand from reaching for my keychain. "You asked for the real tour, so I'm going to give it to you."

"Promise me that you're not using this as an opportunity to take me to a murder spot."

"Has anyone told you that you'd be terrible at committing a crime? I'd be the top suspect if you wound up dead," he says. This time his exasperation doesn't have much force behind it.

"I mean, you have the motive," I say, pointing to his shirt then to mine. "And maybe I'm giving you credit for being smart enough to get away with it. You have this certain Patrick Bateman vibe."

He rolls his eyes and walks to the car without checking if I'll follow.

7

Evelyn

"If you didn't want me to play certain songs then you shouldn't have let me connect to the Bluetooth," I call over the wind and music as I slip my phone between my thighs, securely where Garrett would never dare reach.

I've queued up enough music to last another hour. When we started the scenic drive thirty-something minutes ago, I eased in with one Fool's Gambit song mixed in with other pop hits then I sprinkled in another, then another. With each I've increased frequency to the point that now it's all Fool's Gambit and nothing else.

"You have a gift," he deadpans just loud enough that I can hear him.

Trees tower over us on either side, forming corridor walls leading up to the crystal clear sky. Most are green, but some have given way to the gold and reds of fall. The hues blur together as we rush by, wind causing loose strands of my hair to dance around my face. This is the type of place that sweeps you away, the memory imprinted in the back of your mind long after you leave so you crave it whenever you consider escaping real life.

"I have many to keep track of, which one are you concerned with at the moment?" Amusement threatens to curl my lips, and I have to actively contain a smile.

"The one where you crawl under my skin like a parasite and make my nightmares a reality."

"Too easy. You need more creative nightmares."

"I'll work on that." His eyes remain locked on the road in front of us but there's something in the way that his jaw works that suggests an undertone of humor. "But it can't be too easy since you're the only one who manages to do it so efficiently."

"Oh." Him acknowledging the tidal push and pull we've had throughout the years immediately makes it feel less like a game. For the first time, he's made me speechless.

A few moments later, he pulls into a overlook that butts up against the rolling waters of the Hudson. We exit the car and head toward the sturdy wooden railing, the thick rungs weatherworn. The view goes straight across the water to even more trees as far as the eye can see. Buildings dot the land, and it's tempting to shout and see if anyone could hear.

"It's quite the view," I say.

"Yeah. I used to come here when I needed space to think," he explains. "Made me feel less trapped."

I consider asking what he was breaking free from, but that feels like it would do a disservice to what he's already shared. If he wanted to tell me, he would.

Water laps against the cliff. Birds twitter and chirp overhead. Wind whispers through the trees.

The moment reminds me of a song, "4'33"" composed by John Cage that can be played on any instrument and by any number of instruments. The piece is made up of four minutes and thirty-three seconds without a single note being played. It pushes the boundaries of what is considered music. The song is different every time because it's comprised of what happens during that time. In a theater, that may be the rustle of programs and clothes or a latent whisper. Here, the sounds of nature give their texture and raw musicality. To me, the piece isn't about the silence, it's about listening.

On the drive back, my phone automatically connects to the sound system and I change the playlist to something that's not designed with his torment in mind. When "Dream a Little Dream of Me" sung by Doris Day comes on, he bobs his head along.

"You like this one," I note and instantly regret it when he stops.

"I know it really well. It's one of the first songs I got good at playing on the cello. Pretty much everything I learned to play was from a list of songs Alina liked to sing," he says.

"You said she wasn't your grandmother the other day," I say, inviting an explanation.

"She was my neighbor."

"And you learned music from her?"

"Only the piano. The mayor's wife used to play cello professionally and taught music at the elementary school until she retired. Nothing formal. I just practiced a lot." As he explains his knuckles tighten then loosen again on the leather of the slim steering wheel.

"And how'd you pick up the bass?"

"Wes needed someone to play bass. I figured that out," he explains as if it's that simple to be proficient in three instruments, playing one professionally.

"That's all," I say. "Wow. I mean…it's impressive."

I can play the guitar and I have the finger calluses to prove it, but it's nothing noteworthy. The only reason I'm as proficient as I am at piano is that I've been learning since I was five. Sure, I have a natural skill when it comes to writing and feeling the music, but that's different. I can't imagine picking up an instrument and just figuring it out, not in the way he's implying.

He shrugs. "If you say so."

"You're bad at taking compliments." I shake my head, causing more of my hair to break free and catch in the wind.

"If you say so." This time he gives me a hint of a smirk.

When we pull onto Austen Dr., something in me mourns the end of our day. It's not dark out yet, but it will be soon. The moment I get inside I'll be alone in the house with the reality that even if I used to know what I was doing, I don't anymore. I wish there was some way to stretch today just a little further. One more hour or maybe two. Not that I want to spend time with him, but it's better than my other options.

The convertible pulls to a stop next to my SUV at the end of the driveway and he lazily props his elbow on the door as he turns to me. "We're not done, by the way."

"Is that so?" My hollow longing for company shrinks.

"I have one last stop planned, but it's best if we wait a few hours and we both need to eat."

"How considerate. Will I need to bring anything special? Perhaps a shovel. I'm not sure what's in the shed out back, but I can check," I offer.

"You should change." He gives me a once over, employing one of those looks of his that pierces right through me and causes my stomach to swirl. "I'm taking you to a local's spot so it's best to put in an effort to not look like a tourist. And you're not allergic to cats, right?"

"Noted," I say, "And no, not allergic but thoroughly intrigued."

"Seems like that doesn't take much."

"Hey." With this, I reach over to give a playful shove. His bicep is firm under my touch. Damn.

"I never said that was a bad thing." His gaze intensifies, harnessing the fiery essence of the late afternoon light.

There's a truth that I will never admit because it's rarely ever relevant. There have been a handful of times that Garrett has made my stomach flutter. The instances are so infrequent that I can convince myself they're just the product of his conventionally attractive features or those small flashes of emotion that I draw out of him. But it's never been either of those things. It's those eyes of his, rough cut amber that punctures straight through me, seeing things I'm terrified of anyone knowing about me. He makes my walls turn to glass and I want to tell him to look away, but that in itself would be admitting too much. That I know he's looking.

There was one night in particular that comes back to me in fragments. A rooftop. My dress soaked in champagne. The knowledge that if I ran to him, I wouldn't have to put on a brave face. A suit jacket I've kept ever since.

"See you soon, I guess." The words scratch against my throat as I fumble for the handle to leave.

There's an art to nervously pacing. My tiny apartment in Chelsea is very bad for pacing because what ends up happening is I start walking in circles. If I forget to turn the other direction, my head starts to spin and I get hit with a wave of nausea that tangles with, and then amplifies, my nerves.

The rental, with its expansive living room that stretches into a dining area and floral upholstered breakfast nook, is great for pacing. I can take long unobstructed strides as I peel off pieces of pepperoni from my frozen pizza. I should start getting ready, but I haven't decided on what qualifies as proper attire for the evening. Eventually, I give up and text Garrett.

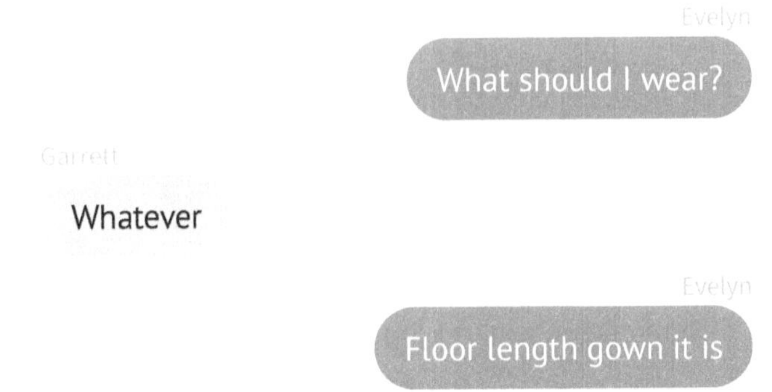

Text dots dance at the bottom of the screen then disappear again. A full minute later a text finally comes through.

Garrett

Don't.

He makes it too easy, and I do have one. I tend to over pack based on a list of *what ifs* that will never happen. I abandon my pizza and wash my hands before heading upstairs.

The black silk dress makes me feel sophisticated in a way that I rarely do. My T-shirts tell everyone what to expect, loud and maybe a little too much. They're my own personal warning labels. Still, it would be nice for someone to see me as someone soft and elegant.

I lift my phone and angle the camera to get the entire dress in frame then send off the picture.

Evelyn

Too late. Unless you have other suggestions.

Garrett

This

He's sent a screenshot from my Instagram. I only have a moment to appreciate the fact that he's taken my words so literally, before I look at the picture that has my stomach tying in knots.

My face is stretched into a rowdy cheer as I hoist a pint glass over my head next to Quinn, who's far more nonchalant with her arm draped around my shoulder. Oliver, whose pint I stole to pose with, took the picture four times because the first time someone else walked between us and the camera, the second and third times the pictures were just bad.

I love Avery and how much closer we've gotten living in the same city, but I miss Quinn and Oliver. I miss going out and talking about work where Peter in design needed to stop trying to find "creative" ways to make Comic Sans a trend or how Kirsten was definitely taking extra product samples from the little bins that we get from brands. Oliver would cheer on the repetitive cycle of petty drama, since he mostly worked virtually and also likes everyone he's ever met. There's a part of me that wishes I could press a rewind button and never sign my record deal. But I made a choice, and now I'm living with it.

My screen goes dark. I tap it once so I can examine the outfit, trying to brush off the aftershock of memory. The jeans are some of my favorites, light wash denim with red stars where pockets should be. I don't have the exact black top because I accidentally snagged and tore it on a fence a while back, but I have plenty like it.

As I'm doing the little jumps that are required to get into the skin tight jeans, my phone flashes with a call. I answer without looking because I assume it's Garrett calling to let me know he's on his way.

"How's Love Land?" Vincent asks and my stomach plummets. This is what I get for not calling him yesterday like I promised.

I put the phone on speaker and place it on the nightstand as I continue dressing.

"It's great. There's this amazing energy here. I wish I could bottle the air," I say as I start to shove my feet into black combat boots.

"So, the writing's going well?" It's the question I didn't want him to ask, but a significant portion of his job is making sure I do my job.

"It's great!" I chirp, hating the sharpness of my voice. "I could give a dumpster fire a run for its money."

"That bad, huh?"

"Yeah. But I'm close." Maybe if I repeat it enough I'll actually get a few steps closer through some sort of willpower fueled manifestation. I don't mention the small issue of my piano needing to be tuned as that doesn't exactly convey that I have everything under control.

Vincent was supportive of this trip because I was excited about something for the first time in a while. I'm not sure how far that support will stretch if I don't show proof of progress soon.

"Just like you were close when you sent me that one insurance company jingle and swore it would make a great hook?" he asks.

Not my greatest moment. To my credit, I've been watching a lot of TV, and those commercials are catchy. I sent him a voice memo with my "amazing idea" only to wake up to his text asking me if I was serious.

"Like one percent closer, maybe two." My attention flicks to the window as a pair of headlights blaze light down Alina's driveway. "Is there something you need to talk about? If not, I should get going."

"Yes. Reverb sent back the changes for your contract renewal," he says with a serious edge that puts me on high alert. "You might want to sit down for this."

We've been expecting them to present a preliminary contract to start negotiations, I've not known what to expect from it. I guess Vincent has the answers.

I claim a spot at the foot of the bed. "Okay. I'm sitting."

"They want you to go public as Lyla as part of the new contract. They think that you're losing public interest and they have the numbers on their side," he explains.

"That's against everything we've been working for," I say, my voice going thin.

I get it. I do. They see all the money they could be getting out of not only my future record but my past ones as well. This was always a possibility, but I thought I was going to have this album as one last chance to prove I don't need to go public. What I've built isn't perfect, but it keeps everything in the balance.

Growing up seeing Avery and Drew in the spotlight I was apprehensive of people, sure. But I made it my mission to make people like me for me, or at least remember me as more than the sibling of someone who they put posters up of in their room. I want to have a genuine connection with the people in my life. People knowing who I am the moment I walk into a room? I don't think I can do it. Even without people knowing my identity, I've struggled so much with reviews and commentaries. If they know who I am, they'll have even more they could tear into. There's no way that some people won't be disappointed. I bet they're expecting someone…more.

"I know, but—" Vincent's voice cuts short, and I look down at the phone thinking the call got cut short.

No. The call is still going.

Just not through my speaker.

8

Garrett

"As Lyla West, without a face or presence, you aren't able to connect with your fan base in the same way other musicians do. People want more than talent; they want to know you—" The male voice stops coming through the Bluetooth connection as quickly as it started and is replaced by Alina's jazz preset station. The abrupt switch is dizzying.

My head thuds back against the firm headrest as shock crushes a breath from my lungs.

This is Evelyn who says every damn thing that pops into her head. Evelyn who wears her heart on her sleeve for everyone to see. *And* she's Lyla West? Fuck.

I've just heard proof of this, but I'm struggling to see how that could be true.

I've known of Lyla West the same as anyone who's interacted with any pop culture for the last five years does. Her first album made her interesting, someone worth talking about. When her second album came out she made her name as a force to be reckoned with. My favorite is her third, even if it is her least popular. It always felt the most familiar.

Evelyn's not someone who I can see keeping that big of a secret and with Drew's relationship with music over the last few years, I can't fathom her doing something that would make him uncomfortable. I guess if he also doesn't know, that might just make sense, be the one reason she'd be able to keep a secret this large.

A blur of movement streaks across the house windows and then Evelyn stops to peer out at me. Her doe eyes are wide but unwavering. She's speaking into the phone but I can't read the words falling from her lips.

I think for a moment she'll hang up and vanish like a ghost. But this is Evelyn. Even if I've just learned that she's also someone else entirely, she barrels things with an unmatched intensity that makes me feel like I'm a pin about to be struck down by a bowling ball. So, I'm not surprised when a few moments pass then she flings open the door and marches toward me.

But then her eyes flicker with hesitation. She just stands there next to the car with her phone clutched at her side. She's wearing the outfit I sent her. Denim hugs her hips, and a thin band of skin exposed between the gap below the hem of her shirt has me desperate to know how my fingers would feel running over it.

Soft. I think she'd feel so fucking soft. For a moment I forget everything else that's happening. There's just her.

Evelyn.

Evelyn, who is also Lyla.

Fuck.

I make an effort to relax back in my seat. There's no point in showing my hand before I know the rules of the game.

In truth, there are very few things that I appreciate about my job, but reading people has always managed to make the list. It's the same reason I hate texting; you lose the nuance of humanity. You can't see someone disguise their sweaty palms over an email or hear the tremor of anxiety that lets you know you can push a negotiation further. It's a skill learned from necessity as a child, knowing when I've overstayed my welcome at the shops around town or when Lana's face would pinch and she'd start reminding me how I destroyed her life with the simple act of being born, as if I asked to be born in the first place.

Everyone has a tell. Evelyn's is a smile that takes an extra few seconds to reach her eyes. It's a brave face, a convincing one for anyone who doesn't know what her genuine smile looks like. I don't know when I started noticing it, but one thing is for sure. Right now, she's doing her best not to show how shaken she is.

Evelyn hovers by the door, her hand floating inches from the handle. An unasked question weighs heavy in the air.

"Get in." I reach over and open the door for her. "We're going somewhere with plenty of alcohol, and you look like you need a drink."

"How do people know if you're actually going to get gas or if you're coming here?" she asks, breaking the stiff silence that's fallen over us during the short drive.

The 'n' in The Gas Station' ancient orange and red neon sign flickers. A handful of familiar cars are parked outside the old converted gas station turned townie bar.

"Context clues, I guess." I pull into a spot under the rusted awning next to a non-functional gas pumps.

"But when someone says, 'I'm taking Darla to The Gas Station' how am I supposed to know if they're taking their unfortunately named car or an actual person?"

The Gas Station is still on most maps as an actual gas station. The odd tourist or two stumbles in because of it, but it's far enough out of the way most people seek out other options for fuel first. But the locals just know. It's one of the few spots besides the unmarked trails around town that we have to ourselves.

I was going to come here tonight with or without Evelyn. I have a soft spot for the place that always has me coming back on my last nights in town.

"Please don't tell me you name your cars," I say.

"Just my piano," she says. "Her name is Meg."

"Meg?"

"Like Meg Ryan," she explains, "I love *When Harry Met Sally*. It makes me feel okay with being single and a mess as my thirtieth birthday creeps around the corner with the voice of my mom asking why I'm not engaged yet. It also taught me how to fake an orgasm at an inappropriately young age."

"I can get behind a piano with a name," I say. My fingers tap nervously along the steering wheel. I guess we're just going to ignore what happened earlier, but my mind is still whirring as I try to slot pieces into place.

Why are you here, Evelyn?

She checks her phone for something. A message from whoever she was talking to earlier? Whatever it was about, it didn't seem all that pleasant.

I nod toward her hands, and she quickly tucks it out of view. "There's a no phone policy. If you take out your phone, you have to buy everyone a round."

"What if there's an emergency?"

"Step outside or there's a payphone," I explain.

"Do some old folks with a vendetta against technology own the place?"

"Pat is turning forty for the sixth time this year, but she's had a vendetta against me since I was a kid."

Evelyn's eyes gleam with amusement. "Are you telling me *you're* the reason for the rule?"

"More or less." I shrug.

The rule has evolved over the years. First, I couldn't bring in textbooks or homework, then it was my school laptop when I'd squeeze in time to visit between classes at Columbia. The phone rule is the most current iteration. The rule was born from the times I would hang around after school. I was definitely too young to be in a bar, but Pat knew it was better than the alternative.

I played pool, or when it was slow Pat would teach me chess. I've never particularly liked people, but I've also never liked being alone. Even if I was by myself in the corner, studying old chess games didn't feel so adrift. I think the sound is part of the reason I miss the city so much. Even if you're shut away in your apartment the world never goes completely quiet outside.

"Anything else I should know?" Evelyn asks as she starts to reach for her door handle.

"If you ask for an off menu cocktail, Pat will try and make it and it will be the worst thing you've ever tasted." The memory of these instances send a shiver down my spine.

"Noted."

Inside, the bartop is constructed out of the old checkout counter and still has the same monstrous outdated register that stopped working last year, leading to some long-time bets to finally be resolved. I'm fairly sure Winnie got upward of a thousand dollars for that one. A group is clustered around one of the two scuffed pool tables tucked in the corner of the bar. Our shoes stick to the checkered linoleum as we head to a pair of red and chrome diner style stools.

Patricia "Pat" Herrington's gaze slips right by me to land on Evelyn. She was in the military before opening the bar and has retained the same short, now graying, pixie cut she's had since she left at eighteen, as well as the muscles she now uses to lug around kegs of local beer. Like most people in town she juggles two jobs, so she also daylights as the high school's gym teacher.

"Rare to see a new face here, especially one with him," Pat says as she hooks a thumb in my direction.

"Oh, I just found him wandering around the parking lot trying to get cell reception. There's no way I'd associate with people who put that much product in their hair," Evelyn says, quick as ever.

Pat slaps the glass counter and lets out a full-throated guffaw. "She's good."

She is. I've always teetered between being wary of people like Evelyn and being enamored by them, because she knows how to interact with people in a way that leaves them feeling lighter.

I might be able to read people, be able understand them, but putting that into practice has never been my forte. If anything it makes it worse. I can see when I fail but not be able to rectify it. It's forced me to the point where I'd rather be seen as cold and indifferent than incompetent. That's part of the reason I'm struggling with what to do about the situation with Evelyn now. There's a fifty-fifty chance that if I say something, I'll fuck up any chance of her speaking to me again.

"She is," I agree, taking the opportunity to look at Evelyn. Despite what I've just learned, she's composed, which only serves to make me question how many times I've seen her like this while there's more going on beneath the surface.

"Did he tell you he's famous, honey? Because you can do better than a washed up C-list celebrity." Pat leans over the counter and lowers her voice conspiratorially, staying loud enough so I can hear her over the Eagles song blaring from the jukebox on the opposite wall.

"I know I can. He's just here to pay for my drinks while I find someone I'd rather go home with," Evelyn says, then does a generous perusal of the bar room. She winks at someone but I don't catch who. This causes my blood to simmer for some fucking reason.

"Slim picking here, don't get your hopes up," Pat warns. "What are we drinking?"

"Two shots of tequila please," Evelyn says.

"I don't drink tequila," I say.

"Good for you. These are both for me." Evelyn flashes a full toothy smile as Pat moves to the other end of the bar to grab chilled tequila and glasses.

"I take it that this is how you're going to cope with what happened?" I ask, finally attempting to broach the topic of what I overheard.

"Well, you offered alcohol and have been avoiding the topic," she says with an indifferent shrug. "In my mind, there's a chance I wake up tomorrow not trying to overthink what you know because I've forgotten. And at this rate you haven't said anything and I'm happy to continue like this."

"Because drinking to the point of amnesia is the best solution here."

"Best? No. Effective? There's only one way to see!"

The moment the tequila shots appear in front of her she slams them back without a chaser.

Alex is sitting on Evelyn's lap looking far too satisfied with his situation.

"Alexander?" she asks with a giggle as he leans into her touch. Evelyn is flushed and in higher spirits after a few drinks. She's also finding everything about ten times funnier than it actually is.

"Yes," I answer.

She looks at Alex and flashes a shameless smile. "You should come home with me, Alexander."

Alex, as one might expect, meows.

The orange cat has one eye and is respectably battle scarred. I'm pretty sure the creature came with The Gas Station when Pat bought the place. Currently, he's found sanctuary on Evelyn's lap in the corner table we've found.

"Many a drunk woman has tried, all have failed," I tell her. I've been drinking water since my first and only beer. Evelyn's drunk enough for the both of us.

"Okay, but we have to stay until he lets me go. It's illegal to move a sleeping cat," she insists.

"I must have missed that chapter in law school. Tell me, is that a felony or a misdemeanor?"

She pauses and considers. Unhappy that she's stopped petting him, Alex wakes up and bumps her hand with his head until she resumes stroking him. "Which one is worse?"

"Felony."

"Then it's a felony." She nods curtly then looks down at Alex, scratching under his chin and earning a rumbling purr. Her expression flattens and her eyes flick to my face then back down. "Why doesn't it seem to bother you?"

"Why would Alex bother me? I don't have allergies."

"No, I mean learning about Lyla." She swallows hard. "It's making me go crazy. Like, I thought the first time someone found out the apocalypse would start and I'd get sucked into a sinkhole or something. I'm just waiting for you to do something with it so I can stop anticipating the worst."

"Are you telling me you wouldn't have downed so much tequila if I told you I don't plan on doing anything with it?" If I knew that, maybe I would have voiced some of the thoughts rattling around in my head.

"No. Tequila was going to happen no matter what," she says, as if that's supposed to be reassuring.

"And you're disappointed because…" I want to give her the reaction she wants, but doubt that's actually to make a big deal of it. I'd rather not feed into the feeling that her world is about to implode on itself.

"I'm not." She trips over her words for a moment. "It's just, I thought you'd have some reaction worthy of the natural disaster brewing in the back of my head for the last five years."

"I thought my eyebrows communicated with you about what's going on in my head."

"Only when you're being judgmental." Her expression softens.

"Well, I'm sorry that my reaction doesn't rival the rapture, but due to the amount of secret love children I draft NDAs to cover up, my threshold is high," I say, but it's more that I keep my reactions to myself.

"Does this mean you're secretly my lawyer? Because last time I checked it was this sweet balding man who insists on me calling him Herb over email," she says. Her voice has a light slur to it. "I like Herb."

"No, I'm not secretly your lawyer. I'll sign something if you want. But if you're worried I'll tell someone, spilling your secret will all but destroy my professional integrity without gaining anything."

"So, not surprised?"

"You're just…" I trail off for the right way to describe it. I'm surprised, of course I am, but it makes sense in a way that I didn't expect. Years ago there would be times when we were writing a new song and Evelyn would be on her stomach, popping candy into her mouth and doing homework. Wes and I would get stuck and start bickering about word choice or a key change and her head would pop up.

She'd say something like "Obviously, the right word is atrophy" then go back down to whatever she was working on. There are so many of her suggestions that ended up in the final product that she should have been given song writing credits.

"Loud, abrasive, not that smart, a bit of a flirt," she finishes for me. Her lashes flutter and she leans in across the table. There's a dangerous light in her eyes that draws me in like a dare.

"I was going to say you've never seemed like the type of person to keep secrets," I say. I guess that's why it's worked so well. Who would guess the girl who lays everything on the table has something like this under wraps.

"It's because there's a tiny, locked room in my head where I compartmentalize those parts of my life. And if you're wondering, that room is on fire right now."

"Might I suggest water. I've heard it helps more than alcohol when dealing with fire."

"But far less fun." She winks and bites at her plush bottom lip causing my blood to heat. God this woman. You'd think she'd flirt less at a time like this.

Alex swipes at me when I start to remove him from Evelyn's lap after last call. Eve's head keeps rocking to the side as she fights sleep. Her eyes keep drifting closed. At least what happened won't be keeping her up at night, granted the amount she's had to drink probably has more to do with that than true peace of mind.

Evelyn reaches for the furball as I pull him away. "No. Bring him back." She moans like he's some long-lost lover and not an equal opportunist already on his way to find someone else to leech affection from.

"You can come back and see him later," I say as I set Alex on the ground. "Come on, let's get you home."

She pouts, but clambers to her feet using a chair to support herself. A hard determination takes over as she walks to the door with all the grace of a newborn deer. Every time I reach out my hand to offer help, she mutters, "I've got it. I've got it."

In the car, her phone connects and a vaguely familiar pop song starts to play, the type that transitions from radio to being played on repeat in department stores. Evelyn is silent with her eyes closed, the wind plastering dark strands of hair to her forehead. The only thing giving away that she's not asleep are the canyons of concentration cut between her brows.

I park at the top of her driveway expecting her to dart out of the car, but she heaves a breath relaxing into the seat. Evelyn's glassy green eyes pool with moonlight as she peers at the sky.

"I'm not really here on vacation," she says.

"Maybe you have decent taste after all."

Evelyn reaches a hand up as if she can pluck one of the stars out of the sky. It's one of the few things I miss when I'm in the city. "Maybe I'll write a song about the stars."

"How would it go?" I ask with genuine curiosity.

"No clue." Her expression slackens into a frown. "That's why I'm here. I need to write an entire album and it's like I've forgotten how. I had this idea that if I surrounded myself with love it would just, I don't know, be easier."

"And?"

"I ended up with a grump in a convertible and what's going to be the worst hangover of my life in the morning," she says, throwing up her hands with this *can you believe the day I'm having* exasperation.

"Sounds terrible."

"It is, don't get me started on how the guy took a cat from me."

"Deplorable."

"The worst," she says. She undoes her seatbelt and gets out of the car. After she shuts the door her hand lingers on the edge. "You're not the worst though, not really." Her eyes latch on mine and it's a marvel she remains soft despite the weight I now know she's carrying. "See you around?"

"Probably not."

"Going to hide at Alina's and avoid me now that the betting pool's not going to come for you?" she teases.

Her references to Alina and the betting pool are such small things, but it's an exchange I've never had with anyone else.

These people. This place. I keep them to myself.

Sharing this with Evelyn, a person who can truly appreciate it even if I can't, was something I never saw coming.

"I'm leaving tomorrow." And I don't have room to regret it. I need to get back to work. It doesn't matter that these twenty-four hours have forced us to share things about ourselves we never would have under different circumstances.

"Oh." Evelyn nods as she digests this. "Well then, I'll see you for our regularly scheduled run-in in a few months."

"Send an NDA and I'll sign it."

Her lips draw into a tight line. "Okay."

The moment she lets go of the door I'm backing down the driveway.

9

Evelyn

A hangover hammers through my skull, scattering my consciousness. As I collect the pieces of myself, fragments of last night dip in and out. All of it plays back like a grainy silent movie with subtitles to commentate on the comedy of errors that transpired.

The new contract with Reverb pushing for a public reveal.

See, look at this idiot girl dealing with the consequences of her own actions!

Waiting for Garrett to say something while I felt like I was going to implode.

Now, over here, kids! This is why you don't insist on being added to someone's car's Bluetooth. At least it wasn't porn!

There's a part of me that wishes it was porn because it would have been just as embarrassing for Garrett as it would have been for me with fewer lasting effects.

He said I could send him an NDA, but I just can't bring myself to do it. First, that would mean admitting to Vincent that I slipped up, and I really don't want to do that right now with so much up in the air. I do trust Garrett. He might think I'm Drew's annoying little sister, but he wouldn't tell anyone my secret.

Eventually, I start my day (read: drag a blanket downstairs and cocoon myself in a hangover nest while wearing sunglasses inside all while cursing my past self.)

I crook my arm out into an invisible embrace and send a picture to Avery. Over the last few months in New York we've spent endless mornings in her bed with its duvet that could make a cloud envious. Sometimes it feels like I'm trying to use her to replace Quinn, but that's not fair to either of them. That would be asking too much of Avery and her busy schedule. Worse, it would also mean Quinn is replaceable.

Evelyn

If you need me, I'll be here rotting.

Moments later a video call comes through. Avery is getting her makeup done, face brightly lit. A brush dips into view, blending out the blush on the apples of her cheeks.

"Two days there and you've already been driven to drinking," she says. The makeup artist lifts the brush as she talks. "Get out while you can."

"Actually, this is how I'm getting in with the locals. They've skipped trying to brainwash me and have started to accept me as their own," I say.

"Are any of the brain washing locals hot?" Right to the important stuff, then.

My mind inserts a picture of Garrett. Garrett, who didn't bat an eye last night and treated me better than I could have hoped for after dropping the weight of my world into his lap. "Yeah."

I'm uncertain what Avery knows about Garrett's background. She was always around the band, but so was I. Based on the fact that when I told her about coming to Hartsfall she didn't mention his connection to it, it doesn't feel right to share it if he's gone to such lengths to keep it a secret.

"Details," she urges.

"Reddish orange hair, scars, a bit of a player." My voice lowers.

"Tell me more."

"A bit touchy, but as we both know I like that in a relationship," I say, drawing out the moment. "Oh, and he meows on occasion, but I think it's part of his charm."

I delight as my words register and Avery's face falls. "I really hope you're talking about a cat."

"And if I wasn't?"

"Then I'd assume that you might have stumbled into a cult and not a cute small town." She cocks her head. "Which would actually be more interesting."

"Okay, well, now I know to bump up alleged culty small towns over cute ones if we ever take a vacation." The blanket rustles around me as I burrow in deeper.

"You make me feel so seen. Well, except for the fact that you're wearing mirrored sunglasses, and I have no idea if you're looking at me or not," she says. "One second." She holds up her finger as she mutters something to her makeup artist. "Sorry about that, I have like five more minutes before the photoshoot for new promo shots with the he-devil." The names she gives Wes have always been a fairly good indicator how she's feeling about him. The more intricate and unique the more likely she's channeled her rage into the identifier. All things considered, *he-devil* is mild. "The shirt he's wearing shouldn't legally be allowed to be called a garment."

"Cropped?" I ask.

She rolls her eyes and says, "It's like he gave a five-year-old scissors and told them to go wild."

"Ahh, as vain as ever, and can't wait to show off his abs to millions of innocent magazine consumers?"

"Yes, you have a way with words."

"I don't and that's a major problem," I groan out.

"So, a tiny naked cupid didn't shoot you in the ass with a comically large arrow then send you writing through the night?"

"Excuse you," I gasp in mock offense. "Cupid wears a very tasteful diaper, or a sash, or something."

"Not in the statues I've seen."

"Well, my modern cupid is aware of indecent exposure laws, and no, I don't have an arrow wound in my ass. My piano needs to be tuned, which I should have expected due to its little road trip, so I'll have to haul someone out here," I say, which reminds me of the more immediate hurdles I need to tackle.

A loud thumping comes and Avery's eyes flick to something off screen. "I've got to go. Good luck."

"I need it," I say, but I doubt she hears me because she hangs up mid-sentence.

I open the house rental app and message Alina, as she's the only other person I know with a piano nearby.

Evelyn

Do you have a referral for a piano tuner?

Alina

I'll send him over.

My stomach drops. There's one option who *he* is. But based on the foggy memories of last night, *he* should be long gone.

10

Garrett

Alina's doing a terrible job of pretending not to eavesdrop through the kitchen window to where I'm standing on her back deck. I never get any privacy in this town. It doesn't matter where I go, my conversation with Holt will be broadcasted through a group chat in a matter of minutes.

"You said two weeks," I remind.

"I said after two weeks we'll reevaluate the situation and if you meet expectations and are ready to get back to work, then you can come back to the office." Holt's voice is measured and unyielding. As much as I want to complain, without her go ahead I won't be able to get past security. Hell, without her I can't even access my email.

"And what expectations did I fail to meet? I went on vacation. I'm ready to come back." I can't afford more time off. It's not that I don't trust the other partners and associates to have helped my clients, but if I take care of something I know exactly how it's done.

"Tell me, what have you done so far on your vacation?" Her words are accompanied by a light, even tapping. I easily picture her walking across the cool marble of her office to the wall of windows overlooking the Financial District the way I've witnessed countless times.

"I've been spending time with my old neighbor. I went home." My jaw clenches with the effort to contain my frustration.

"Do you have any pictures? Did you go out and get some fresh air? I've heard there are some breathtaking views there." Her words are laced with feline satisfaction. She knows me, and even if she didn't, she's a fucking human lie detector. During litigation that's invaluable, but under my current circumstances I'm not the biggest fan. "Tell me, what was your favorite part? Don't spare a single detail."

The deck railing creaks as I lean back against it and heave a sigh. "Pictures weren't part of our deal. But I'm fine. I'm ready to come back."

"There was no *deal*. It's my call and I say no," she says. "I'm not letting you come back if you're just going to push yourself to the brink again. It's a waste of my resources to have you half-assing your work because you're running on empty instead of utilizing the damn PTO you've accrued."

"But—"

"No," she snaps. "Two more weeks. I want to see you use that Instagram of yours with millions of followers and post something. I want to see a picture of you drinking something fruity with an umbrella wearing something that looks close to a smile."

"No drinks here come with umbrellas," I say as if that matters, as if she cares.

"Then I want proof that you're putting your full effort into this. Remember, I know what that looks like." A slyness coats her voice.

She wouldn't act like this with anyone else. But no one else passed out at their desk only to be found by security. Hell, no one else made a quick trip to the ER. If it got out, no one would have their old career become the reason the firm got bad publicity. My grip tightens on the phone, the edges digging into my palm.

"I'm not posting anything that will give away my location," I say. My relationship with Hartsfall has always been complicated. It does fine on its own. Maybe if it needed my influence to boost tourism, I'd use it. But I don't want to disrupt what's here even if I think it's a pretty lie.

"Post or don't. Send me proof that you're taking steps to relax."

"What the hell am I supposed to do here?" I demand, without really expecting an answer. I've already exhausted all of my options because of the two-week timeline I had anticipated. I can't be stuck here any longer. I just fucking can't. It's not like I can join the tourists in their carefree jaunts down Main Street, though that appears to be exactly what Holt is asking for.

"You're the one who chose the location. Figure it out," she says. "I have a meeting. I expect the pictures in my inbox starting tomorrow, or two weeks will quickly become four."

Holt hangs up without another word. Alina gives me a few minutes before the French doors to the back deck fling open letting out the crooning of Nat King Cole. Her shuffling steps scrape against the deck as she walks up behind me.

"I have something to keep you occupied," she says.

After my second round of knocking, Evelyn appears in the doorway wrapped in a thick blanket and wearing mirrored sunglasses. I try to look her in the eye and I'm faced with my own reflection, a reminder that I'm not where I want to be. Instead of a suit, I'm in a navy T-shirt and jeans.

"You look like hell," I say.

"Thank you, it's very in right now. I bet we'll be seeing plenty of it when Paris Fashion Week comes around in a few weeks," she says, not missing a beat.

Even haggard by a hangover, she's acting like last night isn't fazing her. I can throw anything at her and humor will bounce right back.

"Have you eaten?" I ask.

"Why? Are you desperate to take care of me? Have a thing for damsels?" she asks, her lips curling with a self-indulgent smirk.

"No, just wanting to make sure you won't complain about it while I'm here." And yes, maybe I'm worried. She went through it last night—why shouldn't I be concerned?

There's a rustle under her blanket-cloak and a box of cereal pokes out. That's that I guess.

"I thought you were headed back to Manhattan," she says.

"There's been a slight change of plans."

"Oh, care to explain?"

"No," I say and peer around her. "I'd rather tune your piano."

She shrugs, seemingly satisfied with my response then lets me in. I trail behind her to the familiar living room with its thick, plush carpet and walls cluttered with all the pictures she doesn't have space for in her own home. It manages to feel lived in, even with its constantly rotating occupants.

"You never sent the NDA," I remind her since she might have forgotten, given her current state.

"I was never planning on sending you one."

I stop in my tracks. *She has to be joking?*

"You should."

"Planning on selling the story?"

"No."

"That's what I thought," she says. "You might barely put up with me, but I trust you."

Her eyes catch mine as I hold her words for a moment, trying to force them into making sense. Days ago she was going on about the move, and now, she trusts me? I don't get her, but I guess I rarely do.

I need to push past the weight of what she's said, so I cock my head toward her piano. "This is Meg, then?"

The living room furniture has been pushed into a new formation to accommodate the baby grand. Instead of appearing cramped, the living room feels more finished, as if the space has been waiting for the piano to complete it. Waiting for her.

"The one and only." There's an anxious energy to her voice. Her body shifts like she's rocking back and forth on her heels, though I can't see through the fabric pooling around her feet.

"Great. I'll let you know when I'm done." I set the black cloth case holding my tools on a side table then position myself at the piano.

Instead of retreating to a bedroom or some dark corner to let me work in peace, Evelyn opts to curl up onto a couch and watch. Her body is swallowed by the blankets, making her look somewhat like a floating head.

My jaw ticks as I force my attention back to the piano. I find the lip of the keyboard cover and I slip it back. Starting at the far left, I play chromatic chords up the piano to check for any problem areas. It's not terrible. Someone without a good ear could play it as is without being bothered.

Should be simple enough, though it's still tedious. There are two hundred and thirty strings in a piano and each one has to be checked. It's the type of work I love—the type you can't rush. I slip my long length of red felt between the first and third strings of the treble and mid sections to allow me to tune the middle strings first. All the while, I feel a prickle of awareness at the back of my neck.

"Do you have to be in here?" I ask without turning to look.

"No. But I want to be. I'm just actively reconfiguring what a piano tuner looks like in my head." I know her eyes are on me, I always do.

"And what is that exactly?"

"A cute old man who tells me so much about his three grandchildren going to liberal arts colleges in the Pacific Northwest that by the time he leaves I'd feel like they were in the room with us," she explains. "But at least you've got the cute little glasses. That part is spot on."

"Sorry to be a statistical outlier."

"Oh, come on. You love being the exception," she says.

The thing is, I do. Less because of some sense of superiority. But if you are the exception, if you put in the damn work, no one can deny that you belong somewhere. No one can take that from you.

I never did figure out what it was that Lana needed that I could provide, besides money. Growing up there were small things, listening to her stories about her last-minute weekend trips to Boston after not seeing her for three days. Then when I was in middle school there were the shifts she started skipping. I'd go in for her at the pub cleaning tables or spend afternoons watching the register at Love is Brewing. It wasn't legal, but anyone who hired her in town did it out of kindness to support a single mother. And I usually got a free meal out of it. They took a chance on her and she always blew it. Sometimes I think that in trying to be essential to her, I made myself easier to leave. I gave her a safety net I wove out of guilt so she never had to be fully accountable. I grew up so she never had to.

I'm half certain the reason I joined Fool's Gambit was because of how adamant Wes was that I had to be the bassist. It didn't matter that I'd have to learn the instrument, he was insistent. I would try and brush him off with excuses about studying, but that never deterred him. He showed up to my spot in the library every day. When I relocated, he followed. At fourteen, it was the first time I felt like anyone fought to have me in their life. Wes has his faults, but he gave me that. He let me be young alongside him.

He let me be fourteen.

But things have changed. The longer I'm in Hartsfall, the more likely the spot I've carved for myself in the city will become someone else's. The thought sends a wave of tension through my shoulders.

"What if I do?" I ask.

"I do appreciate your help," she says. "I was worried that I'd have to call someone in from the city and who knows how long that would have taken."

"So your album, you think this is the best place to write it?" I continue to work the soft felt between the strings.

"I've been struggling with it. Inspiration. Theme. Every-thing. My last album was a mess," she says, her voice grow-ing heavy. "I thought coming somewhere so dedicated to romance and love would help. Like, if I couldn't draw from my own experiences I could observe other people's."

A spark of an idea starts to flicker in my mind. I might not be able to see Hartsfall the way tourists do, but maybe I don't have to. "So, you're what? Going to all the spots and taking notes? Stalking people?"

"I'm pretty sure a friendly conversation or two will help more than stalking. I'll do all the touristy things for the next few weeks then lock myself away to write with a diet of instant ramen and desperation."

"Don't forget the cereal," I say.

"An essential food group," she agrees. "And because you seem allergic to the idea of those places, even though you'll be here longer you won't be seeing much of me."

"What if I wanted to join you?" I ask.

Despite growing up in a tourist destination, I've never been good at vacations. The empty swaths of time overwhelm me. I need to be moving toward something not sitting in place. The allowances I make to come up here on weekends serve a greater purpose than enjoying the sights. I need to get this vacation right this time around so I can get back to my caseload. If that means asking Evelyn to let me join in on her itinerary, so be it.

"Then I'd assume you'd been swapped with your good twin," she says, then pauses to consider. "Why would you subject yourself to that? You said it yourself yesterday that it's not your thing."

"I'm supposed to be here on vacation. Apparently, I'm failing on that front. So I might need your help."

"Seriously?" The word is accompanied by a chime of laughter.

I finish with the felt then turn. I can't see her eyes behind her sunglasses, but her mouth is turned up in amusement.

"I don't expect you to do it for free."

"Seeing you trying to look like you're enjoying it would be payment enough."

"I'll help you with your album if you help me." I think it's a fair offer, but as the idea enters my mind, I realize I'm anxious for her to agree. If I can do that I won't be wasting my time on the tourist traps and endless miles of hikes. There's a chance I'll be able to experience that same alchemy that washed over us when we played together two days ago.

"You'll what?" Shock has frozen her face in pinched confusion

"I'll help you write," I say. "I wrote half the songs for Fool's Gambit."

It's not something I ever expected to do again. But I used to love it. There was something freeing about creating something, then months later seeing people react to it live, causing a thrum in my pulse that I've never been able to replicate. I shouldn't get ahead of myself. This isn't my album. I won't be performing it, but that doesn't prevent the ache from building in my chest.

"If I agree to this, promise to keep your pessimistic storm cloud in check. If you're coming with me I want you to at least make an honest effort," she asserts.

"That's reasonable," I say. "If possible, I want to know in advance when you want to do things. I might be on vacation, but I like to know my schedule in advance. Also, I need you to take pictures of me."

"Need me to send an invitation with an RSVP every time?" she asks.

"That would be nice."

"I was joking."

"I wasn't."

"You rarely ever are," she says and shakes her head in mock disappointment. "And what exactly are you expecting? I love a good letter, but that feels a bit excessive."

"Send me a Google Calendar invite with the details and I'll show up," I offer.

Her head tilts to either side as she mulls it over. I half expect her to go back and insist on letters just to make things difficult.

"I can manage that," she finally agrees. "So for the next two weeks, you tag along on what I already had planned and then you help me write?"

"Yes. If you're satisfied with that arrangement, can I tune your piano in peace?"

11

Evelyn

“Mom said that you're on vacation.” The upper half of my brother's body fills my phone screen. I have the device propped between my knees as I sit with my back pressed to the bed's carved headboard. Drew is a big guy, not just tall but also broad. Black ink tattoos clutter his arms. He also religiously uses his home gym. But he's a big softy. And while we both have green eyes and brown hair; he inherited all the introverted genes from our parents.

Jazz plays in the background as he cooks, not quite covering the sound of Garrett on the piano downstairs. I meant what I said. It should be illegal to look that good doing something traditionally done by bespectacled older men.

“You mean she managed to make *my* vacation *your* problem,” I say. It's classic Mom. I bet she called him the moment I told her about my trip and then a second time when I arrived. It's another reason I let her put her hands all over my life.

It's our natural order. I “mess up.” They call Drew. And we get to pretend we're healthy communicators. I think sometimes I do things just so they will call him, just so we have to all talk.

"Just asking if you actually were where you said you are." His eyes, framed by thick eyebrows, flick up to the camera.

"I go to London one time and it ruins everything!" I throw my arms up, rocking my body so my back hits the carved headboard. It's a mistake because it causes my head to throb. No more tequila for the next month at least.

Okay, maybe for the next week.

"I think it was the food poisoning that ruined everything."

The trip I took at eighteen with Quinn and Oliver during the spring break of our freshman year would have been fine if I didn't get food poisoning. We were still getting to know each other and when I said I felt like I was dying they panicked and called my family.

"My body is a traitor," I say. "Can I ask something?"

"Only if you take off the sunglasses."

"Fine," I grumble. If I had it my way, I wouldn't have to look him in the eye while I asked this. "Do you ever miss music?" I wish it was a sisterly question instead of something sparked from my own desire for self-preservation. To be Lyla, or to walk away. Those are my options and neither of them feels right. When I consider my possible futures a pit forms in my stomach.

"Where did that come from?" he asks, thankfully without a hint of hurt.

"I ran into Garrett and it got me thinking," I explain. A handy distortion of the truth.

"Yeah, I do. All the time. But I'm not in my twenties anymore. I kinda miss it the same way you wish you could watch your favorite show for the first time. You know?" He shrugs.

"I guess," I say. I do my best to act like his answer doesn't affect me, but a wave of nerves threatens to pull me under.

"It's not that bad, anymore."

"But you're ok?" I ask. I always want to. Sometimes, in the middle of the night, I wake up and type out a text before I know what I'm doing then end up deleting it, only to send it in the morning.

His expression softens as he indulges my question. "Yeah. I am."

The words set something in the back of my mind at ease. *He's ok.*

We talk a while longer until he's finished cooking. His girlfriend, Lacey, pops into the kitchen and says hello. Right now, she's helping him run his bar but she's also a brilliant sports photographer and frankly a bit of a badass. When they hang up, I start scrolling through my phone going back through old headlines, reminding myself exactly what's at stake.

A knock sounds at the door, followed by a rough, "Hey. I'm finished."

"Thank you!" I call out.

"Come downstairs and play to check the piano."

"I bet it's fine." I'm going to be stuck with him anyway, we might as well get a break from each other while we still can.

"I don't want you to have another reason to hold a grudge against me."

"My grudge is completely justified!" Though, with everything else going on I don't really care about the move anymore.

"If you're too hungover just admit it."

His goading gets me. "Fine. I'm getting up, but only because if it's still out of tune I want to see what your face looks like when Mr. Perfect didn't do it right."

"If that's what it takes," he says.

I haul myself off the bed and to the door. I swing it open to find him haunting my hallway, amber eyes twinkling with arrogance. His arms are crossed over his chest, biceps pressing against the fabric of his plain T-shirt. Screw him for having the audacity to look so good while I feel like shit.

I rush past him and down the stairs. If he wants me to check the piano, then I'll check the damn piano as fast as I can. My ass is on the bench before he's in the living room. I run up and down the keys in a chromatic scale to test each tone. Really, I barely pay attention to the sound.

"There," I say. "It's perfect. You can go now."

"Going to write while I'm gone?" he asks, like he actually cares.

"No, I'm going to rot on my couch until I lose all perception of time."

"I could stay." I must make a face that displays the depth of my confusion because he adds, "I told you I'd help you. I'm already here. Neither of us have anything else going on."

Correction—I would like to pretend my problems don't exist while I finish my box of cereal.

Instead of responding I pull out my phone and tap away. His chimes and he pulls it from his pocket.

"'Garrett, did you get a lobotomy?' Seriously?" he says, mouth pulling tight as he reads off the name of the event I invited him to.

"I want to know. It's the only reason you'd go out of your way to spend time with me."

"If I did, life would be far less complicated."

"Well, you got the invite, don't leave me hanging," I urge him, punctuating my words with a nod. A chime sounds from my phone this time, indicating his acceptance of the invite.

"What have you gotten started with?" he asks expectantly as he settles on the couch closest to me.

"It should be a love song." Embarrassingly enough, that's all I've got. Love songs are why I came here. They sell and are what I am—well, *was*—good at. Maybe If I had more time to prepare I'd have something better.

"Play something for me," he prompts. I hesitate and he continues. "I'm not asking you to perform. Just show me what you've been playing with."

I don't want to. It would be like stripping naked here in the living room.

Growing up, piano practice was the one time I felt like I could be quiet, like I didn't need to use words to justify the air I was breathing. It was a bit of a language too, the one way I felt like I could communicate with my family that I never messed up. Drew would be in the garage practicing a groove on his drums and I'd play in the living room with its plush cream carpet, couches with red slipcovers, and the windows that overlooked mom's garden. We'd play completely different songs but depending on our selections, we knew exactly how the other was feeling. It would be similar if Mom put in one of her opera CDs, the entire mood in the house would change based on her selection.

When Drew pulled away it felt a little like I lost someone to have a conversation with. I remember right before I left for college I would play and play and play so the house felt less quiet, but even with all the music I never felt like I managed to do it for my parents or for myself. I want to be able to be understood like that with someone again.

"Fine," I say, then swallow as I spin away from him to face the piano. I steal myself. It's just Garrett. He doesn't give a shit either way.

With one last breath I play a concept I have for a bridge humming along as I go because words have been evading me recently. It has a swing to it, leaning into the feel of Jazz Standards.

"Stop." His voice cuts through the room before I'm done.

"What?" I demand.

His jaw ticks and his eyebrows shoot up in that stupid fucking expression. "Don't pull something like that and waste both of our time."

"I'm not."

"And that's why you played a version of 'Tell Me Everything' slowed down," he says, referencing one of my more upbeat songs from my first album. What's worse is that he's right and I didn't even notice.

"You've listened to my music?" I ask.

"Professional courtesy."

"Fantastic." I roll my eyes, because there's no other reason Garrett would go out of his way to listen to pop hits.

"Are you going to take this seriously?"

"I am. I'm stuck, okay!" I don't mean to shout but my frustration, everything I've been keeping to myself for over a year now, rushes out of me.

"Do you want to write?" Garrett runs a hand through his hair, ruffling the perfect strands before they fall back into place.

"Well, I wasn't planning on it. But I guess I need to."

"That's the problem."

"That I need to write this album? I have a contract and a release date and millions of people who need me to. You invited yourself to stay and help, so help." A simmering feeling starts in my chest.

"Do you want to do it? Do you feel that tug like a chord is pulling you to the piano?" he asks, prompting a phantom sensation to pluck at my heart.

"Not anymore."

His eyes soften. "We're going to spend tonight getting on the same page. I'm not going to help you write until you find something you want to write about. I'm not going to help you try and force something you'll hate. I'm not getting anywhere near that. I don't need you blaming me," he says. "Have you ever collaborated with someone before?"

"No."

Avery has offered, and of course, she's suggested working with Drew, but I've been hesitant to overlap those parts of my life. Bringing someone in on that level opens the door for disagreements that you can't come back from. There's something deeply personal about art, where it's hard to not interpret criticism as an attack. I don't want to ever push the few people I have close to me away over something I've always been good with doing on my own.

Another part of it is keeping my team small. The fewer people who know I'm Lyla West, the better. It's not like I can go and collaborate with people I don't trust on a whim, no matter how talented they are.

"I'm not saying we do nothing tonight. I'm saying we lay the foundation. I told you I'd help if you helped me. So let me." His voice softens with…God, is that pity? "I want to help you, Evelyn."

"How do I know what you're saying is going to work? What if it's a waste of time? It's not like what you wrote for Fool's Gambit is the same as what I'm doing now," I say, scrambling for a justification to stay in motion.

"I'm not promising it will work. But obviously, what you're getting at now isn't working so maybe it's worth trying."

"As if you're still an expert. The last time you wrote a song was ten years ago," I remind him.

"Trust me," he says, voice lowering to a rumble. "I've gotten better with age."

The words skitter up my spine. Sure, there were moments growing up that I might have had something close to a crush on him, but that makes me no different than millions of other people back then. Being in such consistent proximity with him has been a reminder of why, despite his icy exterior, he's hard not to look at. Even now he takes up space like it belongs to him, as if I'm the guest here imposing on his evening.

"Fine," I agree. "But I want to know something too. Why did you stop playing, why did you become a lawyer and give up?"

I feel exposed talking to him about my music. If I can peel back some of his layers, then maybe I'll feel like I'm not the only one.

"I didn't give up." He all but spits the words.

"Sure. You just walked away."

"Fine. I'll tell you why I quit if you tell me how you started," he bargains.

"You have yourself a deal. I was visiting Avery in the Hamptons for a long weekend a bit over five years ago. She was on deadline and we were mostly just messing around," I start. It was a good vacation. We'd lived in our swimsuits and cover ups dancing through every moment making us feel like we were in a golden age rom-com. It was the last night of vacation after she'd put off recording until the end of the week. I was at the piano while she was draped across it in her best impression of a jazz lounge singer. "One night we set up recording equipment so we could send demos to her agent. I guess we left the recorder on, and I sat down and played something for her. I was always writing things back then and

I only had this cheap keyboard in my apartment and the piano at the house was just so nice I couldn't resist," I explain as I glance at my own piano, the one I bought after I signed my contract and got my advance. "She edited my portion and sent it to her connections. She kept my name out of it because she knew I would never want to get something just because of being associated with Fool's Gambit. I told her no for, like, three months before I sat down and really thought about it."

"And you decided to be Lyla," Garrett states more than asks.

"Yeah. Even if I wanted to make music, it felt like if my career was starting while Drew's was still floundering and he was struggling with everything, it would just be cruel. He's doing really well, you know. He's got a therapist and is using his support system. He's happy," I remind myself, even though I just talked to him and he was fine. I'm no better than my parents, worrying over something I can't control. "With my parents…I think they blame themselves and the industry."

I'd come home and overhear them fighting sometimes when he stopped picking up their calls. My parents fought before that, sure. But it was over stupid things that never made them seem like fights, movie captions or if one of them finished a crossword without the other. I was never worried their love story would end.

With Drew, they were fighting to understand something they were never taught to openly discuss. They rarely volunteer information about the mental costs of their immigration to the United States, but from what they've shared, I know it wasn't easy. They likely experienced their own forms of depression, but thought of it as a natural price for the life they were building.

I did what I could. I stayed nearby for school because that's what they wanted. I put up with their constant check-ins and questions because I knew they were more out of worry than anything else, like if they didn't I would slip away. I worked at school for the first time in my life with the help of Quinn and Oliver. I felt good pulling my weight to keep things lighter. I liked knowing that I did that for them. I never had any problems I couldn't fix on my own, and I was happy, so happy, all the time and made sure they could see it. I made sure they didn't need to worry about me when there were more important things going on.

Garrett leans back against the couch and crosses one leg over the other. "So you got the best of both?"

"Or as much of both as I could." It was less about me and more about everyone else. If I juggled both, I could keep everything stable. Though lately it's felt like I've been trying to juggle bowling balls that have also been lit on fire.

I wouldn't be dragging all the people I cared about into a media circus. I could have my normal life with Quinn and Oliver. My parents would be satisfied and not stressed.

"Now what?" Garrett asks.

"Hmm?"

"What's holding you back from going public now?"

Sharing how I got here is one thing. The rest? I doubt I'll ever tell anyone because if I did I know they wouldn't be able to look at me the same. "I told you I'd tell you how I got started, not the rest. Your turn."

"I was always going to quit," he explains. "The plan was once I got into law school I'd leave, even if the rest of the band kept going. That was the only reason I agreed to try in the first place."

"Music was what? The equivalent to a gap year to you?" He had every right to make that choice for his life but I can't grasp why he's so disconnected from something that consumes me. Or maybe I'm jealous that he could walk away when I couldn't.

"It was practical. Don't sound shocked that I chose security." A defensive edge sharpens his voice. "The band breaking up around the same time was a coincidence, really. I made the deal I'd quit when I was ready to go to law school with Wes. Drew and Jared didn't know. I'd appreciate it if you keep it that way."

I've had this feeling since I first saw him here. It's like I've been reading my favorite book, one that I know front to back and could quote at the drop of a hat, but then I find that two of the pages are stuck together. I haven't been able to pull them apart but I know whatever is there is integral to the story, like it will be a different story entirely if I can read them.

It was easy to assume Garrett quit because he thought he was above a career in music, that he had to prove that he was the most accomplished person in any room. Now I'm starting to question if that's the truth or if that was just a simple explanation that he allowed everyone to believe.

I want to see between the pages, but I know if I pull too fast and ignore how delicate the paper is, it will tear and I will never know the truth.

"Do you miss it?" I ask.

"Yes. But even the best songs always end."

12

Garrett

Hours later, we've migrated to the floor, surrounded by scattered notebook pages with old lyric ideas and the empty food containers we got delivered from the pub. The truth is, she has enough here for an album. A good album, but obviously she doesn't see it that way. She doesn't need me; she never really has. Not with the move and definitely not with this.

But I want her to need me here.

It's been so long since I've talked about music like this—playing is one thing, creation is completely different. I want more of this electric hum in my veins even if it's for a short while.

"No, this one," I say, examining the lyrics on one of the pages. "It's pretty much the same as 'Better Not Say'."

"So, you really have listened to my music?" she purrs and plants a hand near my thigh before leaning closer. The glint in her eye tells me that her sultry tone is as intentional as it is artificial.

"I was curious." True, but I also like it. Her voice. Her words. There's this breathy way she sings the word *wisteria* that scratches an itch in my brain that I've played over again just to get enough. "From how I see it, you write about things."

"Ahh, opposed to writing about nothing and screaming into the void." She nods.

"Yeah, but sometimes it feels like that doesn't it?"

Putting music out there is a bit like hoping that the deepest parts of you are worth listening to. Screaming, *tell me you feel this too. That I'm not alone.*

"Yeah." She looks around for something specific in the mess of paper. "If only I could find this one notebook I haven't seen in ages. Not since," she pauses and hurt pinches her face, "well, for a while. It has all this stuff I nearly put in my first album."

"You'll be fine without it," I promise driven by a sudden need to comfort her.

"I guess I have to be." She sags, putting weight on the hand next to my leg, causing the tips of her fingers to brush against me. It's so fucking insignificant, but being alone with her like this seems to heighten my awareness of the smallest things.

The way she rolls her shoulders when she thinks she's messed up. How she bites at her lip when she's particularly proud of something, but waiting for approval. She's not just a pleasant yet sporadic notion anymore. All her parts are coming into excruciating focus. And I don't want to look away.

I inch away as I put the paper down then start to make a stack out of the nearby pages to occupy myself.

"I think we should call it a day." I pull my phone out and pretend to check the time. "See you tomorrow."

"Yeah, tomorrow," she says.

I gather my stuff and walk back from Evelyn's in the dark, using the beam of my flashlight to guide my way. I'm careful not to flash it up toward the windows in case it could wake Alina. Caution is the same reason why I do my best to gingerly ease open the ancient door as I enter the house so my return isn't broadcasted from the wood creaking or the hinges squealing.

"I never thought I'd see the day where I'd get to find you sneaking back after seeing a girl," Alina says from behind me, and I practically jump out of my skin, slamming the door behind me in the process.

"Shit," I hiss, partly out of shock and partly because my foot rams into the wall sending a bolt of pain up my leg. I finish locking the door and then swivel to face Alina. She's dressed in a floor length silk robe and has a cup of water in her hand that she slowly draws to her lips. "I'm not sneaking. I'm just being courteous."

"Being courteous, I didn't know that's what they're calling it nowadays. Make sure to call her when the sun is out. I've had the best night of my life with a man and then he didn't call and I immediately took him off my list."

"We're not sleeping together."

Alina huffs. "A missed opportunity. I set it up so well and you blew it."

"I'm not talking about this with you. I'm going to bed."

"Sex could be good for you. A distraction," Alina continues her pestering. Sure, tonight was the first time in weeks I haven't been fixated on leaving. But anything more besides a bit of songwriting between Evelyn and me is not even a possibility, no matter how appealing the thought of it is.

"Goodnight, Alina," I say, doing my best to shut down a conversation that no one wants to have with their nosy seventy-year-old neighbor. I know if I let Alina go on any longer she'll tell me far too much about her own exploits with scrapbooks used as visual aids.

I head to the guest room and sleep claims me the moment my head hits the pillow.

13

Evelyn

I arrive ten—well, technically eleven—minutes late to find Garrett waiting for me next to the railing of the stairs that lead up to the gazebo.

It's a sight that captures him so completely. Instead of looking relaxed, he's still somehow alert and rigid. I've always thought of him as more predator than prey, but he has this alertness that reminds me of a deer ready to bolt at any moment. It doesn't matter that his attention seems to be on his phone.

"If you're on vacation you shouldn't be doing work on your phone," I tell him in lieu of greeting.

He slips his phone in the back pocket of his tan slacks. With the addition of his green linen button down, the vintage leather watch he always wears, and his glasses, he looks a little like a handsome archeologist. Not the rugged Indiana Jones type, but a version more bookish than that.

His brows pinch together. "Care to explain what today's activity entails?"

"I thought it was fairly straightforward," I say without giving anything away.

"If you mean making a daiquiri at nine a.m. then buying Hemingway's backlist, you might be out of luck. The bookstore's classics section doesn't extend beyond Bronte, Austen, and Shakespeare."

"Let me guess, romance only?" I smile and turn to see if I can spot it from where we're standing. Bound to You has the same idyllic whimsy as the rest of the shops with its large window display and blue trim. Cute as it is, it was never actually on today's itinerary.

"Love stories and romance with a few thrillers and horror because of all the people who come in the fall," he explains.

"That's okay. I have a backup plan," I say, already walking toward our actual destination.

The latticed metal of the cafe chair presses into the backs of my thighs. Per my request, we've been seated in the farthest corner of the outside patio of Butter Half with the other brunch goers.

There's a range of other patrons from the couples in matching workout gear, who have likely been up for hours, to those in sweats and sunglasses that remind me of what I was like yesterday. I mean, it's not like I've put in much more effort with today's T-shirt that says, *Ask me about my lobotomy,* which I chose specifically in reference to the invite I sent him yesterday. Okay after I flung all my clothes on the floor, and it landed near the top. I've paired it with loose Levi's I've worn so many times that the back pocket has faded with an imprint of my phone.

When our waitress comes by, I order a croissant sandwich and a pitcher of mimosas for the two of us. Garrett gets a loaded omelet. The waitress's eyes linger on him as he looks over the menu. He has that effect on people, and I'm not sure if he fails to notice or deems it beneath him to acknowledge. I guess that could be part of the allure for people. The unattainability of the perpetual bachelor.

"You could have had breakfast by yourself then grabbed me after," Garrett gripes.

"I thought I told you to leave your pessimism at home?"

"It's not pessimistic to ask for clarification," he says.

"For one, you need a mimosa or three to act like you actually want to be here," I joke.

"And?"

"This is the perfect spot for people watching."

It was a habit before it was a hobby. In school I always thought that people were more interesting than homework or textbooks. Casual conversations and gossip taught me more about the world than my teachers did. There's something special about getting lost in what other people care about. It could be mundane, but that doesn't make it unimportant. To one person a street corner could mean nothing, and to others it's where they learned they got a promotion or stumbled into the love of their life.

I look around. "We're going to play a game to see if we can spark a seed of inspiration. We take turns picking a couple or a person and come up with their story. Think about what song you'd write about them."

"And that accomplishes what exactly?" he asks, sounding unimpressed. *Lovely.*

"Think Larson, use that stupidly big brain of yours. The reason people like music is it makes them feel something. Like they're part of something bigger, but also have their own experiences. It manages to ride the line between universal and personal."

"That explains why there's so many songs about doing coke in bathrooms, I've always wondered. It's a deeply poignant and personal experience?" His voice remains dry and disinterested, but there's an edge of a joke in there that he's carefully containing.

"See, you get it! I was starting to think I lost you," I say with an extra dose of enthusiasm.

"If your next idea is doing coke in the bathroom, the answer is no."

"No, but those songs make people feel something," I explain. "Like they're young and maybe, just maybe, they can live wild and free and not give a shit about what comes in the morning. It's freedom."

"Then show me how it's done," he says with a note of challenge in his voice.

"Pick a couple for me."

The mimosa pitcher and two champagne flutes arrive while Garrett surveys the other patrons and the meandering couples doing laps through the town.

He takes his time before his eyes fix on a table. "The people who look like they just came back from a run four tables over."

I stretch so I can take an assessing look at them. I let my mind drift back, taking a time machine to who they were before coming to this town. For me, a song, or at least the ones I used to love to write the most were only give or take seventy percent about what was happening in the moment. Break up songs are a prime example of this. There can't be a breakup if there wasn't a relationship before it. That relationship—the good, the bad, the ugly of it—gives the context for the breakup to matter. The pain has to come from somewhere.

I nod as the idea starts to form. "They met through a mutual friend. She started running because of him. She's more than happy to mold to the interests of the people she cares about. It makes her feel closer to them," I say, feeling the momentum of it build. "Still, she's never felt like she's known herself well enough to have any strong special interest of her own, so she's rarely single. He's not the type she usually goes for but he's stable and a bit of a health nut and she'd been wanting to work out for a while, so why not?

"The problem is that she never knows if she's happy or if she's just faking it so well that she even believes it because they never fight and everyone else also says they work so well together. Secretly, she wants to fight and know if he'll fight for her." I close my eyes and feel the wisp of song floating by, but as usual it's like I'm hearing it through a dream. "The song would be about staying even if you're not sure it's the best option because you'd rather be with someone than be alone."

His eyebrows arch. "That's a love song?"

"Love isn't always about making the right choices," I say, but it feels like a futile justification for my own choices. I need the words to be true if there's any hope for me to find anything like what the couples around us appear to be experiencing.

"From the sound of it, you don't need me at all. You could write a whole anthology."

"You're not getting off that easily." I laugh. "Yes, I can come up with these fully fleshed out ideas. I can find a beginning and an end, but I just make it too big. It's like shoving a month-long trip into a carry-on after you took the trip, and for the life of you, you can't figure out how you did it the first time. I have the ideas, I just can't pull it apart and stuff it neatly into three minutes." That, and the few times I've tried I hate every word I write. I can't even be good at the one thing I'm supposed to do; the thing I gave up so much to do.

"So, you're expecting me to do what exactly? Put your proverbial shoes in my bag?" he asks.

"I knew you'd catch on. Afterall, I'm an excellent teacher," I say. "Your turn."

I fill my glass from the sweating pitcher. The cool morning is starting to break into a wave of heat. I've always liked this time of year the most when you can taste summer and fall all at once. My gaze wanders as I raise my glass to my mouth. From my first sip, the fizz of the drink bursts against my tongue.

I want to see Garrett try, but there's a challenge brewing in the back of my mind. I want him to have to admit that there's something worth appreciating about Hartsfall and what it does for people.

"There," I say, tipping my already half drained glass to guide his attention. "The guy in the green hoodie holding open the door while still carrying both coffees."

"If I go with my intuition you won't get mad?" His eyes cut to the couple in question. The woman is wearing an oversized sweatshirt and shorts reminiscent of Princess Diana. A smile brightens her soft features as she talks, like there's no place she'd rather be and no person she'd rather be with. The man is holding open the door as he balances a drink carrier, all the while his eyes never leave her.

"I won't, as long as you play along," I say.

He steals another glance at the couple. "He's cheating on her."

"Seriously, what do you have against this town?" Even though I promised not to say anything, the remark rushes out of me.

"I know this place better than you. You chose the couple, and I'm just telling you what I see. It isn't just people who are happy that come here. You just admitted that." He levels me with a scrutinizing look. "He feels guilty. He's overcompensating."

"Or just wants her to have a good time. Holding doors, actively listening, really putting in that extra effort," I counter. I plant my elbows on the table and lean forward.

A muscle in Garrett's draws closer as he picks up where I left off. "And making sure she notices every single thing he's doing. My guess is that she suggested this place and he went along with it. He more than likely broke it off with whoever else he was seeing before this trip and is trying to redeem himself. He'll make her feel special and wanted and then she'll forget until he does it again." The moment he's done he reaches for his drink and takes a hearty sip.

"You barely looked," I say.

"People aren't all that complicated. You said so yourself. People all like the same song because of some common emotion. Well, they all act the same way if it means getting what they want." His eyes go back to tracking the couple as they walk further away. "It's in the details. Body language, tone, the little habits we hate but can't stop. Those all tell us more than what people are actually saying. Those don't lie." It's like he's reading from some handbook not talking about people, but maybe those two things aren't all that different to him.

Every time he makes a dig at his hometown, I feel like he's also talking about me. Like every comment is subtly saying, *how stupid do you have to be to believe in this shit?* I shouldn't have expected anything different from him.

"Do you moonlight as an armchair psychologist or something?" I pour my flute all the way to the brim with prosecco, not bothering with any orange juice.

"I make more money if I can see someone's holding out in a negotiation." Something in him tightens again, giving me the impression that there's more to his evaluations of behavior. With such a strong response to the couple, there's no way his evaluation was rooted in his love of the law.

"Okay. Then whose song is it?" I ask, trying to get back to why we started this exercise in the first place.

I'm not sure if I would have agreed to our arrangement in the first place if I knew it would be such a hassle. But I'm not one to back out of something like this.

"The person he left," he says. "Maybe they never knew they were part of an affair and are wondering what they did wrong, maybe they're left in their guilt wondering if they should tell the girlfriend. It's them. Whoever they are, they're the most interesting part of the story. The couple gets a happy ending. They're left to manage the fear that the people in their life will always want something better than them."

"I guess I know why we're invited to all the same parties, you really know how to lighten the mood," I say.

"It's just a hypothetical for a song that's never going to be written. For all we know those two are faithful and he just forgot to set the alarm clock this morning." He brushes off the moment with a non-answer.

Our food arrives as we continue. Garrett and I take turns picking tourists and coming up with their stories. An older couple who comes back every year because they want to relive the magic, proof that good things last if you care for them.

"They visit every year," I say.

"And neither of them will admit that it's never the same as the first time," he counters. "But they pretend anyway."

I jump in. "It's better that way because it becoming mundane means they've built something stable that doesn't rely on fireworks."

Another couple walking their dog in silence have come here because they're giving their relationship one last chance and Garrett is determined it will fail because they refuse to communicate how desperately they want it to work.

As we go his cynicism wanes, like he's slowly using up a store of negativity with every critique. Even so, the way he describes his scenarios draws me in. I know that not every relationship ends in a happy ending. I know that some have to end so people can find a better life or chase what they really want.

I wonder sometimes if I've ever really been in love or if I wanted to be loved so badly that I tricked myself into thinking that's what it was. I know what I had with Oliver was special. We took care of each other without having to ask. We had the same friends and liked the same movies. All the important things were there built on a foundation of years long friendship. We worked and he gave me a place where I fit so well. Well, the version of me who was desperate to be loved fit well with him.

It's hard to trust my emotions sometimes about if I want something or if I'm just caught up in the idea of it. I'm terrified of one day thinking I'm in love with someone new only to find myself in that same state of desperation. At least I'm not under any illusions with Garrett—he's with me out of necessity. It's kind of refreshing.

"Holy shit! Is that Garrett Larson, bassist of Fool's Gambit!" a chipper voice calls from down the sidewalk. "Can you autograph my arm so I can get a tattoo of it?"

A few heads whip our way at the commotion causing Garrett to glower.

The man walking toward us has a paper bag hitched into the crook of his arm. His tousled hair is the color of natural clay. Stains are splattered across his coveralls as if someone has used them to experiment with abstract art.

"Fletcher," Garrett says cooly.

The man, Fletcher, closes the gap between us with brisk strides. "Larson, how the hell are you? I didn't think you'd still be around. This is longest you've graced us with your presence since you fucked off to Tennessee. You won people good money staying so long. Not me, but people."

"So, you're Fletcher of pub-slash-garage-fame," I say as I recall my glimpse of the betting pool chat.

"Mostly garage now, haven't worked at the pub since I was trying to earn enough money to impress my prom date."

"Did you?" I ask.

"She married me, so either that or she pitied the hell out of me." Fletcher readjusts his grip on the bag he's carrying mid shrug. "Jury's still out."

Our waitress comes back and she raises a brow as she looks over the knee high decorative fence at Fletcher. "Fletcher, get in here and buy something or stop disrupting the ambiance of my section with your big mouth."

"Annie, I'm wounded. I'm just saying hi to an old friend." Fletcher gives her a pathetic pout.

"We're friends?" Garrett asks.

"I teach this guy how to replace everything from spark plugs to brake pads, and this is the treatment I get." Fletcher directs his words toward me.

"How I remember it, you were eating day-old donuts while Doug did all the teaching," Garrett corrects.

Fletcher tuts. "I was part of some of your formative memories and I think that I deserve some respect."

"I'll teach you some respect if you keep disrupting the peace," Annie presses as she starts to collect our dishes.

"What are you, a cop?" Fletcher slings back then flinches at the glare Annie gives him. "Fine. Give me one minute to ask what I gotta ask and I'll leave your precious ambiance alone."

"Good." With that Annie collects the last plate and heads back toward the kitchen.

"Sorry about that…" Fletcher trails off as he looks at me, and I realize I never introduced myself.

I hold out my hand and Fletcher takes it with worn, grease-stained fingers. "Evelyn Mariano."

"Nice to meet you, Evelyn." He releases my hand then cocks his head toward where Annie headed. "Sorry about that. Little sisters, you know."

"From living my life as one, I have a bit of experience. No offense taken. I make my older brother wish he was an only child."

"Do you actually have something to ask, or are you going to keep hovering?" Garrett's voice cuts in, clear and deliberate, like he's just as annoyed as Annie.

"Didn't mean to interrupt your date." Fletcher's eyes dance with mischief as his gaze flicks between Garrett and me.

"Not a date," Garrett corrects quickly, jaw clenching.

I love it when men are so eager to deny they're with me. Really, a great ego boost.

Fletcher forges on as if Garrett didn't say a thing. "If you have a minute, my apprentice is off today and I'm having a tough time with this old Volkswagen, you know the type. There's this angle I can't quite get. I had a bit of a boating incident that snapped my wrist and the doc doesn't want me to force anything. I'd risk it, but she'll notice if I get home tonight and make a fuss."

Garrett looks at me then to the clock tower. "Evelyn and I are in the middle of something."

"I don't mind, we can include this as part of our outing," I say, trying not to sound like I'm jumping at the opportunity.

Admittedly, I'm curious. I doubt that I'll be offered more from Garrett about the affinity for fixing cars I witnessed a few days ago. This is likely one of the few chances I'll get to learn more.

"We'll meet you at the garage after we pay," Garrett says as he reaches for his water.

"You better tip Annie well with all that fancy ass money of yours. She might be a pain in my ass but she's damn good at her job." Fletcher salutes with his free hand before heading off.

"Do you have an extra pair of coveralls?" Garrett asks once we find Fletcher by the door connecting a small office to the work area of the garage.

There are two main bays. One, as promised, has a boxy, old Volkswagen Golf. It looks like it was taken straight out of a Wes Anderson film with its bright orange paint job and dramatic angles.

"In the back by the bathroom. Haven't moved since the last time you were here. There should be a few clean ones." Fletcher tosses the words over his shoulder as he uses his hip to push through to the office. "Evelyn, you can come with me. Sorry, this place isn't all that spacious. Since I'm walking distance from the shops, people don't usually wait here."

Fletcher holds the door open for me to the room. Cracked leather chairs line one wall. Above them is a peeling paper with the Wi-Fi password. Most of the space is taken up by the type of huge greenish metal desk you can find at military surplus sales.

When Garrett comes back, he's wearing blue coveralls with a blank name tag. Fletcher leaves the office to meet him at the car. I can't make out what they're saying and I doubt I would be able to understand what they were talking about if they were. After a few moments, they stand upright and Fletcher laughs as he thumps Garrett on the back. The sign of friendly affection has Garrett's expression souring. At least he's like that with everyone and not just me.

There's a digital chime as Fletcher comes back into the office. "Sorry for stealing some of your time. He knows what he's doing and the old couple who own this car are headed up to Niagara Falls. I can't, in good conscience, send them up that way in a car that old in its current state."

I nod along to Fletcher's words, but my attention is fixed to where Garrett is selecting his tools from where they're neatly organized on the far wall. The sleeves of the coveralls are rolled up past his forearms revealing the taut muscles and veins running down to strong hands. Those toned forearms of his should come with a content warning. I bet he sits at his desk most days with his sleeves rolled up and those things out there for anyone to see, completely disregarding that he's impacting other people's ability to concentrate.

"Did he learn how to do all of this here?" I ask, seizing the time to get more information.

"Yeah. Annie and him went to school together. His mom, well, she wasn't the most reliable. One day my dad came by with Garrett 'cause she forgot to pick him up. He was even more damn quiet back then. After that he'd come back with Annie and watch Dad, until my old man offered to teach him the basics." Fletcher starts to move to an ancient industrial coffee maker. The pot still holds a generous amount of black steaming liquid. He points but I shake my head. Even if I did drink coffee, whatever he's having would no doubt ruin my stomach lining. "When he went off to Tennessee for that fancy high school he would come back over winter breaks and work as much as he could. I'm not sure if he was bored or what. Smartest guy I've ever met, smartest person besides my wife, Emily, but he's a close second."

Fletcher pours himself a mug from the sizzling coffee pot and joins me at my vantage point where I'm leaning on the edge of his desk.

"I gotta ask, are you Mariano as in the Mariano that was the drummer in his band?" Fletcher asks, then takes a sip and winces at what I assume is the foul taste. Nothing simmering that long can be good.

"That's how we know each other. I'm pretty sure I'll always be his bandmate's obnoxious little sister," I say, ensuring Fletcher has a clear picture of our situation.

"I hope you don't take it personally. I think the only person he actually likes is Alina, and she won't let people not like her."

A laugh burbles from me. "Yeah. I got that impression."

"I know I'm the minority in this, but I really wish he kept up with that band. I mean, seriously, he's so damn good. Like, I'd be pissed about how good he is at shit, but I think it's the universe making up for the cards it handed him. He always planned on getting one of those jobs with a degree that he could frame in a jail cell of an office. Probably felt like he had to since Alina and a few other folks made up the difference to pay his tuition for that boarding school."

"His parents weren't the ones who sent him there?"

Fletcher grimaces for the first time since I've met him. "It was always just his mom and him. But she wasn't exactly the type to show up."

Before I can ask more, Garrett pushes through the door with his elbow and Fletcher tosses him a clean rag with practiced ease. I try to picture a younger version of them doing this. I have the creeping suspicion Garrett had the same severe expression he has now as an adult.

"Should be good now if you want to take a look," Garrett says as he wipes the grease from his hands on the yellow cloth.

There's something about this exact version of him that I want to keep seeing, the one that's a little messy and undone. It's like a secret I want to tuck under my tongue, a piece that I have that he's hidden from everyone else.

Fletcher nods. "Thanks, man. I'm happy I ran into you."

"No problem." A digital alarm goes off and Garrett pulls his phone from his pocket to silence it. He looks at me. "Well, we're done. Time to go."

The statement is jarring. The words take a moment to hit me full force. God. Did he set an alarm to go off at the end time of the invite I sent him? Is that why he was checking the time when Fletcher stopped by earlier, not because he wanted to stay with me, but because he felt obligated? A lump settles in my throat making it hard to breathe.

"So desperate to get rid of me that you set an alarm?" I joke, but at the same time there's a deep ache. He's been clear about not loving the idea of vacation, but I never would have guessed he'd be this eager to get away from me.

"I'm just staying organized," he says.

"Great." I match his curt matter-of-fact tone. "I'll get going then."

"I'll walk you back."

"No, it's fine," I insist as I feel a prickling heat build behind my eyes. "I'll see you for our next appointment when you're obligated to put up with me."

I don't give him the chance to make me feel more insignificant than he already has and walk away.

14

Garrett

"That's one way to end a date." Fletcher fails to conceal his amusement as he lifts his mug to take a sip.

"Wasn't a date," I say pointedly. Maybe for a moment it felt like it was, with her full attention on me and the way that, despite the alarm on my phone, I could have let it go on forever.

"Even if it wasn't, you're still an asshole," he says, then places the mug on the desk beside him. "Just because you're pissed about being here you shouldn't take it out on her."

He's right. I hate the way her face fell before she all but ran out of the garage. I should have gone after her. I should have done something; I just didn't want to make things worse.

I use the rag he's given me to aggressively scrub at the grime collecting in the creases of my knuckles. "That's not what this is about."

"Well, excuse me if I'm making assumptions based on the fact that you treat your visits home like damn business trips and you won't even claim this place publicly as where you're from," he says, and I throw him a look. "Yeah, I've seen the fucking interviews. Everyone loves to paint the picture of the boys from Tennessee who came from middle class backgrounds to become stars. The fucking American dream."

"What if I don't want to be here?"

I come back frequently enough. I check in and keep tabs through the endless group messages. But staying?

I don't have a permanent place here. Alina's guest room is just that, temporary. It doesn't matter if this is where I was born, even when I had a home here it wasn't like it felt like one. This garage is a manifestation of that too. It was a place I'd visit because there was nowhere else to go. I made myself useful enough to be invited back. Fletcher had a spot here because he was born to take over. I always felt one screw up away from being asked to leave.

"Doesn't matter. God knows why she's using that time and spending it with you. So, even if you hate being here, find a fucking ounce of decency and don't waste her time," he chastises, the words pelting me in the chest. He crosses his brawny arms the same way his dad used to when he'd check my work back in the day and found a loose bolt.

"I didn't mean to offend her." That's the last thing I wanted. But there's this constant tug-of-war. Wanting her to be around while knowing it's a terrible idea. Wanting to keep her even if I know that I'll screw it up.

"Words work wonders, you know. I might have a *Conversations for Dummies* guide sitting around somewhere that I can loan you," he says, returning to his usual unserious self and rifling through a stack of documents on the desk.

"Since when can you read?"

"Since Emily said she liked books." He beams. The man would do anything for his high school sweetheart.

"And does the town golden boy have any ideas about how to get a girl to forgive him?"

"You coming to me for relationship advice? If I knew it was my lucky day I would have put more money down on my bet that Sara and Winnie would put passive aggressive Shakespeare quotes on their shop windows this week." His notion isn't that far-fetched since it wouldn't be the first time they used literature to air their grievances.

"I'm not asking you for relationship advice."

"Platonic, romantic. Doesn't matter." He shrugs, and I don't bother to correct him. Evelyn and I know each other but I wouldn't go as far to say we're friends. As of now, we have mutual interest tying us together. An arm's length distance is the safest, but if I want even that, I do have to repair this misunderstanding.

"So, do you have any ideas?" I prompt.

A smile breaks across his face. "Lucky for you, tomorrow is Tuesday."

I text Evelyn first thing in the morning to see if she's free tonight, all I get in response is a calendar invite.

```
Mysterious outing: Tuesday, 7 p.m. - 11
p.m. @ ???
```

Maybe it's not the best sign, with its passive aggressive undertone, but at least she's giving me a chance to redeem myself. I pull up to her place a bit before seven and because she's still not disconnected from my Bluetooth, I get a brief soundbite of what she's listening to.

"—out track nine is objectively the strongest, but is mid-range compared to *Seeing Double* and *Passing Through*. I'd rather relisten to—" The man overly articulates every word, broaching newscaster territory.

I only get the sentence to go off of, but I recognize the names of Lyla West's first and second albums.

Evelyn's albums. I don't know if I'll ever get used to that.

Though I've casually listened to the albums before, I've been relistening to them recently with heightened intent. I tell myself it's for research, that it will help me learn what she's capable of and familiarize myself with her style of writing. There's another layer to it, listening to the songs and knowing that the words are hers makes me feel like I understand her more. There are emotions in the music that I've never seen her outwardly show. Anguish, longing, and an emptiness that never slips onto her face.

The front door flies open, revealing Evelyn hastily shoving a granola bar into her mouth so she can free her hands to grab her keys. Once the door is locked she waves and sprints over to the convertible.

"Hey," she says, the words muffled through another bite as she slips onto the leather seat next to me.

"Were you listening to a review earlier?" I ask.

"Maybe. It's not like you care," Evelyn brushes me off. For a moment, it looks like she's going to kick her feet up on the dash then thinks better of it.

"It's not healthy to listen to shit like that if you're already in a rut," I say.

"I like to know what expectations I need to meet with the album." She shrugs.

I know I'm dipping into dangerous waters with this topic, but I keep going. "I thought we talked about this."

"I don't remember podcasts coming up over the last few conversations."

"Eve, you know what I mean. You're getting caught up in what other people think the album needs to be. Are you actually going to be happy with that?"

Her music is good, too good for her to be seeking out the opinions of idiots who've never written a day in their lives. Why can't she see that?

"Do I have to remind you that it's my album and not yours?" she asks, her smile twitching as if it's an effort to maintain it.

"Are you going to let me disconnect your phone from the car?" I ask, twisting to check the road as I back out of the driveway, my hand landing on the back of her seat.

"How else will you continue to eavesdrop on integral moments in my life?" She sounds winded. When I turn back, I catch her staring at where my hand rests against the leather.

"So if I disconnect it, you'll just add your phone back to the system?" My question has her focus snapping back to my face.

"Pretty much."

The Gas Station has transformed the usual way it does on Tuesday nights. A podium stands at the far end just beyond the pool tables. Rows of metal folding chairs cover the checkered linoleum. Fifty or so people have already shown up and dozens more will trickle in throughout the night.

"What is this?" Evelyn hisses as we claim seats in the very back. Proceedings are already underway with Pat loudly reading tonight's agenda from her yellow legal pad.

"Town-Hall-trivia-night," I say.

"Excuse you," she replies as if I've just sneezed.

"What?"

Her eyes light up in amusement. "You just said a lot of words that make no sense strung together."

"Because the businesses here stay open late most of the week, they close early on Tuesdays so they can come here for town hall meetings then trivia right after. It's more efficient." I maintain a hushed voice as Pat moves onto the first item on tonight's agenda. "They used to have the meetings across town then trivia after, but attendance shot up the moment liquor was involved."

The rumble of disgruntled voices rise around us. In response, Pat thwacks her gavel to silence the crowd. I've always thought it was a bit excessive, but it's better than the whistle she used to use and way better than the attempts at incorporating a megaphone.

It's been years since I've attended one of these. Usually, I only come up on weekends, unless Alina is in dire need of help with a repair and then I'm too preoccupied to spend time coming here. Still, I get the highlights. Every time I delete myself from the group chat designated for updates, I find myself added back against my will.

"Is Pat the mayor or something?" Evelyn's eyes rove over the chaos around us. The energy could rival an auction house, even if they are only discussing the day to release seasonal flavors in town.

"High school gym teacher during the day. The mayor is mostly honorary."

"Hmm."

"Today is going to be mostly Love Letter festival stuff."

"Oh, hell yeah," she emphatically whispers back. "I planned my trip around making sure I could see it before I left."

"Every year it's the biggest fucking headache."

"It can't be that bad. I mean, it looks so fun. Or maybe, it being fun is the entire reason you hate it," she remarks, cocking her head to the side in mock consideration.

"That's because you see the pretty final product for one day that takes months of prep," I say. Hartsfall does well for a tourist town. Money is good year round. In the fall there's the festival and the trees. In winter we are a good place for skiers to lodge, not too far from the slopes and bigger resorts. Spring and summer are nice enough. But the festival is the biggest draw. It often gives families the financial extra boost to buy things they've been putting off or save for the holidays. "Three years ago the gazebo caved in. We had twenty-four hours to replace the entire floor and did it all at night so it wouldn't disrupt the tourists. Who needs a good night's sleep when the tourist might be a little inconvenienced?"

"There's no way."

"Yes," I affirm, my voice rising.

"Thank you, Garrett, for stepping up and showing some festive spirit!" Pat bellows.

Evelyn shrinks into her folding chair. "Are we being reprimanded?"

"I have no fucking clue." When my eyes lock with Pat's, I know whatever's happening is penance for me talking out of turn, even if we're in the back of the building. This is exactly why I don't come to town meetings.

Poppy, a redhead with springy curls who helps run the pottery studio and the inn in town, looks back from where she's seated a row in front of us. "I think you just agreed to go up to the Barlowes' and do the official wine tasting on Thursday."

"No," I say. "I didn't."

"Try telling Pat that," Poppy says as Pat moves onto the next point of order.

"What's wrong with wine tasting?" Evelyn asks.

"I'll tell you later. You'll probably love it," I explain.

The wine tasting is the one assignment for the festival that people avoid like the plague. The wine itself is great. But the Barlowes have been known to change what they donate to the festival based on how much they like the people sent to the taste testing. On some occasions the good stuff has all been "out of stock" other times they give the town extra, allowing the celebration to stretch an extra day with the alcohol alone. So it's safe to say Pat would like me to shut the hell up.

The agenda alternates between things that matter and things that only matter to the town in their own special way. Love is Brewing is thinking about transitioning to a coffee roaster in Rochester. There's a pothole that's given three tourists flats in the last month and simply won't stay filled. The high school band wants permission to change their set list for the festival.

Once Pat gives the final bang of the gavel, everyone rises from their chairs in a practiced but chaotic fashion. People do their best to not drag the chairs but there's a decent amount of clanging and scraping.

"Time for trivia?" Evelyn asks.

"If you want to." It's part of the reason I brought her here, but if she doesn't want to stay we don't have to, even if it means having Alina saying something about it later.

"Do you?

"I'm not allowed to play." My phone buzzes in my pocket and I reach to silence it at risk of angering Pat even more.

"You're kidding." Evelyn's eyes shine with delight. "Got caught cheating? Couldn't handle losing? You're starting to sound like a deviant."

"No. I'm a little too good at winning," I admit.

"Of course that's why." She playfully rolls her eyes.

"The jerk's never lost a game. Not fair to the rest of us who want to enjoy some good competition," Pat explains as she walks up next to us. "He has the honor of tallying points. I came over to tell you that I'm taking drink orders for the next ten minutes before we get going."

Pat gives me a hearty thump on my back before she heads off to tell others to get to the bar.

"So, stay or leave?" I ask, trying not to act like I care either way. I'm hit with an unexpected wave of protectiveness for the town. I don't give a shit about what the tourists see, but this is special. These are people who mean something to me, and I want her to see that they're worth more than the cute shop names and a marketable theme. They are the heart and soul of Hartsfall; the reason people believe in happy endings.

"How do I join in?" she asks with genuine curiosity that puts my fears to rest.

I break down the rules, then Evelyn splits off and joins a group with Alina, Poppy, and Sara. Within moments she strikes up a conversation with them. I shouldn't have expected anything less. My phone starts to buzz again. Probably Wes is just bored, a few hours alone won't kill him. The only people who would call me in an emergency are in this room, so I silence the phone again.

"I could make an exception for tonight," Pat says as I meet her at the folding table that has been set up with the list of questions, a microphone, and score sheets.

"Don't go getting any ideas. I already have Alina's match-making delusions." The last thing I need are more people pushing me in Evelyn's direction. I can handle being around her for two weeks, but it's smart for me to not test my limits to. Anything more than what we're up to is a one-way trip to one or both of us getting hurt. Even if she saw me that way, I'd just disappoint her. I'm not exactly the open, carefree type that can get swept up in the moment with her.

"If that's how you want to play it. Pick up a pencil and get ready to help me read the most god-awful handwriting known to man."

"I'm *not* playing it any specific way."

"And you're also *not* looking over to check in on her every five seconds when it seems like she has a damn good handle on fitting in," Pat says, feigning disinterest while reviewing the first set of questions.

I glance over, despite myself, to see Evelyn talking animatedly, like she's been coming here for ages. For the rest of the first half, each time I look she's cheering or booing along with her team, immersing herself in the game.

By the time we reach the lightning round, my phone rings for a third time, earning me a warning look from Pat. I won't risk pulling it out and buying nearly a third of the town drinks. I can afford it, but it's the principle of it. After the town hall meeting wrapped up, more people have filled the space to the point where it's standing room only. There's likely a fire code being broken, but that's not news to anyone.

"I'm going to get this," I tell Pat after she turns up the music for the one-minute time allotted for team members to deliberate and bring up their answers.

"Take your time. We have a break before the second half starts. Turn the damn thing off before you come back in." She waves me toward the door.

Outside, the parking lot is full. Trucks are parked off the edge of the packed pavement. I walk to a shadowed corner away from the buzzing streetlamp and old gas station sign. My phone goes off again and Lana's contact lights up my phone as I slip it from my pocket.

"Yeah?" I answer, the word heavy on my tongue. My hand squeezes the phone to prevent it from shaking.

"How are you?" she asks cheerily.

"Fine. Is there something wrong with your payments?"

"I heard you were home," she ignores me, but that's to be expected.

"I am." I shouldn't be surprised that town gossip has reached her, but I wish it hadn't.

"What if I came to visit? It's been so long since I've seen you," she says, causing my stomach to twist.

Fifteen years.

Fifteen years since we've been face to face. Fifteen years since she showed up at our tour stop in Vegas. She was smiling and wearing a glittery dress that managed to stick out in a crowd. We talked before I was supposed to go on for a mic check.

It's the only performance I ever missed. The resulting migraine that came made it unsafe for me to be on stage with my nausea and spotty vision. It made me feel so useless. Everyone performed while I was tucked away in a dark hotel room.

Even though I haven't seen her since, Lana and I still talk like this on occasion, or she sends me pictures of a chessboard from a trip to an antique store with messages like *Reminds me of those times I'd come home from work and find you still up at midnight.*

"You know what our deal is." It's simple now that it's been in place for a while. I give her monthly payments on the condition that she never comes back to Hartsfall and never asks for more. It's her hometown, but she was hell bent on making people's lives miserable when she lived here. The town took care of me when she didn't, and I'm returning the favor.

Sometimes, I feel like I've given her a choice. Me and the town or the money; fifteen years and I've never made the cut.

"There are things I want to talk to you about in person, and oh, I miss the fall there. How are the stars? I bet they're so bright. Tell me what they look like.."

I tilt my head to see stars wink at me over the treetops. "It's cloudy tonight."

My attempt to stop her stream of consciousness rambling proves ineffective as she barrels on. "Oh, what about the trees, are the trees starting to turn? You know, when I was growing up, I used to collect leaves. Your grandma and I would try to get the biggest one each year. I think I still have pictures of some of them. Have I shown you the pictures? If not, I can bring them."

I do my best to block out the words.

She always means what she says, genuinely cares as words pour from her lips. That's why everyone was willing to give her chance after chance, no matter what she did. She says sorry and you can't help but believe her. She wants to show me these pictures and share the memories. But that is a foot in the door that has never led to anything good. In the end something else will catch her attention.

I hate thinking about it, but Lana reminds me a bit of Evelyn and the thought terrifies me. They both have this way of drawing people in, making them feel interesting and special. They don't make small talk seem like an inconvenience and they want to share something with you, show you how they see the world in sparkling color. They're fundamentally different beyond that. Lana wants to take, make things hers, make you believe that she is someone you can never leave because she shines so brightly. Evelyn would give her light away if it made you happy. I know the difference. I remind myself of it like a mantra. But it remains as a barrier I have to keep up no matter how much Evelyn draws me in, how much I love when she challenges me and makes me want her.

"I'm busy," I say. This is the last thing I need.

"You can't make time for your mother?" she whines.

Like you made time for me?

I struggle with it. She was seventeen when she had me. I can't imagine having to take care of an entire other person at that age. Sometimes she did a good job, other times she didn't. She'd miss rent payments or forget to get groceries because she ate meals at work. I learned to be self-reliant and careful. I learned everything I could so I could do it for myself.

"I have to go," I say, already knowing this conversation isn't going anywhere.

"Consider it," she pleads. "Please."

"I have." I hang up.

No matter how short the conversations are with her, or if it's been over a year since we last talked, my body feels like it's under attack, muscles tightening for an invisible blow.

I keep my phone out and I pull up the chess app. It's the mechanism I use when I can't sit down and play music. Something that requires my full attention to get a clear-cut desired outcome without any catastrophic stakes. Pat is the one who introduced me to the concept, almost forced it on me, because so many of the things I took up as "hobbies" were more work than play since I wanted nothing to do with people my age.

The bar door swings open and music spills into the night as everyone enjoys the intermission. A few seconds later, Pat turns the corner.

She gives me a once over then wordlessly starts pulling out a pack of cigarettes from her pocket. I hold out a hand and Pat places one of her Marlboros in it. After a flick of her lighter, I prop the cigarette between my lips, taking a long inhale.

I've mostly kicked the habit. I know it only makes my migraines worse in the long run. Still, there's nothing else that quite grounds me like smoking. It was the first act of rebellion I ever took part in. Knowing it was against the rules was a thrill. Now I need it to remind myself that I'm finally the adult who has the power to do what I need.

"You're a bad influence, being a teacher and all," I say as I ash the cigarette.

"Good thing you're too old to be one of my students." She takes a drag. "Who was it?"

"Lana." Her name is sour on my tongue.

"Shit," she spits.

"Yeah." There's something nice about being able to say her name and people knowing. Sometimes I hate the reactions, the pity that melts people's eyes like I'm still twelve and sitting alone on a park bench doing my homework.

Pat's good with it, though. She knows shitty things are just that. Shitty.

"Why'd you bring the girl back?" Pat asks, pointedly changing to what apparently has become everyone's new favorite subject.

"It's not a date." I might have to tattoo it on my forehead at this point.

"Didn't say it was."

"It was an apology," I explain. "We had a bit of a misunderstanding."

"All cleared up?"

"Maybe. It was over the alarms I put on my phone for when I'm done with tasks," I say. It's a technique I've had since I was a kid, so Pat is familiar with it. I couldn't control much, but I could choose how to use my time.

"No one wants to feel like a task, just so you know," Pat says. "A bit dehumanizing. But maybe if she knows why, it'll help in the long run."

"Fuck," I groan. How are we going to get through two weeks if I'm failing after one day?

"People have never been your thing, kid. Doesn't mean you can't learn. Let's get inside before they come and hunt us down."

After trivia, Evelyn helps put up chairs and clean up spills. All the while she talks to everyone. Her laughs break through the music and have other people looking at her with endearing smiles. I think about how she should have been the one from here, not me. She fits in a way I've never been able to, never allowed myself to.

It's past midnight when we leave. Evelyn leans with her head resting on her hand as we cruise. Despite the light nipping breeze, there's a glowing warmth in my chest and she might be the culprit.

"Tonight was fun, the trivia questions made me feel like an idiot. But still, it was a good time," she says as I pull to a stop in front of her house.

"You accept my apology then?"

"You're missing the key part where you apologize. If you need a refresher a good place to start is with 'I'm sorry.'" Her expression grows expectant.

"I am sorry, Eve. I never wanted to make you feel like you were something to check off a to-do list. I am sorry for that," I tell her. I try not to look away as my face heats with embarrassment.

"Honestly, I overreacted a little. I was having a pretty good time, and I thought you were too, so thinking you just wanted to get rid of me pissed me off."

Here goes nothing. "If it's okay with you, I'm going to keep the alarms though, but I'll explain why, if you want."

"If it's because you're secretly a spy and need to check in with your handler I will take it as an acceptable excuse."

"As fun as that sounds, I doubt I'd be able to tell you if that were true. It's just that I like structure and to know what's going on and when. Putting on timers and alerts makes certain I never lose track of that," I explain.

As I was first introduced to a stable schedule, I clung to it. It was something I could control. It's part of the reason I liked boarding school so much. I knew where I needed to be and when. I knew the meal schedule and that the food would always be there.

"Is there a reason you're insistent on me having an action-packed double life?" I'm okay with explaining, but I'm not sure if I want to open myself to more questions.

"It's lonely being the only one, and it's a waste to let your looks not be used for espionage and debauchery. You even have the car for it!" she says then reaches over to slap the dash. "And just so we're clear, you like the calendar invites for the same reason?"

"Yes."

"I'll make sure not to forget them. But I'm going to use my time to the fullest and make you have a little fun." She throws me a wink. "I'm going to get a real smile out of you, Larson, even if it kills us both."

15

Evelyn

The Love Letter Museum has been at the top of my list of places to visit since I first browsed through blogs detailing the local attractions. If I can't come up with my own words dripping with love and sincerity, maybe I can find some glimmer of inspiration in someone else's. It's housed in a robin's egg blue Victorian with a few dedicated parking spots out front.

It's no surprise to find Garrett a few feet from the door tapping away at his phone. I pull out my own phone to take a picture of him and find a notification from Mom waiting for me.

Mom

Your father showed me this article. It's good you're out of the city.

I don't even bother looking at the headline of the article that no doubt details a violent crime. Instead of actually telling me they want me to move back, they usually send articles or news clips to not-so-subtly convince me to come back. There's a universe where I send them crime statistics showing that Nashville has higher crime rates. I don't, I never will, but I like knowing that I have the option to throw an Uno reverse card into the mix. Anyway, what I know they're really saying is *we miss you and we care about you.*

I lightly shake my head trying to dislodge the tense feeling that accompanies these types of texts.

I refocus on Garrett and open the camera app. Taking a step, I make sure to get the sign with the museum name and a small *existed since 1927* in frame.

"What are you doing?" he asks as I press the capture button. With the clouds still blocking the sun, the light coming from his screen casts shadows highlighting the sharp corners of his face.

"Pulling my weight. You know you better come through for our part of the deal on Friday!" I call back then walk up the paved driveway to meet him.

I know the exact moment when he reads my shirt. I have other clothes, sure, but the way his eyebrows pull skyward every time is ever so satisfying.

Today's selection reads, *I wish Italians were real.*

"Aren't you Italian?" he asks.

"And every day I wish I was real. It's really hard work being a figment of your imagination. Living in your head has its downsides. I mean, who gets turned on by dusty law textbooks when there's better stuff out there?"

"I don't think I could make you up if I tried to," he says as his eyes flicker over me.

"I'm just that devastatingly fun and good looking." I sigh as if exhausted by it.

He lets out a huff. "Something like that."

The inside of the museum is reminiscent of a bed and breakfast with its large front desk the moment you step inside. An electric fireplace is running in the corner crackling under the acoustic pop music playing, adding to the welcoming ambience of the lobby.

Garrett goes to the desk to buy our tickets then returns with pens and two pieces of thick paper with uncut edges.

"Love letter supplies, it's included in the ticket cost," he explains as we start to wander into the first room. There's a slight creaking overhead, likely from other patrons, but the downstairs appears to be empty.

Instead of the wooden benches I've seen in other museums, there are loveseats interspersed in the room. Antique pens ranging from metal-tipped feather quills to engraved ball points are arranged along one wall. Further down are an array of signet rings and wax seals. The room appears dedicated to the art of all the details that go into the perfect letter.

"Are you going to write me one?" I joke.

"I doubt you'd enjoy that. It wouldn't stack up to all your other ones," he says.

"You know I'm not like that. I don't float through life on a cloud just collecting relationships dreaming of happy endings," I tell him. Would it kill the man to take me seriously? He's just as bad as my parents with how they act like I never grew up.

"You're right, I don't think that you float on a cloud. It's more of a bubble like the witch from the *Wizard of Oz*." He keeps a straight face and even tone, but somehow that makes it feel even more like a joke than if he had tried to make it funny.

"Glad we have that cleared up. And just so you know, I am not a proud member of the love letter club."

"Really?" he asks. "Because you're the exact type of person guys slip letters into lockers for."

"Yes, of course, since you're an expert on girls' lockers from your time at an *all-boys school*." I slide him a glance.

"You know what I mean."

"I do. But you're still wrong," I say. "I wasn't unpopular in school, but I had a tendency to scare guys off. I had dates to dances and friends, but there was no line of suitors knocking down my door with bouquets of wildflowers."

I didn't hate my high school experience. I'd even say I had fun. But that was back before I knew how to reign myself in. I was constantly in trouble for talking too much in class or being disruptive. It probably had something to do with having a famous brother and needing to feel seen in my own right, but back then I didn't think about it that way. I just wanted to be noticed at full volume. I was fun at parties, but never the girl anyone wanted to sweep off her feet.

"What about that guy you were with who always looked like a Labrador who downed a shot of espresso?" he asks.

It takes me a second to realize first, that he's talking about Oliver—who yes, always had this energy that verged on feeling artificial until you got to know him. Second, there's the fact that he's aware of my dating history. I don't know how to feel about that.

"No love letters there either. That wasn't our type of relationship," I say as I walk over to the single letter in the room. One that's never been opened, its rose-embossed crimson wax seal still intact. Alice scrawled on the front in looping cursive, the intricate penmanship like a fingerprint. Whatever is inside, it never got to Alice and I can't help but feel sorry for the long dead lovers.

"But you wrote love songs about him?" he clarifies.

"He doesn't know they are about him," I say, as if that makes it better.

"And how exactly does that work?"

I've only confronted that question in my head, so it takes a moment to find any words. "We kind of had this low grade happiness. It was good, good enough that it made both of us satisfied that we weren't settling. Our relationship wasn't risky and I think that was a big part of the appeal of it. I think both of us knew that if we really wanted to, we could find someone else to make us happier, but we didn't. It's why after we broke up things were off, but we could still be friends." Or at least, that's why I think so.

Oliver and I had something important in common. We both wanted to belong somewhere stable. He's the oldest and only boy in a slew of half-siblings. I've gone with him to three of his father's nine weddings since we met. Oliver was never resentful. He always had this hope that it would work and always got along with his sisters. But, like me, he wanted something that wouldn't be pulled out from under him. In a world where I didn't have music, I think we would have lasted.

We almost did.

I kept music from him and Quinn because I knew what that type of career could do to people. I saw it happen with Wes and Avery. I saw it with Drew and his bandmates, with Garrett. I saw it with my family. I opted to not talk about music and hoped that would somehow limit its effect on my relationships.

"You still love him?" Garrett asks.

"I always will. Just not that way." I take in a deep breath, ready to move onto something other than the past. "Enough about that. This is a research trip, let's research."

We split off because there's nothing we've established that mandates that we have to spend time together. Still, there's a part of me that is cleaved in two like someone has torn a letter off the wall and ripped it down the middle. Beyond Avery, there's no one else I've been able to tell the truth to, and with Garrett I feel like I can tell him anything. Not because I think he'll care, but because he doesn't.

Unfortunately, the idea causes an old fear to bubble to the surface. I think I need him more than he needs me. He can take pictures all around town without my help. I, on the other hand, really am fucked if I can't finish this album.

These thoughts follow me as I wander through the museum. It's not large. There are five main exhibits with informational materials scattered through the long halls that connect them. The downstairs has three of the rooms. One holds donated letters from the last hundred or so years with words from soldiers to their lovers and sweethearts who maintained their affection across long distances.

There are newer letters too, some from this last year collected from visitors to the town. Another is a room painted from wall to wall with the words of a letter from the town's founder to his wife. I spin around the room reading the words in their clear block letters that thank her for staying with him despite his faults and the time that is spent away.

I have been gone most days, yet you stay. Behind closed eyes I carry your image with me to meetings and across miles. When I return I rest my head next to yours. It is a gift to be the one you trust in sleep. There is no fruit as sweet as the charity you grant me in remaining by my side.

The letter is simple, but it pulls at something in my chest.

The last two exhibits are upstairs. The first has displays discussing how love letters can come in many mediums, music, paintings, monuments. I find Garrett in the last room filled with historic replicas sitting and looking down at his phone. The old wooden floors creak as I walk, calling his attention to my entrance.

"You could leave, if you don't actually want to be here," I say, acknowledging his disinterest.

"It's disingenuous to send pictures pretending I've gone somewhere. And for all I know I'll have a damned quiz waiting for me to recap all of our adventures."

"I just love how desperate you are to spend your days with me," I say as I take a seat next to him. "Enlighten me, then. Why are you so averse to being in the moment?"

"Asking me to ruin it for you?"

"I'm not a five-year-old at a puppet show." I know things are a performance, but that doesn't take away all the joy.

"Sure, but we all have things we'd rather pretend aren't there."

"I promise not to blame you for causing me to get a headache from thinking too hard."

"I'm not calling you stupid. That's never what I mean."

"But I have the energy of a fairy who wears pink glittery dresses and flies around in bubbles," I remind him and playfully nudge his knee. He stares at my leg for a moment before pulling away, creating more distance between us.

"First of all, she's a witch, and second, I firmly believe that she was the mastermind of the film," he says in his standard neutral tone.

"You know, your dedication to fact checking is kind of cute," I say, fighting to contain a laugh.

"Well, the facts about this place aren't as cute. The town is a bit over two hundred years old but the festival has only been going on since the seventies. Tourism was down, but when Woodstock started in '69 other towns had the idea of starting their own festivals to draw people in. Originally, it was in August, but slowly changed to October 14th because of all the leaf peepers."

"Leaf peepers?" I interrupt.

"Tourists. The ones who come to look at the leaves," he explains. "Well, the festival started and Hartsfall changed everything down to its motto to make it work. There was no deep dedication to love, it was always about money." His shoulders heave in a sigh then his gaze roves around the room until his eyes land on a particular letter. "All of these are replicas of the most famous love letters in history. Marilyn Monroe writing to Joe DiMaggio." He points to one letter then another. "Elizabeth Taylor to Richard Burton. The promises written in these letters were lies we use to draw people back every year peddling the same fantasy."

"I don't think so."

"That the relationships didn't fail?"

"The promises weren't lies," I say. "I think they meant all of it, okay, most of it. But life just got in the way."

His eyes narrow. "I thought you wanted my perspective, but if you just want to argue about something we can pick a more interesting topic."

"I do. I'm listening," I tell him then seal my mouth shut.

"You know I don't actually have anything against happy endings or true love. But in these letters"—he gestures to the wall but his eyes jump to mine and hold them—"everyone ignores the truth. Everyone wants to be the exception."

"I don't think love is the exception. Love doesn't have to last to be important, you know." I feel like I'm talking to myself as much as I've been talking to him. I almost believe my own words because I have to. I want what I'm saying to be true, I need it to be. "There is one thing I don't particularly like. These were all private once. I don't mind the donated ones, but the ones that come from celebrities, not so much. They already had such limited privacy and then these vulnerable moments, that just feels too much."

"I think I might be making you a pessimist," he mutters.

"Or I'm a romantic realist and you're finally getting to know me."

We make our way out of the museum after the alarm goes off on Garrett's phone. When we say goodbye and go our separate ways, it's not like he's my favorite person to be around but there's a black hole of unutilized time threatening to consume me. It's not like I'm like Garrett who seems to love schedules and structure.

Before my move I was always doing something. My day job. Music. Going to the brewery Quinn, Oliver, and I found that was equidistant from all of our apartments with its live music and wobbly chairs. Now I feel like I'm drowning in time. Time that I want to be able to utilize, but instead it seems to paralyze me. I've spent days on my couch, balancing a pack of Oreos on my stomach, overwhelmed by the nothingness of it all. It was a paradox. Try and face the reality that all my risks aren't paying off, do nothing and also fail.

I'm halfway back to Austen Dr. when my phone buzzes in my pocket.

Avery

You'd help me hide a body, right?

16

Evelyn

"And we're mad about the flowers?" I ask Avery a second time as I run my finger around the rough edge of the lid of my cup from Love is Brewing.

The text I got a half hour ago, I've learned, would be very incriminating if Wesley suddenly disappeared. Especially after the incident during an after party in LA last night that led to him missing rehearsal this morning. It's taken those full thirty minutes to get through the story as well as the tangents about the best way to dispose of a body if absolutely needed.

I've been slowly making my way along Main Street, window shopping and reading signs that I missed the other day when Garrett breezed by most of the businesses.

"I don't think a dozen roses with a little card that says *It wasn't a threesome!* are something to celebrate. How stupid can he be to think that I was worried about *that*. We have press and, you know, the tour with sold out shows that he refuses to come to rehearsals for starting in a little over a month." She fumes as I reach the sandwich board declaring that Batista's Blooms has discount sunflower bouquets. Flowers would look good in the living room. "If you're going to send apology flowers, at least apologize."

There are three other people in the flower shop. Two older men, one with salt and pepper hair and the other who's gone fully white, are looking at peonies together, comparing two seemingly identical bunches. The other is the woman behind the counter with brown highlighted hair and smattering of freckles. I assume she must be Winnie from what I remember from Garrett's tour. I've been putting off getting flowers for the reason of choosing between the two, but I guess it was an inevitability. I could go to both; I can afford the upcharge from whichever I choose second.

"What did you do with the flowers?" I ask.

"I threw them in the trash closest to his place so he could see them when he walked outside," she explains.

"That's one way to send a message," I say.

I know she knows she's mad about the not-threesome, but she's trying not to be. Wes and Avery care about each other in this all-consuming way that leads them to pretend they don't in acts of desperation and many public affairs that are largely publicized for each other's benefit.

Two years ago, I helped her fake a couples' trip that people had speculated she went on with a mysterious older actor. Her name was trending next to Pedro Pascal's for weeks even though there was nothing to signal they had any association.

"If it wouldn't end my career, I'd quit." She would. That's how she feels about him.

The thing is that Wes is a built in safety measure in my relationship with Avery. I won't ever be her number one person because of him. Even if they despise each other now, they have space reserved for the other no matter what. I don't feel my usual pressure to be the best and most around her because of him. I also know there's no way I can let her down the way he did. Mostly, I hate the guy, but I do benefit from that slightly silver lining.

"I have a question for you. What if after this album, I stop?" I ask.

"Like take a break? Yeah, you deserve one," she agrees as if I haven't all but taken most of the year off to get "settled" after my move.

"I mean…just get a normal job again."

"Why would you do that? You moved to make it easier. You've put in the work and have been bending the truth so hard any reality TV producer would be proud."

There are two sides to this now that I'm standing on the edge. I take a leap and hope all the shit I've done will pay off or I take a dozen steps back before running in the other direction. I've put in the work. I've made a name for Lyla West. I've done the damage. There's just the looming question of if that damage has been worth it.

"I guess you're right. It doesn't make sense to give it all up," I say.

"And that's the thing with this tour, too. I've worked too hard to back out. I'm not going to let a man get in the way of that. He can send all the flowers he wants they're going to keep ending up in the trash."

"Uh huh," I mumble as Garrett turns fully in my direction, and we lock eyes, it's more of a feeling than being sure that we are. It snaps through the air like a rope pulling taut.

He shakes his head in exhausted indignation, and I reply with an exaggerated shrug.

I have to wonder how many times things have happened to Wes and Avery and we've unknowingly been in similar positions with each of us hearing opposite sides of the same conflict. He doesn't look away so I hold up my hand, splaying my fingers then pointing to the gazebo. I mouth "*five minutes*" as dramatically as I can, hoping that will be enough time to ensure that Avery's murderous intent has been forgotten for the time being.

17

Garrett

Through the phone, Wes's voice muddles into nonsense as Evelyn's waving captures my full attention. It's like the world shrinks, it's just her in the flower shop window, framed by draping vines and vases of roses.

She gave me a glimpse of something in the museum. It was similar to what I hear in her music. Raw emotion that she tried to dismiss. She might not think she's the type of woman who deserves love letters, but I think it's a crime no one has written one for her yet.

I almost did.

The thick handmade paper that we got with our tickets is resting on my desk at Alina's. I might have written something if Alina herself didn't call me downstairs to help her open her arthritis medication.

"It wasn't a threesome," Wes says sharply, forcing my attention back to our conversation. I move from the window and go back to surveying the displays for the forget-me-nots that I came to get for Alina. She gets frustrated about not being as independent as she used to and the flowers always brighten even her worst days.

"That is the least important part of this entire scenario." And after knowing him for nearly two decades it's not all that surprising. Wes likes to press a big red self-destruct button whenever things get too good. He tends to be seconds away from this whenever Avery is nearby. We're opposites in that way. I freeze and he reacts. It's not exactly balanced, but it's what we're used to at this point.

"It's very important for me, okay?" he says. "I think being clear about your sexual history is very responsible."

"I think most health teachers would agree. But what about missing rehearsal?"

"Okay, not the most responsible, but I don't know…I couldn't look at her."

"Didn't you promise you'd try to play nice?" It feels like forever since I left Manhattan. Time feels like molasses in Hartsfall when before I was struggling to fit in all my work.

"I wasn't planning on going to the party."

"But you did."

"It sounded fun." He pauses. "She said she was going on a date with her guitarist."

I pick up and inspect a bouquet of delicate blue flowers. "Did she?"

"Maybe." If he isn't sure, I'm guessing that Avery's date was never real. Neither of them shoulder all the blame for the tear in their relationship. But if this were a poker table, Wes would be the one to raise every damn time. "I don't know. I was at the party."

"And?"

"I sent her flowers."

"Not an apology," I tell him, remembering my own slip up with Evelyn and the timer. "You'll be on an entire tour together. Figure out how to string a few civil words together."

"Words aren't exactly my thing."

"You sing for a living, they're your entire thing."

"Well, I don't have to mean those."

"Glad we cleared that up. I have to go." I hang up before he can protest.

At the counter, Sara wraps my flowers in an old newspaper and then secures them with twine.

For the first time, Evelyn shows up before I do. When I arrive, a woman is being swung around in the gazebo as the clock tower chimes marking a newly engaged couple.

I used to think the resentment would pass, the thoughts of that *means nothing* and *what are you trying to prove?* I thought I would be desensitized to it the same way cat owners get with litter boxes or baristas are with steam wands. It's still there no matter how much I wish it would go away.

There's always one person I feel for the most. There's a woman out there who came to this town with her partner only for him to cheat on her with Lana. It's the reason I've never felt particularly motivated to hunt down my birth father. I'm all but certain that woman doesn't know I exist but every single time I remember how I got to be here, I remember her. On some level I'm jealous of her ignorance and hope she's happy. But mostly, I hope she left him.

Evelyn's tender expression tells me she doesn't think about anything other than a happy ending. I don't begrudge her this. I just wish I was able to see those happy endings, even occasionally. After all, I'm the walking manifestation of what happens when Hartsfall doesn't follow through on its lofty promises.

"Is there something you need?" I sit next to her in the space I presume she left for me.

She starts talking and immediately bypasses my question. "You know what this reminds me of?"

"No, but I have a feeling you're going to tell me," I say, pretending I'm annoyed instead of constantly wanting to hear every thought that crosses her mind.

"*When Harry Met Sally.*"

"The movie that infamously taught you how to fake an orgasm," I say, and this earns me a twitch of her lips.

"The very one. I'm so happy that you've taken such an interest in my major milestones."

"I'd like to state for the record that I learned that information against my will."

"Well, there's this scene where Harry and Sally's friends are married and lying in bed and then Harry and Sally call them about different sides of the same issue. Us just now reminds me of that," she barrels on.

"And in this hypothetical we're a married couple." I shut down the image before it has the chance to form in my head.

"Only in the hypothetical. I know from your publicized track record that long term commitment and emotional vulnerability aren't your thing," she says.

I've heard versions of those words hundreds of times, but this time they sour the air around me. Maybe it's the couple still lingering at the fringes of the gazebo. Or it's her, and I don't want her to see me the way other people do. I don't want to be the person who is unable to be with someone longer than a handful of nights.

There was this guy who was getting his master's in counseling who I slept with a few times. I'm convinced he only kept seeing me because he was interested in the psychology of one-night-stands and short term relationships. After the third time we were together he said, "I hope you find someone worth letting in one day," and somehow it only gave me more reason to secure my walls and walk away, like the only allure came from my unattainability.

I look at Evelyn and nod. "As long as we're on the same page."

"Oh, absolutely. I'm not under any illusions that I will be able to change you. Every good town needs a closed-off grump, and I can't deprive Hartsfall of theirs."

"They do just fine without me," I say. "As you've reminded me a few times, I'm the dark cloud on a sunny day."

"I mean, dark clouds bring rain. I like rain."

"You dance in it, don't you?"

She slides me a look. "You know me so well, Larson. Don't go getting obsessed. I know I'm absolutely irresistible. I bring a lot to the table." Too late for that.

"You're sure about that?"

"With this fashion sense? I'm a catch." She makes a sweeping motion with her free hand.

"I don't think my feelings are in danger of changing any time soon." My fucking feelings won't change for her no matter how convenient that would be.

"So the flowers aren't for me? What a shame."

"Alina's arthritis is flaring up. Flowers always cheer her up when it gets bad. When she was performing she'd have forget-me-nots in her dressing room waiting for her after every performance. She told me once that as long as there were forget-me-nots she'd know the show wasn't over yet."

"Besides when you play with her, does she ever still sing?"

"For the festival. If you're here, you'll love it. She does this rendition of 'Funny Valentine' that's something else."

"She really means a lot to you, doesn't she?"

"Yeah, she does. But she pulled some strings to make it happen," I say. "That same thing she pulled with you that first day with the package she did that to me with a letter in the mail. I returned it and the next thing I knew I was being given my first piano lesson. I kept getting her mail until I would come regularly, then suddenly the mix-ups stopped."

"That's sweet."

"She was just bored."

"Why do you brush off people when they obviously care about you?" she asks.

"Why do you lie to the people you love?" I retaliate against the sting of her words.

Alina cares, but that's not how it started. She saw a kid who needed help and it wasn't like they could push me away.

"That's not fair," Evelyn says.

"I'm pretty sure that both questions have nearly the same answer so if you take a minute or two to think about them hard enough."

"You're telling me that we have something in common? That's kinda cute."

"More that you might understand exactly why I hate saying shit like that out loud because you also like to avoid it."

"And the existential-asshole bit is back." She draws out the words to be comedic but I can tell she's hiding the fact that I went too far—again. God. This is exactly why I don't get into situations like this.

"Sorry," I say. Tension builds behind my eyes and I pull off my glasses and rub a knuckle between my brows before replacing them. "I got that call from Wes and then the stuff with Alina. Shit. I just hate that she's getting older. I forget it sometimes then it just hits me. I know it's normal. I shouldn't be taking it out on you."

"Knowing something or it being normal doesn't mean you have to be okay with it all by yourself. Do you have a minute? It won't take long. I just want to show you something in the gazebo."

"I swear, if you're going to fake a proposal I will stop talking to you."

"No. And be real there's no world where you'll ever figure out how to get me to stop talking to you," she says.

"If I see you getting on one knee I'm leaving," I warn.

"Not very progressive of you. But I'll even check my shoes right now to make sure they're tied."

Evelyn makes a point of checking her shoes before starting toward the gazebo. Through the years, boards have been replaced and paint has been reapplied, constantly combating the natural consequences of time. Just another piece of the fantasy. Nothing can stay broken here.

"I came by here the other day to wander around and get another look at everything." She points up and my eyes follow to where she's indicating. "Look."

There's a ledge where the roof of the gazebo connects to support beams. In one of the corners of the octagon, there's a collection of twigs and dried leaves. Something flutters and there's a downy head that peeks out.

"I found the nest and I just stood here for so long I must have looked crazy. You know, I didn't know what to do with myself when I first got to the city. I always liked people watching before, but I really got into it after the move. I think it was more because I finally had all this free time. I went to the MET and the MoMA and I really tried to read the plaques and be a good educated museum goer but the people were just more interesting. I loved it, you know, just remembering that the world is so big and we're just here. There are these little birds and that's just amazing. I might feel like shit about everything I'm dealing with, but there will always be baby birds or people in museums."

I can't pinpoint the moment I stop looking at that nest and start looking at her. There's this creeping understanding that I let in, just this once. She might have baby birds and museum people keeping her going, but right now, I think I might have her.

18

Garrett

"Aren't we going to a wine tasting?" Evelyn asks as her head swivels to read the various welcome signs to the farm, each declaring *Barlowe Berry Farm.* Up ahead little blurs of children running through the bushes that extend for acres. A tractor winds through the neat rows pulling a wagon full of guests.

"Blueberry wine," I say.

"Aren't strawberries the fruit of romance? I mean, I can't dip one in chocolate without thinking about Valentine's day. Whoever is doing strawberry PR is killing it."

I heave a sigh as I maneuver into the parking lot. I choose a spot as far out of ear shot from any of the other guests or workers as possible. "There are a few reasons that no one likes the wine tasting gig for the festival. I told you I'd explain, so I need you to listen because how today goes determines how much wine and beer is donated to the festival and if they have to pay for any of it out of their budget when that should be going to other things.

"The main thing is that all of us have had so much of this stuff that it's just not that great anymore. The second is that the Barlowes are the ones who run the tasting which is really an interview. If they don't like us they'll give us the worst options in the least possible quantities. A few years ago they sent Fletcher and Emily and they made a strawberry joke."

"I'm guessing that didn't end well," she says.

"Let's just say that it was the most sober the residents have been at a festival in a few decades."

"Shit. So we're responsible for everyone's sanity and you're just now telling me?" she asks, her voice rising with genuine concern.

"Glad you're caught up."

Evelyn looks down at her shirt which just says, *I make boys cry*. They've grown on me a bit. There's also the fact she's wearing them for my benefit, which I can't complain about.

"I wish you told me sooner," she says. "I could turn my shirt inside out. Or would that be too obvious and look even worse." Evelyn plucks at the fabric. "I could turn it around and you'll just have to walk behind me so no one can see it."

"I brought something just in case." I reach toward the back seat where I have a bag of options for her. I didn't suggest something sooner because I didn't want to risk her going inside and changing into something more potentially offensive. Then there's the part that this way she gets to wear my clothes. They're old ones from when I stayed with Alina over high school winter breaks and kept a closet of stuff stashed there.

Evelyn takes a moment to riffle through the bag before grabbing a faded red quarter zip sweater and pulling it over her head.

"Better?" she asks.

"Here, let me." I reach over and pull her hair out from where it's tucked under the neckline. "There."

My hand draws a lingering line on her skin as I pull away, causing her to shiver. Her eyes capture mine and I think for a moment something shifts. The world narrows until it's just us in the car. Nothing else exists. I almost fool myself into thinking that there wouldn't be any consequences if I leaned in further, tangled my fingers in her hair and pulled her into my lap.

I've never been fond of physical touch; it was something that came so late in my life that it was foreign. But she makes it feel like the opposite. Something so easy that I feel the urge to fall into.

"Eve—" I start, but she shifts away leaving my hand hovering in open air.

"We don't want to be late," she says, then reaches for the door.

The front desk greeter directs us into a side room that's cozy and reminiscent of the ski lodges around the area. The building itself is cabin style with pale exposed wood and vaulted ceilings. Although it's still reaching the eighties mid-day, there's a fire cracking in the stone fireplace. A landscape painting of the farm takes up almost an entire wall.

The door behind us opens and Evelyn reaches for my arm. It's something so small and unconscious. Hell, her grabbing for me makes me feel needed, feeding my bottomless craving to be necessary.

"Sorry for the wait. There was this kid. Cutest little guy, blueberry coma. His mouth was stained and so were his hands," Millie Barlowe says as she walks arm in arm with her husband Porter.

The husband and wife are the second generation of owners, both somewhere in their sixties. They're wearing matching blue barn jackets and jeans dusted with dried greenery. Porter is a tall man with skin tanned from working outdoors his entire life and iron hard look in his blue eyes. It's easy to tell Millie is the more welcoming of the two with her open features and smile lines framing her eyes are the only signs of age marking her ebony skin.

"Oh, is he okay?" Evelyn asks with genuine concern.

"Happens at least once a week, but always worth checking in on. You let the kids run around and pick their berries and it's just a natural consequence of things," Porter explains. "I'm Porter and this is the love of my life, Millie. You must be the newest pair sent up from Hartsfall."

"Evelyn, and this is Garrett. I've been dying to visit." Evelyn takes the lead on introductions.

"I just love it when a couple comes up. It just embraces the spirit of things, really shows that you're taking the festival seriously," Millie says and she gives us an adoring look that makes Evelyn flush.

"We—" I start to correct her, but Evelyn cuts me off.

"She's right, baby. It's so special to be the ones who get to do this. It's my first time here, and I couldn't have come at a better time." The hand gripping my arm slides up to my chest. It's like she's mapped a trail of fire with how my skin heats.

It takes me a minute to register her playing along. She's the type to. She knows this tasting matters to the town, that's probably all there is to it.

"Great. We're going to go check on the first flight of drinks. We're going to start with a few ales if that's all right. Feel free to get comfortable." Porter gestures toward the two love seats around the live edge wooden table.

The Barlowes shuffle out of the room, allowing us a moment to regain our bearings.

"What are you doing?" I keep my voice low in case anyone can hear.

"Playing along," she whispers back, leaning closer. "They want a couple. Let's give them a couple. It's just a few hours."

"This isn't going to work."

"Why wouldn't it? It's not like you don't know how to put on a good performance. Didn't you guest star on that limited series, you know, the one with the mom who killed all her son's girlfriends?" she asks, referring to one of the acting gigs I was sent on to help promote Fool's Gambit over a decade ago.

"Evelyn, if you have a script you've been keeping somewhere that will help me out in this situation, I'd be more than happy to memorize it in the three or so minutes we have until they come back," I say.

"It's improv, *baby*." She draws out the term of endearment. The word unlocking something I never knew I wanted to hear her say. "Just act like you can't get me out of your head and we'll be fine. There's no reason we can't have some fun with this. A little role-play never hurt anyone." She pats my chest then rises on her toes to press her lips to my jaw. It's fleeting but launches my heart into my throat.

This is a bad idea. There's no logic to why I don't run away and buy the wine for the festival myself. There's just her and she's enough for me to turn into a fool.

"Anything for the festival," I rasp.

After Millie and Porter return, we make it through the ale samples without a hitch, mostly because of Evelyn. She asks all the right questions about the farm and them about their relationship.

"We have a mead, a true blueberry wine, and a Moscato that's a little lighter," Millie explains.

Through Evelyn's questioning we've learned that Porter takes charge of the activities, parties, and other general non-alcoholic endeavors while Millie is the mastermind behind expanding the beverage options. It makes sense because we also learned that she was an intern here studying fermentation science when she met Porter. They found that they perfectly fit into each other's lives and couldn't let go.

Following the way the tasting glasses have been arranged as a guide, we start sipping the mead. The honey that sweetens the drink is cut with lemon which prevents the liquid from becoming too syrupy.

Evelyn gives that quick smile that lets me know it's not her favorite, but will lie about it anyway if she has to. "How do you two do it? Forty years of marriage and working together?"

"You know that saying that relationships are all about compromise?" Porter asks.

Evelyn nods. "Sure."

"It's bullshit. Collaboration. They're all about collaboration. We're partners. We don't always get along but we work through it because this place isn't the dream. We're the dream, our kids and our grandkids too. Never lose focus on that," Porter says in clipped precise sentences, that make him sound annoyed, but appear to be his natural speech pattern. "There were these chickens—"

Millie cuts him off and preemptively waves away the story. "No, we're not talking about the chickens. Enough about us, we talk about us all day. If you read the label on the wine, you can learn half our story right there. What about you two? No, wait, let me guess how long you've been together. I'm good at this." Millie pauses. She adopts the assessing gaze of a psychic trying to collect clues from her customers. Her hazel eyes drift between the two of us. "Under a year, but just barely. But you were friends before that."

"Close. He knows my brother. We've been in each other's lives practically forever," Evelyn skirts around the truth.

Millie offers another one of her adoring looks. "That's nice, isn't it? I bet it gets all the basic questions out of the way." She waggles her brows, suggestively. "You get to skip a few steps and get to the good parts."

I swallow at the implication and try not to think about it too hard so my blood doesn't inconveniently try to relocate south while we finish our trip.

"What flipped the switch? There's always a breaking point with these things. Just snap and it all falls apart and then into place. It was like that with us. You know, there was a strict no fraternization rule when I worked here, and I knew I was the one who was going to get the bad end of it if we got caught. But there was this bonfire at the end of the summer term and everyone came to celebrate before we all went back to our normal lives. One kiss with Porter in the blueberry fields and I had no choice but to come back the moment I graduated." There's a dreamy look in her eyes as she relives the past.

A reflection of the look seeps into Evelyn's eyes as I can only assume she's picturing the future. I can't help the pinch of jealousy that comes when I know I can't ask who's in that image with her.

"There was a party about a year and a half ago," I start before I realize what's happening. I guess the past has a hold on me too. I reach out and the edge of my pinkie whispers against Evelyn's. A small touch to tell her it's my turn in the dance of this minor deception. "A mutual friend was throwing it." Though, I've never been sure if Avery has actually ever considered me as such. "And Evelyn was dancing. She's the type of person who makes everyone want to get up and join her. I didn't, but I watched. She was in this pink dress that kind of floated as it moved, but someone bumped into her and spilled their drink everywhere. Next thing I know, this beautiful woman is standing in front of me demanding I give her my suit jacket."

"I didn't demand," Evelyn interjects, and I wonder if she remembers what I'm talking about. Not that she was drunk that night, but that it might not have been significant to her.

"Fine. You didn't demand, but you asked and I handed it right over. She disappears, and you know what I see a few minutes later? She comes back wearing it as a dress. You know I never got it back." And however good she looked in the dress, she was incomparable in my suit jacket.

"I can fix that, sorry."

"Don't worry about it. My clothes have a tendency to look better on you even if I get them custom made."

There's one thing I leave out about my recollection of the night, the real reason Evelyn started to really drag me under. It was the first time I noticed that tell of hers. That stupid forced smile. For a moment, when she dashed away from the crowd and she looked at me, it was gone. It was like I was a solution, not just my jacket, but me. That's all it took. I don't know what she was pretending to not care about that night, but I'm happy I was there all the same.

After a dinner on the porch of their farm to table restaurant, the Barlowes take us out to the fields just as dusk paints the sky. Strategically placed string lights give the transition into night, a gauzy, fantastical feeling as we meander through the bushes. Millie and Evelyn wander up ahead picking berries. This is likely the last weekend tourists and locals alike will be able to before fall rushes in and the fields are closed to the public.

"You two were quite the treat. Come back next year and you might actually be together with all that's going on between the two of you," Porter says, and I nearly stumble over my own feet.

"Excuse me?" I choke out.

"We got a little ask from the folks in town to give you two a push," he says plainly. "Hold your apologies. I don't give half a damn if you two are a couple or not. It was a good afternoon and you can't buy one of those."

"Any chance there was money involved in other ways?" I hedge my guess about the situation we've gotten ourselves into.

"I might have been promised a bit of a matchmaker's fee. But I don't think I'll take it. This place is a little bit magic; I can't take credit for it or maybe it will slip away." The older man looks toward his wife.

It's not that I want their life, exactly. I don't think I could ever have that. I wasn't raised in a way that I can ever see myself having a family without living in a constant state of fear that I would repeat the mistakes that made me feel the weight of resentment so much of my life. I've made plenty of choices to prevent that. But I want that, to belong with someone so unquestionably you can see it in a passing glance.

"Garrett! We still need a picture. Come here!" Evelyn calls out, her hand waving overhead.

What we have is mutual exchange, even if some roots have grown deeper than intended. But maybe for this next week I can let myself enjoy it. It's fleeting. The moment that holds the last few seconds of your favorite song that has to end, no matter how much you wish it wouldn't.

I stride over and claim the spot next to her, a spot that I force myself to remember shouldn't feel like mine. My arm loops around her waist and I pull her to me so her side is flush against mine. She nestles closer to me, the heat from her body is welcome against the chill whisper of fall. Her soft curves look so good wrapped in my old sweater with my hands pressed into the time softened cotton.

Her face tilts up to look at me. "What are you doing?"

"Let's take one together this time. Today was worth re-membering, don't you think?"

"Yeah," she says. "I think it was."

Before she lifts her phone to take a picture, I already know this one will never make it to Holt.

This is just for us.

19

Evelyn

The Barlowes walk us to the parking lot. My hand is twined in Garrett's partly for show, but mostly because I want to. Because we did this together and it's been so long since I've not felt like I was standing alone.

At the end of the tour of their fields, they told us the list of drinks to expect to have to be picked up next week. From what I could read of Garrett's expression, we won them over. The victory hums through me, or that could just be the small currents I've felt each time Garrett and I touch.

For my own sake, I'll say it's victory. I've grown to value my time with Garrett and I don't want to ruin that with my proclivity to fall for people who show even the smallest amount of interest in me. He's a good actor, he told me so himself, but I think my body has missed the memo.

"You good?" Garrett asks, his thumb running over my knuckles as we walk across the pavement. There are barely any cars left since the farm is about to close. The Barlowes are still standing on the edge of the sidewalk in front of the visitor center, idly chatting to each other.

"Oh, yeah." I bite at my lip. "Just thinking that today was fun."

"Yeah, it was."

"I guess you were able to put up with me as a girlfriend for a day. Hope you didn't suffer too much."

I take a step forward but his hand tugs against mine as he stays in place. "Eve. Promise me something."

I risk a glance up at him and his eyes are trained on me with a brutal intensity. "Yeah?"

"If anyone ever makes you feel like they're simply 'putting up' with you, walk out of their life. They don't deserve you."

A knot catches in my throat. Does he really believe that? Or is he just being nice after helping him today?

"Don't worry. I won't walk; I'll run." I dart toward the car, tugging him behind me. I like that he never lets go when I do this. It's something small but I like the possibility that I might be worth holding on to.

When we reach the car I turn and we almost collide at my sudden stop. His front presses against me and my hands land against his firm chest.

"Hey there," I say, but the words lack my usual confidence.

"Hey, yourself," he mutters.

In the streetlights his brown eyes burn bronze behind the lenses of his glasses. Instead of pulling back, I run a hand up the hard line of his chest so it lands at the collar of his shirt and I play with the seam with my fingers. He melts into my touch. For the longest time I've gained satisfaction from drawing reactions from him because it was something I felt only I could do. This is nearly the same. I want him to react because it's me, because I want to mean something to him.

There's that cliff's edge in my mind, one we've been inching closer toward. This moment feels like taking another step closer to discovering what's waiting at the bottom.

Garrett's face tilts down toward mine and he closes the gap. My breath catches and my fingers freeze, tangled in the fabric of his shirt.

"I don't think we should kiss," he says in a husky voice that makes me want him to be saying the exact opposite. "We don't need to go that far."

The heat building in me fizzles and sparks before I can form a response. Yes, he's talking about the Barlowes who are watching from the sidewalk.

"I guess not." I don't want to confront the tinge of rejection that makes me feel like I'm shrinking. I pull my hands back so they land on the car.

The pad of his finger brushes against my cheek as he guides a strand of my hair behind my ear. "Let's get home, yeah?"

"Yeah."

He unexpectedly leans closer, causing my heart to launch into my throat. Did he change his mind? He should have given me some warning. I suck in a breath and close my eyes as his chest brushes against mine, the friction prompting my nipples to pull tight against my borrowed sweater.

There's a click and then a kiss of night air.

"The doors unlocked for you, didn't want to make you wait," he says.

As my eyes flutter open, I find him holding up the keys when I look to the side then pull at the handle. I'm rewarded with the door hitting the back of my legs.

"Thanks," I choke out through my embarrassment.

Once we're both in the car and he starts the engine, I turn up the music on the radio. An old Willie Nelson song that once finished bleeds into Billy Joel, but neither song is loud enough to drown out my racing thoughts.

Later, when I'm tucked in bed, I pull out my phone to scroll through the photos. Prompted by my earlier thoughts, I swipe my finger to select all of the ones we took then send them to Quinn. If this were last year, it's exactly what I would do. I would call her and we'd spend hours talking that would end up deciding to meet up for drinks. I'd tell her about Garrett and the almost kiss and she'd roll her eyes and say I should have just gone for it.

It's late and I don't expect her to respond, but a few minutes later a notification banner pops up at the top of the screen.

You look happy

I am

My thumbs hover over the screen for a heartbeat before I send a question I desperately want to know the answer to

How are you?

Well, this happened...

Attachments: 5 images

How did they get your latte art to look like a vulva?

And where can I get one?

You don't drink coffee

I would if all my coffee was anatomically accurate

Liar

It turns out that the coffee shop around the corner from her apartment had a new hire who was struggling with steaming milk. For the last month, Quinn's lattes have been borderline pornographic.

I can't help but wonder if I've missed out on any other vulva latte level incidents. It's so dumb, so unimportant compared to so many other moments in our friendship but I want it back so badly.

Evelyn

> The only thing that would make tonight better is if you were here too.

Quinn

> Same here.

> You know you can tell me anything, right?

The light in my chest sputters for a moment, a candle flickering in gale force winds.

Evelyn

> I know

20

Evelyn

"I will. If I ever go out somewhere like that alone I will text you with all the details," I say. My phone is balanced precariously between my ear and shoulder as I open the door for Garrett. "Mom, I promise. I'm fine."

I didn't notice the missed calls from her. She must have tried to call yesterday when we were driving through a dead zone. Like with Avery, it's not my place to say that Garrett is here, so I told her I went to see the leaves on my own. If the last hour I've spent on the phone is any indication, this has turned out to be a mistake.

"There were people in New Hampshire who had to be rescued from that last week. I looked it up. They all got stuck in this bottleneck," she says, and I don't have to check to know that she's already sent me the article she read it in.

"I'm not in New Hampshire," I remind her. "I was in an open area."

"But you went alone."

Garrett looks at me quizzically, and I shake my head as he moves past me. I need to wrap this call up. I was hoping to have something to show to him. I'd been sitting with my notebook with a few ideas I was excited to flesh out when the call came an hour ago. I'm thankful I picked up because, combined with the calls yesterday, if I didn't she would have put in a missing person's report, or something.

"Yes, I went alone. I'm on vacation alone. I'm going to do things alone."

"That's dangerous," she says.

"Mom. I promise. I'll be better about updating you, but I need to go. I'm about to order coffee," I lie and hope she doesn't notice the distinct lack of commotion in the background. *"Ti voglio bene. Ciao."*[1]

I wait in the entryway for a long moment to collect myself before joining Garrett in the living room. Talking to Mom always puts me in a defensive headspace. While I try my best to tell her what she needs to hear, I'm suppressing the parts of me that are desperate to be heard and understood. I wish I could trust that she would understand me, but I can't.

With a deep breath, I plaster on a smile and do my best to move forward. I need to make the most out of my time with

---

1. I love you. Bye.

Garrett to jumpstart the album. I can't let Mom get in my head.

"Everything okay?" he asks, and I wish he didn't.

"Give or take. It was just my mom," I say, doing my best to seem unaffected.

"How is she?"

"Still upset that I moved to New York," I say. She's been more tense since I moved farther from home. I think since that's the first thing Drew did after the band broke up it's put her on high alert, like it's the first sign of me shutting them out.

"They do know you're twenty-nine, right?"

"I can't be too sure about that." I let out a sigh as I slump onto the couch.

"Do they know how you feel about that?" he presses.

"It's complicated," I explain and try to put it into words. "I think it makes them feel better. Like if they can still take care of me that they're able to fix things? They came to the US when they were a bit younger than I am now and they had to do so much for themselves to make it work, not just the paperwork, but adjusting to the culture and making new friends in an unfamiliar place. I'm pretty sure they think they failed my brother, even though what happened to him has nothing to do with them. So, if I can give them peace from letting them into my life this way, I will."

It's not convenient, but I don't want to make them think they've failed when they've given us so much.

"And that's why you haven't told them about Lyla?" he asks.

"I mean, of course, that's part of it, but can we not get into it right now? I just want to start writing since you didn't let me last week," I say, trying to lighten the mood. Desperate to escape from the feeling that no matter how hard I try I can't be exactly who my family needs me to be because of everything I'm hiding. God. This would be so much easier if I didn't need music like I need air. But I do, and right now I need Garrett to help me learn how to breathe again.

"Only if you figured out what I asked you to."

"Yes," I say, relieved to move on. "I also will need to know if you hate it because I'm reaching the point where I cannot fully trust myself to form ideas."

"Great. So if you start describing a Gregorian chant I should stop you." He doesn't miss a beat.

"I think if I do that, it is more likely that I have been possessed because I do not know any Latin," I joke.

"Good to know," he says.

"I'm going to admit that you were right, but please don't get smug because that will ruin this entire thing," I start. "But you're right, I was forcing the entire concept. I was wanting something nebulous and that wasn't getting me anywhere."

"And?" Garrett presses.

For the last week I've spent plenty of hours staring at the piano or my notebook, willing anything to come out. This led to me being frustrated at how much I was forcing it all to try and fill this gaping pit of want in my chest. No matter what I've thrown into that pit for the last few months it never seems to shrink. So, instead of trying to change it, I'm trying to accept it.

"The albums I loved writing were about things I was experiencing and I've lost touch of that. I came here and acted like I could pluck up someone else's love story and it would all work out, even if I didn't put any of the work in myself."

"I need to make sure you're not suggesting that you actually fall in love with someone in town. Because that feels a bit unethical due to the fact that the tourists, present company excluded, are likely all in relationships."

"No. Oh my gosh. No. Who would do that?"

"You'd be surprised," he says.

"The theme for the album will be wanting. That's why people are here, according to you. They're chasing a feeling. And honestly, it's the only emotion I can connect to right now so it will at least be authentic."

It's not that I was expecting the heavens to open or for Garrett to jump up and cheer, but I'm met with silence.

"So…" I prod. "If you're going to tell me it's terrible, could you do it now and put me out of my misery?"

"No. I like it. There's a lot of potential." He pauses for a moment, lost in thought, then says, "Do you have paper?"

"Yeah." I move to the piano bench and snatch my notebook and pen.

"I think you have two options for the structure of the album," he explains as he takes the pen and paper then starts to draw. "You'll build the point where the songs sound like someone is about to get everything they want. That feeling of watching two people neck and neck for an entire race and you're not sure who's going to win." He scribbles one last thing and then turns the notebook toward me. There are two hill-shaped lines, like I used to see in my high school English classes to diagram the flow of a story. One of the drawings curve up at the end while the other goes down.

"What's the difference?"

"Then you have to decide the ending. Are you going to let them get what they want or are you going to take it away when their hope is highest, when they can see it right there in front of them?"

"Like right now?"

"No. I don't think we should decide until the end. The difference between a convincing romance and a tragedy is the end. We have to believe that this album is about getting what we want, then I think the audience will too."

"You really are good at this," I say.

"Will you ever not be surprised by that?"

"Think of it more as basking in awe of your genius."

"How long do you need to bask before we get started?"

"Basking over. I'll be right back," I say as I get up to leave the room.

I go to get a second notebook and pen so we can continue brainstorming concepts. My goal for the night is to send something to Vincent that shows I am worth keeping around.

Garrett and I start volleying ideas back and forth, each of us taking moments to stop and write down lines and ideas that could be built into verses. We're still going when the sun fully sets and we don't stop even as I get up to turn on the lights.

"I think we should start," I say. I have three full pages of notes and a buzz humming through me with the need to create. "From the beginning. I think we need to make this in order, let it all build so it doesn't become disjointed."

"That checks out."

There's a hesitancy that lingers in the air. I know he's listened to my songs. He's told me that outright, but this is vulnerable. There's nothing written. I could sit down and fumble around on the notes and then look up to find Garrett's face screwed up in disappointment.

I just went on about the theme of this album, but taking this next step? It sends me right to the cliff's edge where I find myself over and over again.

"There's room at the bench for two," I say.

"If you're sure."

I move first because if I don't I know I'll stay cemented into place for the rest of the night. I claim the right side of the bench and after a moment he rises from the couch and joins me. I peel my eyes from his form and busy myself with setting my own notebook on the music stand as I feel his body consume the space next to me. His arm grazes against the loose fabric of my hoodie as he places his notebook next to mine. When I look to see what he's written, I release a surprised laugh.

"I think I know where to start," I say as I point to a line on his that matches one on mine. The only difference is that his version is neat and crisp while mine is in a hurried looping scrawl.

End in the beginning

"Fate," he deadpans.

I nod. "Or the universal human experience."

"Or doing lines of coke in the bathroom."

"I'm such a good teacher," I say. "I'm thinking of starting with something like this." I start arpeggiating the chords in A major key with the intent to modulate into chilling minor.

"What about E major instead, it's always given me that action movie feeling."

"The point right after the climax where everything unexpectedly works out," I add.

"But for this song—"

"Things fall apart."

Then there's this moment. No words pass, just his blazing lamplit eyes leaping to mine and then holding there. It's like hearing a story from my childhood that I've been certain that no one else has ever heard, yet here he is knowing something about me that transcends a single detail.

That's where it starts and then the words start blooming like perennials drinking up melted snow to reemerge after winter. It's something dormant in both of us finally bursting to life.

Eventually, our sentences all fragment. I play the chord progression for the bridge and he says, "Yes, but what if..." and suggests a diminished chord instead of a minor. He'll scribble down a line then sing it and I'll scratch out a word and replace it.

"Then the guitar could go fuzzy like..."

"What if..."

"...And the drums would..."

"Not quite."

"But..."

We don't need fully fleshed out thoughts. Like so many of our other moments, picking up where the other left off was always supposed to build to this. Like we've always been meant to do this.

His hands and mine brush against each other as we take turns at the keys until the snippets of sound overlap. The song is a patchwork of moments that slowly takes form. It's like how all the little squares of a quilt stitch together to become something warm and full of love. This isn't what it was like writing my other albums.

This is better. More than just reclaiming my voice.

I've never had something like this before while writing because I didn't allow it. I've always held on to being alone in my music, but maybe that was the wrong way about it.

"That's it," I whisper, keeping my voice low as if not to break the spell we've cast.

"It is," he says.

Our notebooks are a mess of scribbled notes and crossed out lyrics. We've changed the key three times since we started, but we've decided on sticking with E. I don't want to move. I don't want to snap the thread of inspiration tangled around us by calling it a night. Garrett's thigh presses casually against mine on the piano bench, and I don't want to let go of that either.

He's here. I'm not alone.

"We should play through it?" I ask, still feeling a bit winded.

"Just to make sure," he says. There's a hunger in his eyes, something wild like he's chasing down the song.

I swallow hard and stand to let him accompany me on the piano. From the first note a shiver runs down my spine.

In some alternate timeline there's another version of this with me in a shimmering dress, draping myself across the body of the piano. He'd wear a suit with coattails trailing behind him. But I don't want that version, because the one I have here with us surrounded by discarded paper is all this needs to be.

I embrace the feeling. The song is an incantation, pressing pause on everything else. Every worry, every problem that I had before the first note ceases to exist. I'm not alone in this impossible space, and I'm glad I let him in.

With the last chord still quivering in the air, I rush to Garrett. My arms latch around his neck and my knees slide across the surface of the bench to meet the side of his right thigh. We did it. I missed this and he managed to help me find it again.

"Eve," he breathes in that way of his that makes my name sound like a prayer. The sound of it evaporates the heady feeling clouding my thoughts.

I jerk back to sit on my heels, letting go of him as I do. "Sorry. Sorry. I just got so excited."

I don't want to back up and apologize, not really. I want to fall into this feeling. But I need to remember that it will pass. This hum of connection that makes me want to have his fingers reenact what they just did on the piano on my body, it will pass. It will pass and we'll still be friends living in the same city once my time here is over because that's what we are now.

Friends. At least I hope we are.

He's what I need, and I can't ask for more because I've already been given more of him than I ever dreamed of.

"It's okay." He pulls his hands from the keys to his lap. His eyes map my features, parallel canyons carved between his brows.

"What's with that face?"

"You're smiling."

"As I tend to do," I say, then nudge my knee into his thigh. He reaches out his hand landing on my folded leg.

"No." He gives the slightest shake of his head. "This one's different."

"Oh." My heart claws for purchase at the implication.

I take in his face, how he's looking at me but it feels like he's looking into me. Everything in me wants to reach out again, to touch him with intention. We created this song together and it's built some tentative bridge that I want to run across. I want him to let me in more than ever, but not out of pure curiosity anymore. I want to know him. A small voice of wisdom reminds me that I'm probably just associating this rush of feeling from the song with him.

His eyes catch mine, pools of amber that threaten to drown me. Neither of us look away. The moment we do this spell will break. I lean in, so does he, I don't know who does first.

It's late. We're tired. It's a bad idea.

His forefinger starts to make small circles on my knee. I don't look down out of fear that if I do, he'll remember his hand is there and stop.

He's here. I feel more like myself than I have in ages. I'd be stupid to ignore that he's made me feel this way.

"Eve," he says on a breath, and I'm not sure if he's trying to get my attention or if it slipped out by accident. The tip of his nose grazes my cheek. It's infinitesimal but sets off a chain reaction of fireworks bursting from the point of contact.

"Yes?" I ask anyway, hoping that I might be the answer.

If I just tilt my head up my lips will brush against the corner of his mouth. That's all it will take. He breathes and the puff of air tickles my cheek. One small movement to change the course of everything.

I could just lift my face then—

A phone alarm goes off, and I jerk away so quickly that I nearly topple off the side of the stool. Garrett fumbles for his pocket and presses the stop button. When he looks back his eyes flash with panic. The damage is done. Whatever almost happened, that bridge isn't safe to cross anymore.

"It's eight," he says.

"That desperate to get away from me?" I ask but my voice comes out shakier than I would like. "You could stay."

"I think we've hit a perfect stopping point." Still, he doesn't move.

"Sure." My tongue darts out to wet my lips and his eyes track the movement. "I think I need a drink. You know, to celebrate." Among other reasons.

"A drink. I could go for a drink." He nods and now it's my turn to stare as I watch the bob of his Adam's apple. "I'll drive?"

"I think I'm going to walk. It's nice out." And I don't need to be stuck in a car with him right now.

"I'll see you there," he says as he collects his belongings.

The tapping of his parting footsteps syncopates with the anxious rhythm of my thundering heart.

Before I forget, I get the demo recording ready to send off to Vincent. It's a relief to have it done, but I'm having a bit of trouble getting excited about the small victory when every atom in my body is vibrating with need. The ghost of our almost kiss sinks its claws into the back of my mind as I listen back to cut the recording at the appropriate spot.

"Eve?" My name sounds more like a plea than it did before.

Then my breathy, *"Yes."*

21

Garrett

I wish Evelyn didn't look so good bent over a table. The stars on the ass of her tight jeans are the first thing I see when I walk into The Gas Station, and it's damn hard to look away from how the denim hugs her hips.

I'm not surprised she beat me here. I ended up getting a call from Wes, then Alina wanted me to run through a new arrangement for the festival with her.

"I'll have to kick you out for being a creep if you keep staring at her. I suggest you stop looking and grab the beer I have waiting for you," Pat says. I turn to meet her sly smile. She pushes the opened bottle in my direction and I reach for it.

Evelyn and I have only been at this for a week and if my timer hadn't gone off, I would have kissed her. Hell, might have even with the timer if she hadn't jumped away from me. At least one of us seems to have some sense of self preservation. But I'm not sure how much longer I'll last, especially after tonight.

"What? Not going to deny you were staring?" Pat says, prying for more information.

"No denying something plain as day." I walk away before Pat can tell me off. Anyway, there's someone else I'd rather be talking to.

She's breathtaking. But that's not why; it's never been why. Making music with her has only allowed me to wrangle my thoughts and understand them. I feel like myself around her.

Not the boy who did his best to be useful enough to keep around.

Not the bassist for Fool's Gambit.

Not a man itching to work.

Just me.

The crack of billiard balls colliding welcomes me as Evelyn hits them with the intentionality of a sniper. Her lips curl with satisfaction as a red ball neatly falls into a corner pocket.

"Impressive," I say.

She whirls and her gaze trips over me, cataloging my sweater and jeans before it reaches my eyes. "Damn. I was hoping to catch you when you came in so I could scam you."

"You already have my time; you want my money too?"

"I want everything I can get out of you," she says, ignorant of what that would entail. If she had all of me, everything I want to give her, it would scare her off in a heartbeat. Then I'd lose her, and that's exactly why what almost happened earlier can't happen.

"I doubt that," I mutter under my breath.

Evelyn puts up the pool cue then shuffles to reset the table. "I do have a gift for you. I was going to wait until tomorrow to give it to you, but I thought it would pair well with celebratory drinks." Anxiety and excitement battle for dominance in her tone. "Come on."

Before I know it, she's pulling me behind her to one of the red upholstered booths in the corner. A white bakery box rests on the table next to a mismatched set of festive paper plates and napkins I assume she's gotten from Pat.

She releases my hand to fling open the box. "Tada!"

"You set your expectations really low," I say, reading the overly ornate red icing script.

We didn't kill each other!

"The trick with men is keeping the bar in hell so you'll never be disappointed," she explains as she grabs a knife and moves to cut us slices. "You know, I checked three bakeries and none of them had pre-made options. I had to get it special ordered."

"I can't imagine why."

"I know, right?" she says, acting appalled. "It must be a regional thing. I can usually find them so easily."

"It's nice," I tell her.

"You're only saying that because I have a weapon," she says.

The cake has a strawberry filling that, in addition to the red icing, makes the blade look menacing. She continues to cut pieces and put them on plates. Instead of keeping the cake to ourselves, we hand out pieces to Pat and the handful of other bargoers before sliding into the booth.

As we adjust, our legs brush against each other. I expect her to pull away again, but her calf presses against mine. Like if we can't see it we don't have to acknowledge that it's happening.

"You really made it feel like a party in here," I say, cocking my head toward the room full of people.

"If this is the type of party you've been going to recently, I need to get you out more. When we're back in the city I'll take you with me," Evelyn offers then takes a bite.

Back in the city. It's been just under a week since Holt told me I had to stay and I've barely thought of work, barely thought of what this dynamic will look like when we return.

"You're the expert, so if you invite me I won't miss it."

"The other day, why did you bring up that party, I mean, when we were talking to the Barlowes?"

"It's a version of the truth, I thought it would be better than lying," I say, my mouth goes dry, so I take a sip of my beer. "Why?"

"I don't ever really know how to feel about that night. Somehow hearing your version made me like it more." Her eyes dip down to her plate where she's started to absentmindedly push around frosting. "We were celebrating my third album that night. Well, Avery wanted to and I showed up because I'm terrible at saying no, even though I didn't really want to be there. I was supposed to be happy that night. I was supposed to pour champagne to the brim of the plastic flutes we bought to be practical yet celebratory. I was supposed to dance and smile and be on top of the world. I tried but I just really didn't want to. Not that night." She heaves a breath and wriggles her shoulders, as if to simply shake off her discomfort. "It was so weird. All these people didn't even know why they were there. I was so relieved when someone spilled their drink on me because then I could take a break."

"Sorry I brought it up," I say, but I'm not sure I am.

"It's not like you knew." She shrugs. "Anyway, I usually like parties."

"I'm glad, or I would have gone my entire life without celebrating not murdering you."

"Despite the cake industry's best efforts to dissuade me." Her lips curl into a half-hearted shadow of a smile. "But parties celebrating me? I can't do it. I've always had a hard time with birthdays, especially. I hate it when the attention is on me, I feel like I'm being watched and then will inevitably screw up, like when people are singing 'Happy Birthday' and you're just standing there trying to look thankful while not being sure what to do with your hands."

"I promise not to sing happy birthday to you," I say, then make sure to add, "Assuming I'd be invited."

"After what we pulled off with the Barlowes? I can't not invite my partner in crime."

"I'm not sure if pretending to be in a relationship to fool local farmers counts as a crime."

"We have to carry the secret forever or we might ruin the Love Letter Festival's chances of getting donated wine."

"Very high stakes."

"Oh yes. We're permanently bonded." Her features soften, spring-green eyes glimmering. "Seriously, though, after this, if you see me on a street corner, will you look the other way?"

"Never," I say, knowing that if I saw her, a glimpse alone would disrupt my every thought for the rest of the day.

She looks down and a deep flush colors her tan skin. "Good to know." Her eyes dart to the bar and she says, "I'm going to grab water. I'll be right back."

I give in and watch her as she goes up to Pat and they talk cheerily as Pat finishes using a bottle opener to pop off two bottle caps in quick succession. Because I already have my eyes on her, I see Evelyn turn to stone as the door chimes and two frazzled tourists walk in. Their eyes turn to saucers when they spot her. A second later, I'm on my feet closing the distance between us.

22

Evelyn

I need to stop asking for what I want. Or at the very least, I should keep it to myself.

When I said I wished Quinn was here, I meant it. But not in the way that I ever expected her and Oliver to push through the door to The Gas Station.

The moment I make eye contact with Quinn, the world rocks. She is dressed in the same matching olive green sweatshirt and leggings she's worn every time we used to travel. Her black hair is tossed up in a precarious bun. I almost expect her to look at me and say, "*I think ten pairs of underwear is enough for the weekend,*" the way she would whenever I packed the hour before we left.

There must be some part of me that's operating out of habit because I'm taking steps toward them. Before I know it, the three of us crowd the entryway. I don't know where to look. My throat tightens, making me regret abandoning my water on the bartop.

"Hey, Ev," Oliver says, and it shouldn't shake me but it does. It's so casual, so him, that I feel like I've been thrust back in time. What's worse is his easy grin that causes a single dimple to pop on the right side of his mouth. His blue eyes are bright in the way that I used to love, the way that made everything feel like an adventure. But these are the first words he's spoken to me in months.

I don't count the happy birthday text I sent him in June, but maybe I should. In general, I haven't texted him directly much since our break up, hoping to spare him the need to explain, *Oh, she's just a friend. Yeah, we dated three years ago and even lived together, but really, we're only friends now and it's not weird that she's texting me.*

Maybe if I put in more effort to our recent conversations, him being here, in a small town where I'm trying my damnedest to write an album that is in any way as impactful as the one he doesn't know I wrote about our relationship, wouldn't feel like some sort of karmic bitch slap.

"What are you doing here?" I ask, doing my best to sound natural. I don't know if I can even remember what *natural* is supposed to sound like. Are you even supposed to sound natural when your ex-who-is-also-still-your-friend and your best friend who you have been avoiding walk into a bar? Is it rude to sound natural?

"We thought this was a gas station," he says, explaining more about this exact moment in time and less about his and Quinn's proximity to Hartsfall.

"You know that's not what she meant." Quinn cuts a glance in Oliver's direction.

"Well. I guess the truth is…" His hand reaches out to the side and grabs hers. For a moment discomfort pinches her features, then she looks almost sorry? That doesn't make sense unless…

"You're here. Like, *together*?" I ask, then trip over my next words. My heart does some Olympic level gymnastics in my chest, tumbling so violently that I'm hit with a wave of nausea. "I mean, that's really cool…you two together. That makes perfect sense. You guys work so well together and you look great. I know it's only been a few months since I've seen you but so much can happen. I mean, you could have dyed your hair or gotten a face tattoo or something. But this is so much better!"

The three of us were always close. With me gone maybe they got closer. And it's not like I gave them any opportunities to tell me. The few times they asked to call I told them I was busy and would try later until they stopped asking. Is this what they wanted to talk about this entire time? It's been three years since Oliver and I broke up, so it's not like I have any claim over him or his dating life.

"Not that dying your hair is bad; it's just it's nice to see you both looking the same." A hand lands on my lower back. The contact acts as a pause button for my rambling as a familiar warmth spreads through me.

"Hey, *baby*." Two words and Garrett has sent me spiraling all over again, the moment of comfort evaporating. What feels like a kiss is planted at the top of my head and all I can focus on is staying upright. "You guys went to college with Eve. Quinn and Owen, right?"

For the first time in my life I empathize with an overheating computer screaming for proper air flow. God, I need to get outside and jump into freezing water or something to stop my skin from feeling so tight.

"Oliver," I correct as I swallow the very important question of W*hat the hell Garrett is doing?*

Quinn shifts closer to Oliver and rests her head on his shoulder. She's stiff, but she's never been big on public displays of affection. She's always been slow with her relationships, cautious.

How can they be this serious already? I ask myself, as if it's only been one month since I last saw them instead of seven.

Oliver squeezes her hand, and she relaxes slightly into his touch.

"Yeah, college," Oliver confirms, seemingly unfazed.

Garrett's arm slings around my waist and I step back so my back rests against his hard chest. "Welcome to Hartsfall. Where are you two staying?"

"If we can manage to not get lost again, The Ives Inn," Oliver says.

"Cute place for couples." Garrett nods.

Couples. I might throw up. I might throw up and then never be able to show my face here again.

"Yeah, it looks like it. We were lucky they had a spot," Quinn says. "Evelyn, you guys look cuter in person."

"In person?" I squeak.

"Yeah, the pictures you sent," Quinn explains. "From the farm."

"Pictures. Yeah, I remember." *Shit.*

"It's good to see you." Quinn gives a hesitant smile before looking to the side at Oliver. "We should get going. If you could point us in the direction of an actual gas station so we don't have to leave our rental on the side of the road somewhere that would be great."

I tune out the conversation as Garrett gives them directions. I need to get out of here. I need to run, but I can't look like I'm running. I said that I'm good with them being together, so I have to act like I mean it, even if I'm not sure how I feel.

"You guys should tag along with our plans tomorrow," I blurt, because I'm excellent at self-preservation.

"Oh," Quinn stammers.

"That would be fantastic. We didn't have anything planned," Oliver beams. It's oddly comforting that in this moment where everything feels flipped on its head that he still manages to make everything sound like the best idea.

"I'll send you details," I promise. I will send them. I just have to figure out what the hell those details are going to be. I originally planned on taking Garrett to a pottery class, but I'll have to check and see if there's more space.

I do my best impression of a statue as I watch them leave. The hand on my back pulls away and Garrett steps around to face me. To my relief there's no pity in his eyes. He's his same sturdy self, and I really need to lean on someone right now.

"Let's go somewhere you don't have to pretend to be okay," he says, low and reassuring.

"I'm great." The lie comes easily.

"You don't have to be with me."

"So, you have a time machine we can hop in and go back to yesterday?" I choke out.

"Fresh out of time machines."

"Damn, then why do I keep you around?"

Garrett pulls into the same overlook he took me during our tour. Wordlessly, he turns off the engine of his truck and hops out. It's oddly more intimate to be in the old Ford than Alina's convertible. There are traces of him all over even though it's pristine. The fresh, expensive smell of bergamot that clings to the air and the faded leather seats. How the gear shift has been rubbed smooth with a lasting impression of his steady grip.

My phone comes to life from where it's resting on my lap, lighting up the cab.

Quinn

Sorry for the ambush. We were planning on getting a hold of you after we settled in.

Though the text is from Quinn it distinctly sounds like Oliver with the amount of tentative concern strung through the message. No doubt she handed him her phone.

Evelyn

All fine. Talk to you tomorrow.

I tuck the phone in my pocket then exit the truck, the door creaking as I push it open. When I find Garrett lowering the tailgate, he offers me his hand and helps me up. His hand feels like the only real thing, rough, warm, and familiar. Then he's gone again, and I feel like I'm floating. A moment later he joins me, the vehicle dipping under his weight.

The night sky sprawls overhead, a sea of stars with the occasional island of a cloud. I want to get lost in all of it, swim away in the cosmos. I want to feel as insignificant as I do when I'm people watching. I want to feel like a speck of dust and that my problems can be carried away in the wind.

Garrett's low measured voice breaks through the night. "You know, I'm fucking terrified of the day this truck stops working. Fletcher's dad was the one who gave it to me when I was sixteen. It's like this deal with the universe. If I keep fixing the truck and if I keep coming back to help Alina with her house and play music for her, then I can still belong here. I can still keep coming back even though I promised I'd get the hell out and make a good life for myself," he says. His words loop around me like we're two rock climbers tethered on a mountain and he's the only thing keeping me from hitting rock bottom. "When I came back for my first winter break, I was scared that people would just forget me. It sounds so dumb but I was fourteen and I didn't have a house here anymore. My mother had moved to Florida on a whim, and I hadn't heard from her for months. I told you I have a tough time with this place, that's true. But I'll never be able to let go of it because it's proof that I'm worth something."

"Why are you telling me this?" I ask, awestruck by his rare moment of vulnerability.

"Because I want you to know that if you have things you feel like you can't tell anyone else…you can tell them to me. You don't have to, but you can."

It's like all the conversations I've never had rattle on the shelves where I store them in the back of my mind.

I try to return his leap of faith with the truth. "I just want them to be happy. I know that sounds like a cop out, but that's all I've ever wanted for them. I think it was just the shock that rattled me. Like I was really coming to terms with all the distance between us." For so long, not responding, not talking, has allowed me to pretend that the three of us were frozen in time. But that's just a pretty lie. Of course, life kept going. Going without me. "We used to do everything together. Now, I guess, they're doing everything without me. I should have known that already. I needed to see it."

"I'm sorry."

Guilt lances through me. I chose this. No matter how lonely I feel, I don't get to feel sorry for myself. There's an ache in me in the chamber of my heart I carved out for Oliver and Quinn. A monument. Over the last week, I started to forget it.

"It's not like it's your fault." I nudge Garrett with my knee. "You didn't have to do that in the bar. Pretend to be with me. Thank you, though."

"I didn't want you to deal with that alone," he says. "And I'm pretty sure they thought we were together before they stepped foot into the place. You know me, I like to exceed expectations."

"I swear, if I told people how funny you can be they'd never believe me."

"Maybe that's on purpose," he says, looking at me in that secret way. No one would believe me because to them this man didn't grow up here, getting his hands dirty as he learned how to fix trucks and coming up on weekends to help his neighbor. They only get the smallest possible piece of him.

But I get this, however much that amounts to.

"Still, you didn't have to do any of that. I can figure it out."

"I owe you for the Barlowes."

"And they say chivalry is dead." I huff a pathetic attempt at a laugh.

"Sounded better than saying I still need your help as my vacation expert and camera woman," he says.

"You're agreeing to pretend to be with me for purely selfish reasons? Got it."

His eyes narrow, snaring my gaze. "Eve. When it comes to you, everything I do is selfish." His voice threatens to liquefy me.

"Well, I'm glad I get to reap the rewards."

His eyes hold mine until the whispering of the wind and rippling of the Hudson are drowned out by the unsteady thudding of my heart.

Bad idea. Bad idea.

A bad idea that's never looked so good. One that made me feel alive when his hands brushed against mine as they danced along piano keys.

"But I mean it's only for a week, since you're supposed to be out of here next Monday, so you won't have to suffer too long," I remind the both of us.

"Yeah, just a week." Garrett clears his throat. "I guess I should ask, what happened between you and Oliver? What did he do?"

"Nothing." The thought of Oliver is sobering. I look away and draw my knees to my chest. "I was the one who left. Sorry to shatter your jilted lover image of me. I dug this grave."

I told him part of the truth our first time at the museum. But the rest? That's twisted into the fabric of my mistakes. Pull one thread and everything will unravel.

"So you left. You did what was right for you."

"You're still giving me too much credit." A dam breaks and the force of everything I've been holding back rushes out of me in a flood. I need it out in the world, the reason I can't trust myself with Garrett. Not when he's starting to mean something to me. "I shouldn't have stayed as long as I did in the first place. I had been making music as Lyla officially for two years by then and I should have told him about it. He was *the* person I should have told because I was building a life with him. But he was finishing his master's then starting a new job. There was excuse after excuse. The truth was that we fit as Evelyn and Oliver. We didn't fit if I was also Lyla. I knew if I told him he would stay because that's the type of person he is. He's someone who takes care of people, a good person. So he would have stayed and encouraged me to chase my dreams even if it went against his picture of a simple content life.

"I couldn't promise him it would stay a secret. So I didn't tell him. I stayed anyway. It was so fucking selfish." My chest heaves as I relinquish the truth.

I think about the ring pressed into Oliver's hand. The weekend I spent in my childhood bedroom. Then two weeks after the break up when we were at our favorite bar and he was fine. I hated myself more that night than I did when I ended things. I wanted him to hurt. I wanted to mean something to him. But at least it showed we'd be fine.

Ever since, Lyla has been the shield I've used to never get close to anyone again. Never get close enough to hurt them with my own ambition. It's dangerous with Garrett, there's no shield. How can I know I won't hurt us both when I get caught up in the idea of something I can't follow through on, just because I want to be someone to someone?

"Sounds lonely," he says, causing the back of my eyes to sting as the urge to cry tightens my throat. Part of me wishes that he said anything else. Instead, he's cut me right to my core.

"It was my choice." I shrug. "If you do want to pretend to be together, we should probably make some rules then, figure out how all this works so it doesn't get messy…" I trail off sheepishly as memories filter in. Nimble fingers stroking keys in a way that caused my mind to wander. A flow of inspiration that blended with passion exploding between us. The way he left when I wanted him to stay.

"Not going to sleep with me?" he says teasingly. I appreciate how he's trying to lighten the mood even if it doesn't come naturally to him, but it causes heat to flare across my skin.

"I have this tendency to develop feelings hard and fast. So, unless you want to be stuck with me forever, maybe not the best choice," I say.

"There are worse fates."

"I'm glad being stuck with me isn't nightmare fuel." I roll my eyes, starting to feel a bit better. "I have to ask…how do you do it? I mean, just move on from someone and be okay. I feel like I've stopped being able to trust if I'm actually feeling something for someone or if I just want to be wanted so badly that I just throw my all into it. I feel like I'm missing something."

"I go in knowing I'm not the type of person people end up with. It has to end, so it does."

Before coming to Hartsfall, I had the impression he thought he was above it all. Better than something as feeble as love. It never occurred to me he thought there was something wrong with him, that he was never supposed to fit anywhere. His mom. The band. This town. He convinced himself he was the person others left behind, like it was a birthright.

Garrett must mistake my silence for offense, or something of the sort, because he adds, "I admire how much of yourself you can give others even when you keep parts so hidden. There's nothing wrong with wanting to belong with someone. I think it's the most human thing you can feel."

"Do you want that too?"

"I'm not sure that matters," he says. I see it in his eyes, lurking along the edges, that he does, even if he's lived a life where survival was contingent on never admitting it.

"I think it does. I think you belong with someone."

"Maybe." But he says it in a way that makes me think he's only playing along for my benefit. Like he really doesn't believe he deserves what everyone else deserves.

"Maybe while we're here, pretending, we can belong to each other for a little while."

The corners of his lips flirt with a smile. "For a little while."

23

Garrett

"What do you mean the money got sent back. Is the account closed?" I ask Denton, my accountant, as I wait in line at Love is Brewing. They've updated their menu to include fall drinks, so people are taking roughly twice as long to decide on their order only to inevitably buy a pumpkin spice latte. It's good, it just shouldn't be a decision that takes someone three or more minutes to make.

"No, it was sent back. I checked to see if there were any abnormal explanations, but everything checked out. I was calling to see if the payments need to stop."

"Try to send it again in a few days," I instruct. There's an off chance that Lana sent it back on a whim and will regret returning the money. It's happened one time before, when I called to check she gave me a long waxing lecture on pride and how she doesn't need my hand outs. That lasted about forty-eight hours before an inbox full of missed calls saying it was a joke, and I should have sent it again. *That I should have known.* This time I'm hoping I can skip the calls altogether. "Anything else I need to be aware of?"

The line moves another foot forward but the couple at the counter is starting to point to each menu item, so I still have plenty of time.

"That's all."

"Thanks for letting me know about the issue. If anything else happens let me know," I say, despite hoping there won't be another call anytime soon.

I don't like the feeling of having the money back in my possession. It makes things feel unbalanced. Things will never be steady with Lana. Blame and blistering bitterness. Those aren't emotions that provide a reliable foundation. Money and the deal we've made, it's an attempt at something close to normal. Whatever the fuck that means.

When I reach the front of the line, the frazzled barista looks relieved I know my order. I get a drink for Eve too. Her light was on until two in the morning, and I want to check on her. It's odd seeing her like this. When I learned she was Lyla she didn't seem to care. I fix things. It's what I'm good at. But I'm not sure I can fix this.

I open the chess app on my phone and start a game against a computer as I wait for the drinks at the end of the bar. I sink my concentration into it and find a moment of calm until the barista calls my name, and I slot the drinks into a carrier and head toward the door.

Just as I reach for the door, it pushes inward and I'm face to face with a startled Quinn.

"Oh hey," she says as she brushes off our near collision and claims a spot at the back of the line.

I eye the door. If only the line hadn't been slowed down by indecisive pumpkin lovers, I might have been able to skip this interaction all together. "Hey. No Oliver?"

"He's working. We both can do what we need remotely, but he's on deadline for the software he's working on," Quinn explains as she eyes the drink carrier in my hand.

I nod. "How long are you two staying in town?"

"If Ev asks us to leave, we'll go." Her lips tighten into a thin line.

"She won't," I say. I know Evelyn, she'd rather suffer in silence than turn away her friends.

"You're right, but this is me letting you know she has that option."

"And if she doesn't ask you to leave?"

"We're hoping to stick around for her birthday. We've celebrated it with her since we met so I guess it's worth it for tradition's sake," she explains.

I nod as I take in the information. Her birthday is on the 12th, two weeks away. "I'll let her know."

Quinn starts to turn away then shifts her attention back to me, as if remembering to share something. "You know, I'm impressed with how okay you seem to be with all of this. Not every guy would be chill with their girl's ex-fiancé coming into town, even if he was in a new relationship."

"Ex-fiancé?" The word slips out with all my confusion before I can bottle it up. I knew they were together for years, but not on that level.

She sighs. "Shit. I would have thought she'd have told you. I mean, at least after last night. I should have guessed, though. Oliver was the one who told me about it, I had to wait a month before she even mentioned it," she says apprehensively. "She's always had this way of talking to people, making sure you feel seen and heard and then you leave a conversation and realize you barely learned anything new about her. Like she doesn't think she's significant enough to matter. I've always thought it had to do with growing up around you guys. You know the fame, secrets, and all that."

"Knowing doesn't change anything for me." Doesn't change that this isn't real so either way I have no right to feel jealous. I do, though, the feeling clawing at my chest, demanding to be acknowledged. But I can pretend I don't at least until I finish this conversation.

"There are things she'll never share, but I've come to terms with it." An unreadable expression flickers across her face. "You might have to, too."

Quinn steps forward in line and gives me one last glance. "I guess I'll see you tonight. Could you have her send us the details when you get the chance? I haven't heard from her since last night."

"I'll make sure to remind her," I say, playing along with the promise Evelyn made yesterday.

As I leave, I give Quinn a quick attempt at a wave with a drink in my hand. I take the walk to Evelyn's as an opportunity to roll over the new knowledge in my mind. Evelyn was engaged. From the timeline that she's told me and from what I've seen on social media it was three years ago, but that's still a significant event to just brush over. What else isn't she telling me?

Evelyn opens the door a minute or so after I knock. She's yawning as she takes me in. Using the heel of her hand she rubs the sleep from her eyes.

"What's wrong?" she asks. The corners of her mouth drag downward with concern. "Did you get called back to the city?"

"Why would I be leaving?"

"You showed up in person with the gift of matcha. It's ominous."

"Me being nice is ominous? That's concerning to hear. But no, this isn't apology matcha and I'm not going back early. I'm still here to help you fake it for your ex-fiancé," I say and I immediately wish I went about it a different way. I thought she trusted me. It hurts that I was wrong.

She flinches. "I don't remember telling you that."

"I ran into Quinn," I explain. I could have tried to get it out of her more naturally, less accusatory, but I don't want to have to play a game to make it feel like it was her choice to divulge information I already know.

"All right."

"You could tell me about it."

"It seems like you're caught up. Is there anything else you need?" Her voice manages to walk the line between charming and guarded. If I wasn't in the position that I am I'd take it as an opportunity to walk away.

"Evelyn, if you want me to help you, if we're actually a team, it would be nice to know I'm not flying blind."

She mulls over my request for a moment. Her eyes dart between me and the drinks I'm carrying.

"Fine, come in, but only because you brought me a drink," she says dismissively and moves from the door to let me in. "It's not like it's a big, crazy story or anything."

We move inside to the living room. Her body folds into the corner of the couch while I settle into the armchair that's positioned between her piano and the fireplace.

"What's the story then, if it's not big and crazy?"

"It really isn't a big deal," she bites out.

"How is it that you being engaged is not a big deal? It seems like the exact type of thing you'd care about," I press. It feels like a thumb digging into a fading bruise. Hartsfall is the rawest part of me. I just thought she was sharing those parts of herself too.

"It was only for forty-eight hours. I'm not sure it counts." A self-deprecating chuckle cracks out of her. "I didn't tell anyone until Quinn. Even then, I almost didn't. It's like if we pretended it didn't happen, we could just move on. We treated the whole break up that way. We talked about it enough to make sure we were still friends and just moved on."

"And how is that working out for you?" I ask, not fully managing to contain my hurt.

"He seems happy," she explains, avoiding my question.

"I didn't ask about him. I asked about you."

"I came to this town because the last time I was able to write good music was when I was with him. So that's how I'm doing. Not great." She glares at me. "Is that what you want me to say? Do you want me to admit I feel like a fucking failure whenever I think about how I walked away from Oliver to pursue something I'm not good at anymore? There are so many times when I think about that ring and wonder if I screwed everything up on a whim. Can you blame me for not wanting you to see me that way? I like the way you look at me. I don't want to give you a reason to look away." Her face is flushed pink with shame and frustration.

"I'm looking at you now." When am I not looking? When am I not wanting more of her?

"How long will that last? When will you get tired and turn away?" she asks like it's a foregone conclusion. I've spent years wanting her. This might complicate a few things, but it doesn't change what matters. And what matters is her. Hell. It's always her.

"I'm here, Evelyn," I tell her. "I see you and I'm not looking away."

Not now. Not ever. I watch as her features shift, softening as she accepts that I mean it. She's not losing me over this.

Her chest heaves as she takes a deep breath. "Thank you."

"Are you doing all right? I mean, you still love him and he's with your best friend" I ask, not sure I want the answer. But I need to know.

"I don't love him anymore, not like that. I care about him, so yes, if he's happy with Quinn, I'm happy for them," she says with fierce adamancy. "He'll always be important to me, but at the end of our relationship I started feeling lost and I've been trying so hard to find myself again. Anything else you need to know to make sure you have a clear picture of everything?"

"That's it," I say, feeling unsteady with a relief that shouldn't matter. Even if she doesn't love him, that doesn't change who we are to each other.

"Good. Then can you go? I need to check and see if I can edit my reservation for the pottery class I had scheduled for us," Evelyn says as she gets up from the couch and grabs her phone from the side table and walks away.

24

Evelyn

I stroke my hands up, applying constant pressure along the slick surface. "Does this seem erotic to you?"

"Yes, but I think it's generally frowned upon to say it out loud," Garrett groans like I hoped he would.

"Makes sense. Didn't take you as an exhibitionist," I say as I lift my hands from the cone of clay I've been working to center on the pottery wheel.

I wasn't exactly paying attention to our instructor, Poppy, when she was enthusiastically walking us through the process. Right now, she's hunched over helping another one of the attendees on the opposite side of the semi-circle of stations. Her red curls are pulled back with a bandana and her striped overalls are smeared with dried clay.

The studio should be the perfect place to relax. Finished projects rest on shelves along the brick walls. The brown and green earthen hues of the plates and bowls match the plants strategically placed in corners or hanging above the register, vines creeping up to the ceiling. But there's the simple fact that my best friend and ex-whatever-Oliver-qualifies as are also here. I can't focus or fully relax the way I want to.

Still, the class structure is working to my advantage. I rarely find advantages to my perpetual tardiness, but tonight it was a convenient excuse to show up right as the class was starting. There wasn't any room for much conversation other than a standard exchange of hellos. After this morning's conversation with Garrett, everything is even more uneasy, thus the necessary integration of innuendo.

I should have told him, but I've spent years repressing those forty-eight hours. Mostly, I try to forget them because they should never have happened. I never should have been with Oliver long enough to picture forever. It's taken years to systematically sort through the reasons and lock them into a fireproof safe in the back of my mind.

"I think that is something good to be on the same page about," Garrett says.

He's successfully formed his clay into a puck on the mat and is now dipping his hands into the bucket of water at his station. His khaki button-up is rolled to the elbow, exposing the contours of his forearms. He goes silent as his attention fixes on the clay, dipping his fingers into the center to open it up then guiding out the edge. It's impossible to stop watching the shifting of his muscles. He makes it look so easy, the clay obeying his every touch. He's in absolute control with his strong hands and laser focus.

My body buzzes and heats, tendrils of electricity collecting low in my stomach. It would be easy to attribute the warmth to the nature of what we're doing, the imagery of it. But that moment between us yesterday is still raw. And this morning when he came over earlier, I walked away to check on the class because I needed to remember how to breathe around him rather than being upset about him learning about my engagement.

He cocks his head, effectively breaking my trance. "Are you going to try?"

"Hmm?" I ask.

"Are you going to make something now you've centered the clay?"

"I think it's fine as is. Quit while I'm ahead, and all that." I look at the puck lazily spinning on the mat affixed to my wheel. In this form is pure potential. In the right hands, with the right choices, it could be anything. I'm having a lot of trouble thinking I'm capable of that right now.

"You're allowed to mess it up." Garrett's voice is soft. I think he's also on edge and trying to figure out what's safe between us.

"Says you." I nod toward the bowl he's formed.

"You think I did this in one go?"

"I think your skill set has more in common with a genetically modified superhuman than the average American, so I don't think you being able to do that in one try is off the table."

"There are about ten things you could do in this town growing up. Most of them involved having friends to do them with and I didn't really meet that criteria. So no, this isn't my first time here."

"I'll try," I say.

"That's all you're here to do."

I feel his eyes on me as I guide my attention back to the wheel. I wet my hands and place them on the cool clay. It's an effort to recall Poppy's instruction, mostly because all that comes to mind is a 4K replay of Garrett's hands. Eventually, I let the visual take over because I'm a masochist.

Tucking my arms in and leaning over the wheel, I start. Well, I try. I reach the point where I'm pulling the walls up into something cup-like and I'm feeling good. Then without warning the top lip crumples inward and splits, rippling and distorting the entire piece.

"Well, I guess that's it." I shrug, trying to play off the bitter taste of disappointment. I just want something, anything, to go right.

"It fell apart one time. Try again." His voice is so tender. I want to tell him not to feel bad for me, but I don't think it's that. I think he wants to be soft with me. He looks up and across the room to catch Poppy's attention. They make eye contact and he gestures toward me.

"I might be a bit of a lost cause," I explain as she eyes my piece.

"Garrett, don't be lazy. Help your girl out." I watch as Garrett opens his mouth but Poppy stops him. "And don't say you're out of practice." She points at the bowl on his wheel.

"You okay with that?" Garrett asks. He swallows hard and I track the bob of his Adam's apple. His eyes leap to mine. He'll have to touch me to help and the fact that it is a completely normal thing Poppy is doing with everyone else doesn't detract from how it makes me feel like a blushing teenager.

"I don't want to monopolize her time if others need help."

He grabs his stool and sets it next to mine. When he sits our thighs press together and I nearly pull away to make room but my legs have nowhere to go with the pottery wheel between them.

"You were putting too much pressure on the walls, that's why they collapsed," he explains. "I'm going to put my hands on yours. We'll do it together."

"Do you always talk people through it?" I tease, hoping it will offset the molten feeling in my stomach.

"Is your mind always in the gutter?" He leans in and lowers his voice to a whisper that breezes across my ear. "But for the sake of our charade, maybe you should know. Yes, Eve, I like to talk through it, all the way. I like it when I can help make sure people get exactly what they want."

I suck in a breath right as his hands land on mine, and I wonder if he can feel the fire burning right under the surface of my skin. It takes me a full thirty seconds to regain the ability to speak. "Well, if it casually comes up in conversation, then I'll be prepared to share that interesting fact. Couldn't help yourself, could you?"

"You seem to have a lot of fun flirting with me, so I thought I'd try it out." His words are a current tugging inviting me to play with him even more. "Look at the clay, Evelyn. Don't look at me; you'll have plenty of time for that later."

He drags a thumb over my knuckles, as if to direct my focus but it only make me more scattered. I force myself to take in a full breath, and once my attention is firmly on the wheel, he presses his fore and middle fingers down against mine. Controlled and firm, working with the clay, not against it.

"Good. Now we're going to pull up the walls," he guides. We wet our hands again and I let him reposition them, one on the inside and the other on the outside. Even with his assistance I wait for the clay to fold in on itself and become useless. "Steady," Garrett mutters. I release a breath as I match the pressure he's applying. "There it is. Atta girl."

The praise thrums through me. I consider failing on purpose to do this all over again and see if he'll say it one more time.

Our hands leave the bowl, and I gasp at the product. "You did it!"

"I was just the training wheels. You deserve the credit for trusting the process." He nudges my knee with his.

"Because you're preternaturally gifted at everything," I say. "Even before I came here I knew you as an excellent musician and someone who graduated from a top law school. Now I know you fix houses for old ladies and casually can help at a mechanic's garage."

"Not to shatter your reality, but I wasn't good at any of those things naturally."

"Bullshit," I call out loud enough a few people look up from their stations.

"I never had much going for me, so I changed that."

"By being the human equivalent of a Swiss army knife?" I ask, like, *come on, seriously?*

"I'd rather be the most useful person in a room than be asked to leave," he explains.

The more I see the full picture of who Garrett is, the more I hate it. I want him to see how extraordinary he is, how he's like no man I've ever met. I want to paint over his self-portrait, show him the way I see him, capturing the details of the resilient, caring, talented man who I'm growing to know.

"Well, I like being in the same room as you. Swiss army knife capabilities or not," I say, and I hope he believes me. I really want him to see he's worth caring about because of who he is and not because of what he can do for others.

"All right, everyone! If you have a piece you're happy with, make sure to put it on the wood board next to your contact information," Poppy calls out, reminding me we're not the only people in the room.

I look up and there's a brief moment of shock when I also remember Oliver and Quinn are here. Garrett just draws me in so completely the rest of the world becomes irrelevant. I guess there was something to those mindfulness articles.

The Lost and Found wine bar is far more suited for tourists than The Gas Station. The warm lighting is romantic but it's so dim that it's a challenge to properly read the chalkboard menu above the counter. Oliver was the one to suggest a drink because we weren't able to catch up during the class.

It's true, but I was half hoping that we'd be able to ignore that. Mostly, there is the fact that there's only a handful of things that are safe to share with them.

There's only one table with four seats available and this leads to an uncomfortable moment of deciding who should go get drinks, leaving the others to guard the table. The weirdness stems mostly from the fact that it seems like we're all doing mental calculations to determine which two of us should stay and which two should go.

In the end, I stay at the table with Oliver.

"So, how are you?" he asks and it manages to sound light and not accusatory. It's not that I expected it to, but it was definitely a fear.

"Honestly? Tired and homesick."

"I'm sorry to hear that. You sounded excited about the move when you were getting ready for it. I've always pictured you as this person who could live anywhere."

"I always thought when I left, I would feel great...you know?" The admission awkwardly slips out of me before I can stop it. I guess I've been wanting to say it for a long time now.

"That's exactly how I felt when we were freshmen. Remember how you guys called my dad for his chicken noodle soup recipe and made it for me on that hot plate you had to hide in your ottoman so the RA wouldn't confiscate it?" To this day we haven't revealed that the recipe is just a very specific brand that we had to go to Whole Foods to find. "I was so sure I would love being away from my family and finally not having to fight my sisters for the bathroom. It just made me realize why I loved it so much." He pauses then looks over toward the bar. "She told me you didn't want to talk about it until after your vacation, but I have to ask. What are you thinking about the job offer?"

The question momentarily throws me for a loop. Over the last week in Hartsfall I've only been worried about music and my outings with Garrett. If I thought that writing would give me clarity on what I should do next, I was wrong.

"I'll probably at least interview. It's not like I actually got an offer," I say, trying to dismiss the possibility so I'm not tempted to grasp for it. Still, Oliver and Quinn are here. Maybe that's for the best? This could be our chance to work everything out, so if I do take the interview we'll be good as new. We could go back to the familiar rom-com marathons and after work drinks with a side of office gossip.

"From what I heard, it's a formality. I don't want to push. I mostly wanted to say that it would be nice to have you back. It's not the same," he says, and my stomach tumbles. I want them to be happy, but knowing they miss me? It shouldn't feel this good since I know that means they might ache the way I do at the memories.

"It can't be all bad. You have Quinn. It seems like me being gone helped you guys figure things out," I say, trying to convince us both.

I can't help but wonder if they've felt something for each other for longer than they've been together and were holding back for my sake. Quinn wouldn't. She'd tell me to my face, but Oliver would. If he can do something to make someone's life easier, he does. It's always been a problem for him at work, taking on too many projects or assisting his coworkers when they have any questions. He's the guy you go to when you're floundering or just need support. But it also means that he tends to never make himself the priority. It's why we worked the way we did. Our people pleasing tended to cancel the other's out, so we found a way to meet our needs without having to communicate all that much.

"Yeah, things are different…" he starts, and the fact that he's not comfortable enough to say more tells me all that I need to know. Instead he changes subjects. "How's your brother? Still good?"

"Yeah," I say, and a true smile forms on my lips. "He's also great at telling us when he's not at his best, you know, which is something I never thought I'd be happy about. But the fact that he's honest about it and not just trying to hide his bad days, it's a huge relief."

"You deserve to be happy. I know you're saying that the city isn't working out the way you planned but it seems other things are." He makes it sound so simple.

Garrett and Quinn return, each holding two glasses of wine. Garrett settles in next to me while Quinn slides in right across the circular table next to Oliver.

She takes a sip and hums with approval as she sets it down. "So how exactly did you two go from not talking to this?"

"Quinn," Oliver snaps.

"I'm sorry, was I not supposed to ask how the guy who didn't show up to help her move is now on vacation with her?" she asks, brows arching.

"He helped. He sent movers," I say then take a hasty sip of the pinot Garrett picked out for me.

"Well, the last time we talked, you weren't all too happy with him," she says, and it stings. Has it really been that long since we had a real conversation? It can't be. I do the mental math over and over until I can't ignore that she's right.

"Don't worry, she made me make it up to her," Garrett says. "Really made me earn it."

Quinn smiles but it looks more like she's baring her teeth. "Good."

The air goes stale as we all simultaneously reach for our glasses.

"As you can see, we're all good now! What about you two?" I ask, desperate to keep the conversation moving.

Oliver and Quinn share a look then Oliver finally says, "It just sort of happened. Isn't that right, honey?"

"Yes, *honey*," Quinn says. "But why stop there, tell them the whole story."

"If you want them to know, why don't you?" Oliver says as he leans back in his seat.

"Oh, because you tell it better." Quinn leans forward and props her elbow on the table. "Really, I can't do it justice."

"Okay, so there was this concert we went to for my birthday which was a fucking disaster," Oliver starts.

"And after she saved me from the port-a-potty, and we had missed the entire concert because of it, I had to buy her dinner." Oliver says then reaches for his wine glass only to find it empty.

The tension in the air split the moment he detailed the panic that gripped him the moment he realized that he was locked into the port-a-potty at the outdoor concert venue.

"I made him change first," Quinn adds. "There was no way that I could eat with the smell clinging to his clothes."

"Okay, so I changed, bought her dinner and never wanted the night to end. That was a pretty good birthday in the end," Oliver says as he looks at Quinn and reaches for her hand.

We don't stay much longer. Even though we're not as on edge, it doesn't seem necessary to draw out the evening any longer when we seem one topic change away from souring the light mood.

"We should do this again," Oliver says as we walk onto the mostly empty sidewalk outside the bar.

"When are you guys free?" I ask, feeling more optimistic about the idea than I did when I blurted out an invitation yesterday.

Quinn throws me a look. "Pretty much whenever. Vacation and all."

"So, tomorrow?" I ask.

"We can go to Bethel. They have a ton of stuff dedicated to Woodstock, and we might be able to catch a concert," Garrett suggests.

"Sounds good," Oliver gets out through a yawn.

"Goodnight." Quinn grabs Oliver's hand and steers them toward the inn.

I watch for a second before I catch myself and move to walk toward where Garrett is parked. Garrett's hand lands against the small of my back, stopping me.

"Is everything okay?" I blink up at him. I thought tonight ended alright. But is this too much for him? Quinn has made it clear she's not exactly his biggest fan.

"I think I should kiss you."

I sputter. "What?"

"If you were here with anyone else, would you kiss them?" he asks. "It would be normal for you to kiss me right now if we were actually together, right? And they'll see us, but it won't be like we're throwing it in their faces."

"You don't have to."

"Let me." I pick up on something dangerously close to desire in his voice. His eyes are hooded, and I want to pretend I don't see it because I *want* him to be looking at me like this. I want him to mean it and be able to keep meaning it after this.

"Okay." I give in because I have an excuse to, and I really want another taste of his touch.

I expect him to just do the damn thing but he pauses to say, "Tell me how it would go."

"You'd go in for a peck," I start, testing the waters.

He leans in and brushes his lips against mine. It's a feather-light whisper of affection. "Like that?" He speaks against my mouth.

"Yes," I breathe.

"What would I do next, now that I've had a taste?"

"You'd come back for more." Every cell in my body screams *please, come back, please!*

"How much more?" His voice runs jagged.

All of me. If he asked, right now, I'd give him everything. "As much as you can get."

"Fuck." I know he says it, but I don't register it fully because his lips press into mine, coaxing my mouth open. He steals a breath from me as he nips at my bottom lip.

My hands thread through his hair and my body leans into him. He pulls me even closer as hands skate up my sides. Fingers catch on the hem of my shirt, pushing up the fabric so his calluses drag against my waist.

His tongue slips against the seam of my lips, a question. *More?*

My mouth opens in answer. *Yes, more.*

My body arches into him to find that he's hard, and I do my best to gain more friction. I'm chasing so much. Him. Me. The life I think I still have but might have thrown away. But this right here, the electric current that is looping through me? It's a reprieve. His palm traces the curve of my spine.

Up. Up. Up.

Then his mouth is gone and I'm still left wanting. Hungry. The inches between us could be an infinity as far as I'm concerned.

"Good?" he rasps.

"Yeah." I nod and my tongue darts out to wet my lips. He tracks the movement and I'm tempted to do it again. I want to watch him as he watches me. Before I go deeper into dangerous territory Garrett looks up and past me.

"I don't see them anymore. We should get going now."

Garrett turns up the radio the moment we get to the car. How can he just move on from a kiss like that? Is that what it's like for him, a moment of high floating relief and then on to the next? Neither of us say a word until he pulls up my driveway.

"How do you think it went?" Garrett asks.

"I kind of wish I had something to compare it to. Like was that a normal amount of conversation or not enough," I say as I sag against the car seat.

"If only this was the second time you encountered an ex who was dating your best friend," he muses.

"If only I were so lucky to be able to repeat this experience." I throw my hands up in indignation. "At least it wasn't as bad as it could have been, and without you here it would have been worse."

"I do enjoy when people keep me around to make sure things aren't worse."

"Garrett," I say as I remember our conversation during the pottery class. "I do mean it when I say that I would rather be doing this with you than anyone else."

"That makes sense. Unlike most fake couples, we've already had practice."

"I wish it were appropriate to send the Barlowes a thank you note for their service. But even without that, I like knowing I can rely on you and that…" I scramble for the right words. "We're good together. Good at this."

"We are," he agrees.

"I—" I hesitate, wondering if I should ask if he wants to come inside. "Just thank you. I couldn't have survived tonight without you."

Without waiting for his response, I push open the car door and head toward the house.

25

Evelyn

We silently agree to take separate cars to Bethel. We'd all fit in Quinn and Oliver's rental, but I think the elephant in the room would have a hard time fitting in the trunk.

This morning when Garrett picks me up, I try to play off my silence as being tired. I'm pretty sure if I speak, something like "Could you kiss me again—you know, for science" will fall out, which would make the car ride even more super fun and pleasant than it already is.

I stayed up for hours feeling the specter of his touch trail over me until I had to put my vibrator to use. His name tumbled from my lips when I came, not on purpose, but the shape of it fit perfectly in my mouth.

"Eve?" Garrett asks, and my cheeks flair with heat.

"Yes?" I chirp.

"Could you tell them we're about fifteen minutes out from the museum," he directs, his attention fixed on the road.

Our first stop will be The Woodstock Museum at Bethel Woods, dedicated to the groundbreaking festival and the artists who performed at it. There is a Woodstock, New York, but there's close to a two-hour drive between the two.

Once we arrive, we meet Quinn and Oliver who are already outside. Garrett and I got a late start—only a few minutes, but still. The building is a series of wood sided octagonal spaces connected by long halls.

"Hey, pumpkin, look who decided to show up," Oliver says to Quinn.

"Pumpkin?" Quinn sounds nonplussed, her eyebrows arched.

Her tone doesn't seem to bother Oliver, though. "I'm trying something new."

"And you're immediately failing at it." Quinn shakes her head then turns to me. "Do I look like a pumpkin to you?"

"You have a certain rhubarb quality, but definitely not a pumpkin," I say to ease the spark of tension. A great sign since we have yet to make it inside.

"Ahh, see, that's probably what I was picking up on." Oliver nods then slings his arm around Quinn's waist before starting toward the entrance.

We scan our tickets and shed our jackets as we push through to the main hall. The colors of the exhibit are decidedly psychedelic. A painted bus and VW Bug take up opposite sides of a walkway, each with their own intricate swirling patterns of flowers and starbursts. Overhead, film footage is projected on panels.

"I think I found your time machine," Garrett says, leaning close enough that I'm met with his clean scent of bergamot and lavender.

"Close enough." Though, this isn't exactly what I meant.

Quinn and I end up next to each other watching concert film from bean bag chairs. Jimi Hendrix, Janis Joplin, Santana, and others from the lineup each performing to a sea of people all caught up in the same moment. Collective effervescence, one of those things that make you believe there's a touch of magic in the mundane. Strangers becoming friends through their love of music.

"Would you want to do something like that?" Quinn asks.

"Go to a music festival? Maybe?" I shrug. "I'm not exactly the biggest fan of camping but I could make it work."

"No, go on stage." There's a rustling from her bean bag, and I turn to find her facing me. "And be in front of a crowd like that. I bet you could, with Avery, and play the piano or something. I mean, if you still practice now that you're in the city."

"I think I'd be too stressed about all the people. Like one mistake and it will live forever on someone's phone."

"Really?" She sounds shocked. I guess it makes sense why. Between the two of us I was always a bit more performative.

"I mean in this hypothetical, it could be fun," I say and let myself dream. A crowd singing along as I play. People dancing. Strangers sharing this one moment. I *could* like it.

"Yeah, well, I think your hypothetical self would kill it," she says then hesitates. My bean bag crinkles as I turn to face her. Her bottom lip is pulled between her teeth, a question caught in her eyes. "We should talk about Oliver."

"I don't see what's to talk about. You're together. I'm with Garrett. We're good," I insist, despite my stomach starting to flip. There's nothing more to it. Nothing that's going to change by making a fuss of it.

"Ev, I'm serious."

"So am I." My eyes nervously dart around the room to land on a group of five glancing our way, waiting for us to give up our seats. "The film is about to restart. Let's give them our spots," I say, then stand and call out to the group. "Hey, we're done if you want our seats."

"Evelyn." Quinn stands and tries to reach for me, but I pretend not to notice as I hurry to the next part of the exhibit.

I find Garrett and take his hand as we meander through the space and then outdoors to view the sculptures. Every now and then I make him pose so I can take pictures of him, which he sends off to his boss. I'm running on the logic that if I make sure I'm not alone with Quinn then the conversation can never really happen, and if the conversation can't happen, then it can't implode our current delicate balance.

"You're part of Fool's Gambit, right?" A woman's voice comes in a hushed question. I whip around to find two women standing in front of Garrett with hopeful bright eyes.

"Yeah." Garrett nods. His hands are thrust deep in his pockets. His attention flickering between the women and the stage for the performance getting ready to start in the pavilion. We're on the grass near the back because we got waylaid by a vegetable stand where Oliver found an impressively large zucchini he *needed* to buy. Quinn managed to talk him out of it, but only after she took a picture of him cradling it.

Things are *normalish*. But I'm not sure if that's us in our default setting, years of history winning out over the last few months of distance, or if things are actually okay.

"Could we get you to sign something?" one of the women asks.

"Sure, do you have a pen?" he replies. He's not eager, but he also doesn't seem put off by it either, which surprises me.

Quinn and Oliver approach, carrying popcorn and drinks to where I'm resting on the red gingham picnic blanket we bought in town.

"That seems fun," Oliver says.

"It happens all the time." I shrug, as if Garrett and I have done this before.

"The moment you post with him online you're going to break so many hearts," Quinn says as she sits next to me, working to not spill the butter drenched popcorn.

"Thanks, I've always dreamed of crushing thousands of people with my happiness," I say.

Quinn shakes her head. "Don't sell yourself short, definitely hundreds of thousands."

"Sorry about that," Garrett says as he walks back to us. When he sits down, he brushes against me, his hand landing on my knee and resting there.

"Completely unrelated question, do you have any spare bath water," I ask.

"Let me think," Garrett says. "No. I don't really bottle that up for special occasions."

"A shame. Ev, you could make a killing. I mean, nothing's stopping you from selling off the odd pair of underwear," Quinn suggests.

"Please, don't give me a reason to hide my belongings," Garrett bemoans. My attention fixes on his thumb trailing up and down, burning through the fabric of my pants.

"You're killing her entrepreneurial spirit. Don't let this man limit you, Ev," Quinn says.

Applause roars, rising in a wave originating from the stage as the opening act walks on. A warm weight wraps around me. I stiffen at the unexpected embrace before settling in Garrett's arms.

His chin rests on my shoulder so when he speaks his words are for me alone. "You okay?"

"Why wouldn't I be?" I reply in a hushed voice.

"It was a long day."

I consider lying. Saying that I'm perfectly fine and pretending I have yet to have a real full conversation with Quinn. "Yeah, it was."

"I'm here."

"I know." I wrap my arms over his, hugging him to me the best I can. "Thank you."

The headliner is a bluegrass trio whose music has a few of the couples around us on the lawn getting up to dance. I can't help but smile at the energy blooming all around us even as the cold night nips at our noses and paints our cheeks pink.

Quinn and Oliver leave before the set is over since Oliver has a meeting in the morning with the rest of his team. I can't help but think it also has to do with how things are between us, that they need distance.

Garrett and I stay, wrapped up together until the final note. For warmth, obviously. On the way back, he blasts the heat in the car and suggests we stop for food. I readily agree, happy that tonight there are no timers or quick getaways.

"I wonder if this was an old Burger King and they were too lazy to come up with something new," I say as we pull into the lot. "Or the owner has a one-sided feud with the chain."

The menu is so big that I can make out parts of it from the edge of the asphalt. Vintage illustrations of ice cream and burgers dance along a white background. There are three other cars besides ours in the lot. A truck has its tailgate down and a few teens are clustered into the back with their grease-stained paper bags scattered around them. The other two are empty and must belong to employees.

King's seems like a place that's seen countless memories. It's somewhere I can imagine parents bringing their kids to so they can share the taste of the food, passing down the experience like an heirloom.

"What if he blames chain restaurants for the downfall of his marriage? Imagine him toiling away at home, grilling burgers flavored with his family's secret seasoning?" Garrett catches the end of my hypothetical and runs with it. A smile melts onto my face.

I continue helping the story take shape. "And the wife and son come back with burgers and won't eat his. But this isn't the first time. Each time it happens he pushes himself to make a better burger and, in the end, his family never even tries them. They don't know what they're missing out on."

"You should write a song about that," he says, maneuvering into the parking space furthest from the teens.

"The rise and fall of a New England burger entrepreneur?" I ask.

"If you write it, I'd listen."

"You might be the only one," I say. "But I'll put it on the list of ideas to workshop."

"Who wouldn't want to hear about the epic highs and lows of owning a drive-in burger joint?" His voice drips with astonishment at the idea as he turns off the engine.

"The general population, but why would I cater to them?" I say, trying not to remember that I have to do exactly that. I shove the thought away.

"I'd listen either way." He turns and his eyes hold mine. All of his edges and shadows are exaggerated with the buzzing light coming from the drive-in. He's a study in angles. If we weren't us, I'd run my hand over those edges to see if they're as sharp as they look.

The moment shifts as he cocks his head toward the building. "What do you want?"

I give him my order, and he goes to the counter where a teen in a paper hat helps him. I'm doing my best not to think of what will happen after this weekend.

I've always tended to hold one crucial part of myself back from people. More often than not, it's music. For some reason it feels like if someone doesn't have all of me then if they don't really like me then I can blame it on the fact they never had the chance to know all of me.

Garrett has learned so much more about me than most people ever have. The versions of us here aren't the same as who we are in the city. He's not someone who I can pull through blueberry farms and museums, and I'm not someone who can pretend I don't want more of that. We've been those people before, but the shape of who we are now isn't something I want to let go of. It fits so well in my hands, into the cracks in my heart.

Garrett walks back to the car with greasy paper bags that make my mouth water. He hands them over to me as he climbs into the car. When I look inside my brows pull together.

"Why didn't you get the burger? Mr. King lost his family so you could try it," I tease.

"I'll just have to have a bite of yours," he says as he reaches for his bag.

"That's awfully presumptuous of you. I respect this man's hard work, and I'll savor every bite."

"Chicken tenders are easier to eat if I want some while driving and they won't get soggy if I wait too long to eat them," he explains.

"Let's stay here and eat," I say, but then add, "Unless you have somewhere you need to be."

"No. I just need to be here."

The night air fills with the crinkle of wrappers and foil being stripped from food. I trade some of my burger for a chicken tender. When our food is gone, he goes back for chocolate shakes. The night continues to stretch, and my heart seems to patter out a rhythm.

More. More. More.

After the first sip of my shake, I hesitate for a moment. The words burst out of me at a sprint. I can't stop what comes next. "We're friends, right?"

"Is that a trick question?" His brows pinch in their usual way.

"I promise I wouldn't give you the verbal version of a check yes or no for a trick question," I joke through the embarrassment heating my cheeks.

"Yes, we're friends, Eve," he says. His face softens. "I thought it was obvious."

"Maybe it should be." I look down to where my hands are wrapped around the plastic cup. "I guess as adults we're just expected to know when we transition from people who spend time together to friends without asking. I'm just out of practice with this whole friend thing. It just felt pointless to meet new people who I couldn't really open up to when I moved to New York."

And now with Oliver and Quinn, I have no idea what I'm doing either. Who I'm supposed to be with them, to them, now that they have each other. Do they even need me anymore?

"It's hard picturing you alone like that." It's not the first time he's said something like it. In some ways, I'm happy he sees me in the way I present myself to everyone else.

"I never thought I'd end up that way," I admit. I always thought I'd have Quinn and Oliver; I guess I still do. I just don't know how to have them in my life without the potential of hurting them. I've already done it once. "And it's not like you noticed. You were too busy ignoring me."

"You're impossible to ignore, even if I wanted to."

"Good to know I'm starting to win you over." I tap my melty shake against his.

"It's not like I ever did—want to ignore you, I mean." The heat in his words causes me to take a long sip, but that does nothing to dampen the intensity.

"I guess you can keep me as your emergency contact then," I tell him, trying to sidestep how that makes me feel. "But seriously, getting to know you here...I don't know, it's like I'm meeting you for the first time, even though I've known you almost all my life."

"You weren't missing out on much." And I can tell he believes it.

"I think you're wrong about that." I reach out my hand. "I'm Evelyn, by the way."

He plays along, the way the Hartsfall version of him has grown to do. "Garrett." His hand wraps over mine.

"Thanks for letting me know you."

26

Evelyn

I look at the text again.

Garrett

Work thing. Can't make it. Is that ok?

Evelyn

Yeah, that's ok.

"Is something wrong?" Quinn asks as she stretches her calves using the trailhead marker for balance. The plan was for all of us to meet here at eight but I got the text just as I was leaving.

"No. Why?" I ask as I shove my phone into my shorts.

"Because you've checked your phone about ten times in the last five minutes," she says.

Closer to twenty, but who's counting?

"It's nothing, just checking to see what's up with Garrett," I tell her.

Oliver finishes taking a drink from his water bottle then looks our way. "Is everything okay?"

"I think so." I really hope so. Work isn't a casual thing for him and it must be serious if they asked for him.

"You can go," Quinn says.

"Would you guys be okay with that, going on the trail all by yourselves?"

"You know these things don't require adult supervision. Even if they did, we are adults so I think we'll be just fine." A wry smile pulls on Quinn's lips.

"If you're sure," I hedge.

"You're not going to let us down if you leave," Oliver adds. "We have another week and a half here." It's what I need to hear and the moment his eyes meet mine, I know that's exactly why he said it.

"We'll do something tomorrow. Anything you guys want," I say, my eyes already on the short path to the parking lot.

Quinn considers for a moment. "Dinner at the house you and Garrett are staying at."

"I'll take care of everything!" I promise as I start to dart off.

When I reach my SUV I pat my pockets looking for my keys. When I don't feel them I check again as if they somehow got lost in the thin fabric of my exercise shorts. I keep my eyes on the ground as I make my way back to the trailhead, searching for any hint of metal or my black fob on on the packed earth.

Snippets of hushed voices cause me to slow down. I only catch parts of the sentences and they sound agitated.

"Do you think it's necessary?" It takes me a moment to realize it's Quinn because of her agitated tone.

"But what if?"

"I don't see how? I'm still not sure—"

"We should. It's for the best—"

I'm torn between hanging back for a few moments to let them finish whatever has them sounding upset or going for the keys.

When I reach the top of the rise, I see my keys at the edge of the trail, half-covered in a pile of leaves where Quinn and I were stretching. When I look up, I freeze.

Kissing. They're kissing. Oliver's hand cups the back of Quinn's head, her dark hair flaring between the gaps in his fingers. It's not a long kiss. I breathe and it's over.

They're dating. I know they're dating, doing far more than this in private. But I guess seeing is believing, pushing unconscious understanding into stark reality.

The jealousy that settles on my tongue has a confusing flavor to it. I want to spit it out.

It's not because Quinn is with Oliver. No, it's the type that comes when you're watching a rom-com and think *I want to belong with someone like that. I want to belong so bad it hurts.* They found it without me. Together.

There's another fraction of a second where they look at each other. Oliver's blue eyes shine for Quinn in the way that everyone wants to be looked at. He sees her, only her.

But Quinn sees me, all but jumping away from Oliver's hold as she does. She stumbles over the rock she was using earlier to prop up her leg and Oliver reaches out to grab her. His arm snakes around her waist pull her back to him. The moment they're both upright, they're putting distance between them again.

I hold up my keys and then point at where I picked them up from the ground. "I lost these." My voice comes out robotically before I turn and head back to the cars.

"Ev, we—" Oliver starts to say.

"No. Stay," Quinn says, effectively cutting him off before there's a light thud of footfalls behind me. The steps slow as she closes the distance. "I'm sorry. You didn't need to see that."

"I'm not upset," I say.

"Yeah, right."

"I'm not upset that you guys were kissing," I clarify.

"Then why won't you look at me!" she demands, causing me to stop in my tracks. Quinn kicks up dust around her as she works to not run into me with her forward momentum.

"Because you practically shoved Oliver away to not touch in front of me," I say. "I don't want it to be weird. If you guys want to touch, touch. I don't want to be the reason you can't."

"Stop it!" she shouts.

"Stop what?" My voice rises to match hers and my muscles tighten in my shoulders.

"Stop it," she says softer this time, but only slightly. "You're doing that thing I hate where you act like nothing can touch you if you decide that it should be okay. You've been doing it all week. Barely talking to me at the wine bar then avoiding conversations yesterday."

"It *is* okay. Haven't I said that already?" *Haven't I said that enough? Can't we just move on? Please, can we move on?*

"Maybe things aren't supposed to be okay. Maybe we should talk through things because we're friends and it's been a while since we've seen each other, and I don't want to act like that doesn't matter?"

"I don't want to fight. We don't fight." We all have our reasons for it. When we all met each other, we were thick in the magic that's reserved for new beginnings.

In those days, we always ended up in Oliver's room because his roommate had upperclassman friends who lived off campus and Quinn and my roommates liked to use our rooms for studying. I had a fake ID and bought us a box of wine, a shitty red blend that we still buy on principle and not for the taste even though we can afford much better.

The first time it happened was during the third week of classes. Nothing mattered besides finding a place to belong for the next four years. Secrets and hidden thoughts bled into casual conversation, until we could never be strangers ever again.

It was the time that Oliver told us about his sisters and how they were his favorite people in the world. How he delayed college by a year because of his dad's most recent divorce.

Quinn told us about her parents. How they couldn't stand each other and were only still together because of their staunch religious beliefs. That she lies to them about going to bible study and church every Sunday. We promised to be her unconditional alibis if she ever needed us.

For me, it was the first time I talked about my brother. It was the first time I told anyone about my deep need for things to be okay. We all cried and let it be okay to cry.

My eyes catch on a red sedan pulling into the parking space.

"Then why are you running from us? If everything is fine, why did you leave?" she asks, and I don't think we're talking about their kiss anymore.

"I didn't think it was right to stay."

"You can tell me if there's another reason. You can tell me anything," she says, opening an opportunity with her words. An invitation I nearly take.

"Not right now," I say. It's not the right time. "And also, I'm not all that into voyeurism, so I thought walking away was an okay response."

"Can you at least admit this is a little awkward?" Her plea is purposefully exaggerated. "Can you at least do that because I feel like I'm going crazy. Oliver is doing the same exact thing because that's what both of you always do."

"Fine." A laugh soars out of me. "It's definitely awkward. But I really do just want you two to be comfortable and happy and know that I'm okay with it. That's always going to be true."

"You're not going to pay off townspeople to spit in our food or anything?"

"Of course not," I deadpan. "If I was going to be petty, I'd be far more original than that. Spitting in food has no shock factor."

"If the hot water is suddenly shut off at the bed and breakfast?" she presses.

"Then you have a reason to be suspicious," I confirm. "Now, go enjoy the hike and I'll see you two tomorrow for dinner."

"Will your fancy boyfriend be offended at the sight of boxed wine? Because if he will be you have to get rid of him," she says seriously, and I know she's not joking. Few things are sacred to Quinn, boxed wine is near the top of the list.

"He'll survive," I say.

"Good."

When I reach Alina's house, I hesitate for a moment deciding if I actually should go to check on Garrett. It's not like he gave me any indication that anything is wrong. Still, if this means he's headed back to the city earlier than he planned, at least this way we can talk about it as soon as possible. That doesn't exactly appeal to me, but I'd rather know now than let it loom over me.

I park in the driveway behind his truck so I don't block Alina in if she needs to leave. There's something about coming here casually. There's so much purpose to how Garrett and I meet up. We have our calendar invites that set clear boundaries, but over the last two days we've started to test them.

I'm almost tempted to send an invite to announce my presence, a gesture that would feel like a shield for the concern that's building in my chest like a rapidly inflating balloon. At the door I take the lion's head knocker and release it to percussively hit the metal plate behind it.

When the door opens a few minutes later, Alina is on the other side. She's dressed in an orange kaftan and slippers. Her face is painted with a full face of makeup and reading glasses are perched at the end of her nose.

"Hello, dear girl."

"Alina, it's good to see you," I say, a bit disappointed she's the one to greet me.

"No need to flatter me. I know you're not here for me," she says curtly, and my cheeks heat.

"Is he still busy?"

"He's finished with work." She hesitates before adding, "but he'll be upstairs for a while."

"I can come back later." I'm already shifting my weight to leave. This was a bad idea to show up unannounced. I should have at least texted to ask if it was okay to come over. I guess I just didn't want him to say no.

"It should be another few hours before he gets up," she explains, stepping back into the house to welcome me in.

"Up?" *What is she talking about?*

"He's sleeping, managing a migraine. If he caught it in time it should only last until the afternoon," she says plainly, like this is common. "But you're here so you might as well keep me company. I know I'm entertaining enough for it not to be a chore. People don't pay me like they used to, but I still shine."

"You know what? I would love to stay a while."

We head inside and I follow her to the kitchen as she starts an electric kettle. The backsplash is hand painted tile in shades of soothing blue. The oven is an old gas one. There's a hominess to this place that I want to wrap up and reconstruct for myself. I have a moment picturing a younger Garrett here. I know this wasn't his home, but I get the impression that he spent enough time here to at least consider it a secondary landing place during his childhood.

The China selection today is gold plated with clusters of little yellow flowers.

"Are the migraines new? I mean, when I visited the band on tour he never seemed to have them." Or at least any that were bad enough to call attention to. Granted, I was usually spending time with Avery or Drew, but still I think I would have noticed.

"You knew him when he was doing music, yes?"

"Yeah, for the most part." And even then I really only knew him in theory, as proven over and over again since I arrived here.

"He was happiest then. There were less things to be stressed about. I taught him to play and he had *it*," she says. Glowing pride is etched in every corner of her face. "You know what I mean, you have *it* too. Music likes you and you like it back. There are people who think it's just playing the notes. Those are people who will never be good enough to be anyone."

"And you had it too."

"Of course I did. I had it and God, did I make sure everyone knew it," she says, adding a subtle shimmy to her shoulders. "Our boy, oh, he seems like a show off, but he's just that good. He might not be mine by blood, but I was always worried he'd pick up my bad habits. I was selfish when I taught him."

"It doesn't sound like you were." From everything I've gathered, Alina's home has always been a haven for him.

Alina tuts. "Good things can come from misguided intentions. You see, my children, they're dull and greedy. I wrote them out of my will, but they don't know that so they're waiting around for me to die so they can inherit it all," she says then presses a finger to her lips and winks. "I wasn't a good mother. I traveled and I hired nannies to do all the work I didn't want to do. When I saw that boy continue to go home to an empty house when his own mother was off to who knows where, I took it as a second chance."

"You found someone who loves music the same way you do," I say. "That's special what you gave him."

"Yes, but he got it in his head that he needed to do more. We wanted to give him more, this town. He stopped the music and went to law school," she tells me, as I recall the version of the story Garrett's told me. "I think that's when it started. He looks terrible when he comes back. That's why I make sure he does. That job of his is no good. He doesn't need it no matter what he thinks it proves to us. He hates it but he'll never leave."

Even when he told me about this from his perspective of duty and a need for a stable career it sounded clinical. After

Friday night, it's hard to imagine him choosing a life like this over one he obviously loved.

I feel like a hypocrite at the thought. Even if I struggle to picture it, right now I'm caught in that exact web. But I liked my job in PR; what he's doing, it sounds miserable. And for what? Guilt? Obligation?

"That's a shame," I say, even though it hardly encompasses the reality of it.

"It is."

27

Garrett

I listen to Alina play as I tip back into consciousness. The pulsing pain that was thrumming through the right side of my head before I turned off the lights has dissipated. My eyes adjust slowly to the dark room. Light filters in through the crack in the curtains, reminding me it's still daytime. I might still be able to meet up with Evelyn and the others at the tail end of their hike. I still feel like shit for canceling. The whole point of this was for me to help her.

Holt had called asking for help with a client I've been working with since I started at the firm—a paranoid New York Times Best Selling thriller author. Their ability to see conspiracy theories in everything likely has helped them creatively, but it also means they're consistently in need of swift attention. Usually, we work directly with their agent, but there was a mix up and the author wouldn't have the video meeting without me.

Getting back online meant that I got access to my email. I shouldn't have looked. I did anyway. Each of the thousands of unread messages hit like a brick crumbling from the ceiling and right onto my shoulders. That's when the migraine aura started to form in my vision. Little blurs dotted the world, and I knew I had to stop and go to my stash of pain medication.

I usually can manage the stress that leads to the tension building to this point by staying on top of things. But the reality of being away from the office for nearly four weeks came down all at once.

The song stops downstairs then another one starts. But it's not one that Alina would know because it's one I helped write on Friday. This thought reminds me of what I should already know, but my mind is still a bit foggy. Alina hasn't played for at least four years. She's not the one playing. But as I listen, the smooth articulation of a legato stringing the notes together tells me exactly who is at the piano. The way she plays is like a fingerprint with how distinct it is to me.

I grab my glasses from where they're resting on the nightstand and head to the stairs. I'm careful to skip the creaky step halfway down. Alina and Eve are both so caught in the song that neither looks in my direction when I tread into the room and lean against the wall.

She's hypnotic. Every inch of her body is dedicated in worship to the act of bringing out the potential of the piano and the song, *our song*. It's a pocket universe where sound breathes through her. I know how it feels. God. I know how good it feels.

The room seems to vibrate even when she stops. Her fingers hover over the keys for a moment before they land in her lap. She's dressed for the hike. Athletic shorts and a tight fitting long sleeve shirt.

Alina claps, breaking the silence. I join in and both of them turn in my direction.

"I don't remember you buying tickets to this show," Evelyn says, her eyes scanning over me, assessing.

"I thought you were heading to the falls or I would have made sure to stop at will call," I say.

"Something more important brought me back," she says. Her words hit me full force. People leaving? I'm numb to that. But her coming here? She makes it so hard not to want her.

"I didn't know that living room concerts were a high priority for you," I quip.

"There's nothing more intimate than live music in your own home," Alina says, adding to the flow of conversation. "But I have to cut this short." Alina rises to her feet slowly then brushes her hands down the skirt of her kaftan.

I raise a brow. "Where are you going?" As far as I know she didn't have anything planned for the afternoon.

"Out," she puts simply as she comes closer to where I'm standing to get to the door. She pauses as she reaches me then lowers her voice. "Anywhere else."

"Subtle," I mutter.

"I don't need to be. I'm too old to waste time being clever."

"News to me."

Alina moves past me and further into the entryway and there's a jingling of keys followed by the sound of the door as she leaves.

"So, what would you be up to if I weren't here?" Evelyn asks still watching me from the piano

"Trying to snoop?"

"Or just interested in what you're like when no one else is looking." A tempting edge cuts into her voice. As more time passes it's getting harder and harder to write off the invitation in her flirtations. But there's one thing I don't have to write off. She's shown up here without going through all the hoops that we tend to jump through to spend time together.

"What if it's boring?"

"I know for a fact Alina wouldn't keep you around if you were boring in your free time. And I don't think there's genuinely a single person who is boring." Her words cause the corner of my mouth to tug upward. I guess Alina talked to her about her children then. "There are just people who don't know how to ask others the right questions."

"But you have all the right questions," I state.

"I try to. I think it makes up for having none of the right answers." Doubt flickers on her face in a way that lets me know she's gone straight into that place that makes her intensely aware of everyone around her.

"I think you know more than you allow yourself to believe. You're pretty damn smart," I remind her.

"Playing nice?"

"Telling the truth."

"So, what are we going to do?"

"Chess."

"You're saying that if it were just you here, that's what you'd be doing?" Her brows pull together in confusion.

"That or playing music, but I don't think that fits the criteria you're looking for."

"I think I'm more caught up on the part where you play chess alone. You know, the game that traditionally takes two people, a board, and pieces that are supposed to emulate some sort of feudal system court dynamics?" she teases.

"It's what I'm usually doing on my phone. Not answering emails, just so you know. I do it when I'm stressed," I explain, setting the record straight.

"You were stressed waiting for me?"

"You make me nervous, Evelyn." Always. For the last few weeks I've logged more hours than I have in years.

"Do I still? Am I right now?"

"Yes."

"I guess that means we should play some chess then," she says.

"Okay, to recap, so this one goes on a diagonal?" Evelyn asks, pointing to the bishop. "Knight is two in one direction, then one in the other. Why the hell do people say it moves in an L? It's so ambiguous?"

"People like patterns," I explain. "They like seeing how things fit together and make sense."

"Is that how you feel about work? That there are things that fit together?" she asks, and with how quickly she jumps to the question, I have the feeling Alina said something about my time upstairs resting.

"Sometimes, sure. I think that's why I chose it over other things. It's not always black and white but you have problems and you have solutions. It makes sense," I explain. The structure of it, the endless rules and regulations to reference were part of what attracted me to working with contracts and negotiations over specializing in anything that could put me in a courtroom."

"Do you like it?"

"Why do you care?"

"C'mon, Larson, I'm allowed to care about you," she says. "We're friends, remember."

I'm really starting to hate that word even though it means we get to have moments like this. Alone, together.

"Then, no, not particularly," I admit.

She hesitates before saying, "You could go back to music."

"I'm not sure that's a good idea." I try to brush it off.

I've thought about it, sure, but what if it's not the same? What if I go back and it lets me down? Then what? I'm left with two realities I don't want, drowning in dissatisfaction. It's the hope that kills you, and I rather like surviving.

"Why not. You're amazing at it. Fuck. You were the best," she says, and I almost ask her to repeat herself so I can hear her say it all over again.

"Don't let your brother hear that."

She scoffs, waving a hand and nearly swiping away pieces from the board. "He's an adult and he can handle the truth."

"Wes is the one who went solo. He's probably better," I say, as if it's a good excuse.

"Bullshit."

"It's not stable."

Evelyn crosses her arms over her chest, unimpressed. "You don't need the money. I bet you could retire right now and buy a mansion or two while you're at it."

"That's not the type of stability I'm worried about. With music, one day you're in, the next you're not. It's not predictable. With the firm I know my trajectory. I know how to get clients and negotiate. I know how to be valuable to them." I know how to be integral enough that I'm needed. I have a spot there that I earned, that can't be questioned. Earlier today, even with the mountain of stress that piled on to me when I saw the work piling up, I also had a sense of reassurance that I was needed there. "I owe Alina, Pat, and the rest of the people here who sent me to Tennessee. I had merit and need based scholarships to St. George's, but they covered the rest, as well as the plane tickets over the winter holidays. They invested in my education and I'm making sure they get a return on that investment."

"I doubt they think you owe them. They care about you and just want you to be happy," she says.

And maybe she's right. But if she is, that doesn't matter. I need to see this through, I need all the late nights to be worth something. If they aren't, then what have I been working toward?

"I thought you stayed to play chess." My voice comes out gruff.

"We can play." She nods, hesitantly accepting the end of the conversation.

We get through two games before we take a break. I grab us some water. Evelyn's approach to chess is similar to how she approaches life, aggressive but aware. She's constantly on the offensive but manages to maintain a solid defense. She doesn't win, but she puts in a solid effort without ever asking me to give her any suggestions for her next move.

"I don't want to cancel on you again, but on Wednesday the wine is supposed to be ready for pick up and Thursday afternoon is the rehearsal for the festival," I say. I didn't tell her sooner because I didn't want to cancel, but I've never missed a rehearsal.

"Is there room for another set of hands?" she offers.

"You want to help?" I ask, but honestly, what else did I expect from her?

"I would, but if it's just a town thing I can't get into without a special membership card, I'll figure something out."

I shrug trying not to reveal how much I would really like her there. "If you want to, sure."

"Do you want me to? We've been with each other pretty much non-stop, so you can tell me you need space."

I don't want space when it comes to her. I know that, but that's not something I can casually slip into conversation without imploding things. "If I need space from you, I'll just decline one of your calendar invites."

"So that's why you like them so much. Because you can reject me through a workflow management system." Humor lightens her voice, but the trace of relief isn't lost on me.

"My methods have their benefits." Really, it's like I have this vampiric need to be invited to places in addition to my love of knowing what's going to come next in my days.

"And if I come to the event, people won't get mad?"

"I think Alina is half in love with you from making sure I get out of the house. And everyone else likes you more than they like me."

"No, they don't," she says as she averts her gaze.

"Based on the fact that there's a few thousand on us ending up together, I think their feelings are pretty clear."

I pull out my phone and show it to her.

Fletcher

50 on the under

Winnie

50 it doesn't happen

Annie

50 on the over

"Over and under?" she asks.

"Ten days."

"They sure do think you act fast."

"Between the two of us, I'm not the professional flirt."

"Fair enough." She heaves an exaggerated sigh. "And this prep is what exactly? Do I need to bring my pink hard hat?"

"No hard hat needed."

"I do appreciate that you've accepted the possibility that I have one," she says.

"Underestimating your ability to create a shock factor is just asking for trouble. But the festival prep is essentially a rehearsal in the high school gym. Vendors test out recipes and activities." I start to explain one of Hartsfall's most beloved traditions. "I'll be rehearsing with Alina. Because most people are working the main festival, it's a way for them to enjoy everything. If Oliver and Quinn want to join, they can."

"Speaking of them, I kind of invited them over for dinner tomorrow to make up for today," she says as she nervously presses her finger into the top of her king and rocks it back and forth.

"You invited them to the house we've supposedly been staying in together for the last few weeks?" I ask to confirm we're on the same page.

"Shit." The realization hits her and I can see her scrambling for a solution.

"I'll come over tomorrow with some of my stuff and we can make sure the story checks out." It shouldn't be too hard, especially since we're just across the street from each other.

"Have I mentioned recently how I think you'd make an excellent spy?" She gives me a once over. Her eyes trailing from my face to the rumpled button down then all the way to the reset chessboard in front of us. "I mean, this is really selling it for me."

"By some miracle, you've managed to restrain yourself for nearly a week."

"Truly an act of God," she agrees.

"That or everything has gone to shit."

"Or that." A smile brightens her face.

"Want to keep playing?"

"You teaching me a hobby that will give me a sense of intellectual superiority? Yes, please, keep talking dirty to me." Her voice turns low and sultry. The way she messes with my head when I know she's only joking is fucking criminal.

"Incorrigible."

"Always."

28

Evelyn

"You cooked?" Quinn embraces me with her free arm inside the entryway. She's started using her fall perfume, transitioning from florals to warm vanilla. I was starting to think I wouldn't be able to experience it this year.

"I did. But just know if you go to the pub and it tastes the same, they stole my recipes. Not the other way around," I say. I am a nightmare in the kitchen. The first time I'd "cooked" to try and impress Quinn and Oliver, I'd plated Olive Garden alfredo and soup to pass it off as my own. It worked up until Quinn found the bag in the trash.

"I love it when you host. I always know I'm going to get restaurant quality." Oliver throws me a conspiratorial wink. A drizzle has started outside and a cool breeze floats in before he shuts the door.

"Only the best for my esteemed guests. I see that you've brought the finest vintage to pair with our meal." I cock my head toward the hand Quinn's using to clutch the box of red blend.

"I couldn't break tradition," she says. "You really think your man will be able to stomach it?"

"He doesn't drink much so he'll probably take one sip and then dump it out in the sink at some point when no one is looking," I say, already imagining how he'll go about it.

"Not everyone can have our refined palates," Quinn says disapprovingly.

I usher Quinn and Oliver the rest of the way into the house. When we reach the dining table, Garrett is placing a tray of mini sliders next to the bowl of mashed potatoes.

He and I spent the last few hours prepping. He brought over a suitcase with clothes and toiletries to make it look like he's been living here with me. Oliver isn't exactly the snooping type, but I've been right alongside Quinn at house parties when trips to the bathroom turned into self-guided tours.

Tonight is the first time I've used the table since I arrived—well, at least for its intended purpose. I had to clean off stray papers and to-go cups before we could put down the emerald table runner we found in the linen cabinet.

There's always been something special about sit-down dinners for the three of us, even at restaurants. It doesn't matter that I didn't make the food or that we used to eat off the cheap plastic plates that every college student bought for their first apartment.

It was our way of making time for each other.

Quinn adds the box of wine to the table and Garrett raises his eyebrows but plays along and fills his glass. I don't think he takes a single sip. When Oliver's fork clatters to the ground Garrett offers to get a new one and takes his glass with him. I share a look with Quinn when he returns with an empty glass.

"Wow, you really downed that," I say. My knee nudges against his under the table. When I start to pull it away his hand lands on my thigh, keeping it in place. The touch is warm and steady like he's done it a hundred times before.

"I couldn't help myself. It was too good to just sip," Garrett says.

"I'll make sure to tell Pat to get some at The Gas Station," I threaten.

His lips twitch in an entertaining mix of a smile and a grimace. "Maybe we should just keep it for special occasions."

"Tell me, what notes did you pick up on?" I press my leg further against his. In response his thumb glides up my inner thigh. Heat flashes through me, landing low.

"Earthy. Definitely earthy." The gravel in his voice skates against my skin.

"You know, not everyone picks up the dirt aftertaste!" Quinn chimes in. Her cheeks are slightly flushed from her second glass.

"I didn't say that. I will say the tannins are impressive." Garrett picks up my half full glass and gives it a swirl. "Decent legs." On the word legs he squeezes my thigh, prompting me to reach for my water to cool off.

"You can say it's bad. We know it's bad," Oliver volunteers, as an olive branch.

"Because you hate yourselves?" Garrett asks.

"Sometimes," Quinn admits as she reaches for more fries. "But there's this liquid nostalgia to it that is impossible to replicate. What seasoning is on these? There's something spicy about them that I can't place."

"Ahh, that's the essence of ghost pepper, I think."

"You really have a way with ingredients." Quinn nods approvingly then takes another bite.

We all settle into the night slowly spiraling back to who we are, a mattress that remembers the shape of the bodies that have worn their impressions into it. Quinn and Oliver spare no detail telling us about the birds they spotted on the hike yesterday and the loose gravel that almost sent Oliver to the hospital with a sprained ankle. The trays empty as we refill our plates. Eventually, we're left picking at scraps, savoring everything left at the table.

Oliver's face brightens when he notes the state of the food and then calls out, "Capitals!"

"Wait," I say and put up a hand to stop the progress. "Let me explain it to Garrett first."

Quinn raises a brow. "Do you think he'll have a fighting chance?"

"They don't let him participate in local trivia, so I think so," I say.

"What am I missing?" Garrett looks more amused than confused.

"It's what we do to determine who does the dishes after a meal," I say. "We pull up this website and whoever gets the least amount of capitals of countries right in under a minute has to do them."

"Can't we all just help out?" Garrett offers a logical, albeit boring solution.

"When Quinn and I lived together we had this tiny kitchen and only one person could actually fit in it," I explain.

"It didn't even have a full-sized fridge," Quinn adds.

"And practically no cabinet space," Oliver jumps in. "Remember that time you stored those plastic cutting boards in the oven and we forgot to take them out."

Quinn's face scrunches her nose. "Even thinking about it makes me get this phantom smell. God, burning plastic was the worst. And then we had to use those shitty lighters to melt the plastic off because we were all too broke to get new oven racks."

"Like we could find ones that worked with that ancient oven," I say. That apartment was one of my favorite places. It was cramped and we were always finding mold, but it was ours.

"So, are you in?" I ask Garrett.

"If you'll let me," he says.

I text Garrett the link to the website. It's a bit jarring to take a look at our messages; there have only been a few. Most of our exchanges have been through calendar invites.

The website has a timer built in so we don't have to synchronize our start times. There's a few seconds between each of us finishing. As usual, Quinn wins with forty. It's less that she likes being the best at things and more that she hates failing. Oliver gets thirty-five and I get thirty-three. Surprisingly, Garrett gets twenty-four. Accepting his fate, he grabs a stack of dishes and heads through the door to the kitchen. I wait a beat before collecting an armful of trays and serving utensils.

The dishes clatter as they jostle in my arms causing Garrett to look up from where he's turning on the sink. "What are you doing in here?"

"Helping. There's room for the two of us and they're my friends. You don't need to do this alone," I tell him as I unload my armful onto the counter.

"I lost on purpose so you could spend time with them," he says in that weighted way that forces me off balance. "You guys looked like you were having a good time."

"Are you just saying that so I think you know more capitals?" I tease, instead of acknowledging the gesture. An aftershock of heat climbs to my cheeks as I also remember his hand on my leg. Then there was the kiss from three days ago, the way he asked how I wanted him to kiss me, tender then ravenous.

"I could start listing them if you need proof," he offers.

"Feeling confident?"

"Minsk," he says, then turns off the water.

"Easy."

"Brussels." He takes a step closer and my heart thunders.

"Basic," I breathe.

"Helsinki."

"Obvious." I lean back against the counter and his body eats up the remaining space between us. His arms land on either side of my hips, caging me in. Bergamot and lavender wash over me.

"Port au Prince."

"Passable," I say. His eyes are on my lips. He's not even hiding it. I want to reach up and pull him in. I want him to close the distance. "What else do you have for me?"

"I'm coming in to get water!" Quinn shouts a second before she strides in. Garrett doesn't move an inch. It takes me a moment to remember that it's good for Quinn to catch us like this, acting like a couple who'd casually occupy each other's space.

"Thanks for the announcement," I say, trying and failing to keep my voice steady.

"I just ate, no point in ruining a good meal by walking in on something pornographic. It looks like I got in just in time. Cups?" Quinn asks, and I point to the cabinet to my left. She navigates around us, selecting a commemorative Love Letter Festival cup from 2016 and then going to the fridge to get the Britta.

"Can you blame me? She's the perfect dessert," Garrett says as he runs the cold back of his hand against my flaming cheek.

I gasp into his mouth as his lips seal against mine. My chin tilts upward guided by his thumb and forefinger. My eyes flutter closed. The kiss is over a moment later, but I still feel it everywhere. Not just this kiss but a collection of all the moments he's touched me. Calluses skating across my skin. Fingers in my hair. The seer of his fingers through fabric.

"I'm going to go finish the boxed wine in hopes I forget I heard that," Quinn says to herself. "Carry on, but please keep any moaning to a minimum."

"Go make out with Oliver on the couch," I say, and it feels more natural than I would have thought.

Quinn halts in the doorway putting a hand on the door jamb and considers. "Tempting. I'm more of a rendezvous in a bathroom gal."

Even as Quinn leaves, Garrett doesn't pull away.

"You didn't have to kiss me," I tell him.

"As long as they're here, you're mine," he says, guiding my chin up so I meet his heavy lidded gaze. "That's the deal right?"

His. I like that too much.

"Yeah," I breathe out. "I just don't want you to do anything you're uncomfortable with."

"Don't worry, I'm very comfortable with kissing you," he says. His body holds in place one second longer before moving to the sink and turning the water back on. "It seems like things are better between the three of you."

"Yeah, we're getting our footing again. We've never been so out of sync before. Not even when Oliver and I broke it off," I admit, thankful for the subject change.

"Do you think there's a reason for it?" he asks as he plunges his hands into the mountain of suds growing in the sink. "You dry, I wash?"

I move to his other side and grab a towel. "Sure. I think there's a part of me that was hoping they'd just forget me? I have always had this tendency to build in these excuses for people to leave or to push me away. Like, if I can know the reason, then at least I can understand it. But then they showed up and we're in different places."

It's a hard truth I've been grappling with. If I can control why I'm alone, if I can make it my fault, then at least there's a justification. It's better than being left with an explanation of *just because* that sends me spiraling. But also it's hard to trust myself to not do what I did to Oliver with someone else.

"That's fair."

"I think it's part of what terrifies me with Lyla. If I go public, there will be plenty of people who hate me for no reason. I know that's normal, but I don't know if I'm strong enough. I mean, I obsess over podcast reviews and they don't even know anything personal about me," I say.

"From what I can tell, you're not obsessing over them anymore." His focus is directed to scrubbing. "But things would change. People start caring about you when they used to act like you were never there. I hadn't seen my mom for almost four years at the time we started touring."

"You were what, seventeen? Eighteen?"

"Eighteen."

"I'm sorry," I say.

His eyes jump to me as he hands me a plate and his expression shadows. "Don't do that."

"What? Acknowledge how much that fucking sucks? Because it does." I hate thinking about how he went through all of that. How, even though I thought I knew him, I didn't at all. How maybe if I paid more attention I could have done... I don't know. Something?

"I'm just saying you're right to expect a shift and there are things that are shitty. I have my career. I was able to make it work," he says, voice turning hollow. Sometimes when he talks it's like he's telling me a story about someone else, like it wasn't him it happened to. Maybe that's his way of coping with it, being someone else.

"A career you seem to hate." I feel compelled to remind him.

"One that I'm good at. One where I'm valued and I earned everything I have," he says, but I'm not sure who he's trying to convince. "One that I'm going back to on Monday."

"You don't have to."

I don't want this version of him to disappear, the one who jokes about wine and holds my hand at museums. The one who gets lost in the moment when he plays music. He's the man that I—well have this massive feeling that blooms to life in my chest when I think about him. Impending dread blankets me, struck by the feeling that if he starts working again, he won't stop. And it will be like these past two weeks never happened. I'll lose him. But I think he'll lose himself, too.

"Eve, of course I do." His shoulders slump and he looks away. It's like he's tugged on a thick winter coat. One that he's so used to wearing, so he doesn't seem to notice that it's weighing him down.

"Those things you just said also go for music. You're still great at it. People valued what you did." I almost don't say it, but after a moment I add, "I know you miss it."

That should matter, not just the validation it gave him but the way it made him feel. If he wants that life, he should have it. But why can't he see that as a relevant variable in his decision?

"It wouldn't be the same, I'd be alone this time around." His attention snaps back to the sink. "Let's not talk about it. I'm going back and if you're worried about what to tell Quinn and Oliver when I leave, I can take care of that," he says, then hands me a knife. "Careful. Make sure to grab the handle."

We finish the rest of the dishes in taut silence. No matter what I've learned about Garrett, I have to come to terms with the fact that our friendship is still new. Sometimes I feel like I'm navigating a minefield. He's not explosive, but it makes me ache whenever he tucks himself away from me.

Once done we head back toward the living room.

"Coming in. Please pull on any discarded pieces of clothing!" I project my voice with a similar warning to what Quinn had given to us earlier.

"Get over here. Cuddle me." I think Quinn is the one to say it but I'm not sure based on how low and hushed the words are.

"Ow. Watch your elbow," comes a second voice.

"Do you guys need a second?" I ask, not quite sure what we're interrupting.

"We're decent!" Oliver croaks.

Quinn is reclined on Oliver's chest holding a mostly empty glass of wine on the couch. His arms encircle her and rest on her stomach. It feels more different than uncomfortable to see them like this. I think I've settled into the fact that the awkwardness I do feel is because it's as if I missed out watching a season of our favorite show with them. They know all the details and subplots, what characters have been written off, and I'm reading into every context clue I can get.

"Do we have time for a game?" I ask, looking between them as I try to regain the connection we had during dinner. "There's Monopoly and a few others in the closet."

"Actually, I think we're going to call it a night," Quinn says.

"We have to pick up the wine for the festival tomorrow at this berry farm. You guys should come!" I say. A few days ago, spending the car ride with them would have been impossible. Now, I think we'll be able to survive it.

Oliver and Quinn exchange a look and a silent conversation passes between them.

"Could be fun," Oliver says as he shifts to skate his hands up and down the sides of Quinn's arms.

"I'm not sure you guys are going anywhere unless you brought a kayak with you," Garrett says. I turn to find him looking out the back window toward the deck. Sheets of rain are coming down obscuring the usual view of the trees

"The car has four-wheel drive," Quinn counters. "It's less than two miles."

"Good for the car. The problem is the road. It turns into a river in weather like this. If you don't believe me, go check outside." Garrett raises his arm gesturing toward the door.

This prompts Quinn, Oliver, and I to go look. I know Alina told me the road has drainage problems, but there's no way it's that bad. The moment I open the door I realize how wrong I am.

If I didn't know there was a fully paved road at the base of my driveway, I would have believed there was always rushing water there.

"It's a low priority project for the town. The water will clear up a few hours after the storm breaks," Garrett says reassuringly, but that doesn't seem to comfort anyone.

"We can walk," Quinn says.

"You mean swim," Oliver corrects. "Then get hypothermia. I'm sorry, but I don't exactly want to spend my vacation in bed."

"We have a spare room," I offer.

"Oliver, you can borrow some of my clothes," Garrett says. When I look at him he has this self-satisfied expression that clearly says, *Good thing I was thorough.*

Garrett's clothes in my closet remind me about another key factor in this very fun, super voluntary, sleepover scenario. Oliver and Quinn aren't the only ones stuck here.

And it's not like Garrett and I can sleep in separate rooms.

29

Evelyn

"When have you been going to sleep recently?" Garrett asks as he walks toward the right side of the bed. I look up from where I'm lying and rotate on top of the covers as he picks up the pillow and pats it into what I assume is his preferred position.

We've each taken turns in the en suite bathroom, changing and showering. I had to stare very hard at my phone when he came out in sweatpants and a pale blue shirt clinging to his damp skin. He might as well be naked.

Okay not really, but close.

"Ha." The sound escapes from me in a gust of air. "Sometime between one and four in the morning. You know, that type of sleep where you close your eyes and everything is just hazy."

"You wake up and never know if you actually slept." He follows my train of thought.

"Reminds me of seltzer water."

"Or those lime tortilla chips."

"Yes. Exactly that." I almost cheer as I sit up and point. I'm so close that my finger lands on his chest. I pull it away faster than if I had touched a hot stove.

His eyes follow my hand and his brows pull tight. I used to think that the expression indicated he was judging me, but now I'm not so sure. With how familiar I am with that expression, how often I've earned it in response to stupid jokes, that would mean he's spent a lot of time thinking about me. The possibility makes my mouth go dry.

Him thinking about me is one thing. Him thinking about me the way I've been thinking about him? That's entirely different.

"So, I guess we have a few hours to kill, unless we want to stare at the ceiling and pretend we're sleeping, but I get anxious breathing around people when it's super quiet," I say, unable to stop the already mounting anxiety to turn into a ramble.

"That seems wildly inconvenient."

"Okay, that's not what I mean," I stutter, then force myself to breathe. "I used to wear headphones and listen to music while I was walking around and then I just felt like I was breathing too loud in public so I would just, like, hold my breath."

"Oh," he mutters, but I'm looking away so he can't see the pink flush I know is on my face.

"Yeah, I know, it's embarrassing. I literally would stop myself from breathing if I thought it would bother someone," I say as I start to turn to the night stand in search of my laptop. "Let's just watch a movie or something."

Garrett reaches, crossing the gap between us and holds my hand, drawing me back to him. I risk looking at him and am met with tender caramel eyes. "It's not embarrassing. I mean, I hope you are comfortable breathing around me. You care about people so much. Sometimes I'm around you and it feels like you are on this earth to balance out all the people who don't care enough."

"I can breathe around you." Most of the time at least. The exceptions are always moments like this when he steals the air from my lungs. I swallow hard as I work around the words caught in my throat. "So, a movie?"

"Yeah. You pick."

I pull my laptop from the nightstand and position it between us. I'm navigating to Netflix from my browser's bookmarked websites when lighting strobes through the sky. The lights flicker, fighting to stay on before the room goes dark. The only light left comes from the screen. I optimistically click my profile and the server shows an error.

"I guess we're not watching a movie then," I say and start to feel panicked. I need some sort of distraction if he's going to lay next to me all night.

"Wait." The bed dips as he turns away. "I have something downloaded on my phone."

"*Wizard of Oz?*" I ask, teasing.

"*When Harry Met Sally.*"

"I thought you said you never watched it, because if you have you could have spared us my very long explanations," I say.

"I haven't. That's why I have it downloaded. If you keep making references, I want to understand them," he says. "I was planning to watch it this weekend."

His words sound startlingly similar to *I want to understand you.* I need to find a way of stopping this line of thinking if it's what I fall into when I'm around him. He doesn't see me that way. He doesn't do relationships. Hell, based on so much of what we've talked about, I don't know if he even believes in love that way for himself. And I struggle to stay casual with things. If something happens I'll keep wanting more.

"Oh," I say. "It's going to drain your battery."

"It's your favorite, right?"

My eyes are still adjusting to the darkness, but I know his every outline. I could close my eyes and it wouldn't matter. If I was an artist I could draw him from memory.

"Yeah."

"Then, it's worth it."

With the phone instead of a laptop we have to lean closer. Each of us tilt toward the screen, but there's intention in how we keep an inch or two of distance.

Thirty minutes in, something relaxes between us. We meet halfway. His thigh pressing against mine. My head on his shoulder, obviously so I can get a better view, though I'm struggling to follow the movie. I convince myself that the only reason I'm not paying attention is because I've seen it so many times. I feel the flow of the movie like my own heartbeat. A heartbeat that I'm worried that he can hear thrumming loudly.

I blink and the credits are rolling. Even when the screen turns black, Garrett holds the phone in place, like he knows if he lowers it we have to move. This position is an excuse we only maintained because of the movie, but now it's gone.

"Sorry about earlier," Garrett says when he finally lowers the phone.

"It's fine," I say, even though I'm not exactly sure what I'm saying I'm fine about.

"I don't like how I snapped at you. I might not want to talk about work, but there was no reason to do that."

"We all have our weak spots. No one is an island or however that saying goes."

"Let me be sorry," he insists. "You deserve more than that."

"Maybe." I give a wavering smile that he might not see in the dark.

"You do. You deserve so goddamn much." The sentiment is a caress I dismiss.

"Says my fake boyfriend."

I don't know what I deserve. Who am I to judge that? In recent years, my wants and the wants of those around me have twisted and knotted together. As I've pursued the one thing I thought I wanted, I've driven a wedge between me and the people I care about.

"Maybe that's what I am," he says, not sounding pleased with it. "But, remember, as long as they're here in this house, you're mine."

My mind goes to wondering what that would look like, only to conclude that I already know. I know how his hands feel pressed over fabric, on skin. How his firm mouth can work against my lips.

"Am I?" I utter.

"Why is that a question?"

"Because if I was, things would be different right now."

"Eve. Please," he rasps. "Don't."

"Don't what?" I ask. He shifts, pulling the blanket so it drifts across my heated skin.

"I want to read into every word that's coming out of those pretty little lips." The words press against my inhibitions.

"As if you can see me in the dark," I taunt.

"I don't need to. My imagination is enough to torment me." And he does sound like he's close to anguish at the admission. The thought does me in. Neither of us will get any sleep like this.

"I'm yours." I swallow my last bit of hesitation. "Read into it."

I expect him to collide into me, for both of us to let whatever has been building burst at the seams.

But he doesn't. His hand cups my face, and he's so careful as he brushes his lips against my cheek, where a tremendous amount of heat is gathering.

He pulls back, his nose trailing a line against my cheek. "Tell me what you like."

"You keep asking me what I want," I say.

"Why shouldn't you have it?" Teeth skate along my collar bone. "Why can't I be the one who gives it to you?"

My lips part as I form an answer and his mouth finds mine, swallowing any words I could have said. I'm thankful for it because I don't know what I would have anyway. I want this moment. I've wanted this moment for so long, I doubt I even knew I was craving the press of his fingers into my side when I was lonely.

He pulls away and one of my thoughts breaks loose. "What happens next?"

"Tonight. Give me tonight." He rakes me across the gravel of his voice. His fingers creeping up my ribs persuade me.

Tonight. I can give us tonight. "Have tonight. Have me."

I'm not wearing a bra so when he reaches higher, he palms my bare breast, his thumb brushing over a peaked nipple. My teeth catch at his bottom lip and I rock into him. His erection presses against my stomach. I steal a groan from him as my hand meets the taut fabric of his pants.

The knowledge that I did this to him stokes my own need to see more of him. My fingers tug at his shirt. He moves back from me to aid in the process of discarding it, but the moment it's off, I'm back to touching him.

The occasional flash of lightning allows me to see him more clearly, how his stomach muscles ripple as my hand drags across them.

"Fuck. How is this so much better?" he groans.

"Better than what?"

"You touching me without anyone looking," he gasps. "When you're not thinking about anyone else."

The thing is, whenever he touches me it's like the parts of my brain thinking about anything else shut off. Like I'm physically incapable of not thinking about him. Instead of saying any of this out loud, I press my hand to his chest and guide him to lay on the bed. I sling a leg over his hips so I'm straddling him. My lips find his, and I grind against him trying to use the friction between us to ease the ache between my legs.

Snaking my fingers through his hair, I revel in knowing that I'm allowed to mess him up. He messes me up as well, makes me a fucking disaster in all the best ways, so we might as well match.

"Eve," Garrett says. His hands land on my hips stopping my desperate movements. "Is this all you want?"

"Are you offering more?"

"Yes, but I won't be able to last much longer if you keep up with what you're doing. At this rate, I'm going to come in my pants."

"I don't have any condoms. Did you pack any?"

"No, that wasn't exactly on my list of essentials," he says. "I'm clean, I've had a vasectomy. But if you're not comfortable without one we don't have to."

"You do?"

"I got it when I was eighteen."

"Very responsible," I say. "And I got tested two months ago, and haven't been with anyone since."

"Then, Evelyn, can I please?" Garrett asks as he hooks a finger under the waistband of my shorts.

"Are you going to be gentle with me?" I gasp.

"You're the only person I know how to be gentle with," he murmurs into my skin, causing my stomach to flutter.

I don't want to admit that even before it's started, I don't want it to end. That I'm breaking the feeble promises I made to myself. I'm about to fall so far there is no coming back.

But I think it might just be worth it. We might be worth it.

He stares at me for a moment then kisses my cheek. His lips trail a meandering constellation, stars rising to prickle under the surface of my skin.

Cheek. Nose. Cheek. Corner of my lips. Neck. Lips.

Lips. His firm lips against mine. Asking. Wanting.

He pulls back and touches his forefinger against my lower lip. I pull the finger into my mouth, swirling my tongue around it. The action draws a groan from him.

"And what if I don't want you to be gentle?"

"Whatever you want," he says as he lifts the hem of my shirt. His stare tracks each inch of exposed skin. "But you better be quiet or your friends in the other room will know exactly how obedient I can be."

I impatiently help him the rest of the way, rolling my hips against him and his fingers latch on to my waist. "Show me exactly what you meant. Show me how you want to treat me like I'm yours."

"How wet are you?" he demands.

"Why don't you check?" I bite at my lip.

I lift my hips and plant my hands on his shoulders as his hand drags down the plane of my stomach. His hand slides underneath the elastic waistband of my shorts and over the cotton fabric of my underwear.

He pushes aside the fabric and slides a finger into me. "Soaked for me. Fucking hell."

I grip his shoulders harder and attempt to swallow a moan. He adds another finger and works in and out of me as I match his movements with my hips. The press of the palm of his hand sends the most delicious feeling I've ever experienced rocketing through me.

"Fuck, Garrett. Yes," I pant.

"What a fast learner. So fucking smart," he says, and I moan. "Do you like that? Me telling you how fucking good you are?"

"Yes."

He leans in so his words sweep against the shell of my ear. "So intelligent. Incredible at getting what you want, making yourself feel good. Is my girl going to come on my hand before she comes on my cock?"

"Yes." The word rolls through me as my thighs start to shake.

The orgasm floods my system and Garrett holds me through it. Simultaneously breaking me and keeping me together.

"Are you okay?" he asks once the electricity under my skin fades, and I sink back into this gauzy version of reality.

"Yes. I would like another one of those please," I say as I collapse on the bed next to him.

"Then I'll give it to you." His low chuckle rolls through me as he pushes upright so we're in the opposite position as we were before. "Lift your hips for me so I can help you take these off."

I do as I'm told. My shorts are gone and then so are his pants. I get a better look at all of him, but only for a moment before he demands my attention. "Is this how you want it to be?"

"Only got one position in you?"

"Once I'm in you, it will take everything in me to last, so you better tell me exactly how you want it."

"Like this," I say. I just want to see him, what I do to him, who I am to him. Only for tonight.

My leg hitches over his hip. He lines himself up and eases into me. I relish each inch of him. My body can't comprehend anything outside of us. I clench around him.

"I'm almost there," he coaxes.

"God. There's more?" I'm not complaining by any means.

"Breathe, baby. Let your body learn how to take me." He moves slowly, deliberately until we're flush against each other. "Fuck, Eve," he says into my hair.

He starts to move, picking up pace with every thrust of his hips. Frantic, trying to make up for everything that won't come after this. Like every other moment dominated by his touch, I lose myself. My identity weaves itself from the fabric of my immediate reality.

There is no tomorrow, just now.

Now. Now. Now.

Us.

30

Evelyn

I roll over then spread out on the bed. When I open my eyes, I have to take a moment to adjust to the sunlight. I can't remember the last time I slept until the sun was all the way up. The sound of running water starts, coming from the bathroom. I guess that's where Garrett went, then. He's still here, which is good. He didn't run, but what does that mean for this morning? How do I continue at the level we got to before bed last night in front of Quinn and Oliver? Especially now I know exactly what it's like to be with him.

The door to the bathroom swings open. My eyes take their sweet time skimming from the waistband of his low slung sweatpants up his torso.

"Having a good time over there?" he asks as he twists to close the door behind him.

"It's a good view," I croon. "So…" I trail off inviting him to play along.

"Quinn and Oliver headed out. They knocked on the door this morning pretty early to let us know," he rushes to say.

"Oh." I guess that's it then, and now I'm sitting on the sheets feeling like a horny idiot. "I guess it's good that we shared the bed then, since they saw."

"Thought you'd want to know. And yeah, it worked in our favor," he says. A blush creeps up his neck to reach his ears. Okay, at least he's not completely unphased. "I'll finish getting ready in the guest room. I just wanted to make sure you knew I didn't just leave."

I nod dumbly for a few seconds. "Great. Thanks."

He leaves and I wait until I hear the sound of the guest room door closing behind him before I grab the nearest pillow and scream into it. This, of course, was a mistake because it smells like him.

Stupid. How could I be so fucking stupid? Why did he have to be cute by going and downloading that damn movie? All it took was a few flirty touches and a genuine moment of interest and I latched on to the most relationship-adverse man I know.

We manage to maneuver around each other throughout the morning. I walk into the kitchen to grab cereal just as he's finishing his bowl. I accidentally bump into him, causing the milk to splatter all over his shirt, so he has to go change.

Nice, smooth fucking move.

He's still upstairs when a knock sounds at the door just before ten. I empty my bowl and hurry to the entrance. "Garrett! They're here!" I call up the stairs as I pass by.

When I open the door, Quinn's attention keeps shifting to something I can't quite see.

"Hey, I'm ready but give me five to make sure Garrett is done putting product in his hair," I say. One of the sole benefits of this morning is now I know my belief that he takes longer with his hair than I do is completely founded.

"Yeah," Quinn says, then her eyes flick to the side again. "Can you get him soon because there's this lady on the swing who says she's his mom."

"I'm sorry, what?"

"I mean, they look alike if you ignore the clothes. See for yourself." Quinn hooks her thumb, and I lean out using the door frame for support to poke my head around the corner.

Sure enough, there's a woman with gold blonde hair tied up in a ponytail using one leg to rock herself back and forth on the porch swing. A leather jacket is draped over the legs of her faded light wash jeans. When she turns to wave at me, I get a good look at her blue eyes. They're not Garrett's eyes, but many of her sharp features are so close to his. The flat tip of her nose, the expressive lift of her eyebrows, and other small things that I recreate in my imagination more often than I care to admit.

"Do you know if they have a phone charger in the car? I still haven't had a chance to recharge my phone after the blackout," Garrett says as his footfalls thump down the stairs. I can't even appreciate that he was so in the moment last night he didn't care about his phone.

"I think someone's here to see you." The words tear out of my throat as I watch Garrett peek outside to see what the rest of us are already looking at. He doesn't shatter the way I know I would.

He turns to ice, cold and stiff. Old Garrett.
Not mine, not mine at all.

31

Garrett

"Hi, Lana," I say, when all I can think is *you shouldn't be here.*

You shouldn't be here. You shouldn't be here.

A record skips over in my brain, demanding that I let the words out, but I can't.

I have to be in control of this situation for as long as I can, but I can already feel that slipping from my grasp. The moment I do, I'll get caught up in whatever she's up to.

Hartsfall has always been safe to come back to. Our deal that I would pay her to stay away guaranteed I didn't have to worry about her. She liked her bank account far more than the town she blamed for all of her shortcomings. Early on it felt like a test. Me or the money. Risk coming back and making amends or show me how little you care. I don't know what outcome I wanted, what constituted failing, but she was consistent for fifteen years.

"So serious calling your mother by her first name. But you always have been." Lana smiles, flashing perfectly white teeth.

With a sweep of her legs she swings upright while slinging her jacket over her shoulder.

"You know me so well." I keep my tone level. Evelyn and Quinn are still here, looking at me for directions. Directions I have no idea how to give because I feel like the wind's been knocked out of me.

"Didn't you get my texts this morning? I've been trying to call but you didn't pick up," she pouts and tilts her head so the others can also see.

"My phone is dead. There was a black out," I explain.

"That's so unlike you," she chides in a tone that could be misconstrued as motherly. "He was so much more responsible than me. Did you know that this guy helped me with my taxes every year? I was so bad at it and he'd sit with me until we got it all figured out. I can only assume he got his brains from his father. That and his eyes." She taps a finger against her temple so the others will note her blue eyes, ones that she loves to point out.

Lana is magnetic and she basks in it. She used to tell me she had a superpower, that she could get anyone to look at her by walking into a room. When I was a kid I believed it because it happened over and over. Before I knew better, it made me feel special to know someone so loved was my mother.

An errant breeze catches the door, slamming it against the wall. I'm half tempted to go back inside, close the door, and walk right back out. The same way I check the fridge sometimes expecting new food to appear.

"We're about to get going," Quinn says and gives me a look that hinges between concern and confusion.

"Ooo, where? A day trip?" Lana's voice drips with interest.

"The berry farm," I say.

"Barlowe's? God, I loved that place, field trips, holidays, birthdays. It's the place to visit, or at least, during the summer and fall," Lana chimes her approval.

Quinn tries again. "Yeah, Oliver is in the car. Let's not keep him waiting."

"Are these all your friends? God, it's so good to meet everyone. Girlfriend?" Lana asks and her eyes ping pong between Quinn and Evelyn then shoot to a sleeping Oliver, who is resting, unaware in the passenger seat. "Boyfriend?"

I can't help but wonder if she actually knows I'm bisexual or is just guessing. Then there's the embarrassment pattering against me, reminding me how little this woman knows me, but more so how little she seems to care.

"I'm the girlfriend," Evelyn volunteers brightly.

Looking at her stokes the embers I haven't been able to put out since last night. I've been avoiding her all morning because I've been scared of being alone in a room with her and having to hide how hard I get just remembering how she said my name last night. And I need to talk to her before I hear back from Holt about heading back to work after this weekend.

"Oh, you're gorgeous!" Lana then launches herself at Evelyn wrapping her in enthusiastic embrace. "How long have you been together? Months? Years? I want to know everything. I've never seen him with anyone before."

"Can we get in the car, please?" Quinn cuts in again, seemingly as uncomfortable as I am.

"Great idea." Lana nods, stepping away from Evelyn. Before any of us process what's happening she's opening the back door and sliding in. We all watch as Oliver startles awake then looks behind him to see a complete stranger in the backseat. After a moment he is caught in a conversation with her.

"Did she just…" Quinn asks, aghast.

"Invite herself? Yeah," I answer as Quinn starts to march off the porch and to the SUV. "Fuck. I hate parents."

Evelyn grabs my arm then pulls away, obviously not sure how to handle last night. I was hoping we could talk once I could think straight. Right now is not the time. I'm just hoping I will find a time before it's too late. Before the weekend has gone by and I'm still making damned excuses. "We have room in the car, but do you want her here?"

"I'm not sure we'll be able to get her out of the car until we get to the farm."

"I can ask her to leave."

"No, it's fine. I need to figure out why the hell she's here."

Also, now I don't particularly want to learn what lengths it will take to get her out of the car. At least I can ride the knowledge that people can't help but get caught up in her whirlwind. Quinn still looks apprehensive when we reach the car, but I have no doubt she'll flip within the next two hours.

"Your legs won't fit," Evelyn says as she moves in front of me to take the middle seat. From the look in her eyes, I can tell that she's also doing it to give me the illusion of space.

Tension starts to build behind my temples and we haven't even left the driveway.

"And I'm still not sure if the swamp guide was alluding that he dumped bodies there or that he knew people who did. Either way, after the trip he told me where to find the best Cajun food. If you're ever in Louisiana, let me know and I'll send you all the details," Lana says animatedly. She's been talking with her hands so much that Evelyn has to lean into me to avoid a collision.

From the driver's seat, Quinn mutters something like, "I can think of one body I might need dumped."

She throws me a glance through the rearview mirror that conveys the depth of her annoyance, which I answer with a nod. Between Quinn's looks and Evelyn's concern, I don't feel completely adrift with Lana, though the close quarters of the car are less than ideal.

"I had a similar experience in the Florida Keys," Oliver replies. "The amount of people you meet out in the world is always so surprising."

It's been an hour of this. Lana eagerly has shared her cross-continental adventures spanning the last decade, each of them so detailed that I doubt they were made up. The dune buggy race she accidentally entered and then won in Colorado that ended with her being invited to Vienna, where she went to a masked ball. Then there was the week she spent in Vegas with a food critic. Oliver and Evelyn have been there to pipe in with appropriate comments and enthusiastic nods.

Each story proves again and again how little I know about this woman. There's the jealousy that intertwines with a tainted type of relief. She's living a full life. She can't complain any more about what I've taken from her because I gave this to her. It's not that I wish I lived that life. Some of the stories she's telling with all the people and unexpected turns sounds like my personal hell, but her life sounds so vast, while mine is contained.

Usually, I like it that way, but being around her reminds me of my social distance from most people. Before I realized it didn't matter who I was or what I did, I wondered if we'd have a better relationship if I was more like her.

Quinn slows and pulls into an exit with a gas station. The moment she's parked by a pump I push my door open, heading for the convenience store. I go straight for the single occupant bathroom and let out a sigh of relief when I find it unlocked. I don't bother to turn on the light, I just lock the door and brace myself against the sink. The touch of cool porcelain is calming. I turn on the water then splash it on my face twice.

We only have a bit longer before we get to the farm. At least then we will be in a wide open space instead of being pressed together in a car.

One last breath and I leave the bathroom. Evelyn is standing there in the dingy hallway next to a corkboard boasting events from last February. She has a neon-blue sports drink and a bag of sour gummy worms clutched in one hand.

"I'm not going to ask if you're okay on the off chance you'll lie, but do you need anything?" Evelyn asks.

"I'd go for a cigarette, but I'm assuming Quinn will do terrible things to me if I get close to the car with one." I'm itching for one. Lana has always been my biggest trigger.

"Probably." She half laughs. "Your phone is still dead, that's why you haven't been playing chess on it, right?"

"Yeah." I had hopes of charging it the moment I got in the car but Lana had already managed to claim it for herself, then Quinn had to plug hers in so it wouldn't die while she was using it for directions.

"Mine is pretty charged and I downloaded an app if you want to use it."

"Thanks."

"Also, if you need it, I have a bottle of Excedrin in my bag, just in case," she offers.

"You didn't have to do that," I say.

She shrugs like it's no big deal. Maybe it's not. Maybe I just haven't had the right people around me. "I just thought if I made good use of the information you gave me, then I could bribe you into telling me more about yourself."

"So, you'll only give me pain relievers and your phone if I tell you my secrets?" I ask.

"I'm glad you're catching on to my master plan," she says. Her smile is strained as if she's about to ask something else, but Quinn strides around the corner looking a little dazed.

"I think I just became friends with your mom on Spotify. Or at least I think I am because I didn't even know that was something you could do. I'm pretty sure she's added me to a joint playlist. If you guys have your gas station snacks I encourage you to hurry up." Quinn throws a furtive glance to the wall of windows. "I left Oliver with her because I didn't want to risk her taking the car and trying to street race it in broad daylight. We shouldn't leave them for too long because if she starts trying to plan a trip to Dubai with him he is incapable of saying no."

32

Evelyn

Once we're done with the farm's handful of off-season attractions, Garrett goes to check on the beverage donations while the rest of us, including Lana, explore the two-story gift shop. I offered to help, but he insisted he could take care of it alone. Beyond that, he hasn't spoken much. On the rest of the car ride, I looked over his shoulder as he played chess. Out of all the matches he played, he only lost once. The entire time his side was pressed against mine, and I couldn't help but feel that I was an anchor to reality while his focus was devoted to the games he cycled through. I like being safe for him the way he's become safe for me.

We got lunch at the cafe where we all had the shared experience of blueberry white cheddar grilled cheese sandwiches with a balsamic glaze. After, we explored the kids' craft corner with its coloring sheets until the next tractor ride was available. It's a far more touristy and less romantic version of the time we had with the Barlowes.

Now, I'm standing in front of a blueberry bath mat that turns blue when water gets on it with my phone tucked next to my ear. It rings twice before Avery picks up.

"Is Wes there?" I ask.

"Yes, my day has been going great. I even got a fake tan to look like I've been able to go to the beach between rehearsals. And, oh yeah, are you in a hostage situation because that's a request I thought you were physically incapable of making?" Her voice remains fairly even until the last sentence. The reality is that if I were in need of a signal to covertly convey I had been kidnapped, asking about Wes would do the trick.

Since I don't have Alina's contact outside of the rental app and no other way to get information I might need, Wes is unfortunately the best option.

"I wish I could explain, but it's not my business to share."

"You promise you aren't in danger?" Her voice lowers. "If you are, say Jeff Goldblum, and I'll use the Find My Friends app to send authorities to your location."

"I'm fine, now can I talk to Wes?" I ask.

There's a muffled shout from her end as if she's covering the microphone with her hand then a slight scuffling noise.

"I'm here, by popular demand," Wes says.

"Garrett's mom is here." I cut to the chase, not wanting to waste any more time.

"Where's here?" From the way his voice turns serious I know I took the right risk in assuming he would know.

"Hartsfall. Well, technically, a farm a few hours away, but she showed up in town this morning."

"She's not supposed to be there. God, I hate her," he bites out. My stomach sinks. This is Wes, perpetually happy and carefree.

"You've met?" I ask.

"Once in Vegas, while we were on tour," he says, and I briefly wonder if it's the same story she was telling us on the drive over. "I've never seen him the way he was—or not to that degree. Like he's completely shut down and doesn't talk unless he has to."

"Yeah," I confirm, thinking about the silence I used to expect from him, but feels so uncharacteristic now. "Is there anything I need to know?" I pick up a soap dish to do something with my hands.

"She'll ask him for money," Wes explains in a taut voice. "That's the only reason she ever shows up, even though he gives her plenty already."

"She'll what?"

"It's not like we've really talked about it. But they had a deal. She would leave him and Hartsfall alone and she'd get an allowance. If she's there, it's not a happy healthy reunion. The sooner she leaves the better." He releases a heavy sigh. "She might be his mother, but it's that town that raised him. That's the way I've come to understand it over the years, he's not liberal with the specifics."

"I'll keep an eye on her," I promise.

"I appreciate it. I'm glad someone's there with him," he says. Wes hands the phone to Avery and I say a quick good-bye.

I leave the home goods area in the far corner, walking past overpriced hot pads, soap dishes, and a slushy machine. I wouldn't be surprised if people who live nearby come here to shop instead of department stores if it's closer.

"What are the chances we buy new outfits and walk out of here as walking blueberry advertisements," I ask as I find Quinn in the center of the clothing section that contains everything from briefs to an interpretation of formalwear.

I scan the rest of the open area and spot Lana talking to an employee in the middle of restocking candy and packaged baked goods near the checkout counter.

"Out of ten?" Quinn asks.

"Sure."

"Zero," she says, then reconsiders. "Actually, one. It is the one thing I'm more likely to do than ask Lana about her tramp stamp." We discovered the tramp stamp during the tractor ride when Lana convinced the driver to let her sit up front with him. The rest of us were in the attached wagon bracing for the moment when she managed to switch places and take complete control of the vehicle. It never happened, but I'm pretty sure if the ride was five minutes longer it would have.

The thing is, I get it. Lana is the type of person you meet in a bar bathroom and then go on an adventure with. She is pretty, funny, and stories pour out of her at a rate that should be studied in a laboratory setting. I'm pretty sure the only reason I'm not getting caught up in Lana and her stories is because I know Garrett. After talking to Wesley the sour taste in my mouth has only worsened.

"Because she'll ask if you want to get a matching one?" I ask as I run my fingers over the plush fabric of a blueberry embroidered bathrobe. Not bad for something that would make you look like that one girl from *Willy Wonka.*

"Because she'll offer to be the one to give it to me and then somehow convince me it's a good idea. How the hell does she do that?" Quinn shakes her head in astonishment.

"I think it has something to do with her ability to deliberately ignore negativity," I say. "I don't think it's technically considered gaslighting, but it sure as hell is disorienting."

There's no malice in what she's doing, but it's like being knocked off your feet over and over again until you convince yourself it was your idea.

"Whatever reality she's in, I'm both terrified of it and want to experience it for about an hour so I understand it on an anthropological level."

A dressing room stall door swings open to reveal Oliver in a novelty suit. "What do you guys think?"

"You look like Dionysus," Quinn says, giving him a bemused once over.

"The god of grapes?" I ask.

"I think it's more like wine in general." Oliver does a turn, assessing himself in the full length mirror.

Quinn scrunches her nose. "You're not seriously considering getting that."

"If I can get it tailored, then it wouldn't be so bad. I saw a matching dress over there. The perfect date night attire, don't you think so, sweetie? Or maybe I'll wear it to Dad's tenth wedding."

"The only thing that can fix that suit is a vat of black clothing dye."

In my periphery Lana hitches her tote with her purchases over her shoulder and then saunters out of the gift shop. So far, her and Garrett haven't been left alone together and on Garrett's part that seems intentional.

"Hey, I'm going to be right back. If you find any berry paraphernalia you think I can't live without, don't hesitate to grab it for me." I'm already moving. There's a significant chance that Lana will be wandering off somewhere else or that Garrett actually wants to talk to her. Either way, I'm going to show up for him. If he doesn't want me there, then I'll leave. I'd rather him know I care than leave him stranded.

My eyes take a moment to adjust as I step out of the gift shop. The sun has crested in the sky and the world is glaringly bright. I head to where Garrett pulled the car around to help the workers load up the cases of wine and beer.

"We could go up to Niagara. I have my passport on me, make a whole trip of it," Lana says, brightly.

"You came here to invite me to Niagara?" he asks, indignation coating his words.

"God, you've grown up so handsome. I can't even remember what he looks like but I think you got the better parts of him." Lana reaches out to pat Garrett's cheek. I half expect him to flinch away, but it looks like she's touching a statue. Her attention snaps to the side as a man walks by and she starts to pull away. "I'm pretty sure I met that guy at Burning Man once. I'll be right back. If I'm right, he has these pictures I've been dying to get my hands on."

Garrett stands there like even if a truck were coming at him full force he wouldn't notice.

"Hey," I say softly. He blinks then turns toward me, but it still feels like he isn't completely here. "How do you feel about a blueberry themed home?"

"What does that entail?" he asks with an attempt at levity.

"Everything you currently have but covered in a pattern that slowly works away at your sanity." I shrug. "Crock pots, dog bowls, towel covers."

"When you put it like that, no."

"I did want to check, how are you doing? Full transparency, I called Wes to help me understand the situation," I say. I don't want him to feel like I've gone behind his back.

"You hate him."

"Sure, I hate him, but I like you more." It's the truth. We might never talk about last night and given the circumstances, I'd understand that. But that doesn't change how I feel about him as a person. "Are you, I mean…not okay, but how do you feel?"

"If I knew, I'd tell you. She feels like a stranger, and I've never been good with strangers. Then there's the part where she absolutely shouldn't be a stranger and I should already know all the answers to the most basic fucking questions, but I don't."

"Do you want to sit in the car?" I ask, because it's the most private place I can think of.

"Sure."

We slip into the back seat of the car.

Evelyn
> Can you find Lana? I lost her

Quinn
> AirTags were invented for people like her

Quinn
> Would it be so bad if she ran off with the rodeo.

Evelyn
> Please

Quinn
> Fine. Only because Oliver is one minute away from getting me in the dress that matches his suit.

Evelyn
> There's nothing stopping you from trying it on

> If you find her - text me and I'll let you know when we're ready to leave

"We can stay here as long as you need," I say. I want to take care of him but I'm lost on how to. So much of what I do is centered around avoiding moments like this. My whole brand is keeping it all together so other people can stay happy. Still, I know moments like this, the ones where the emotions hit you squarely in the chest and refuse to be ignored, are unavoidable.

He crumbles into me and I pull him close before he can back away and block me out.

"It's so fucking embarrassing. I feel like I'm ten when my teacher had to come out and she asked if someone was coming to get me and I didn't know how to answer. I don't know how to react." He buries his face in the crook of my neck and I squeeze him to me. "I used to be so jealous of you and Drew. At first I hated going to practice in your family's garage. I knew at the end of the day you had somewhere you belonged, all I had was a dorm at school and a guest room. It was probably a year before I stopped feeling that way. Your garage, the band, that was the first place I ever felt like I belonged. Like I truly was wanted there. It wasn't given to me out of pity, or charity. I earned it. I haven't seen her for years. She doesn't know me and it just reminds me how little there is to care about."

"Garrett. It's *her* fault she doesn't know you. None of us think it's your fault. It doesn't make you look bad—it makes her look bad. It's her loss for missing out," I say, though the words aren't enough. I want to pull him into me, let him hide if he needs to. I want to take it away.

"If you say so," he dismisses.

"After the last few weeks and then nineteen years before, I think I have enough experience to say that you are worth knowing," I say. "Also, there's the fact that if I give Quinn the option she will leave Lana here."

"She'd hitchhike back and somehow manage to beat us to Hartsfall."

"Probably. Do you want me to get the others? We can leave whenever you want," I offer.

"Let's stay here. Just for another minute."

"You can have as many of my minutes as you need."

33

Garrett

It's a bit past four when we pull up the driveway to Evelyn's place. Quinn turns off the engine then exits the car so fast she might set a new world record. Everyone is notably more on edge than when we left this morning.

"Lana and I are going to head to town," I say before she can weasel into making more plans. "Are you guys going to be okay with bringing the wine to the festival practice tomorrow? It's at the high school. I can send directions."

"Yeah, that shouldn't be a problem," Oliver says.

"All right." I turn to Lana. "My truck is parked at Alina's. We're getting coffee."

Lana starts walking down the drive and toward Alina's. I'm about to join her when a hand lands on my arm. I look over to find Evelyn.

"Come back after you're done. I'll cook dinner." It's not a question but from how she stiffens I know she's braced for an answer.

"Based on the last meal you 'cooked', how can I say no?" I ask.

"Then don't say no." Something like fear glistens in her eyes and it slams into me.

I don't want to slip away from her. I don't want to shut her out. But I can't promise I'll be pleasant to be around after my talk with Lana. "Come back to me." Her voice softens and just like that, the raging sea in my head calms.

"Okay."

By the time I make it across the street Lana is already leaning against my truck. She's impatiently picking at her nails like she's been waiting for me longer than a handful of minutes.

"You got this from Doug Fletcher, right?" she asks, patting the side of the truck bed.

"Yeah," I say as I mechanically unlock the door.

"God. I have so many memories in that truck bed. Not with Doug, he was already with Kirstie then, but his friend Marty. Let's just say we did our best to be discreet."

"Thanks, I really needed that image in my head."

"Well, what did you expect?" she scoffs. "This thing is a piece of Hartsfall history."

"What are you in the mood for in town?"

"Let's get something pumpkin flavored that will go straight to my ass." She slaps her side for emphasis.

I keep her in my periphery as we get coffee. She does her usual thing, complimenting a stranger's geode necklace then pulls up a seat at their table. It's the reason she always kept her waitressing jobs the longest. She was able to upsell the shit out of things and get great tips.

Her distractibility was also usually how she got fired. Still, the money was always the best then, and I was able to hide generous amounts away for when we needed it.

I risk a glance at my phone since she looks settled for at least a moment.

Eve

Ok?

Garrett

I've got it handled

Eve

Promise to tell me if you need reinforce-ments?

I hesitate for a moment; not about what to say, but to feel the weight of truth the word holds. I trust her to show up if I need help and it's a relief to send my reply.

Garrett

I promise.

With her pumpkin spice iced coffee and my cappuccino in hand I head to the table with the young couple who are completely under her spell.

"Here he is. You have to know his music; you must have heard of Fool's Gambit. He plays at the festival, you know. I watch the livestream every year." Lana pats at her jacket and then starts to dig into her bag. "I have to have a pen somewhere. I bet we can get an autograph."

"Yeah, sure. That would be great," the man says, even though he doesn't sound completely certain about the situation. The woman next to him is wide-eyed and eagerly nodding.

I usually avoid being recognized in Hartsfall. Mostly, the couples that visit are so involved with each other they rarely pay any mind to anyone else around them.

Lana finally manages to pull out an empty envelope and a pen. "Here, sign this. Oh, do you want a picture?"

Going along with the situation, I sign the paper. Its edge is coffee stained and I have no doubt it will end up in the trash or run through the wash after it's forgotten in a back pocket. "Let's get going, Lana. We're interrupting."

I don't leave it up for discussion and she must hear it in my voice because she gets up and replaces the extra chair.

"Come on," I mutter.

She loops an arm over my shoulders and I try to ignore the weight of it. She's only a few inches shorter than me thanks to the platforms on her shoes, so she's able to manage it. "Don't be like that. Let a mother be proud."

"You watch the festival live streams?" I ask.

"Last year I watched from Paris. The time difference was a bitch. I was in one of these hotel robes sipping on espresso and the Eiffel Tower was sparkling in the background. Almost as good as being here in person. You loved the festival so much even before you were in it. There was that fortune teller you went to every year. Remember?"

"Yeah." I went every year with one question. The poor woman with her shitty smoke machine had to come up with new answers each time. *Is it going to be an okay year?* Even then, I didn't ask if it was going to be good, okay was fine enough.

I force my mind to only grab at the relevant details. I don't know how to feel about her being supportive. It could be for show, for attention, that's not out of the question. It's the first time since she showed up on Evelyn's doorstep this morning that I'm truly tempted to entertain her. Could she actually be back because she cares?

Honestly, it's fucking confusing. Why the hell is she here if she knows it will jeopardize the money I've been giving to her? Her watching live streams is nice and all, but it's not like she's been sending her appreciation my way. No doubt she's been doing exactly what she just did in Love is Brewing. I make her look better. It's what I'm used to, it's the dynamic we've always had.

"A place in Paris that close to the Eiffel Tower must have been nice." I start my investigation. That's what it is with Lana. She gives you the bread crumbs then I'm left to pull out the red string and make sense of it all.

"Yes, it was a great anniversary. I've dated the guy for that long, doesn't feel real. It was just as good as the year before. We went on this Nordic Fjord cruise and fell in love with everywhere we went so we kept hopping around to all the sights in Europe. Oh my gosh, I have to show you this picture of the tulips in Holland." As soon as the thought hits her she rummages for her phone again.

"I don't have to see them. I've already gone."

It was a shoot for Vogue for an April issue years back, for the band. A part of me is vindicated that she doesn't seem to know this. But also, there's the part of me that reels at hearing about her life, a full life. The one she always wanted.

"Oh. Okay." Her face falls, and I'm hit with regret.

"Let's sit somewhere. If you came here to talk, then let's actually talk." We get to a bench facing the gazebo.

"You know, I thought I'd get engaged right there. I know it's a tourist thing, but I always liked the idea of it, everyone cheering." She chuckles to herself then perks up. "That reminds me!"

I hand over her drink, and as she reaches for it I almost lose my grip. A ring with a massive diamond on it glints as it catches the golden late afternoon sun.

"What the hell is that?" I demand. My stomach launches to my throat.

"Oh, you know, I've had it in my pocket this entire time, but I was waiting for the right moment," she says casually, like she's not holding a massive fucking engagement ring. "I saw your friends and didn't want it to be a huge deal in front of them."

"Congratulations."

"After we got all the excitement out of our systems you were on the list of people to call, but I wanted to tell you in person. You said you were busy, but I knew you weren't too busy for this."

A list I bet she got to the bottom of before remembering me.

"Where did it actually happen?" My stomach drops as I ask exactly what I know she wants me to.

"Lake Tahoe. It was the most incredibly clear day two months ago. We had just gotten back from David's neighbor's place. Well, maybe not neighbor, we had to take a boat to get there. But it was a good day."

Two months. She waited two months before deciding this was a good reason to drop in.

"So, you don't need my money anymore. Is that what this is about? You have his?" I demand.

She has everything she's wanted. Anger and bitterness batter my insides. She did it, and what the hell have I done? What the hell am I doing? Why does she get to be happy while I've been living a life defined by her mistakes?

Lana's face crumples like paper. "Ouch. God. I deserve that, don't I?"

"Yeah," I bite out.

"I came because I wanted to tell you to stop sending money. But not because I have his. He does well for himself. Has a construction company in Chicago. I told him I wouldn't accept a ring until I was able to take care of myself with my own money. I'm doing all right. I'm a secretary for this travel magazine editor. That's how I get to go on most of my trips. It's not crazy money, but it's enough that if I need it I can support myself."

"You're doing all right with everything else?"

"Got a nice therapist. He's got these French bulldogs I just adore. We do video calls and they always pop up in the back. I know it's a health concern, but I love those squashed little faces.

She looks to me for a reaction that I don't give. Her eyes dip down to her drink as the smile is wiped from her face. "I know I've made a lot of excuses over the years. I kept telling myself I was a kid."

"You were," I say.

It's a fact I've reminded myself so many times. She was a kid, but right now? The last fifteen years? The person next to me is a woman, who has proven that with the right motivation, when someone else came into her life, she could put in the right effort.

"Yeah, but you were too. I let it be an excuse, even when I stopped being a kid."

"Is that why you're here? To see how I turned out? To make yourself feel better because I got the fame and the money and I'm fine?" I snap.

"I guess that's a bonus, seeing you fine in spite of me. But I guess I wanted you to see I'm fine too. That we're both okay. I mean, look at us!" she says like it's something that we actually share.

"Sounds like you've been okay for a while," I say.

"It took some work. I had some really bad years. I went to rehab four years ago. A nice place, thanks to what you gave me." Her attention stays fixed straight ahead, focusing on nothing. I want to care more than I do. But when I search for our connection, there's nothing but the distance she's been all too comfortable creating between us. "Nasty time. I had enough of the right people that were putting up with me that I got the help in time. Real friends, good people. Indy, oh, she is one of the photographers the magazine works with and just the best type of person. So sturdy."

"And now?"

"Sober since," she says, beaming with pride. "I was scared it wouldn't stick. I was going to keep going every day and at least try. I wanted you to be able to look at me and not feel like I failed us both."

She does look good, more settled into her life. Maybe everything she's saying is true and she's ready to slow down. She's engaged, after all, and I never thought I'd see the day.

"You could stay, you know. The festival is coming up. The show's better in person than it is over live stream." She's trying. She's here. In the same way I've felt obligated to help her, I want to repay the effort she's made to come here.

Her fingers start to tap out a nervous rhythm on the side of her cup. "I don't know. I mean, I have work and I have a return ticket."

"Don't do that," I tell her.

"I have important things to do."

"I'm not saying you don't. I just want you to give me a straight answer."

Lana finally has everything she wants, but I know I've never been on any list of priorities. I shouldn't have gotten my hopes up even if it was for a moment. I know better. I know better than to read into one moment of effort. So what if she traveled here? So what if it felt like an opening for something real without the complication of money? So fucking what? I've always been the adult. Today's no different.

"Make an effort or don't." I do my best to not crush my cup. The words come out clipped, but level. "This isn't a clean slate. This is a choice. Stay or go. Tell me what you want. I'm not asking you to choose me. I'm not going to beg you to care. Choose what you want so we can both go on living. The gray area isn't an option anymore."

Her expression morphs, sliding between possibilities. Defeat is what eventually wins out. Her eyes fix straight ahead. She wasn't a good parent, but the deal between us kept her in my life. I'm forcing both of us to face who we are to each other head on and I can tell she doesn't want to.

"I can't stay."

"Then go. Don't drag this out."

And freedom turns out to be a lot like goodbye.

We sit in silence for a few heartbeats before she tells me she parked in town and should get going. The hotel she's staying at is a town over anyway and her fiancé is waiting there for her. I wonder if she wanted us to meet. It doesn't matter. We've severed the chord we've been using to tie ourselves together.

I continue to sit while she stands. There's a moment where I think she wants to hug me, but I'm not sure we know how to, not on a logistical level.

She walks away, leather jacket over her shoulder. She doesn't look back, and I'm happier for it. Looking back means regret, and finally, I don't feel like my image comes into her mind when she thinks of the word.

There's a possibility that if it weren't for my promise to Evelyn, I would have found a way to throw myself into work.

I would have read and reread contracts and proposals until my eyes were dry.

Instead, I go straight back to her. The moment I open the door and the three people sitting on the floor eating pizza cheer, I know I made the right decision. The moment she spots me, Evelyn leaps up and almost loses her balance in her hurry to get to me.

It's nice to be seen and welcomed on such a basic level, yet it wasn't ever something I thought I could attain. At least, not again after the band. I thought I got lucky that one time. But I guess I had a little luck left over.

Her arms land on my shoulders and she says, "You came back."

"You asked me to." *I wanted to.*

"Food is in the kitchen." Evelyn pulls away from me and points toward the scraps of pizza still remaining on their plates.

"I'm going to wait a minute. I'm not hungry yet." My body is still catching up to my head. I'll probably be starving later, but right now my emotions bear more than a passing resemblance to a knotted ball of yarn.

Quinn's legs are fully stretched out with a plate balanced on top of her thighs. Oliver, on the other hand, seems hyper aware of the space he's taking up and has folded himself into a pretzel.

"I got it! You know who she reminds me of?" Quinn exclaims then trains her eyes on Oliver. "Your dad's sixth wife."

Evelyn's brows furrow as she asks, "The one who he got married to after a one-night stand?"

"No. I forgot about that one. The one who had the psychic on speed dial," Quinn corrects.

"Oh, that was number seven. Number six was the one with the farm he refused to move to because he genuinely thought she was going to sell it and move to the city." Oliver nods along.

"I liked her. Actually, I can't remember anything except for the horse ride we went on, so I guess I liked her horses," Quinn says a bit wistfully before looking at me. "I'd apologize for being rude, but the first thing she did was jump into my rental car without asking for permission. There are other things too, but I'm going to be nice tonight."

"Your dad's really been married seven times?" I ask.

Oliver shrugs. "Nine, actually, but after number four my rehearsal dinner speeches really started to plateau."

"You can't blame yourself for that," Evelyn says.

"Yeah, there are only so many ways to nicely say that someone's marriage might be doomed, but you hope it isn't." Oliver's tone remains purposefully light.

"Imagine, without them we wouldn't have gone horseback riding," Evelyn reminds them.

"You wouldn't have to spend so much at Christmas for all your sisters," Quinn counters as she picks up the remnants of her crust.

"Money spent on a good gift is never a waste," Oliver says.

Quinn breaks off a bit of her crust and tosses it at Oliver without much force. He manages to catch it between his teeth as Quinn says, "I see you're still reading the quotes on the inside of chocolate wrappers."

"I'm actually starting to get a bit hungry, does anyone want more?" I ask. I need a minute. It's nice to be around people and not collapse into myself as I deal with the cocktail of relief and grief fermenting in me.

I get water as I collect myself, staring out the small window over the sink when Evelyn pads in.

"Has Oliver's dad actually been married that many times or was that for my benefit?" I ask.

"Yeah. He jokes about it and makes it all sound like an adventure, but it does weigh on him. I think the fact that he really does care about all his sisters makes it better. They have a group chat that is impossible to keep up with," Evelyn explains as she starts putting all the stray pizza slices into one central box. "And it was for your benefit. I'm not going to share Quinn's personal stuff because that's not my place, but most of the first year of college was bonding over our dysfunctional families."

The look of concern on my face tells me there are questions she's stopping herself from asking and I'm thankful for her patience.

"Sounds like I'm in good company."

"You are. Having people like them around doesn't fix everything. My brother still wasn't communicating with us about what he was going through. My parents still are on my ass about everything like I'm sixteen sneaking out my window."

"You snuck out?"

"All the time. I had places to be, parties to improve. Really hard work." She collects the empty boxes and piles them near the trash for later. "Shit was still bad, but at least I wasn't alone in it."

"You guys don't have to get up in arms for my sake. I know she's likable, it's fine," I say.

"She is literally a woman who crashed our trip and we have no investment in. Sure, she knows a hitman water guide in Louisiana and would be able to sneak us into a concert or something. But I care about you," Evelyn says, and my heart catches on her use of *I*. Not *we* care about you. *I* care about you. "And if it makes you feel better, Quinn will be holding a grudge against her until the end of time. She's like that."

"Yeah, it does make me feel a bit better."

"Good. Now grab your pizza, and you have our full permission to feel like shit or not even talk, but for us that's a group activity."

I grab a plate and load up on the misshapen pieces that the others passed over. When I try to take a seat on the couch, the three of them boo and I settle on the floor.

"It's a very important part of the process," Evelyn says.

"How?" I ask.

"If I could go back ten years and ask our drunk selves I would. It's just part of it." She shrugs.

"All right then."

Oliver and Quinn stay for another hour before they say their goodbyes and promise to see us tomorrow at the practice festival. Evelyn walks them out as I collect their crumb-covered plates.

"Do you want to talk about it?" Evelyn asks hesitantly.

"Not particularly. She left. I think this time it's for good." That familiar guilt calls for me. I should care more, is what it tells me. I should care, but the memories I've been clinging to have the stability of a house of cards on a windy afternoon.

"What do you want to do now?"

"Honestly, if you're up for it, I'd love to write something."

"Good thing I'm behind. I have about eleven songs to finish."

"So convenient," I say.

It's hard to believe that it's been less than a week since the last time we sat at the piano together. I feel like I've aged years. Now I let the need to process my feelings through song bubble to the surface. I want to topple into this, the ability to pour everything bottled up in me into a stream of notes.

Evelyn pads to a side table and picks up her notebook. "We have a plan, but we can also throw away the plan. What we make tonight doesn't have to make it on the album. It can just be whatever you need it to be. I don't want to force you into any corners."

"I have a feeling whatever we come up with will work perfectly." It's what we do. We work.

Tomorrow, I'll talk to her about what happens after I leave on Monday. Right now, I just need to escape.

34

Garrett

The last note plays and Evelyn reaches over to her phone to stop the recording. "I'll never get over this."

I don't think I will either. In some ways, thinking about the person I was performing and writing with Fool's Gambit, I don't think I've gotten over it. There's this part of me that's been in a deep hibernation, finally yawning open. Like I was waiting for her to come along and wake me up.

I shift in my seat on the piano bench so I can properly look at her. "Me either."

A blush blooms on the apples of her cheeks and she bites at her lower lip. "Anything else you need before tomorrow?"

I know the answer, but words fail to capture the depth of my need. I cup her cheek and kiss her. Her mouth parts for me. My hand slips to her lower back and she arches under my touch, drawing closer. I pull away for a moment and am met with wide green eyes.

"This." My chest heaves. "This is what I need. Tell me to stop if you don't need it too." I need to know. I'm about to topple right into her if she doesn't stop me now.

"Don't," she says. "Don't stop."

And that's all I need to hear. Her fingers work at the buttons of my shirt and I pull at hers. Our clothes land in a heap.

I move so sitting with my back to the keys and she's lowering to kneel between my thighs. Her fingers go to my hair, my neck, my arms. Her touch is fucking everywhere. Physical touch has never been something I crave, not like this. Not before her. It's like she's knitting me back together.

"Stand up," she says, breaking away from me.

I rise from my place on the bench and she pulls at the button and zipper on my pants. She drags down the waistband a few inches before stopping.

"What is this?" she asks as her fingers ghost against the jut of my hip. She shifts back from the red heart inked into my skin.

"It's part of a set, matching the rest of the band. We each have a card suit."

"Why the heart?"

"Because I'm heartless," I say. They thought it would be ironic. It was funny in the moment, but the truth was I had reached a point where I clung to that part of myself. If you're heartless, there's less of you to break.

"You're not heartless, you just hide it better than the rest of us. I wish I was like that," she says with a soft, sad smile.

I pull her back, pressing her to me and planting a kiss under her ear. "Never hide part of what makes you special. You helped me be brave with that big heart of yours."

"Garrett, tell me you need me," she begs.

"I need you." My lips feather against her skin. "I want to see you."

"What do you want to see?"

"Show me how you make yourself feel good, show me exactly how you do it," I say. "I want to be able to picture you, every face you make when you're alone."

She pulls back so I can see the flush dominating her cheeks. The pink of her tongue slips out to wet her parted lips. "I've never had someone watch me like that before."

"Don't if it makes you uncomfortable."

"I want to," she says without hesitation. "But I might have to get used to it. I don't want to disappoint you."

"You couldn't if you tried," I promise.

She steps back from me and slips off her pants at a painfully slow pace that makes me groan. She could ask me to do anything right now and I would. Her chest flutters with a breath before she lowers to her knees in front of me. Lazily, she drags a hand along her body and aching progression from her breast to the valley between her thighs.

Her lips form a silent "O" as she presses against her clit. It's impossible to take my eyes off her. I like knowing she feels good, seeing the pleasure painted on her face. As she continues, I watch her muscles tense and shift. I memorize the erratic rhythm of her breath. She sinks a finger into her entrance then another.

She bites into her bottom lip, stifling a cry. I catalog every movement, everything that she likes to do to herself so I can replicate it later. I've never thought of sex as beautiful. But that was before her.

In truth, when I was younger, I struggled to view sex as a positive experience. There was more anxiety when I had sex with women than with men. The potential for an accidental pregnancy haunted me until I got a vasectomy. The thought that I could bring life to this world unintentionally without being able to say for sure that I could love them? It sickened me.

It took years for me to shed the fear. From that point on I viewed sex as a destructive, yet pleasurable act. The moment I slept with someone it was one step closer to a guaranteed ending. Pleasure that would be used up.

But this view. This perfect view, I could never get tired of it. I want to undo her and make her whole at once. Over and over again.

Sex with Evelyn makes me realize why people make art dedicated to the act. If I were to ever carve a statue it would be to immortalize the bliss that consumes her face as she climbs to the point of orgasm.

"Am I doing a good job?" she pleads.

"You're fucking yourself with your fingers so well. Add another and tell me how it feels." My voice is low and hungry. I want to consume her as much as I want her to consume me.

She does and gasps. "It feels full. Good. But full."

"Fuck, you don't know how much your pleasure turns me on," I tell her, fucking transfixed by the woman I have the privilege of being with.

"Let me touch you, please. Let me help you feel good too." She gazes at me through dark lashes and I nod.

She crawls across the plush carpet, hands and knees sinking into the fibers. Her full hips sway as she takes her time closing the distance. Those green eyes of hers never leave me.

By the time she reaches me, I've tossed away my pants. Evelyn stops to kneel at my feet as I stand in front of the piano. Her hand skates up my thigh, slow. So fucking slow. The groan rips out of me just as her fingers are inches from my cock.

But I stop her, my hand landing over hers, so I can make one thing perfectly clear.

I tuck my forefinger under her chin and guide her to meet my eyes. "You are not allowed to stop touching yourself. Do you understand?"

"Yes," she says on an exhale.

She presses her pillowy lips against the tip, sending a jolt of pleasure through me as she takes me into the wet heat of her mouth. Her head bobs an easy rhythm as her tongue expertly swirls.

I lightly thrust, slowly picking up speed. Looking down I see that two of her fingers are dipping in and out of her pussy at a similar pace. Her mouth vibrates around my cock as she moans. It's fucking glorious and I nearly come. My arm reaches back to crash into the keys of the piano, sending a discordant scattering sound through the room.

"Stop," I demand.

"Why?"

"You're going to play me a song."

Her lips pop open and her eyes are glazed with lust. I watch as she muddles through the moment of confusion. "What?"

Reaching down, I weave my fingers in her hair. "I'm going to fuck you while you play our song. And you're going to keep playing until you come."

And if I have it my way, even after I leave on Monday. Anytime she plays this song. Anytime she even hears it all I want her to think about is me buried in her. *Us.*

She shifts away and then on to her feet. I turn to face the piano and pull the bench back, taking a seat on the cool wood.

"Come here," I beckon.

I spread my thighs so she can fit between them and stroke my cock. Carefully, she steps into place. I line myself up with her entrance and she cautiously shifts down.

"Sit, Evelyn. I know you can take me after getting your pussy all nice and ready, so sit."

She does, slamming down the rest of the way until I'm completely inside her. A breathy gasp breezes past her lips then she readjusts, lifting and lowering.

Have you ever been to heaven? Because this is it. *She* is it.

I gather her hair and move it to one shoulder then press a kiss to her neck. "I'm not starting until I hear the first note. Or we can stay like this as long as you like, I don't mind."

"Fine," she snaps. She tips slightly forward to reach the keys, fingers delicately taking position.

She presses down on an E and I thrust, snapping my hips.

"Shit," she groans. "You're going to mess me up."

"Count on it," I promise as I rock into her again.

Evelyn squares her shoulders then starts again with a new determination. This time she gets past the first three measures before making a mistake. She plays through it.

I follow her tempo and her intensity, matching my own rhythm to what she's playing on the keys. I can tell the moment she catches on because she speeds up and my movements quicken, the percussive sound of our bodies a back beat to our composition.

She punches out a rapid staccato and I reach up to roll her nipple between my fingers.

Her body grows tighter as we reach the final chorus as if she's holding back her orgasm. She clenches around me, testing my limits along with hers.

But this is music. Raw. Perfect. Music. A performance no one else will ever get.

The last strains of music ring through the room, growing louder through a roaring crescendo as I surge into her.

Giving her all I am, all I have, until she comes. And then so do I.

35

Garrett

I wake up and look over at Evelyn. All of the emotions from the last few days have a moment to settle in my mind as the barest traces of dawn steal through the gap in the curtains.

She's sleeping easily; moments ago, I was too. Acknowledging the comfort I feel in the spot next to her terrifies me.

I want this. To belong in the silent moments with her. Fill the gaps of life with her in my arms.

The thought starts to tear at me the more I watch the rise and fall of her chest. It only eases up when I'm out of the bed, looking away.

Before I know it, I'm out the door and driving. I pull over an hour later to send a text, but I keep going. I'm running—I'm just not sure if it's toward something or away from it.

It's a blur. The red and gold trees. The city grows closer on the horizon until it swallows me into traffic. The elevator I've taken countless times over the last seven years moves too fast and slow all at once. I sink into a chair on the other side of Holt's desk and I know this is it.

"I'm going to ask a second time. Are you sure?" Holt asks.

As she tilts her head, the light filtering in from the office window catches on one of her diamond stud earrings. It's the first time back at the firm in over a month and it's disorienting to see everything exactly the same as when I left.

I don't hesitate. I've played this out in my head over and over all the way to the city. "Yes."

"All right then. We'll discuss next steps on Monday. Please, make sure to block off two hours to meet with me in the morning and I'll be sending an email to make sure everything goes smoothly."

She stands, and I know I've been dismissed. Over two hours driving for a meeting that lasted fifteen minutes.

"I'll keep an eye out for it," I say.

"And, Garrett," she says with a rare softness.

"Yes?"

"I do appreciate how seriously you took your time away. I know it didn't come naturally to you, but relaxation suits you."

"I can't take all the credit." My lips threaten to turn upward despite the current melancholy.

"Then thank that photographer for me."

"Who?"

"Unless you were set up with a tripod, there was someone there with you," she explains.

"Oh, yeah. Well, I'll add it to the list of things I need to say to her."

"Good. Talk to you again soon, Larson."

I leave with only one thought in my head: *I have to get this next part right.*

36

Evelyn

Squeaks fill the air as shoes scuff across the linoleum flooring of Hartsfall High School's gymnasium. Long white plastic tables line the perimeter with different vendors testing out their foods and services. Hand painted signs are being touched up at the far end away from the main entrance where coordinators are checking in volunteers. We join the short line and I check my phone again. I stopped counting how many times I've reached for it an hour ago when the number hit an embarrassingly high double digit.

Garrett

I'm in the city. Talk soon.

Evelyn

Why didn't you wake me up?

Garrett

You haven't been sleeping well. You needed to sleep.

I've drafted and redrafted messages, but none of them have felt fair. We made no commitments to each other last night. It wasn't about me at all. I'm not the one who severed ties with the only parent I've ever known. No matter how much him leaving for Manhattan feels like a knife in my gut, I understand it.

He's going back to somewhere safe, somewhere without all the memories. He needs that, and it was always supposed to be the plan. I said yes knowing I wanted more, betting on being strong enough to turn off the emotions that are now swallowing me whole.

He left and didn't say goodbye. It's just a few days early. I can't be upset about something that was lurking right around the corner.

So, I deleted the texts and told Oliver and Quinn he'd be here late. I'll come up with another excuse about his absence later.

The pair in front of us finishes and I sign us in. As I scrawl our names, I do my best not to look for any evidence that Garrett could be here. He's not on stage with the other musicians or mingling with the crowd. Quinn and Oliver didn't originally have placements, but Poppy is the person who is checking us in so she's able to help us find places for them to fill in for people who are sick or will only be able to work the actual event in a week.

Quinn joins me at the face painting station while Oliver helps with the cider. Between every person who sits at my station, I make any excuse I can to get up and look around. The moment we run out of paper towels, I head out to find a bathroom to get more. I offer to grab water and refreshments. I probably only paint one person's face for every five anyone else does.

Before I can get up again, Fletcher slides into the folding chair across from me.

"What will it be? I can do hearts, flowers, or hearts," I offer. Though I've worked in design before, Photoshop is a completely different ballgame than a tiny plastic brush against the contours of a human face.

"Hmm, I have a novel idea. What about hearts?"

"Might be hard, but I'll try my best. Color?"

"Purple. Special request, can I get an F plus E in one, like a doodle in a notebook? I gotta remind the world who this ugly mug belongs to." A crooked grin cracks across his face.

"Is Emily here?" I ask.

"Nah, it's flu shot season so she's helping with that, but I'll be damned if she doesn't come to the real thing with me."

The door behind me opens and clatters closed with more arrivals and before I can stop myself, I turn to look.

"He'll be here," Fletcher says as his eyes soften. I look away and focus on perfectly coating my brush.

I take my time with little hearts making them almost look like freckles. "I don't know what you're talking about."

"Sure you don't."

"But if I did? I mean, know what you're talking about." I give in slightly but don't dare break my forced concentration. I try to dampen the hope building in my chest.

"I'd tell you he's never missed a rehearsal or the actual festival. Not when he was touring or when he was in school.

He made it work, made them write into his contract and everything. He has his rough edges but he's reliable as hell." A woman painting the face of an apple-cheeked child huffs her disapproval and Fletcher corrects. "Excuse me, reliable as heck. Forgot we had some tender ears around here. That's why they tuck me back in the da—darned garage."

I cover my mouth to hide a smile. "Even when he was touring? There's no way that people didn't recognize him."

"Well, he doesn't sing. He just plays because of Alina. Then there's the wig."

"Wig?" I choke out the question through a laugh.

"Yeah, wig. It kinda looks like a fucking"—the lady throws him another look and he cringes—"dead rat. And he takes off his glasses."

"Now *that* I need to see."

"Hell, it'll change you. That's for sure," he says, giving me a wide-eyed, haunted expression.

"Let me finish you up before you say something that has parents pulling out soap to wash your mouth with." I hold back a laugh as I pull back my hand so I don't leave jagged scribbles on his face.

A few flicks of my brush later and I send him on his way. He grabs a donut then bounds over to help someone move speakers.

"Hello, everyone!" Pat's voice booms through the gym in a way that probably gives some of the younger people flashbacks to when she was their teacher. "I wanted to thank all of our volunteers and business owners for making today possible. Every year, you are the folks who make the magic happen for everyone who comes to town on the 14th of October to experience the Love Letter Festival. We know you've been waiting for it, so the music is about to start."

Alina and then a younger blonde woman walk on to the stage. The woman settles at the piano and Alina in front of the microphone. Then, there he is carrying a cello case and wearing an impassive expression. An expression I want to crack open to know how he is. I wonder how long he's been here, what side door he used to come in.

Even with Fletcher's reassurance I had doubts, but he's here. The conversations of the community members dominate the space as the trio finishes setting up.

A bow stroke carries through the gymnasium. Everyone stills with anticipation. In practiced unison, the pianist and Garrett start a familiar swinging tune, and Alina starts to sing "Dream a Little Dream of Me." Couples start to form in front of the stage, dancing however they see fit, gentle swaying to seemingly choreographed routines. I pay them little mind. I only care about the man with his arms in an embrace around his instrument. He looks up and catches me staring—I don't look away because I can't. Not when he looks at me like I'm the only person in the room.

In the universe.

"Hey, Ev," someone calls, and my attention is forced back to where I'm sitting. Oliver is standing to my left. His hands are shoved deep into his pockets and he's rocking back on his heels.

"Oh, hey. Do you need something?" I ask, actively having to pay attention to Oliver and not Garrett. Not Garrett, who I still don't know how to feel about right now.

"Dance with me?" he says. The question itself is complete, but my mind tacks on *like we used to*. "I mean, if you want."

"What about Quinn?" I ask, looking to where my friend is meticulously cleaning her station.

"You know how she feels about being perceived with the potential of publicly failing or anything like it," he says with a light smile. Quinn notoriously only dances when the lights are low and the music is deafening.

"If it's okay, then sure." I give a nod and he gives me his hand. As I drape my fingers in his, my first thought is to compare Oliver's soft ones to Garrett's calloused ones.

We join the rest of the dancers, slipping into a gap a few feet from the stage. There's no strict pattern to our movements, just intuition. I lead as my body is swallowed by the aching strains of music, and Oliver follows.

We've experienced so many shades of this before, even when we weren't together. The first time was at a sophomore year bonfire. We'd driven out of the city with a group of people Quinn and I knew from our major, and Oliver tagged along like he always did. Two beers and mystery shots later I was insistent on teaching someone to waltz.

"I'm sorry, but I have no need for ballroom lessons, I don't intend on having to go through archaic courting rituals," Quinn said from her place on her log-turned-bench.

"You're right. I much prefer our modern ones that involve watching potential love interests slam cheap shots as proof of their courage," I said, recalling an event from a few weekends ago when a guy misinterpreted Quinn's indifference as a drinking challenge.

Quinn mulled this over a bit. "I could settle for something arranged and loveless with a few affairs." She'd been making light of her own parents' constant cycle of infidelity. That night was before their long-awaited divorce.

Oliver walked over with a fresh drink and his permanently bashful smile. "Why is Quinn considering marriage? Has something changed since she rambled on about how she would be a child bride last week to her mom."

"She doesn't want me to teach her how to waltz," I explained.

"As usual, a perfect line of logic." He nodded then handed his neon plastic cup to Quinn. "I've always wanted to learn. I guess now's the perfect chance."

I always liked how serious he was about all of it. Nothing was stupid if it was something one of us cared about. Really, I only kind of knew how to waltz, but I had gotten so swept up in the idea of it I couldn't back down.

Oliver and I arranged ourselves with one of my hands on his shoulder, one of his on my mid back, and the others linked.

"It's a box step. Start with your left," I said as he moved toward me. I'd continued to give my instructions until we were tilted away from Quinn. "Thank you for playing along."

"I just like dancing."

"You're good at it."

"I'll tell my ballroom teacher that," he said, then his eyes crinkled. "I have three sisters who took lessons, and I wanted to know what it was all about."

"You already know how to waltz," I concluded.

"I was in need of a refresher."

There were times at friends' weddings and bars when he wanted to pull me close and rock back and forth, even as the music urged us to flail and bounce. I've missed it, but not because I've missed him.

I'm flung back into the moment as Oliver briskly maneuvers us from getting hit by overly enthusiastic swing dancers.

"You're still so good at this," I say.

"I'm a bit out of practice, so I'm happy this is passable."

"Does Quinn still threaten arranged marriage as a way to get out of it?" I ask.

"We don't dance," he says and his features shadow into something unreadable then quickly bounce back. "But she is still a fan of the arranged marriage bit. Not great for my ego."

"You two make sense together." I swallow and keep going. "Like a boat and an anchor."

"Going out on a limb and assuming I'm the boat here," he says, flashing me a timid smile.

"A very handsome boat named after someone's twenty-year-old mistress."

He nods. "As the best kinds are."

"And Quinn is a very sturdy anchor," I say. "The kind you can rely on in a storm."

Growing up I wasn't good at making friends, I was loud and didn't understand how to reel myself in. But I had Drew and he was my best friend, until he was in Fool's Gambit. I wasn't close to my parents in the same way some people are, because they were always worried about what I'd do. Then there were the small things. I couldn't connect with my quiet father or cook like Drew did with Mom. Even with Avery I've been in the backseat because Wes will always be her person on a level I can't fully grasp. I didn't fit anywhere until I met Quinn and Oliver. Fitting with them made me more aware of the loneliness that came before, but I was sure it was over. And I really had started to think I might have a place with Garrett.

Oliver spins me around, the move requiring me to concentrate to keep my balance. He pulls me back in then stops short on the next step.

"Can I cut in?" The low voice is cold but it invites me in like the urge to crunch through fresh snow.

"Of course." Oliver's hands leave my body, but I don't feel bereft without them. At some point they just turned into hands and not the tactile things I constantly wanted pressed against me. "If you need a waltz instructor, she's great."

Garrett's light brown eyes clash with Oliver's brilliant blue ones.

37

Garrett

She's trying her best to not look at me. Her hand might be draped in mine and my hand might be resting on her back, but she's doing her best to avoid me. I know I have no right to be jealous, but I couldn't help but feel like I caused her to run from me and dance with him. It's my own damn fault for waiting to tell her what I was doing this morning. I just needed to follow through first.

"Eve," I plead.

"I get it." Her false smile lags before falling into place. "It's fine."

"I sent a text."

"You know what text no one wants to get? Any variation of 'we need to talk.'" Her eyes flare as they fix on me. There's also that damn fake smile of hers. Fuck. She's hiding again, hiding from me. "Like I said, I get it. You don't do relationships. We said we shouldn't sleep together when we first discussed this. I could have said no, I had that choice. If you want to go back to New York and work, that's fine."

I spin her around to get out of the way of someone who's turned the slow song into a whirling swing dance. "I'm not going back. Can we talk? I can explain. It wasn't something I could have explained over text. And you haven't been sleeping well. I didn't want to wake you up."

"Five minutes. I'll give you five minutes."

"I'll make them worth it," I promise.

The song stops and I take her hand to lead her out of the gym. We rush past lockers and the open doors of classrooms where teams are assembling signs.

"Wasting your five minutes on a tour?" she asks as I pull her along.

"Based on the conversation we're about to have, I thought you'd value privacy, unless we want everyone in our business via text chain within the next hour."

It should be here somewhere. I'm not very familiar with the layout because I never went to school here myself, but I've come to enough practice festivals over the years. Around the next corner I find the door I'm looking for. I test the knob to find that it's unlocked. After a twist and a push, I walk into the dark room then pat along the wall for a light switch.

"Supply closet, very classy," Evelyn says. She steps in behind me with her arms crossed defiantly over her chest.

"If you want, I bet the cafeteria is unoccupied but I didn't want to waste any more time."

Evelyn strides past me to an empty bucket, which she grabs and turns over to use as a chair. She crosses jean clad legs and folds her arms over her chest. It isn't lost on me that she's wearing the sweater I gave her last week.

I don't know what it means that she still chose to wear it despite being upset with me, but I want to.

"Did you go to the office this morning to meet with your boss about getting back to work?" she asks.

I can't blame her for the assumption. It was all I had wanted when we first ran into each other in Alina's driveway.

"That's where I was," I start, and her face falls. I walk over to her in two quick steps. My knees fall to the hard ground. "I went there to quit."

"Huh?"

"I went to the city so I could quit in person. I met with Holt and put in my notice. That's what I was doing this morning. That's why I left and couldn't explain over the phone because I didn't want to tell you until it was done and I was standing in front of you and could have this conversation." The words fall out in a rush. I need her to know, but also there's this electric feeling that comes with the adrenaline of it all.

"You quit your job for me?"

"No, I quit my job because I should have left a long time ago. Talking to Lana got to me. She's living a life she can't shut up about. I've been going through life without living it like I was playing out some self-imposed sentence," I explain. "And yesterday you showed me how good it could feel to go for what I want. I was happy making music for years. I want that again. Actually, I want more than that, because now when I think of music, I also think of making it with you."

She reaches out to cup my cheek and I lean into her touch. I'm here on my knees praying she won't give up on me. "Does that mean…"

"Yes, I want you. Only you. All of you."

"And you're not freaking out." Her voice breaks into a quiver. "Because I am still freaking out. Because you say that and I feel like there's this nonstop earthquake and I'm the only one experiencing it."

I put my hand over where hers is resting on my face. My thumb rubs against her knuckles. My eyes latch onto hers as I say, "I'm fucking terrified. But I know that's because what happened between us mattered. You matter so damn much to me, Evelyn. I drove to the city scared out of my mind that when I came back you'd be okay with keeping things the exact same. But I had it in my head that if I quit then at least I was doing something right for myself. For the record, I would never run away from you. If anything, I'm running from myself. I see all of you and that's a fucking gift. With you, things make sense."

I spent so long running from her. So long doing everything I could to keep her at a healthy distance. I'm done with that. Running back to her is all I ever want to do from here on out.

"Garrett." She nods and her face finally softens. "That makes me feel a bit better, but I'm not sure if that's the shock. Promise me one thing. If you leave, make sure not to give me a cryptic text that leads me to question everything."

"I promise."

"What happened to your feelings never changing?" she asks, and for the first time today, I'm gifted with a genuine smile from her.

"Well, that's what happens when you go assuming you know exactly how I feel."

"You…" I've made her speechless and I might deserve some sort of award for achieving that.

"Have felt this way about you before you walked up Alina's driveway and crashed my vacation. Evelyn, you get under my fucking skin, but I want you there. I need your dumb T-shirts and jokes that you make up just to make me uncomfortable because when you're next to me, well, I breathe easier too," I say. With each word her expression brightens, until her eyes blaze with emotion. "When I'm with you, I don't feel like I'm falling behind."

"Well, if we're making confessions. I do have a folder of photos of you on my phone from this trip and no matter how hard I tried…none of them turned out ugly."

I can't help but laugh.

"So, we're together," she confirms.

"We are," I say, and her smile grows.

"And you were jealous when you saw Oliver dancing with me?"

"Yes."

"You don't need to be. I just want to make that clear."

I squeeze her hand. "Well, I was and I needed to touch you."

"You're barely touching me now," she says, her voice lowering.

"Should I be doing more? You already have me on my knees."

"That's a stupid fucking question, Larson."

My hands sweep up her sides, and she starts to strip off the sweater, revealing a sheer blue lace bra. Her legs spread and

I press my body into the space she's created for me. Space here, space in the future. I'm not under the illusion that things are perfect, but maybe this right here can be a small type of perfect.

"Tell me what you need," I murmur into the soft skin of her stomach.

"Convince me all over again that you were always going to come back. Show me exactly what you would have missed if you didn't."

"These." I cup one of her breasts then press my mouth to the other, swiping my tongue over the lace straining against her peaked nipple. "I fucking would have dreamed every night about these."

She moans arching into me. "What else?"

I start to work at the button of her jeans. "Stand up and I'll show you."

The bucket she was sitting on scrapes against the floor. Her hands press into my shoulders as she rises. She starts to move them.

"Stop. Keep your hands on me, you might need a little help standing," I tell her as I pull down the jeans over the curve of her ass. Lifting my hand, I ghost my fingers over the thin cotton covering her pussy. I pull back and her fingers dig into my shoulders, as if she's fighting the urge not to touch herself. Instead of teasing her more, I pull down her underwear.

"Touch me, Garrett, please, fucking touch me," she begs.

"How can I say no now that you've asked twice?" I ask, lowering my head to settle between her thighs. The flat of my tongue swipes along her and she lets out a muffled sound. I stop then press a kiss to the rise of her hip.

I continue the progression across the plane of her stomach. She squirms, so when I press my thumb to her clit she starts to rub against it. I make slow circles as I feel her continue to get wet. My hand sinks lower to cup her.

"I would have missed this, Eve. I would have missed how you turn me on with every sound you make. I would have missed seeing my fingers fuck you," I say, punctuating my words with a finger slipping into her. I put my mouth to better use than talking as I lap at her clit.

"You're such a good fucking boy. Maybe you're allowed to send me stupid texts if you apologize like this," she groans out.

I like that. God. My cock stiffens pressing harder against the fabric of my pants. I want to earn that from her again and again.

One of her hands leaves my shoulder to tangle in my hair. She moans as she pulls on the strands and a pleasant shock of pain zips through me.

I sink another finger into her then curl, pressing against her walls. Her hips buck forward, and my free hand grips her ass, fingers creating divots in her soft skin.

She begins to quake. "Like that, exactly. Oh. Like that."

I want her to give me everything. I want to give and give, so when she gets what she wants, I'll know I was the one responsible.

Eve sits on my lap to get as close as possible. I like her this way. I've been pulled to the face painting station to act as another test subject for Evelyn's attempts at honing her skills before the festival. After our time in the closet, I was called back on stage to run through the songs I skipped out on. I should have known that Alina would have insisted. It was worth it.

Around us, most of the vendors are breaking down their stations since there's barely any food left. With the musical acts wrapped up, '90s rock hits crackle through the ancient sound system.

"What are you painting?" I ask as Evelyn nibbles on the end of her cheap paint brush.

Using her thumb and forefinger she moves my head from side to side for inspection. "Hearts for now, but I'm thinking about putting my name all over you."

"Any particular reason?"

"Because it's a bit more subtle than yelling that you're mine from the rooftops."

"I appreciate your self-restraint. But if you wanted to, you could. It wouldn't be too much," I tell her. "You're never too much."

"There's the other fact that I'd have to stop touching you to go up to said rooftops."

"Smart choice. I like you where you are." I pull her closer which causes her to drop her hand. When I have her where I want her, I run my nose along her neck until I reach the collar of the sweater and I plant a kiss there. Delighted laughter bubbles out of her.

"I thought so. Now hold still," she commands then leans back.

She dots the brush into the paint then grabs my face again. The brush is cool as it swirls across my skin. It's an effort not to kiss her again right on those lips that are parted in concentration. After a few more brush strokes she gets more paint and deposits more hearts on my face. Once she's done she leans back and nearly tips off my lap. My hand steadies her.

"Almost," she says as her eyes narrow. A spark lights her eyes and she smiles. In a swift motion her body dips down then she presses her finger into the paint then swipes it messily on her lips. She leans in, planting her lips firmly on my forehead then moves to either side like she's working a stamp. She does it again and again. A smile tears across my face, growing wider with each kiss.

When she's done, red is smeared all over her soft lips. Using my thumb, I swipe some of it away. I paint the remnants on my own lips and return the favor. The marks are faint where I've pressed them to the apples of her cheeks.

"How do I look?" I ask.

"Like mine."

38

Evelyn

"I can't believe you drove to Manhattan and grabbed a chess board," I tease as I lose again. I don't care, losing to him is winning in my book if it means we can spend time together.

It's been two days since he went to the city. The last two mornings he's had to spend taking phone calls with clients. A benefit of his recent vacation is that many of them have been working with other associates and partners at his firm so the transition will be less painful.

During this time, I've headed off with Quinn and Oliver. This morning, we left Hartsfall on a mission to visit where they filmed *Dirty Dancing*, only to realize part way through the drive that it was actually filmed in North Carolina and Virginia. Still, we ended up going on a gondola ride at one of the expensive resorts in the area.

"I had to change outfits since I was going to meet with my boss. Well, ex-boss. I grabbed it so we could play here," he explains and starts to reset the board. The pieces are metal, bronze and silver instead of white and black, and the board is painted to look like marble. My heart keens knowing that even when he was in the middle of changing his life, he was always intending on coming back and sharing this with me.

"What's next? After you have everything with your clients ironed out."

"I still technically have an agent to help with the occasional deal for our music in movies and my likeness being used for things. I'll probably reach out to her. I still don't know what I want this to look like. The first time around I was part of something, one of four people making the decisions. I was never alone in it." He puts the final piece into place. "You go first."

I take my first move and advance a pawn. Garrett quickly follows by moving his own pawn.

"You don't have to be alone in it. If you want me there, like we've been, I'm in."

"Have you decided what you want to do with your contract?" he asks.

My stomach sinks as I pick up one of my knights. "Not yet. In the mean time all I want is to enjoy making this album."

My fingers hover as I consider my next move then I reach for my next piece.

"Wait," Garrett says, stopping me before I make my selection.

"What is it?"

"If you make that move the game will end."

"After two moves you can't be serious," I say in disbelief, but even so I pull back from the pawn.

"You move that piece and you give me a direct path for my queen." My eyes snap to the board and trace the path he's indicating when I look up his lips tug upward. "It's called a Fool's Mate. Or maybe you might be more familiar with the name Fool's Gambit."

"Are you telling me you named the band?"

"I might have made a suggestion."

"And you chose a losing move?"

"It's a move that makes you vulnerable. A risk. Sometimes you need to be brave enough to dream," he says with a wistfulness that sounds like a memory.

Without hesitating, I pick up the piece and place it how I intended. Garrett counters with his Queen but from the gleam in his eye I know we're on the same page. A risk worth taking. A dream worth having.

We continue to play. Well, I continue to lose over and over again while Garrett humors my efforts.

"What will you give me when I finally win?" I ask as I give in for the evening and reset the board a final time.

"So you can redeem it in a hundred years?"

"Rude." I press my foot against his under the table.

He presses back, his eyes intensifying. "I'll give you whatever you want."

"You're a brave man."

"Based on the fact I'm already prepared to give you anything you want, I think I'll survive."

"You don't really mean that. What if I ask you to grow a mustache or be a part of a flash mob?"

"Okay, you might have a point. Mustache maybe. Flash mob, I think those should never have been invented and I would happily live in a timeline without them."

I throw my head back in a laugh as my phone chimes with an incoming text message.

Oliver

Do you have a minute?

Instead of texting back, I immediately call. Last time he played this exact scenario out, he was in the ER. He wasn't hurt but his roommate's appendix had burst and he was trying to manage all of it by himself.

"I'll be right back." The words rush out of me as I climb to my feet. I nearly topple over, but catch myself on the arm of the couch because my leg feels like TV static after falling asleep from how I've been sitting.

I press the call button as I teeter into the hall and Oliver picks up on the first ring.

"You didn't have to call," Oliver says by way of greeting.

"Knowing you, you're likely trying to act as a first responder without any training, so I think I did," I say. It's part of the reason we've always complemented each other. Neither of us like asking for help, but the other would always know exactly when it was needed.

"I was CPR certified." He pauses for a moment.

"Ten years ago, when you were a camp counselor," I say. "What's going on?"

"Quinn's period hit and you know how bad it gets the first few days," he says.

Quinn has endometriosis. Her cramps and nausea can keep her in bed for days, especially if she doesn't have all the small things with her. They don't make the pain go away, but definitely better.

"Shit. Do you need me to go to the store?" I ask as a grocery list starts to form in my mind. Even with birth control and painkillers that help with the worst of her symptoms, Quinn frequently called out of work sick.

"I'm at the store, but when I got here I realized I have no idea what she regularly uses and she was asleep when I left so I don't want to ask her. I've been standing in front of a wall of tampons and pads for ten minutes." His words cause me to smile because who else would rush out like that without batting an eye to pick up feminine care products? I know it's because of all of his younger sisters, but not every brother is like that.

"I'll meet you there, give me a few minutes and I'll make sure we get everything she might need," I say before hanging up.

Garrett is studying the chess board as I reenter the living room.

"I need to go run a quick errand with Oliver. Will you be here when I get back?"

"Of course." He nods. "Go."

Oliver is still standing in front of the pads and tampons when I find him at the small grocery store. The grocery basket slung on his arm is empty. His expression eases the moment he spots me.

"Thanks for coming," he says. "I'm seriously blanking. I actually loaded up with the stuff I'd usually grab for Kate and Yosalin, but then remembered that's not who I'm getting anything for."

I inspect the aisle for a moment searching for the exact brand that Quinn prefers as well as the size. "These. Super plus is what she needs on the first few days. Let's grab some dark chocolate and see if they have a heating pad."

We find a heating pad a bit further down the aisle because all the health items are all in one spot. The box doesn't fit in the basket, so I carry it as we start walking toward the candy section.

"You've always been a good boyfriend," I say, then try to back track. "Shit. I mean, not everyone would come out and do this. I know you're chill with it, but I know it must still mean a lot to her."

It's taken years for me to put words to it, why Oliver and I could still be friends after the break up. Really, we just wanted someone to belong with. We gave each other the stability that we didn't have in our families, but had proven through our friendship we could provide to each other. We found that stability again after, even if it looked slightly different. But he made me realize wanting to belong with someone isn't enough of a reason to actually be with someone. It's haunted me a bit, made me second guess what my future will look like.

In some ways, being Lyla has been a crutch. Being her lets me always have a reason to question my relationships, hold back just enough to evaluate if I'm scratching an itch or actually falling. With Garrett, without that crutch, I think I finally am.

"It's okay." He laughs. "This is odd, isn't it?"

"Yeah." I laugh, relieved we can admit it.

"I feel like we skipped past the awkward stage and it's finally crept up on us."

"All at once," I add.

"When we're finally with other people," he says.

"Was it really not weird for you? It was for me, at least for a while, and then you just seemed fine and I guess it helped me feel fine," I say.

"I mean, I wasn't." Oliver's voice turns scratchy. "I watched my dad implode so many times and let us all scramble to keep everything together while he forgot to get groceries and shit. So, I guess I just shut down. I didn't want to be him, so I wasn't."

There would be nights when we were out having the best time and the energy would be high until Oliver got a call from his dad. He'd walk outside for half an hour and then pretend he was okay, like he didn't have his father needing to lean on him for emotional support at the slightest inconvenience. Quinn and I would always work harder to bring up the energy after, not to make him forget, but more to say *"we see you, and we're here."* With Oliver's need to be the happiest person in the room we tried to compensate so he didn't feel like he had to do it all alone.

I should have realized that was exactly what he was doing for me; instead, I used it when it was convenient. I knew he would act happy, the same way I have so many times, and pretended he was actually okay because that's what I needed to think.

"I'm sorry," I apologize, knowing no matter how many times I do it will never be enough.

"I know you are," he acknowledges. "You were back then too."

The two of us turn the corner and walk past vibrant packages of sour candies and the jumbo bags that are on display for Halloween. There are five options for dark chocolate with varying percentages of cacao.

"Talking to Quinn about it is what helped in the end," he says as we stand side by side reading the labels. "Not that we were together or anything. Especially not back then. But you know how she is, cutting through the bullshit and saying what you need to hear."

"We're definitely better for it. How many times would we have been left without the extra dipping sauce we ordered?"

"She saved us from such tragic fates." He looks at me and we share a tender look before shifting our attention back to the chocolate. "But yeah, she basically told me that if I wanted it to work I could and to not ignore emotions so they didn't go nuclear."

"I'm happy we have her and I hope she'll be happy to have this chocolate," I say as I grab a bar to stop stalling.

At the checkout I insist on paying even though Oliver tries to slide the cashier his card. He might be Quinn's boyfriend, but I'm the best friend who hasn't been there to step up for a while.

39

Evelyn

Garrett is slightly drunk on sleep, and he tries to hold onto me as I get up.

"Where are you going?" he asks. His voice is rough from disuse. A new part of him that I've been happy to collect. Sometimes, I compare the image I had of him before I came to Hartsfall with the one I have now. It reminds me a bit of an artist comparing old work to what they're capable of now. The first image rough with potential. The more recent work vibrant and fleshed out.

"The inn to check on Quinn." Instead of going to the closet to get fresh clothes, I grab his button down from the floor. I pull it over my shoulders and button it most of the way up, leaving the top few undone for a relaxed look.

"You could grab a clean one," he says as he surveys me.

"But this one smells like you."

"Are you saying I smell?"

"Good." I crawl onto the bed and press a kiss to his mouth. "Your three-hundred-dollar cologne is doing some heavy lifting."

He shakes his head. He's not wearing his glasses, so his eyes are slightly unfocused. Morning Garrett. A new version of him I get to cherish. "Five hundred."

"Of course it is." I go back to getting dressed, hopping into my jeans and searching for matching socks in the dresser. "I was going to ask them if they wanted to go on a day trip to Manhattan. I'm assuming you have stuff in your office to clean out, so if there's a day that's best…"

"Let me know what they say. I'll tell Holt I'll be in the area."

I go to Love is Brewing to get ginger tea for Quinn. We used to stock up on it in our apartment for this reason. I also grab a coffee for Oliver and a matcha for myself.

The inn has massive rose gardens fanning out along its sides. Stone paths wind through the flowers and the benches that are spread out at regular intervals. It's the exact type of place I can imagine someone renting out for a wedding.

No one is at the front desk inside. I wait five minutes before peering around the corner to where I hear casual chatter and the clinking of utensils on plates. In what appears to be a dining area, I spot a familiar redhead with springy curls is speed-walking around the dining area to drop off orders. After she slides a steaming plate of pancakes and sausage onto a white linen draped table her eyes flick to me.

"Hey! I'll be right with you," Poppy chimes with an enthusiasm that is at least a little bit because of the rush she's in. She does another lap collecting plates, darts through a swinging door that I assume is to the kitchen, and then finally strides to me.

"You're not checking in, right?" Her eyes flicker with uncertainty. "I didn't see anything on the reservation books for today."

"Sorry. No. I was just wondering if I can get these delivered to a friend? I wanted them to be a surprise," I say.

The man at the table closest to us knocks a mug onto the floor with his elbow and the entire room goes silent for a heartbeat before returning to its steady murmur of conversation. Poppy is doing her best not to wince through her customer service mask.

"Quinn and Oliver? You were at my pottery class with them the other day right and at the festival prep?" she asks as her eyes fix on the mess on the floor. There was little coffee in the mug, but porcelain shards are strewn across the carpet.

"Yeah."

"Okay. I shouldn't do this but we're understaffed and fully booked. Garrett likes you too and that's good enough for me. Room 8. It's at the end of the hall on the first floor."

Thank God for small towns.

"Thanks." The word isn't fully out of my mouth before Poppy is headed to start cleaning the mess.

The flight of stairs up to the first set of rooms is lined with paintings of flowers in gold and brass frames. My steps are muffled by the thick burgundy carpet that starts on the second floor. Each of the rooms are marked with a gold number and they all have actual keyhole locks instead of electronic ones.

I knock when I reach the door at the end of the hall. After a moment I hear the familiar sound of Oliver's voice. "It's probably just housekeeping. I'll tell them we'll be inside all day so they don't come back if you're sleeping or something."

The door opens and Oliver fills the gap with his body. He's in sweats and wearing blue light glasses that have that yellowish tint, so he must be doing work. There's a second before he seems to register that it's me and not housekeeping and he nearly shuts the door.

"Ev. Wow," he stammers then pulls the door a little more closed. "Didn't expect you to stop by."

"Well, I still need to pick up the clothes you guys borrowed from the other night and I brought ginger tea. I forgot to tell you to get it while we were at the store," I say and hold up the drink carrier. "Brought you something too, didn't want you to be left out."

"Thanks."

"Is everything okay?" I ask. I rise up onto my toes to look over Oliver's shoulder. A bolt of confusion courses through me when I spot two full beds. "What—"

"Oh, thank God." Quinn joins us and forces the door open. She's in an oversized shirt, and probably shorts, but the shirt is so long that it hovers at mid-thigh. A hand is propped on her lower back, a sign that her cramps are still giving her hell.

"Here." I hold out the cup with her tea and she grabs it greedily.

"Hmm," she hums with the first sip. "If you were to ask me to drink this medicinal tasting shit any other time I'd hate it, but while my uterus is actively out to kill me, it is my favorite thing in the world."

"Can I stay for a bit? Watch TV or something?" I ask. Since dinner a few nights ago I've been hoping to spend more time with just the three of us, just to see how things are without Garrett as a buffer. If I do go back to Nashville, it'll be the three of us. With Garrett's work situation up in the air I know he could join me, but that would be too much to ask. Still, after the last few days of writing with him, I'm more conflicted than ever. It's addictive. I want to write like this with him over and over again.

Quinn waves me in. "Sure."

A low-budget Christmas rom-com is frozen on the screen, the female lead encountering a smalltown baker/carpenter/coffee shop owner. Quinn climbs on the bed then repositions the hot pad Oliver and I got her last night so it's under her back. In the far corner, Oliver's computer is set up on a massive oak writing desk. Then there's the second bed which has obviously been used. Did Quinn not want to sleep next to him last night? I know some people like to sleep alone, but I know that's not the case for either of them.

"Can I?" I ask, pointing to the empty bed.

"Go for it," Oliver says as he pulls the chair from his desk to face the TV.

"Did they have too many beds or something?" I ask, gesturing between where Quinn and I are reclining. Okay, so maybe bulldoze right into a conversation.

"It's what they had available. A shame, but we're making do. Isn't that right, sweetpea?" Oliver maintains his usual playful lilt to the pet name he calls her, but there's something unreadable in the shift of his eyes.

Quinn shakes her head. "That's not what happened."

"What?" I ask just as Oliver says, "Quinn…"

"No. I'm tired of this. I'm tired of you calling me terrible food nicknames," Quinn snaps.

Oliver frantically glances between Quinn and me, eyes wide and words flying out of him. "We should have talked about this."

"I tried to. I didn't want to do this in the first place, but you were the one who grabbed my hand. You were the one who said it would be best to make it less awkward. But I've been so stressed that my period came late. When were you planning on stopping anyway? A month? A year?" Quinn demands.

"I bet there's a jewelry shop around here, who says we need to stop? I mean, it would cut down on rent to move in together." Oliver shrugs.

"Should I go?" I look between them, feeling the need to bolt as tension boils over.

"No," Quinn says to me before her attention returns to Oliver. "Be serious."

"Fine. I was impulsive, but it worked, right?" he counters.

I hold my hands up to stop whatever's going on before I get even more lost. "Can we slow the hell down. What's worked?"

"Us pretending to date," Quinn says.

Pretending? That's what this is? But…I scramble to re-structure the last week around this new information. Quinn's insistence on leaving the other night. The hushed discussions.

All the moments of hesitancy and discomfort that I misread as them not knowing how to act around me, were them putting on an act.

"Great minds think alike." The words slip out as my brain plays a game of connect-the-dots in the shape of our current reality.

"What?" Quinn and Oliver ask in near unison. Quinn's face pinches with confusion while Oliver's features brighten with excitement.

"Shit." I never planned on telling them Garrett's and my relationship wasn't real. I really wish I could rewind the last ten seconds. "Well, that's how Garrett and I started."

"How you *started*? But now?" Oliver presses.

"Yeah. We're together." I bite down on my smile. "Very much, very real."

"When did that change?"

"We got together the night of the blackout and then again." I blush and I can't help but be excited that we're back to talking about things like this. "We talked at the carnival and it was all good."

"Don't tell me that you hooked up in a classroom. There are cameras in there," says Quinn, practical as ever.

I shake my head. "Supply closet."

"The classier option, obviously," Oliver asserts.

"So, the beds?" I cock my head, still waiting on an answer.

"The plan was to come here, hang out, and have a real vacation. They only had one room but, luckily, everyone else wanted the ones with one bed. Couples destination and all that," Quinn explains, "thus the fake dating ordeal."

"Dating me isn't an ordeal," Oliver complains, shoulders sagging.

Quinn continues. "It was partly because you sent all those pictures from the berry farm and there was that picture of the two of you in it. It was supposed to be a backup plan, but Oliver, here, got a bit trigger-happy and jumped the gun before we were sure about the situation."

"If you didn't come to tell me about you two being together then what would the vacation be for?" I ask.

"Come on. We miss you," Oliver says.

Quinn shrugs. "Maybe we should have told you, an ambush obviously didn't work the way we planned, but you've been averaging mostly one-word responses or just sending thumbs up emojis. I took the time off months ago, just in case you wanted to invite us up to New York for your birthday."

Everything she's saying hits me right in the soft tissue of my heart. I pushed them away. I gave them a good excuse to let me fade. Obviously, they've had each other, even if platonically; still, they came after me.

"What the hell did you do the other night with the guest room?" I ask, remembering a night that was good for me, but as I'm learning theirs is a very different story.

"I slept in the bathtub. With a pillow and a blanket, it's not that bad." Oliver says, then rubs the back of his neck.

"Oh my gosh." A laugh launches out of me. This is all so stupid, the lengths we've all gone to are so fucking ridiculous.

My phone vibrates in my pocket.

Helping Alina with groceries. Probably will
get roped into rehearsing a bit. Let me
know when you get back and I'll come over
if you want me to.

I will and I do.

Anxiety funnels into my thoughts. Garrett and I have talked about us. We're official. This revelation about Quinn and Oliver shouldn't change anything. Still, that's not a conversation I know how to have.

"That him?" Quinn asks, suggestiveness dripping from her voice.

"Yeah, he's just checking in."

"I don't feel weird about it," Oliver reassures me. "Just so you know."

"I don't either," I tell him.

"Wow. You know what I love? Communication. Imagine. We could have just had this conversation a week ago and I wouldn't have had to live through Oliver calling me food themed nicknames," Quinn says.

"You know, cannibalism is a common metaphor for love," I say.

Oliver throws out a flailing gesture that I assume is supposed to mean something along the lines of *See!*

"Damn. I wish I had someone eating me," Quinn deadpans as she presses the play button to start the movie, setting the meet-cute back in motion.

"Is this the one where she sleeps with her boss' twin brother?" Oliver asks, leaning forward so his elbows rest on his knees.

"No this is the one where she's the twin of his ex-fiancée," Quinn says, eyes locked on a scene I know she's watched a dozen times.

"My bad, wrong twin plot contrivance."

"Honest mistake," I say. "Happens to the best of us."

It's a simple thing, a TV show we've watched before. Commentary we're repeating for the hundredth time. Moments that shouldn't mean anything. But to me, I know we're one step closer to who we were.

But there's one thing getting in the way of crossing the remaining distance. Me.

No matter how much I want to stay after the movie is done, I leave. I need to find a solution. I can't lose them again.

40

Garrett

I'm glued to my seat with my cello resting between my thighs until Alina and I run through the entire festival setlist. It used to be an hour, but gradually we've shaved off a few songs, now it's just over thirty minutes.

"Follow me on the last notes. If the crowd wants more, I'll hold it. I'll show them exactly what this old lady can do," she corrects.

"Of course," I readily agree.

Alina has mellowed through the years. Journalists still list her in articles about classic divas through the generations. If she wants to opt up in a song or hold a note just because she can, she will.

"I have a few meetings this week to finish helping my clients transition, but otherwise I should be free to rehearse."

"Unless you're with your girl."

"We're probably going to go to the city. I'll make sure to stop by that bakery and grab you those macarons and croissants you like." It's her one request. She says they remind her of the ones she had in Paris, a taste of a different time. A time when she had the world in the palm of her hand.

"I say good riddance to that part of your life," she scoffs. "The sooner you're done, the better."

"You don't have to say that just to make me feel better. I know how much you invested to help me through St. George's."

"You think I care about that?" she scoffs.

"It's what you helped set me up to do" I say, mostly to myself.

It was the plan. Get out of Hartsfall, be the best, find something that shows I was worthy of all the opportunities that I'd been given.

"You act like music was a pit stop, not a destination. I taught you how to carry a tune. It was my whole career. You think I cared if that's all you did? You were chasing a dream. Dreams like that are rare and you treated it like it was anything else," she says, running her hand lovingly across the surface of the piano.

"This is the first time you've said that."

"And if I said it before? Hmm?" she presses and starts toward the couch. "You had those ideas drilled into you. *You have to be something. You have to give back to us.* Foolish boy. Love isn't a debt you have to repay. You give it and maybe some finds you. Maybe Lana coming back has messed with your head." Scorn blankets her words as she sits. "I was more than happy to tell her to never knock on my door again."

I jerk back at this, I'd assumed she knew the same way everyone already knows, but I should have guessed she looked for me here first. "You didn't say she stopped by here."

"Where do you think she came first? I only talked to tell her to go away. But she seemed to slither right to you," she says in a huff.

"Well, she's gone for good now." I search for a tinge of regret and fail to find it. I doubt I'll ever be truly free of Lana, that would be erasing a part of myself that would undermine so much good. Despite her faults, even if unintentionally, she gave me Hartsfall.

"I'm happy that you are taking life by the balls."

"Alina," I cough out.

"I said it. Live with it. Now, do that last song again," she prompts.

We play through "Put Your Head on My Shoulder" two more times. The only reason I don't get asked to do a third is because my phone starts to ring.

"Yeah?" I ask wearily.

"I have a favor to ask," Fletcher says, without greeting.

"Another old Volkswagen?"

"It's Annie, she's got a stomach bug and can't make it to Butter Half for her shift. I normally wouldn't ask if it was a slower season," he says.

I know what he means, it's fall and everything has been booked out. Most businesses are struggling to keep up with demand.

"If there's no one else, then I can stop in for a bit," I say.

"There really isn't."

"Thought so, I'll head over."

I've stepped in over the years at plenty of the shops and businesses around town. First, it was because Lana would miss shifts and I was trying to make it up to the business owners who went out on a limb to hire her, despite her reputation for being unreliable. As I grew older, it gave me a comfort that even if I didn't fit somewhere specifically, I could step in as needed.

I text Evelyn that I'll be at Butter Half, but I don't get a response by the time I arrive at the cafe. There is a line of people trailing around the corner waiting for an available table. I give a nod to the hostess before heading to the back and grabbing a spare apron and server notepad.

The tide of business drags me in. I carry hot plates loaded with the special, eggs benedict and bacon, refill the diner-style mugs over and over with the house roast coffee. Time loses meaning in the familiar monotony. It's past two when the shift lead asks me if I can roll silverware before I head out. I walk out from the back to find an empty table to sit at as I work. The crowd has subsided, and the outside patio has closed since dark clouds have rolled in.

"Hey, didn't know you'd be here," Oliver says, looking up from his menu. Quinn is seated across from him sipping tea, but there's no third menu.

"Yeah, just helping out for the lunch rush." I prop the bin of silverware on my hip as I settle into the conversation.

"Glad we missed the crowd." Quinn folds her menu and places it to the side.

"Good to see you're doing okay. Evelyn told me she went to see you earlier," I say.

Oliver's brows inch up his forehead. "Oh, she told you?"

"Of course. Why wouldn't she?" I ask.

Quinn lets out an exaggerated breath. "Thank God. I was hoping she would tell you. I'm too tired to keep pretending to be dating Ollie. I just want a shit ton of bacon and a nap."

"Can you please stop acting like dating me was the worst thing to happen to you?" Oliver winces. Poor guy. "I'm an excellent fake boyfriend."

Fake.

My expression falls. "What?"

"Yeah, there was never anything between us. We just did it to make you two feel comfortable," Oliver explains, and his good humored expression makes me feel like I'm in a fun house.

My grip tightens on the bin causing the edge to dig into my fingers. That doesn't make any sense. But if that's true…God. If Oliver cared enough about Evelyn to fake a relationship, then who knows how he still feels about her. He's the better option. They have history. They built a life together. Hell, they were engaged. I can't promise her the same simple things that she knows she can get with him.

My throat tightens as I feel history repeating. There's always someone better. Always a person more worthy of their time. I'm just a pit stop that tricked itself into getting used to the idea of something permanent.

"Where is she?" I croak.

Quinn and Oliver share a glance then Oliver says, "I think she went on a hike on that trail you guys missed out on a few days ago."

The words are barely out of his mouth before I'm dashing back to the kitchen and apologizing as I put down the bin of silverware. It's not real until I hear her say it.

Until then, she's still mine.

41

Evelyn

"I need more time," I say. The remains of a crumbling log crunch under my sneaker as I walk through it and further up the trail. The ground is littered with fallen leaves, softening the sound of my footsteps. Overhead the clouds have completely claimed the sky and rain has started to fall and darken the earth.

"I—" Vincent sighs and a lump forms in my throat.

"Please."

"Evelyn, I want to give it to you, but you know I'm not the one making the calls. Reverb has been breathing down my neck as is, waiting for the album and for you to agree to take Lyla public." He sounds exhausted. He's done so much for me already, still I'm desperate for this.

"I just need a few months. That's it. I need to be able to get some things figured out first." The words come out in a flurry and heat builds behind my eyes. I'm alone on the trail, so at least there's no one to see me cry over my own stupid decisions.

All I am is pathetic, begging for a chance to do damage control.

"I'll see what I can do. No promises," Vincent says, and I know he'll ask even if we both know the answer.

We've reached the point of no return and it's all my fault.

The first year of being Lyla West was a dream. I was on top of the world, feeling I tricked an industry well known for exploitation. I had my friends, and I had music; neither had to impact the other. God, I was so stupid. So stupid and naïve. I didn't trick anyone, except myself into believing that it would work. And ever since I've felt like I've been trying to win a race, but I'm the only participant. So, even if I win, I'm also destined to lose.

I had so many chances back then to say something. But now, even if my career choice doesn't change things between me and the people I care about the most, I can't change that I've spent years hiding things from them. What's worse is I don't know if I can let music go. Then there's this part of me that's desperate for the damage to be worth it, for it all to work out because if it doesn't, that's further proof of how stupid I was in the first place.

I just need to—

My phone chimes.

Quinn

Kind of fucked up

Thought you told Garrett already

"Shit." My toe catches on a rock sending me sprawling. Rough earth digs into my knees, my skin stinging. My phone flies from my hand, tumbling down the trail and thudding against a protruding boulder. A laugh rips from my throat, ugly and feral. Hot tears leak from my eyes, mixing with the cold rain that has started to pick up in intensity.

Of course. If I'm not careful I'll prove my mom right and get lost out here too. Now, wouldn't that be the perfect way to end the day? I don't bother getting up. I just keep letting out my emotions until my throat is scratched raw and my jacket is fully dampened with rain.

The thudding of rapidly approaching footsteps breaks the moment and I go silent as my heart races. This is a popular trail, but with the gloomy weather I haven't seen anyone else out here. I'm alone out here and whoever is coming my way is moving fast. I scramble on my hands and knees to retrieve my phone. Shit.

"If you are a serial killer, please give me a head start! I just had a shitty phone call, so if you could give me a fighting chance that would be great," I say, still a bit slap-happy from being battered by the current state of my life.

A shadowy form turns the corner, and my damn body stays in place.

Move Evelyn. Move.

"Evelyn, why the fuck would you say that if you really thought I was a serial killer? Do you have a fucking death wish?" Garrett says. His chest heaves as he gasps for breath. Damp strands of hair are plastered to his forehead. And speckles of rain have collected on the lenses of his glasses.

"What the hell are you doing here?" I ask, then my attention lands on his clothing. "Are you wearing an apron?"

"I came from Butter Half. I ran into—"

"Quinn and Oliver, I heard." *Shit. Shit. Shit.*

He closes the distance between us, his hands coming up to cup my cheeks. There's a frantic, almost feverish, look in his eyes I've never seen before.

"I'd get it," he says then takes a deep inhale. "I need you to know that I'd understand if you chose him. But I really don't want you to and maybe I'm a terrible person for saying this, but I can't fucking lose you, Eve." The words rush out of him in a torrent like now that he has his hands on me he can no longer contain them. And he's saying my name in that way that makes me feel like the center of his universe. "Not now that I have you after so long. I can't. Give me a chance."

My hand falls over his. "I don't understand?"

"Oliver's single and you're out here in the woods by yourself? Of course you're considering it."

"Garrett, look at me," I say. "You said you wanted to be with me. Did that change?"

"I do, but that doesn't mean you owe me anything. I want you to be happy and I want you to stay, but I won't assume those are the same thing." He shakes his head and squints his eyes shut as he spirals, that logical mind of his battling his desires.

"This is me telling you that me being with you and me being happy are the same thing," I say calmly.

This man, who is so used to being left behind, thought it was happening again and ran to me in the pouring rain to tell me this. He thought he wasn't enough, even though he's the only thing keeping me intact. I make a silent promise to myself that even if it's the last thing I do, I'll make him see that he is worth staying for. Worth keeping.

My heart melts in my chest. I wish I could carve it out and hand it to him so he could see how completely it belongs to him.

"And I want to believe that. But he's a guy you've literally written love songs about. He's stable and good. Fuck," he says, pressing his forehead against mine. "I hate that I like the guy, but I do. And the only reason I have to hate him is because he has a shot with you."

"He doesn't have a shot with me. That's what I'm trying to tell you," I insist. "And you're right. I came here for something like that. But I was wrong, I was chasing disaster. Despite that, I found you. Maybe you're not used to it, maybe I need to say it more, but Garrett, you're the only person on my mind. Maybe you're used to people walking away. But I've told you a time or two that I'm a bit obsessive, and I'm completely and utterly consumed by you." I reach up and swipe at a damp strand of his hair. "I'm pretty damn sure you're my happiest possible ending."

"You really think I can give you that? Your happiest possible ending?"

"Yes. There is no one better for me than you." I barely utter the word before his lips crush against mine. His tongue coaxes my mouth open then glides against mine.

I pull back for a moment and slip off his glasses then tuck them into the collar of his shirt. His eyes are blown with lust and something softer. That part of him that is all mine. And I'm not sure I can grasp the reality of how precious that truly is.

My hands slide up his arms to land in his hair. I pull, and he grunts then nips at my lower lip before pressing a hot kiss behind my ear. He guides me backward until tree bark digs into my back as I thud against the tree. The bite of the uneven surface pressing through my clothes is a good type of pain, the type that keeps you in the moment.

I grind against him, and he hoists me up so my legs are wrapped around his waist and his hands are cupping my ass. Each time I circle my hips, he lets loose a new delicious sound.

"Eve. You're everything. The best damn thing that's ever fucking happened to me." Garrett pants against the side of my neck. "I waited for so long. I used to think about that party all the time. And it nearly killed me when you showed up here, but I'm so glad you did."

"The party?" I ask, still swept up in the press of him between my thighs. It takes a moment to register what party he's talking about, then it shifts into place—the album release.

"Seeing you on that rooftop. I meant every single word I said at the farm. You were the most spectacular thing I'd ever seen. I was gone then, maybe even before." His eyes search mine and he grows impossibly still beneath me as he waits for my reaction.

"I thought I annoyed the shit out of you," I admit.

"You have always been the only person who's terrified me to get close to because I knew the moment we did, I'd either have you or lose you forever. You're not someone I could risk losing." He reaches out and twirls a loose hair around his finger then slips it behind my ear.

I'm glad he's holding me because if he wasn't, I'm sure I'd have to sit down. That long? He's wanted me for years. I can't fathom it. I've always felt so temporary in all my relationships, like I was always on the verge of messing up and disappointing whoever I was with if I showed too much of myself. But for Garrett, who has known me through nearly two decades, to want me? It overwhelms me with relief.

"You have me. You won't lose me," I promise with a steady assurance that I've been longing to feel.

"Thank God." His face nestles into the crook of my neck, and he takes in a heaving breath that reverberates through me.

I shift and the friction of the seam reignites the building ache to be touched by him. "Garrett. I want you here. I don't want to wait until we get back."

"Evelyn, are you saying…" Garrett starts to ask then trails off. His hand trails around my thigh to pull at the waistband of my pants.

"Yes," I moan. I want all of him right now. I need to feel him too. I writhe against his erection to provide further confirmation.

"Baby, are you really going to let me fuck you against this tree?"

"Only if you hurry up."

He eases me to the ground then grips my waist and turns me so I'm facing the tree and my palms land hard, pressing into the bark to brace myself. At the sound of his zipper, a mental image of him quickly comes to mind, and I arch my back, pushing my ass out in anticipation. *Now.* I need this now.

A hand settles on my stomach, slipping down slowly before landing on the button of my jeans. I shift, ready to lift my hands and tear off the pants myself.

"If either of your hands leave that tree I'll stop. You're going to come on my cock, and I'm going to be the one to undress you. Understood?" His rough voice makes my stomach dip with pleasure and anticipation. A weight lands on my back as he leans over me.

"Yes." My thighs clench and it's an effort to keep them apart so he can slip my pants and underwear down to catch around my thighs. The cool air and rain kiss my hot sensitive skin, adding a new welcome sensation to the mix.

A thick finger spreads me and teases my entrance before it sinks into me. I rock my hips back and grind my ass against the hard length of his cock as he works me into a frenzy. When I demand more, he adds another finger. His other hand joins rubbing my clit.

It's all so much. The edges of the bark against my skin. The prospect of getting caught sends my heart racing. The rain. Him.

Him.

"Garrett. Fuck me. I need you right now." I beg.

I hold my breath, gasping as he presses into me. Slow, achingly slow, ensuring that I'll always crave the feel of him. One of his hands lands over mine, tangling with my fingers, my callouses scraping against the tree. He thrusts sharply, intentionally.

"You could ask me to do anything, and I would," he rasps as he drives into me. "Anything."

"You're mine," I promise. "Only you can make me feel so good."

Teeth skate against the back of my neck as he whimpers. "Fuuuuck."

His thrusts pick up speed, wild and messy. Fingers dig into the soft dip of my hip then let go to snake up the shirt plastered to my skin. He strips it away, reaching up to palm my breast and squeeze. The act wrings a groan of delight from deep in my throat.

With a final press against my clit, my thighs shake and the orgasm washes through me. I squeeze my eyes shut and sparks of light play against the back of my eyelids as I cry out his name. "Garrett!"

He fucks me through it, then slows as if to draw out this moment. Like no matter how many times we do this, he'll never get tired of me.

I hold my hands to the heating vents as Garrett drives my car. We left his truck in the parking lot to pick up in the morning because its heating isn't nearly as good. The rain started coming down in white sheets as we came down the trail and we're both in desperate need of a hot shower. Both of us have stripped down to our underwear and are wrapped in blankets from my trunk.

"Holy fuck. If we ever do that again, let's check the weather first." I shiver.

Garrett's mouth quirks into a smirk. "As I recall there was very little planning involved with what we just did. Why were you out here anyway?"

"I was calling Vincent," I say. "I went out there to think and I ended up calling him to see if there was a way to extend my contract."

I've told Garrett about the album, but not the rest. Not on purpose, but I didn't want to face it, so I pretended it wasn't going to happen. Very healthy, like the rest of my coping mechanisms.

"Why do you need to do that?" he asks, eyes flicking to me then back to the road.

"Because after this, either the world learns I'm Lyla or I say goodbye to all of it. I think if I can get a little more time, I can figure it out, but I already know that won't happen. Vincent is great at his job, but the label execs have been subtly hinting at this for a while."

"That second day here, that's what the call was about?" he asks.

"Yeah, they want all of me. But I can't help feeling I'll disappoint everyone."

"What makes you say that?"

"I'm a nepo-sibling who talks too much. They like my music, but after five years of waiting there's no way that I'll live up to that."

"Fuck them."

"What?" My face pinches with confusion.

"You heard me. Fuck them. You're my favorite person, Eve. And if they don't like you, they're wrong. Make music and be happy if that's what you want," he says with a firm conviction that sets free a swarm of butterflies in my stomach.

For a moment it doesn't matter what anyone else thinks, because he believes in me.

"I don't know, that sounds great but doesn't change the rest with all the lies I've told."

"It doesn't. That's a risk you'll have to take if you want it. Do you?"

"I don't know. Nothing seems right. I feel like I've been waiting for a third option to just fall in my lap, and it hasn't. I can't keep waiting, but whatever I choose is going to define everything." I shrug, I wish I could give him a better answer.

"Not everything. Whatever you choose. What we have, that will stay the same," he promises. His hand reaches over to squeeze mine.

42

Evelyn

When I first arrived in Hartsfall, I imagined a soundtrack to a romance I never expected to have. Honestly, it's a soundtrack that doesn't fit the one that I've found. But if it did, the current days would be set to the light interlude where time melts into a montage.

We take Quinn and Oliver into the city. It's long overdue, but this way I can show them all the spots I've come to frequent. For the last few months, I've felt stuck where I am, but pointing out things like the yoga studio in Midtown I went to once and the taco truck with the best al pastor tacos I've ever had and I realize there was so much around me I never truly appreciated. I can step back and see all the pieces, even if I feel like I'm still missing a few. When we go to The Met, Garrett gets a T-shirt from the gift shop and changes into it in the bathroom.

"Are you trying to use novelty T-shirts to seduce me?" I ask.

He picks at the fabric of the simple black shirt with its red serif lettering. "That depends, is it working?"

"Completely." *Always.*

I kiss him on a street corner, hard and long, to the point passersby whistle and call out to us. We still might be on some version of vacation but stepping out of Hartsfall and into the city solidifies our transition from daydream into waking reality.

Afterward, we go to a comedy show at a dingy little bar in The Village. The floors are so sticky that I stumble when one of my shoes gets stuck halfway through. Quinn looks at me with wide eyes and whispers, "I'm pretty sure we saw this guy bomb at a party once."

"I think you're right," I say, recalling an unfortunate open mic night in college where we saw a variation of the act being performed now.

After I confirm this she turns to Oliver and he nods. I never thought a bad comedy show could ever make me feel so good, though the jokes have nothing to do with it. We're back, not the same as before, but that was never going to happen. We've changed, but we survived it.

"What is it?" Garrett asks, and I explain, sharing more of myself with him, something inconsequential that means more because he's the one who I get to tell it to.

As the days pass, Garrett and I continue to exchange calendar invites. When I have nothing to do or we're in the middle of a drive, I scroll back through them.

> *Feed me grapes and call me pretty:*
> *Today, 1:27 p.m. - 5:30 p.m. @ in bed*

> *I'm sitting on the back deck: Tuesday,*
> *8:41 p.m. - 11:59 p.m. @ deck*

> *Come over, I miss you: Today, 3:13 p.m.*
> *- 8:00 p.m. @ Across the street*

I lie in bed the morning of my birthday answering texts and calls from family. My head rests on Garrett's lap as he braids and unbraids my hair. He massages my scalp halfway through talking with Avery, and I moan into the phone.

"What the hell was that?"

"Wait, FaceTime me," I say, then press mute. I look up at Garrett and ask, "Is that okay?"

"You wanting to share us with the people you care about? Yeah, that's okay," he says as a rough finger swipes a stray strand from my face.

A second later the FaceTime comes in and my video shows my head on Garrett's lap with his hand tangled in my messy strands.

"Holy shit. You found a local!" Avery yelps and her eyes sparkle.

"You know what? I think he qualifies." I smile as I tilt the camera up to show Garrett's still sleepy face.

"No fucking way. Did Drew freak the hell out? Did your parents ask you guys to get married on the spot?"

"Only Quinn and Oliver know, and you," I tell her, and she beams at the sentiment that she's in the select few who know.

"What's going on?" Wes's face pushes into view as he looks at Avery's screen. "Is it a Grammy nominations predictions article? I heard Variety put one out." Wes pauses then nods. "Oh, that's what's going on."

"What the hell does that mean?" Avery demands. "How does he know?"

"He knows we're both here from that time when I needed to borrow your phone, remember? Where are you guys?" I ask as I inspect the bare white wall behind them.

"Rehearsal." Avery switches the camera to show the room. Dancers are stretching and checking their phones. "We have five minutes so I'm going to grab headphones and you can tell me everything as quickly as possible without anyone eavesdropping." Avery swivels away from Wes and grabs headphones.

She takes a seat on the pale wood flooring as I tell her the CliffsNotes of the last month and a half. Garrett slips away and leaves the bedroom as we catch up. I confirm with Avery that yes, I got the T-shirt with the Sleepy Time Tea bear on it from her to add to my collection and that I will be wearing it today. There's a sharp clap and a call for break to be over. We say our goodbyes.

There's a slight chill in the house, it's been dipping down to the thirties at night with fall in full swing. As I promised Avery, I pull on the shirt she sent in addition to sweatpants before heading downstairs.

I have to catch myself on the wall of the entryway when I see what's been waiting for me and a laugh rockets out of me.

"I decided not to ask, and I still don't want to," Quinn says, glaring at the cake that reads *We made it out alive.*

"They didn't have anything else," Garrett explains.

I walk to him and he settles his hands on my hips. I go in for a kiss but at the last second brush my lip to his ear. "Liar. Does this mean you're also not going to sing me 'Happy Birthday'?"

"I would never. What would you do with your hands?" he murmurs, and my heart sings at the simple fact he remembered.

I cup his jaw and my lips melt into his. Not just my lips, my bones, my soul. It all melts knowing that he's there to catch me.

"I got you something," he says against my mouth. Garrett pulls back and grabs a rectangular package. "I had to bribe a bookseller for this."

I tear apart the wrapping and the back of my eyes sting with how perfect it is. It's stupid to get this emotional over something I won't ever crack open.

"I didn't know you read Hemmingway," Oliver says.

"I don't, not really." I shake my head.

"Thank God," Quinn adds. "I can put up with a lot but you becoming a classics snob is where I draw the line."

"Okay, good, now I know how to get rid of you," I tease.

There's a handwritten note on the inside.

Every shrine has to start somewhere. Let this one start with me.

Realistically, I know he could have bought me something extravagant. He didn't. Instead, he used his gift to me to say something far more important. Even the small moments we've shared matter.

"We went in on it together." Oliver hands over a package with crisp corners.

Quinn's somber eyes latch against mine. "It took a lot of time and emotional labor to return to purgatory."

I tear open the wrapping then open the plain box inside to find more blueberry products than a person could ever need. I pull out tissue paper revealing more treasures as I go: lotion, a T-shirt, a book on the history of blueberry farms.

"You asked for paraphernalia, and we went back and got all of it."

"Is this a bong?" I manage to get out through gasps of laughter.

"Due to its lack of ventilation," Quinn says, "I think it's a vase, but I was sorely disappointed after I went through the same thought process at the store."

"We could have a completely different day. But I guess we can get a different type of flower," I say and place the vase on a side table.

"What do you want to do? There's this pedal tour on a railroad through the Catskills that looks interesting," Quinn suggests, then looks between the rest of us for our thoughts on the matter.

"There are many things that could be fun, but that sounds like endurance exercise and I've never dreamed about that as a birthday activity," I say. "It's your last day in town. Let's just wander."

After a breakfast of pancakes drenched in locally sourced maple syrup we go into town. No matter how much I'd like time to come to a standstill, it keeps moving. Oliver and Quinn will be leaving soon, but so will I. My rental is over the morning after the festival. My time here wasn't supposed to be any more than a research trip. I tried to keep some distance, but I've still managed to fall for it.

It's the best type of day for doing nothing, the sun is bright, but the air is crisp. Leaves have been raked into piles. After stopping at Love is Brewing, Oliver takes a bite of Quinn's apple cider donut while she's turned away. She catches him which prompts a chase around the gazebo. He lets her catch up and they tumble into a pile of leaves, her landing squarely on his chest. Leaves poke out from their hair and Quinn breaks off another bite of the donut before stuffing it in his mouth.

"Here, have more if you want it so much," she says.

I walk over to them and say, "Where's my bite?"

In response they pull me down with them, and only then am I given a piece of the cinnamon sugar dusted fried dough. When Quinn starts to get up, I say, "Wait. Let me get a picture."

Holding my phone above our heads I drop it and am saved from a broken nose only because Garrett catches it. He flips it and takes the picture for the three of us.

We're still picking leaves out of each other's hair an hour later. Quinn stops me on the sidewalk to pull one free.

"I wouldn't normally bother you, but I have to ask," says an unfamiliar voice behind us. I turn to find a man talking to Garrett, who appears unfazed. "I was hoping you could help me with a proposal. You see, my girlfriend's sister's flight got canceled and she was bringing all this stuff with her and now she's stuck in Nebraska. We've been together since high school, and you were her favorite back then."

"What exactly are you asking?" Garrett questions.

The man appears to grow more nervous with all four of us looking at him. "Could you sing something for her?"

"Anything in particular?"

"Would it be weird to ask you to sing someone else's song? You were her favorite back then but now she's super into Lyla West. There's this song, 'Sundays in July' that she loves, and listens to it every morning," the man explains.

"I've heard of it. It's a good song," Garrett says, his eyes cut to me with the truth only the two of us know. "We're in the middle of something, so I'd have to ask."

"Yes, of course we can help." I jump at the opportunity. It's not lost on me that Garrett is willingly helping with a proposal. "We can help set it up. That would be perfect."

"You want to help with someone else's proposal on your birthday?"

"And help be a part of one of the best memories they might ever have? Of course."

"I'll do it on one condition," Garrett says, then reaches back to hold my hand. "Eve, accompany me."

I haven't performed in front of people for years. The last time was when I was twelve and almost threw up taking the stage for my piano recital. It was fine during the performance, but the pressure and expectation even then got to me.

Garrett squeezes my hand. "You can say no."

"The stakes are too high, I can't sacrifice someone else's happy ending," I say, because I want to, but also because that's the answer I've always been wired to give. For so long, everyone else's happiness has been my primary concern. "What do we need to do?" I ask.

The answer: pretty much everything.

The man, who finally introduces himself as Javi, tells us about his hopefully soon-to-be fiancée Kathrine. Pretty much everything he had planned was riding on the sister and now it's all up in the air. What results from this is a bit of a scavenger hunt. We all break off to put the plan into motion. Oliver, Javi, and Garrett take Garrett's truck to borrow a piano from the high school.

Quinn and I head to the Love Letter Museum to ask if we can reserve space for a private event this evening and let us keep the piano there until then. Haven, the owner, readily helps. In the end, we have to go to both Winnie and Sara's flower shops to get enough daisies for our vision, the upcharge for crossing enemy lines is worth it. When we leave the second shop we're so laden with daisies it's hard to see

Quinn's face, but I can tell she's enjoying it. It's a reminder of the true magic of this town, the people behind the scenes to give couples moments to cherish.

We set down the crates we've been using to transport the three loads of daisies to the museum and lean against the siding.

"You should go get ready," Quinn says, then pulls in a deep breath.

"I'll stay and help. It's fine."

"I'm sorry, but if I was getting proposed to, I wouldn't want the pianist to be covered in leaf debris and dry sweat. I'll help Oliver set this up and change too. We'll meet back here at five."

I blow a strand of hair out of my face. "Okay, you have a point." I close the distance between us and wrap my arms around her. "Thanks for playing along. I'm assuming you didn't think you'd be doing labor on your last day in town."

Her grip tightens around me as she says, "I think it's what I get for suggesting endurance exercise this morning."

43

Garrett

For the first time in my life, I understand why grooms cry when they first see their brides walk down the aisle. I'm not hearing wedding bells necessarily, but the moment Evelyn walks into the hall of replica letters wearing the dress she sent me a picture of the first time I took her to The Gas Station, I could weep. She's incandescent.

I used to think of her as a whirlwind. She is definitely a force of nature, but something less disastrous than what I used to think of. To me, she's sunshine cutting through the clouds. A rush of light that forces your eyes to adjust and view the world differently.

She does a spin. The black silk flows like water against her form. "Too much?"

"If it wouldn't ruin everything we've done for Javi, I would pick you up and carry you away." I walk up to her and pull her flush against me. I kiss her cheeks before finding her mouth.

"I think I would let you," she says.

"Noted."

She twists in my arms looking around. "This looks great." The normal array of couches has been pushed to the corners of the room. The piano and a microphone have been set up along the wall furthest from the door. Buckets overflowing with daisies have been positioned along the perimeter.

"Are you ready?" I ask.

"Nervous, but in a good way. I haven't performed one of my songs before. This will be my first time, even if I'm only at the piano and not singing."

"Well, I haven't performed one of your songs before either, so it will be mine too."

"That's such a bad joke," she says but still lets out a light laugh.

"I know what you mean, though. It'll be great and I'll be right there with you," I tell her.

Quinn walks into the room dressed in all black in the style of a stagehand or non-descript photographer. She's agreed to slip in and film the entire thing.

"Javi just texted they'll be here in five minutes. I'm going to turn off the light. He'll flip it on when he comes in and that's your cue to start," Quinn instructs, adopting an all-business tone.

"Got it," Evelyn says. We pull apart and take our positions, her at the piano and me behind the microphone, then the room descends into darkness.

Neither of us risk talking on the off chance we'll ruin the moment. The first sign for us to prepare is the warm, purposefully too loud greeting from Haven.

"Someone must have turned off the lights," says Javi.

Even though I was expecting it, the sudden light takes a moment to adjust to. Still, we only have a second to jump into the song. I give Evelyn a quick nod while the world is still coming into focus and she starts, not missing a beat. The intro is short, but just before I start singing there's a quick gasp.

"Dance with me?" Javi asks. Kathrine nods through her awe and he pulls her close.

They sway together as I sing, and Evelyn plays along.
I'm in a rush to do nothing at all, except to do nothing with you.
It's Sunday in July and I'm exactly where I'm supposed to be.
As close to you as the sun when it kisses your skin.

At the end of the song, Javi sinks down onto one knee and starts to talk. I don't listen, I'm caught up watching Evelyn. Tears are collecting along her lower lashes and her eyes are on the couple. This woman did this for perfect strangers. Sure, I might have said yes without her. But if it weren't for these last few weeks, I'm not so sure I would have.

She raises her hand and wipes away a trailing tear.

"Yes, of course I'll marry you. Yes, a thousand times yes," Kathrine says, and I'm pulled back into the moment.

I move quietly to join Evelyn on the piano bench and start to play another of her songs. Her eyes gleam, and I lean in. "I told you I listened to them. I might have forgotten to say I learned them too."

She kisses me and I don't know how I manage it but I keep playing, it's probably because I've played it so many times that I don't have to think any more.

I continue through Lyla West's slower songs until Javi and Kathrine are done. Quinn sends them the video and then they're on their way to dinner.

"Is being a proposal planner a thing? We'd be great at it," Oliver says, still riding the high of the day, a grin splitting his face.

We're all back at the rental, doing our best to stretch the day as far as it can go. For the first time, we've set up the fire pit and we're clustered around, sitting on Adirondack chairs.

"If you're interested in a massive pay cut," Quinn says pragmatically.

Oliver tuts and shakes his head. "You can't put a price on love."

"Well, you can put a price on rent and basic needs." Quinn takes the poker that she appointed herself in charge of and pushes at one of the logs. "You like eating out too much and you're still paying off your student loans."

"Okay, fine. Kill my dreams."

"Drama queen," Quinn says.

I look down and see Evelyn beaming at her friends' interaction.

"Let's promise that this won't be a one-time thing," Oliver says.

Evelyn looks up at me. "Can I convince you to come visit with me?"

"I think I can be persuaded," I say, and she nestles closer.

"I mean, if Ev moves back then you'll have even more reason to replicate this with us. I mean without the fire pit because both of us are in apartments," Oliver suggests. Evelyn stiffens under my touch, it's the only indication she gives that she's uncomfortable with this turn in conversation.

Evelyn swallows hard then tilts her face so our eyes lock. "I have the opportunity to interview for a position at my old job, a better position. I still haven't given my answer yet."

My stomach churns. She told me about her options, but the fact that there's an actual job and not just some what-if possibility makes it more real. She doesn't want to be in the spotlight, so what would that mean for us if I start up a solo career? I could just write songs. I think I could be happy with that. We can make it work. When it comes to her I'll make sure it works.

But there's another thing that starts to tear at me. Every time we've written or played together it's been impossible to see a world where she stops. She is music to me, in so many ways. After today, after having her song be a part of someone's love story like that? It's hard to see the woman I know shy away from what she's so gifted at. I just don't get it.

"I know they've gotten a few good applicants, but if you're not interested, that's fine. We want you to be happy in New York, if that's what you want," Quinn says and there's something odd in her tone, apologetic almost.

"Thanks." Evelyn gives a soft smile.

"Okay. Something more urgent to think about," Quinn says, "What the hell are we going to do with all the daisies?"

Oliver and Evelyn let out startled laughs and Quinn forges on. "I'm serious. We spent hundreds of dollars on those and have nowhere to put them."

"I'll take care of them in the morning," I promise. "Pat will put them to use for the festival."

The rest of the night goes with the same ease that comes after a collective victory. Slowly the fire starts to crumble into glowing embers. It's just past eleven when Oliver and Quinn head out. They still need to pack for their early afternoon flight out of JFK tomorrow. Evelyn and I end up at the piano and she starts recording on her phone as she starts to play and jot down notes in her nearly full notebook.

She talks through the next three songs she wants to write. We still haven't decided on the ending, up until now I thought it was obvious. I do my best to shrug it off. It's her choice. Still, I can't manage more than short answers.

"I like that," I say after she works through a potential key change.

The corners of her mouth are drawn downward as she lifts her hands from the piano and puts them in her lap. "What's wrong?"

"I'm fine," I say.

"You're not okay," she says. "You're hardly talking to me."

"I just didn't realize you had actual jobs you were considering. I should have assumed. It's nothing."

"I didn't tell you and I should have," she says and her shoulders slump. "I guess I got swept up with being here and wanted to forget I had to make the decision. There's no going back after I take the leap, you know? I've been in limbo for so long, and now it's all or nothing." I expect her to look away, to hide from this moment but she reaches for me. "I got the email on my second day here. With everything going on it felt like the best plan B I could have."

"I don't know how to feel about that. I mean, am I just someone for you to get swept up in when you need a distraction?" I don't want to believe it, but she ran here to hide from things, this isn't the city. This is a vacation and just like songs, vacations end. "I know I'm dealing with shit, but that's the first place my mind goes. I can't help but think that when you're done with your album and have to make decisions, you'll realize that this won't work anymore."

"It will."

"How do you know? Can you tell me right now what you want to do with the job offer? What about the label and your new contract? Those are your two options, right? Going back to a normal life or going for music?" The frantic questions spill out of me, and I feel like I'm losing her even while she's next to me. I see it play out in front of me, the exact thing I've been avoiding by not being with her.

I'll go back to the city where I've lived for so long. I'll write music, like I used to. The days will pass. But I don't want to learn what that would look like without her. I used to be content with life, but now she's breathed a purpose into me that has irrevocably changed me. Content will never be enough for me again.

"I don't know. What do you think I should do?" she asks earnestly.

It takes everything in me not to tell her to take the leap. I think it's the right decision from what I know, but there's so much I haven't been in her life for, how could I make that choice?

I pull in a sharp breath. "I can't make that decision for you. I won't."

"I just need an answer, you know." Her voice cracks over the words. "Flip a coin. Shout what pops into your head first. Anything."

"I wish I could give it to you." It would be so easy, but I can't. I just can't and I need her to know why, but that requires me to break out truths I hate voicing. But maybe it's time.

I reach out and grab one of her hands and my thumb immediately starts to trace lines across her knuckles.

It takes another moment for my thoughts to collect. "I'm going to tell you this because I need you to understand why I can't tell you what you should choose."

"Okay," she says.

"You know why I got a vasectomy?"

"I'd just assumed you were being cautious."

"When I was eighteen, Lana came to Vegas. She ended up running into Wes and I before the show and she just went off on me. Some of what she said I doubt she meant, but there are things that got to me. Things she'd said before, how I was responsible for depriving her of the life she always wanted to live. That she was better off without me." *If she never had me.*

"I got one of my migraines after and never made it on stage. I made the appointment the next day. I never wanted my actions to cause someone to resent me the way my mother did; I never wanted to risk the chance that I would bring a child into this world that I would resent either. I lived it. No one else needs to. I want to be with you, but whatever choice you make can't be because you want to stay with me."

I've lived so much of my life trying to make up for choices I had no part in. I want to support her, I want to be there for her, but I can't make this choice for her. I can't tip the balance of her life pushing her toward something because of her desperation to keep things stable between us.

I can't make Evelyn love me. I don't want to make her love me. I want her to choose to, the same way I've chosen her.

"It wouldn't be like that," she insists.

"Are you sure? I am one of the only people who know your secrets and it's not because you told me. I stumbled on them. Yes, you've let me in, but I have to question if you would have if I didn't know the rest. Did you choose me because I was the only option?" I don't like admitting these thoughts, but I need her to understand. I need her to see that we are my favorite coincidence, but that doesn't change everything else. "You never had a chance to hide from me."

"You are the only option, but not for any of those reasons," she insists. "God, Garrett. When I'm around you I'm never scared that you'll look away. I know that if I'm too much for others you won't feel that way. But also because silence doesn't feel like silence with you. I'd do anything with you. I do want the answer about how to keep you. But if that means I have to find it myself, I'll figure it out."

"I know you will." I need to believe in her. It's hard to relinquish this, but for us to work, I'll trust her.

"I will. I'll figure it out," she echoes. "Give me until the end of the festival. Let me think about it and we can enjoy this time."

44

Evelyn

G arrett and I did it. After yesterday, we only have one last song to write. This is what I came here to do. But my stomach sinks as I read the final lines of the message.

I have two days before I promised Garrett I'd have an answer. Vincent can wait that long, too.

"I'm going to get caffeine!" I call out as I swing my legs off the bed. Garrett's reply is muffled by the sound of running water from the shower. He's been so understanding, but right now I need a minute alone.

I don't bother changing out of the shirt I slept in. I throw on a coat and sweatpants then head outside to be greeted by a rush of cold air. Once I leave the neighborhood, there's this prickling awareness that crawls up my neck. Do I usually make this much eye contact with people? I check to make sure my clothes aren't on inside out after a woman gives me a once over as I pass the gazebo.

Okay, weird.

When I get to Love is Brewing a couple walks out of the shop and the moment they see me, their casual conversation sputters out.

I give them a wave as a knee-jerk response, which only makes it worse. They give me tight smiles then rush away.

Right before I push through the door, my phone rings in my pocket. I pull my coat tighter around me then take a seat at one of the empty tables in front of the shop.

"Hey, you called yesterday. But I'm not opposed to more birthday wishes," I tease my brother.

"Ev," Drew says.

"What's wrong?" Panic quickens my pulse, mixed with the weird vibes I've been picking up today, I already feel like I'm going to throw up.

"Are you dating Garrett?"

"What?" I blurt. "Did you hear from Avery and Wes?" Avery and my brother might be on good terms and Wes might be his old bandmate, but I doubt either of them would say something to him.

"No. Wait, how do they know?"

"I told Avery, and well, Wes was kind of just there." My thoughts stumble. "How do you know?"

"God," he says on a huff.

"I really doubt God told you," I say because I can't help myself. "How do you know?"

"Fuck. Just. Fuck," he says, almost to himself. "I'm not the only one who knows."

"Great, keep it vague," I say, rolling my eyes even though he can't see.

"There was an engagement video that took off overnight because the guy got her favorite singer to sing her favorite song, I'm assuming you know the rest because you were in it."

I realize exactly who he's concerned about. "Mom and Dad."

"If they haven't called yet, does that mean you aren't…" He trails off, letting me fill in the implications of his words.

"Yes, we're together," I say. I won't ever deny it, not now when it's inconvenient. If I do, how do I deserve him when it's easy and straightforward.

"Do you want me to call them?" Drew offers, and I'm tempted to accept.

"I mean, that would be nice," I say, "but I should deal with it."

"Ev, I am happy for you," he says, and it's a nice consolation prize considering what's to come.

"It is nice that you're not going to threaten to punch the guy," I prod because I can't help myself.

"I mean, I'd win in a fight," he says easily, "but that would be a lot of effort to get all defensive over my adult sister. I've got to go. Love you."

"Love you."

I push into Love is Brewing and take my spot at the back of the line. For the last few weeks I've been so good about not checking Lyla's name in headlines, but now as I check for my real one, I'm sucked back into the vortex.

"Viral Proposal with Fool's Gambit Favorite reveals secret relationship."

"Sparks fly with Fool's Gambit bassist and drummer's younger sister."

"Avery Sloane's close friend. Garrett Larson's new fling. Who is Evelyn Mariano?"

Each time I tap a new article I feel like I'm slipping further and further from my body. This is what I've been avoiding for so long. Three seconds at the end of a video did this. Three seconds caused my name to trend on social media and send an influx of followers. In less than a day journalists and gossip blogs have discovered enough information to make me feel exposed in front of millions of digital eyes. If this is the reaction to something so small, what would happen if they found out that I'm Lyla?

In some ways, I've known. I've seen how Avery and Drew have dealt with media attention. I was already terrified of it, how people will pick apart every small part of my life. I can't help but think about Oliver and Quinn, how being close to me would put them at risk of similar privacy violations.

I shuffle along with the line on autopilot. The barista's voice startles me back to the moment when I order and it takes me long minutes to remember the names of drinks I've asked for hundreds of times over the years.

"Don't you usually get the matcha with oat milk?" the barista asks.

"Oh, yeah. Thanks," I say.

"We all have those days…just means you need your caffeine fix, right?"

"Yeah," I readily agree and tap my phone that still has the article I was reading pulled up. I catch the barista reading the headline the second before my card pulls up on the screen. Great.

At least the moment of embarrassment makes me exit out of the browser so no one else can see that I've Googled myself.

I make it out the door and a few feet down the sidewalk when Mom calls. I know it's her before I take out my phone, like I can feel her frustration through the radio waves.

"Hey!" I answer, refusing to implicate myself until I need to. For all I know she's vowed to not go on the internet.

"Why is it I heard from Lori this morning that you are in a relationship with Garrett? You know how embarrassing it is to have to play along like I knew? My own daughter doesn't tell me something but everyone else already seems to know," she reprimands, and I feel myself shrinking while wanting to give the exact right answer to placate her.

"I was going to tell you," I say.

"But you didn't," she snaps.

"It's new, I didn't want to say anything until it was official," I say, still trying to mend the already fraying threads of this situation.

"It looks official now."

I jump to explain. "We didn't post the video. We were just helping someone and they posted it. I'm still on vacation."

"So you go on vacation with him and you still don't think that's important enough to share? The only man I've gone on vacation with was your father."

I don't know if it's the pressure or the exhaustion that causes it but I snap, not completely, not the way that I would have as a teenager, but more than I have in years. "I am a grown woman. My relationships are *my* concern, not yours. I'm thirty. This isn't a guy who's taking me to homecoming."

"But you didn't tell us."

"I didn't," I echo. "I should be allowed to choose that."

"What else aren't you saying? First, an entire relationship, what else are you comfortable keeping from us?" she demands.

"I have to go," I say. I can't do this right now, not when she won't listen. Not when I know the only thing on her mind is Drew and how he pulled away. This conversation isn't about me. It's never been about me. I wish it was. Maybe then I'd actually be comfortable telling them things instead of doing it to appease them. I hate that they make me feel so young sometimes, but I guess that's what parents do. They have a special gift, to tear you down to an early version of yourself even when you've grown.

"No, we're talking." Her voice sharpens further, but I can't take another cut from the words she's wielding against me.

"No. You're talking and I can't do this right now. Maybe you should ask yourself why I didn't tell you." I hang up the second the words are out. She calls back again. The notifications keep popping up as I text Quinn.

I can't do this.

Evelyn

I'm doing the interview.

Quinn

I'll pick you up in an hour.

45

Garrett

"I just think it's better this way, you know?" Evelyn's voice cracks over the phone. She told me not to come over, to let her pack in peace.

"I told you I'd be with you no matter what you chose and support you. That hasn't changed," I soothe. I want to tell her to change her mind and contradict everything I said last night. "Are you sure you don't want me there?"

"Yes," she says. "Quinn will be here soon. I don't want to make her late for her flight."

"Tell me how it goes. I'm rooting for you," I tell her. "Call me when you land."

"Ok, I will."

She hangs up to finish packing. My head falls into my hands and I groan. A need to do something, fix something, make this all better for her itches against my bones. But I can't. This isn't something I can solve by taking her to a greasy drive-in or changing my own life.

If she gets the job offer, which there's no doubt in my mind that she will, I'm ready to move back to Nashville. I have a soft spot for the city, and it wouldn't be a burden. I can write music from anywhere. But I can't shake the feeling that this isn't how it's supposed to end.

"Garrett. There's a guest for you." Alina steps into the living room where I was practicing for the festival before Evelyn called.

I put my cello securely back in its case before heading to the door. Before I reach it, I know it won't be Evelyn, Alina would have said something different if it were.

Quinn stands stiffly as she waits. Her eyes move across the panels of the house as if counting them to distract herself.

"She's coming with us to Nashville," she announces.

"I know," I say.

"What are you going to do about it?"

"Why do you think I should do something?"

"Because I know it's a mistake. You know it's a mistake too and you're not doing anything," Quinn says, putting in effort to make sure I can read between the lines. I do, and that doesn't change anything.

"Tell her that."

"I told someone I would wait," she says then looks toward the road.

That someone I can only assume is Oliver. If that's true, then I'm right to stay out of this. This is about the three of them and their friendship now; in some ways it always was.

"I trust her to figure it out."

"What if she doesn't?" she asks, the iron in her voice turning to a soft desperation.

"Then she'll have plenty of chances to change her mind. I know I did. It took me fucking ages. Maybe I waited too long. Or maybe I needed to realize certain things before that choice made sense. Maybe I needed the exact right person to tell me some tough truths," I tell her.

I'm not the right person, not just because of what I need for my and Evelyn's relationship to succeed, but because this was never about me. She never had the chance to hide from me.

"You know she's making the wrong choice"—she waves from me to the house across the street—"and you're just standing there."

"And you sent her the job opening in the first place," I remind her. I sort of hate Quinn for it, giving Evelyn this way to abandon everything she has sacrificed so much for.

"I shouldn't have." Quinn grows more agitated, but I have the impression that it's more at herself than with me. "You're seriously not going to talk her out of it?"

"No," I say. "Is there anything else?"

"Just that this conversation has been wildly infuriating, and the only reason I'm not calling you an asshole is because I love Evelyn more than to insult her boyfriend to his face."

"Somehow, you still managed to tell me exactly how you feel," I say and earn a faint, knowing smirk. "I hope you get what you want out of your trip."

She gives me a clipped "Thanks" before walking away.

The door creaks as I watch Quinn back down the driveway then turn toward the house across the street.

"You're really letting her go," Alina says as she sidles up next to me.

"I have to at least give her a convincing head start." I sigh.

There's no guarantee today will play out in the way I hope, but I'm not the one she needs to talk to. I already believe in her, but my perspective isn't going to help. She'll have me either way, but I have to trust my gut. It's been the thing telling me to chase her for years and I have to give that feeling some credit.

Alina lets out a shuddering cough that causes every muscle in my body to tense.

"Are you all right?" I ask.

"Nothing tea can't fix." I give her a concerned look and she tuts. "I'm not a child. I will call Emily if it makes you feel better. Don't you dare hover and crowd me like I'm some feeble thing. This body held up for five hour shows while wearing a corset, I am fine."

"Call Emily and I'll drop it."

"I call, and you make sure to leave in time to get your girl." Alina raises a hand to point at the car driving away with the woman I love.

"Deal."

46

Evelyn

I nstead of driving myself to the airport I ride with Quinn while Oliver drives my car. Besides the fact that out of the three of us I'm the worst behind the wheel, I'm also drained. I've turned off my phone so I don't have the urge to check social media or my texts.

I've been better these last few weeks about not checking for Lyla in the headlines, but this is more personal. It's me, or at least about me, because the few that I saw did address me as "bandmate's sister." The way it was phrased poked at a long-term fear that only recently went dormant. It's not just my life that would be under the lens if I went public as Lyla West.

I would be putting Drew under that old scrutiny all over again. The people who I care about didn't sign up for their lives to be torn through and their privacy invaded.

"Didn't you want to see the festival?" Quinn asks. "That's part of why you came here in the first place."

"I can come back next year." I feel detached from my words as I look out the window.

"Will you, though?" Quinn presses.

"If I can get the time off, I don't see why not," I say as I sink further into my seat. "It's just a festival."

"You really want the job?"

"It's the best option." It's the one that works. It's a solution instead of the Band-Aids that I've been constantly reapplying to the situation. This can be permanent. I need it to be.

"Fuck. Fine. I guess we're doing this right now," Quinn mutters under her breath. It's the only warning I get before she jerks the wheel to pull over to a small rest area. I grapple for the handle above the door as my body slams to one side.

"Is everything okay?" I ask, eyes shifting around us.

"No," she bites out. "It's not, Ev."

What the hell? Does she not want me back there after all after this weekend? At the same time, it feels like she's wrestling with herself, not me.

A call comes in with Oliver's name flashing on the display. "Did you guys just pull off? I think I just passed you."

"Yes. We did. I'm going to talk to Ev and tell her what we came here to discuss in the first place," she says with no room for argument. "See you at the airport."

"Wh—" Oliver starts but Quinn firmly presses the hang up button before he can continue.

"Quinn, what's going on?" I ask. What they came here to discuss... I thought we already talked about everything.

Quinn turns in her seat. Her seatbelt digs into her shoulder as she leans toward me with blazing eyes. "You're acting like an idiot."

"Excuse me?" I'm still too startled to be anything other than confused.

"You're out here repeating history. You've already done this," she starts, her voice raising with indignation. "You're running away from what you really want. Why? Because you have an easy out? Because it's easier to leave before it gets too real?"

"Are you mad at me for something? If you are, can you at least explain to me what the hell you're upset about so I can understand what's going on?" My mind starts to race in time with my heart. I'm tired, not just from today, but the weight I've been carrying for years is pressing down harder than ever before.

"Yes, you know what? I am." Quinn unbuckles her seat, turns off the car, then stomps around it. By the time I follow suit she's already working to open the trunk. "Where the hell is it?" she mutters to herself as she starts to dig through Oliver's blue duffle. She pulls out clothes that have been recklessly shoved into the bag and then dips her hand into an unzipped side pocket.

My pulse quickens, thundering in my ears, drowning out the sound of cars breezing past us. The only thing I can think of…but there's no way. Yesterday when Garrett and I performed, he was the only one who sang. She can't know. I've been careful. If she knows then all of it is over. The damage, the lies, all of it has been for nothing.

I gasp for air trying to break free of where my mind has jumped to in way of explanation.

She holds up the embossed floral journal like it's a weapon to be wielded against me.

"You know what this is?" she asks. I do, but my mouth has gone dry and I'm not entirely sure I'm asleep and this is some sort of dream. The journal in her hand is the one I used to write "Seeing Double" and a few other songs that I never followed through on. I lose my footing, my body tilting until I catch myself on the side of the car.

No. There's no way.

That's supposed to be with the rest of the notebooks I brought with me to Hartsfall. "This is what Oliver found in a box he forgot to unpack after he moved out. That time I was off work for a week because I had pneumonia. I was actually just so pissed at you that I couldn't risk coming into work because there was a chance I would leak your secret to everyone."

"I brought you soup," I say, my mind reeling, scrambling to play catch up. Quinn and the journal. To parts of my life that don't make sense sharing space with each other.

"You did, and honestly that's part of the reason I tried to be patient with you. But I'm so fucking over it." She frustratedly tosses the journal back into the car and it lands with a soft thump. "Evelyn, I really need to fight with you right now."

As someone who grew up around parents who never got along and made that clear to anyone within earshot, Quinn avoids fighting. It's part of the reason the three of us worked together for so long. We all had our own reasons to avoid confrontation but now I'm wondering if that stunted our relationship, deprived us from our full potential.

"Okay, then let's fight," I agree. I owe her this and I need this. I need to take this and face what I've been sprinting away from at a full tilt for years. If she wants to fight, I'll fight with her, even if it's the last thing we do as friends.

"Why didn't you trust us? What the hell did I do to make you think you couldn't come to me?" Her voice doesn't waver as her words hit home.

"Nothing. You did nothing! I just didn't want anything to change. I wanted everything to be the same and keep going out with you guys and not make you carry around a secret with you. What else are you mad at me for?" I demand. I want to get it all out. I want to carve out the bad parts and finally make room for the good.

"I'm mad that you stopped talking to me. You're my best friend. I've never had someone like you in my life and then it was like you didn't want to talk to me. Yeah, there's Oliver, but I wanted to be around you sometimes because you let me be an ass when I need to and borrow your stupid T-shirts and order too much pizza. And I knew you were in New York to chase your dreams, and I sent the damn email anyway."

"Did you not want me to reply?"

"Of course I did! I wanted you to tell me all about your life and that you were happy so I could finally be happy for you. I wanted you to say you made the right choice so I could know that all the secrets were worth it!" She stamps her foot on the ground kicking up a cloud of dust.

"But you don't want me to do the interview. If you want, you can just leave me at the airport and you don't have to see me ever again," I choke out around the knot in my throat.

"No. That is the last thing I want you to do. I'm mad because I want you to stay in my life and you fucking left over something we should have talked about ages ago," she says. Guilt fissures through me, cracking the walls I've spent so long building to protect me from this. "I want you to have everything you want and that's not waiting for you in that damn office in Nashville when you can make music with a man who looks at you like you hung the damn moon. Honestly, I don't think you made a mistake breaking up with Ollie. I think you need to talk to him about why and tell him the truth so he can get closure. You guys never pushed each other. You lived in this no-conflict bubble and you two were good together, but both of you deserved more."

No sinkhole opens to swallow me whole. Fire doesn't fall from the sky. The world keeps spinning and Quinn doesn't hate me. I was petrified by the thought of this happening for so long, bracing for the collapse of my relationship with my favorite person. But she's still here, standing her ground, explaining to me how ridiculous I've been. And I've been so stupid not to trust her with this. So fucking stupid.

"Can you forgive me for any of this?" I ask.

"Yes, but only if you don't make this same mistake again. I'm so tired of seeing you not go for what you want and not leaning on anyone. Tell me what you want, Evelyn. I know you know, so tell me," she says firmly.

And for the first time, it feels like it's all in reach. *This.* This is what I've been bracing for and running from.

"I want to have you and Ollie back in my life and share everything I've been doing. I want to make music. I want to be with Garrett, even if it scares the shit out of me that it might not work," I tell us both.

"Okay, then what's stopping you from having all of that. Who said you had to choose?" she asks, which seems to give my building tears permission to fall because they start to stream down my cheeks.

Me.

I'm the one who told myself that I had to pick. Is it really that easy? Just asking for all of these things that I want.

"I really got in my own way," I say.

"Sure did. I am proud of you, too, you know." A smile teases the corners of her lips.

"You are?"

"Of course I am. My best friend is an internationally renowned superstar and I've been waiting ages to tell her how talented and gifted I think she is," she says like it's obvious. I'm not sure if I would have done this differently if I knew, but the fact of the matter is that we have right now and that's what's important.

"Even if she's an idiot?" I check.

She rolls her eyes and pulls me into a hug. "Yes, even then."

"Do you know how much I missed you?"

"I think I might." She squeezes me tighter and it feels like all my fractured pieces are mending themselves. Quinn's shoulders start to shake and I pull away, but instead of tears streaming down her face I find a wide grin.

"All good there?"

"I was just thinking how I nearly got a tattoo of your song lyrics, you know before I found out?"

"I don't think that's a reason to stop you."

"Nah, I have to keep your ego in check." Her smile softens. "I know you weren't there all the time but when I listened to your music, it was always like you were."

"But I should've been there."

Her hand slips down and finds mine. "We have time."

We stand lost in the relief of having everything out in the open, until we can't justify it anymore because Quinn still has a flight to catch. There isn't enough time to head back to Hartsfall and Oliver is driving my car so I have to get to the airport anyway.

Quinn speeds the rest of the way to JFK and once we arrive, it takes us half an hour to drop off Quinn's bags and shuffle through security. All the while I'm buzzing with anticipation to turn back but I need my keys to do that, and I need to talk to Oliver even more.

We find him at the gate, balancing a cardboard drink holder on his lap. A tea for me and a sugary frozen drink for Quinn are nestled into opposite corners while he sips his own drink and flips through the first few pages of one of those thrillers that only seem to exist in airport bookstores. He fits here so perfectly, softly. I'm happy I get the chance to talk to him now.

We'll always belong to each other like the first and last chapter belong to the same book, different parts of the same story.

"Hey, Ollie, walk me to arrivals while Quinn watches our stuff?" I ask, my heart caught in my throat.

"Sure thing." He closes his book and hands us each our drinks.

I give Quinn one more hug and it feels good knowing it's far from the last one and that there's so much less distance between us. Oliver and I set off for the arrivals area so I can get to my car.

"Quinn told me you guys know," I say.

His hand nervously runs through his hair. "Yeah, that was one wild thing to find out."

"Why did you tell her not to ask me about it?"

"How do you know it was me?"

"Because you always look out for me, for both of us," I remind him as I think about the choice he made. He didn't owe me time to process this but he chose kindness. He chose to trust me in a way that I wish I trusted him.

He shrugs. "There wasn't any other way I could think about it. You'd told us about your brother and all the stuff with your family and I think I got it. Music was something you loved but you also knew that it could be something that ruined things. Not saying that I love the choices you made, but I've had time to sit with them."

"I am really sorry. I should have told you. I left and I know I hurt you."

"You did, but I really don't think about it as much as I did three years ago, but if I think about it really hard, I'm still hurt," he admits. "The important thing is you're telling me now."

"If you need to talk about it more…I can and I will. I'll put in the work I should have in the first place," I promise. It's the least I can do.

"What about your family? Do you think you're ready to tell them?" he asks.

Yesterday, it was an impossible question, but talking to him and Quinn has made it less daunting. "I think I need to figure out how to. But talking to you both has helped me learn I'll live, even if it isn't perfect."

And it won't be. Mom will no doubt volley questions at me like they're fiery arrows trying to convince me the choices I've already made should be taken back and reconsidered. Dad will give me a look of silent support. Drew, well, I wonder how my brother will take knowing that I have more Grammys than him, but otherwise I know he'll be in my corner. But I know their happiness isn't my responsibility, no matter how much I've tried to take on that burden.

"I'm glad you're able to work through it." He nods.

"Thanks to Quinn." I have to give her credit. If it weren't for Quinn none of this would have happened.

At her name Oliver's expression fades a shade, his lip tipping downward. "Yeah, she's the best."

"You know, you could go for it."

"I don't think she's interested." He shrugs.

I think about what Quinn said, how Oliver and I didn't push each other. It's true, I'm not sure if that would be the same for them. Quinn needs a soft love, and Oliver needs someone to tell him he can do more than he thinks he's capable of.

"Or she's scared to take the leap. I know my best friend. She wouldn't just pretend to be with just anyone. And seeing you two together made sense. I can't think of anything better than you two being happy together. I meant it then and I do now," I tell him. I want them to have the same joy I've found with Garrett, the type that can only come when you break past the fear of being seen to find the one person who makes you feel known.

"And it won't be weird?"

I laugh then lightly shove his shoulder. "I think we're way past that. These last few weeks helped us get that out of the way. We all survived it," I say and mean it on many levels. We survived this, on the other end we're rebuilding what worked and what needs to change. Because change is needed and it's perpetual.

"Somehow, yeah, we did."

"I do mean it, we can talk more about this if you need." I reach out to grip his free hand and give it a squeeze.

"I will at some point. I've gone to a lot of therapy, so really, I've been talking through this for a long time and I also had Quinn to talk about this to. But I'm happy to know that door is open whenever we need it."

It makes me feel a little better. I put him in this situation so there's only so much relief I can allow myself to accept.

Eventually, we reach the doors to the arrivals that say no reentry beyond this point. The point of no return and I'm finally brave enough to see what the other side has in store.

47

Garrett

"This is a funny place to find you." Her voice cuts through the yelling of the airport attendants and angry clamor of car horns.

I look up from my phone right as a black pawn captures one of my knights. She's far more enjoyable to look at than the 2D graphics that I've been focusing on to distract myself. "Unemployment has given me plenty of free time."

"And the airport arrivals area is where you've decided to spend it?" She crosses her arms over her chest, seemingly unimpressed. My heart races at the sight of her, the way it always does.

I considered running in, buying a ticket, and waiting at her gate. But there was a chance Quinn wouldn't confront Evelyn with the truth. I don't need to know what they said, but I know something happened or she wouldn't be here. Evelyn needed to know her worst fears weren't what she imagined them to be.

"You see, there's this one girl I was hoping would come back to me and I wanted to be here in case she did. I told her to go when I really meant to tell her I wanted her to stay. But I knew if I asked her to stay then she wouldn't have been able to talk to some very important people. It scared the shit out of me because there are about three things in my life that make me happy."

"And she makes you happy?"

"Happy doesn't begin to describe how I am with her."

"How'd that turn out for you? Did she show up?" she asks, slyly as her eyes rove over me. "If not, I'm free right now. You're hot enough that we could have some fun together."

"Maybe you can help me find her. She wears these stupid T-shirts I can't ever tell her that I love, and I'm pretty sure the only reason I love them is because she's the one wearing them. She's also a hopeless romantic and gets offended on behalf of happy endings," I say, sweeping my gaze across the sea of people leaving the airport. My fingers itch with the need to reach out and hold her.

"I don't see how that second one will help me."

"You can see it in her eyes. It's the way she sees the best in everyone," I tell her. "Even me."

Finally, she steps closer. Her shoulders shake in nervous, silent laughter. "You're here."

"So are you."

"I had a flight to catch, what's your excuse?"

"You."

"Really, no other reason? I'm not sure I'm worth the drive."

"As far as I'm concerned, you're the best reason to do anything." I say, then take a deep breath to steady myself. "Because I love you, Evelyn. I love you and the person I get to be because of you. I meant what I said, I'll be here to support you through these moments, as many as you have, because there's no limit to what I'll do when it comes to you," I tell her, freeing the emotion stored deep in my chest.

It took me far too long to learn that you can't make someone love you. You can be everything they need and it doesn't matter if you show up for them every time, they might never do the same.

Then one person finds you and their love is so loud you wonder why you craved anything quieter.

Evelyn chose me. And I get to choose how I love her. So, I'm going to love her out loud so there's no doubt in her mind about how I feel.

"I love you. Dammit. I love you too. And it scares me, but I know that's only because of how much I want this." Tears start to well in her eyes and she falls into me, her face pressing in the fabric of my sweater. "And I really hope you mean all of that because I think my life is about to get very intense."

My arms wrap around her, holding her and this moment as tightly as I can.

"Does that mean…" I let my words trail off.

"Yes, but I'd prefer that I don't leak my secret at JFK in front of an audience," she says, then pulls back from me to look around. Beyond the people in a rush, there are a few people waiting for rides that have definitely been listening in. "So, what if we go back to Hartsfall and talk?"

"I think that's a good idea."

Evelyn and I get her car from airport parking then drive it to the garage where she stores it so we can head back to Hartsfall together. We stay in the city for lunch, going to a Thai place she suggests. Under the table her leg stays pressed to mine. Each time one of us adjusts the other follows suit so we are always connected. She might have come back, but I don't have any intention of stopping myself from touching her to remind myself she's here.

"I'm pretty sure Thai is the sixth essential food group," she muses between a heaping fork full of flat Pad See Ew noodles.

I nod as I spear a piece of broccoli. "Yes, next to pizza, off-brand cereal, unlimited breadsticks, street tacos, and pasta."

"The USDA should hire us to make the newest graphic to show in schools."

"Because we are very qualified to do so," I agree.

"Exactly, now all I have to do is find the right email."

"The youth of America depend on it." My phone vibrates in my pocket. I put down my fork and I'm ready to silence the call and send a text that I'll call them back later until I see the caller ID.

"Emily?" I ask cautiously.

"Hey, Garrett," Emily's light, almost airy voice comes through. "I've got Alina here and she insisted that I call to tell you that she followed through on her end of the deal, whatever that means."

"Can you tell me how she is?" I ask.

"Yeah, she gave me permission to. Actually, she insisted on making sure you knew that it wasn't life threatening and I quote 'has done just fine without men telling her what to do.' It's a cold. I am suggesting vocal rest," Emily says, not sounding all that happy about playing messenger.

"I bet she loved the sound of that," I say.

"She was more compliant than you'd think, but after we got through that part of the discussion she told me to call. Oh, yes, the last bit of what she wanted me to tell you." She goes back to her notes. "Call Pat and fill in for her tomorrow at the festival."

"I appreciate how she found a way to make it my problem," I grumble.

"She told me if you said that to remind you that's what you like to do."

"Of course. Can you send me a list of anything I should pick up for her from the store?"

My phone buzzes with the incoming list then we say goodbye. I hang up and pinch my brow. There always has to be something, doesn't there? But at least now the most important things are taken care of.

"All good?"

"Alina might have just bribed a doctor to lie to me, or she's actually sick. I don't know which one is better."

"Is that legal? Actually, wait, don't answer that, I don't want to force you into accidentally lawyering."

I let loose a laugh. "Even if it isn't, I'm not sure that matters. If she wants something, she finds a way to get it. I need to call Pat and tell her the Love Letter Festival curse has struck again."

"Go make the call, I'll pay."

I go outside and call Pat who answers immediately and is already in festival crisis mode. I explain the situation as traffic zips by. After being in Hartsfall for nearly two months the speed of the city is slightly disorienting. It's hard to imagine going back to moving at that breakneck pace again.

"Oh, thank God." Pat sighs with relief.

"Interesting choice of response," I say.

"I mean, I've been waiting for something to go wrong. Everything going so smoothly up until now has been very concerning. You've got it handled?"

"Yeah. I have an idea or two." I spare a glance toward the restaurant door.

"Let me know if you need anything to make it work. Just remember no pyrotechnics," she says firmly. "I can't have another tree catching on fire."

"Wasn't that was ten years ago?" I ask, despite the fact that none of my ideas require fire.

"Yes, but Fletcher is still Fletcher."

"True." I'll give her that. "I'll let you know what I come up with."

"Bye, kid."

The door to the restaurant swings open as Evelyn pushes through. She tucks her arms tight to her body to brace against the gust of cool wind cutting through the air.

"Everything okay?" she asks when she's next to me.

"I think so," I answer as I mull over what we can do now that Alina isn't going to perform. "Evelyn, the fact that you're here means you've decided what you want, right?"

"Yes, I'm planning on calling up Vincent after the festival and letting him know. Why?" Her brows pull up quizzically.

"Depends on if you're willing to spend the rest of our day rehearsing classic love songs," I start, inviting her into my train of thought.

She presses a hand to my chest and looks up at me through her lashes. "Only if I get to decide how to use our breaks."

"I'm assuming we'll be emailing a custom graphic to the USDA," I say.

"Something like that," she murmurs. "Actually, something completely different. With no clothes."

"I was hoping so," I say. I pull her closer and run my hands up and down her arms to warm her up.

"Good. Because I'm vastly unqualified to educate anyone's children."

"I wasn't going to say anything but—" I start, but the rest of my words fall away as she kisses me on the sidewalk.

Mine. All mine.

48

Evelyn

"Y ou're sure about this?" Garrett asks.

"It's a little too late to change my mind," I say as I glance to my left.

The high school's band concludes its rendition of "Can't Help Falling in Love" and applause erupts from in front of the gazebo. The festival is contained within the limits of the town square. Shops have adopted more formal displays compared to what they had set up at the practice event over a week ago. Hand-painted menus and tablecloths in reds and pinks have been added. Closer to the gazebo are activities that can be accessed using tickets, including my abandoned face painting post.

"I think you have a good ten seconds," Garrett notes over the clamor.

"And if I say yes, are you going to run onto that stage and stop Pat?" I challenge.

"If that's what you want," he says, then pulls me to him. His hand lands splayed on my lower back before he continues in a husky tone. "I will calmly walk on to the stage and tell her you've changed your mind."

"See, this is why I keep you around." I press against him and pull his face to mine in a kiss.

When I let go, I find him smiling down at me. "I'll add conflict management next to novelty shirts on the list of things that turn you on."

Pat walks to the front as students start to pack up their instruments, music stands and chairs. "Thank you to Mr. Cohen and the students of Hartsfall High School for their performance." Pat continues on providing a brief history of the town and the festival.

"I'm still disappointed you aren't wearing the infamous wig." I reach up and brush a strand of his hair.

"If I get to perform next to you, I want to do it as I am with no synthetic hair."

"A shame. A damn shame that you are depriving me of my deepest desires."

Microphone feedback cuts through the moment as Pat continues, "Our live entertainment will continue with a special performance. For the last twenty years, Alina Nicolescu has graced us with her voice, and we want to thank her for it. In a last-minute program change we have asked another musical talent to step in. Please welcome Garrett Larson and, for the first time ever, Lyla West."

A breath catches in my throat. It's happening—it's really happening. It hits me far harder than it did when I called Vincent yesterday to move forward with the Reverb contracts and propose this reveal. He had less than twenty-four hours to get the go ahead from Reverb and set up all the necessary PR measures. There's no more planning. No more running.

I'm Lyla West, and it's time the world found out.

Whispers rise from the crowd with a frenzied energy, but the hushed words are impossible to pick out.

"Okay, let's go." I wipe my sweaty palms against my jeans and take a step forward.

Before I get any further, Garrett reaches out and spins me back to him. "One more thing."

His hands land on my hips and I instinctively wrap my arms around his neck. The kiss is quick, but it still manages to settle some of the nerves caught in my gut.

This wasn't the easy answer. If I wanted to, I could draw my anonymity out for a few more months until the album was officially released and Reverb could strategically use the reveal as a publicity stunt to boost sales overnight. I don't want to wait.

I want it all out in the open before I can shy away from one of the best things that's ever happened to me. After tonight, Garrett and I will go back to Nashville together to visit my parents and go through the explanations in person. I considered telling them before the performance, but I don't want them to talk me out of this.

The first thing I notice when I step on the stage is a sign being held up by three friendly faces. "Lyla West's biggest fans." Avery, Oliver, and Quinn are all beaming, which causes my heart to melt. Scanning the crowd, I spot more people I know and love.

They're here. My composure waivers as my knees go weak.

I turn away from the microphone to where Garrett is settling his cello between his thighs. "How is my family here?" I whisper.

There they are, mixed into the gathering crowd. Mom, Dad, Drew, and his girlfriend, Lacey. Pride shines from their expressions and the last of the knots in my stomach loosen.

"You only get to do this once. You deserve to have everyone you love cheering for you."

"How?" I ask in awe of the man I love.

This man who helped me gently find the courage to be on this stage. But that wasn't enough. He knew how important it was and made sure I could share it with the people I care about most in the world. There are a thousand ways to say I love you, and he's teaching me a new one every day.

He presses a kiss to my cheek. "I told them it would be important to you and that's all they needed to hear. You're a very easy person to show up for."

The back of my nose prickles with the threat of tears. I take a deep breath and readjust my feet to ground myself. There will be time to get choked up later. Right now, I'm going to give back to a town that I have completely fallen for.

I give Garrett a nod and he lowers his bow to play the first strains of "Funny Valentine." The energy around us swells in anticipation and when I join in I know I'm exactly where I need to be.

Once the song is over the cheers wash over us. The crowd is at full attention, cameras flashing to capture every second.

"We love you, Lyla!"

"I can't believe you're here!"

"It's really her. Oh my God. It's really her!"

It's a wave that crashes into me, and I can't contain the impossibly wide smile that stretches across my mouth. This is what I've been choosing to go without, feeling connected to so many people with something simultaneously so grand and simple as a song. I'm a part of this.

It's immeasurably better than seeing people dance to my music. Here, we're sharing this moment, one that I might be able to repeat, yet it can never be truly replicated. Love blooms from between my ribs. This is what I've been missing out on. These people. This feeling of being swept up in a collective experience that's only possible because of them. I'm already addicted to the high, and I won't be coming down any time soon.

"Hello, everyone, thank you for coming to Hartsfall's 52nd Love Letter Festival." My first few words come out as shaky as I feel. Singing old favorites is one thing, but what is coming next feels like handing over my heart. It's scary, but it's supposed to be, because I care. "I've been so lucky to spend my time here writing and becoming inspired. You never stop falling in Hartsfall. We have a few more surprises for you tonight. I have an album in the works, and it would be a shame to not share one of my favorite songs. So here is 'Stop Falling'. I hope you enjoy it."

There's a swell of commotion, cheers and whistles cut through the air. Behind me Garrett moves from his cello to take over at the piano.

Darling, hold my hand on the knife's edge.
Dance with me until we fall.

Spin me around again.
I won't break apart. I won't feel the fear,
As long as I'm the one you hold dear
Come with me over the edge.
Invite the rush of the wind and hope it never ends
Because I never want to stop falling, falling with you.

At the end of the performance my friends and family are waiting at the edge of the gazebo to be the first to talk to me. Avery's security personnel, a burly man and a stocky woman both wearing casual clothing but are identifiable from their wide stances, are likely the reason there's a good distance between us and the rest of the crowd.

My eyes sting and I stop holding onto the tears, good tears from my emotions overflowing and needing to find a way to leak out. Everyone waits their turn for hugs.

"Are you mad?" I whisper into my brother's ear as he wraps his arms around me.

"Only that you have more Grammys than I do."

"I'm just getting started," I promise.

"Good."

"If you're ever ready, I want to write a song with you." I brace myself as the words fall from my lips.

"The moment I am you'll be my first call," he agrees, and I'm hit with that same aching relief. We'll get there, back to the place where we can talk through the songs we share. It might not be soon, but eventually is all I need.

I step away and look at Avery. I can tell she's doing her best to not to say *"I told you so,"* but it's right there in the curve of her smirk. If she did say it, she'd be right. The hug she gives me is absolutely bone crunching and an "oof" escapes my lips before I return the hug.

"I wouldn't have any of this without you, you know?"

"I do, but you wouldn't have any of this without you either. I just struck the match. You took it and lit the fuse," she says.

"I'm ready to set the world on fire," I promise, and she squeezes me tighter.

"You know this means you could open for us on tour at a show or two."

"I would like that," I say. I know it will take more than a simple yes to make it work. After today there will be a lot to juggle, but I'll make the effort for her. Without her generous shove toward my passions five years ago I wouldn't be here. I glance over to Garrett. This is the life that brought me into his orbit.

The air goes stiff as I turn to my parents. The last time we talked it wasn't great. I said what I needed to but there's so much more we need to discuss.

"Later," Mom says, as if reading my mind. "Tonight is for celebrating. Tomorrow is for fixing things."

"Thank you." Tonight is the start of so many things and the end of others. My relationship with my parents has been frozen in time, locking me in their minds as sixteen for fourteen years. Time is finally starting back up and we'll need to decide what that looks like together.

I shake my head as I turn to the final pair.

"I thought you both were desperate to get out of here. I ask you to stay and you say no. Garrett asks, and you come right back? Should I be worried I'm getting replaced?" I muse.

"Funny thing happened. We got off the plane, got this text explaining things and we had no choice but to come right back. Your friend only ever has one performance where she outs her real identity to the world," Oliver explains.

"That and the blueberry wine," Quinn adds wryly, holding up a plastic cup. "I came back for the blueberry wine."

"How many flights have you taken for me at this point?"

Quinn makes a show of counting on her fingers. "By the time we go back it will be four."

"Don't worry, when you start touring you can just get us the most expensive tickets for free," Oliver says, shoving his hands into his pockets.

"They're yours. Your sisters are welcome too, Ollie, just say the word," I promise.

Every show. Every moment. Every triumph and pitfall. If they want to be there, I will invite them in.

I have wasted so much time dwelling on the worst-case scenarios in the back of my mind that I never let myself consider how good it would be if it all worked out. And it feels like this.

It feels like knowing this is just the beginning of so many moments that will string together for us to look back on and find them shining like Christmas lights.

The moment breaks as a crowd starts to form, I hear both my name and cheers calling for Lyla growing louder. I turn to find Fletcher and Pat attempting to hold the people at bay as they attempt to shove forward.

I reach out and take Garretts's hand then say, "Don't let go," before I take off running. He runs with me for a few feet before tugging me to a halt and lifting me in his arms. Then he carries me away from the crowd and all the rest of the way to the rental house.

49

Evelyn

Mist blankets the town, making the morning feel suspended in time as if it would last forever with all of my favorite people crammed inside one house. Last night, Mom and Dad took the largest bedroom, Drew and Lacey took the guest room, and the rest of us crammed into the living room on the couch and an ancient air mattress we found in the linen closet.

I'd woken up in the middle of the night, nose to nose with Garrett and said, "I did it."

"You did it," he'd said, and I'd cried. I'd cried silent tears of relief in the arms of the man I love while everyone slept around us.

We all have to be out by this afternoon. Alina has rented the house to a couple who are expecting to love their stay as much as I have. She offered to let us stay in her house, but I think this is supposed to end. Or maybe this is how it's supposed to begin.

Avery is the first to leave. Technically, she was going to leave last night but something made her stay. I pull her into one last hug before she steps off the porch.

"I'm going to perform with you one day. It's going to be fucking great and we're going to wear so much glitter," she says into my messy hair.

"We are and it's going to be amazing," I say as my throat thickens.

"Because you're amazing. I'm just so happy you're being brave enough to share this part of you." With those words she pulls away.

I wait until her car turns off Austen Dr. before I head inside. Everyone is up and cluttered around the table with their various cups of coffee. Lacey brought her own coffee maker; a cheap one she used to brew coffee. It smells foul but she seems to like it.

"I'm going to get pastries in town. Who wants to come with me?" Quinn asks with a pointed look around the room.

"I'm good," Oliver says, then there's a light thud under the table. He straightens in his chair and mugs clatter on the table. "You know what? I would actually love to get up and move."

That's all the convincing everyone else needs to vacate the room, leaving only me and my parents.

As he passes by, Drew squeezes my shoulder. "I have a good feeling about this."

"That makes one of us," I joke. I feel okay about this. Not great, but definitely okay.

I said what I needed to get out in the moment during the last time Mom and I talked, letting out feelings that have festered for years until they turned ugly.

"I forgot how beautiful your voice was," Mom says, her voice hesitant as I feel.

"I'm sorry," I start, still feeling shaky despite how much practice I've gotten talking about this recently.

Dad shakes his head then sets down his mug shaped like a giant blueberry. "No. Don't apologize. Never apologize for something you do so well."

"But I am sorry," I say. Not for music. I make a silent promise to myself to never feel sorry for my music ever again. "I could have told you, maybe this would be different if I had."

"Maybe it would be different. I wanted to help you and your brother, but I didn't know when to stop. You're all grown up…but I remember when I had you, all I wanted was my mother, but she was so far away," Mom says. God, she looks so old in the gray morning light. My strong mother who tirelessly still takes care of us and looks out for us even as adults when she did so much of this on her own when her and Dad came from Italy. I ache for her and the woman she was, raising two kids and sharing her love of music that reminded her of home. "I'm glad you made your choice before we learned the truth. This way I can't try to save you from your dream. You forced me to think why you'd hide anything in the first place. I wasn't doing the saving, you were. You were saving yourself and us."

"You did such a good job," I say. "I could have done a better job."

"You shouldn't have had to in the first place," Dad says. "*Ti voglio bene.*"[1]

My eyes blur and then I'm wrapped in their arms.

I'm safe. I'm loved.

"I'm so proud of you," Mom murmurs as she tenderly strokes my hair. Tears spill from my eyes as my heart bursts.

I always told myself I'd be fine without hearing those words from her. I'd convinced myself for so many years I was happy doing this alone. I'm starting to lose count of how many times I've been proven wrong over the last few days.

We talk a little longer and once we've had a moment to collect ourselves, I text Drew.

Evelyn

You guys can come back now.

Drew

Everything ok?

Evelyn

Not perfect yet. But really good

The day remains hazy, but the rental feels like a lighthouse with how it glows with the joy radiating off it. Throughout the day people head out. First Drew and Lacey, who are going to visit her friend who's a professor upstate. Then my parents leave in the early afternoon. Oliver and Quinn linger as long as possible before leaving for the fourth, and hopefully last, flight of their trip. I promise to visit.

---

1. I love you.

"Are you ready?" Garrett calls from the doorway to where I'm standing by the piano. Most of my bags are still in my car from the last time I tried to leave and his are waiting by the door next to our shoes.

I shake my head. "There's one last thing we need to do." My fingers float over the closed key cover. Meg is getting picked up in the morning and Alina has promised to let me know when the piano is headed back to the city. "It feels wrong to finish the album anywhere else."

It would be a betrayal to the house that saw us through it all to not let it witness this last memory.

"I agree." Garrett steps up behind me and runs his hand down my spine then rests it on my hip. "Have you decided how it ends?"

"I think life decided for us," I say.

"Oh, really?" I tilt my head up to look at him. The smile on his lips tells me he knows the answer but he wants me to be the one to say it.

I lean back into him. "You're my happiest possible ending. Remember?"

"How could I forget?" he asks, reaching past me to uncover the keys. His hand dips down to play the first chord.

For the last time, the house fills with music. It sounds like forever, it sounds like us.

Evelyn

1 YEAR LATER

"What does it feel like coming off the final leg of your first tour?" Clement Meryl asks as he leans over his mic.

The *Get Out of My Head* podcast studio is designed to be comfortable and allow guests to unwind. Clement and Walt share one of the blue mid-century modern couches while I share the other with Garrett. A custom green neon sign in the shape of the show's logo is mounted on the wall over the hosts.

"I feel like I'm ready for a very long nap. I think I might start experimenting with hibernation," I say as I stretch my arms over my head so I can loop one around Garrett as he sits beside me.

"So, you're not jumping into your next album?" Walt asks a new version of the same question they've asked three times already, but I don't mind all that much.

"Stop Falling" peaked at number one on the charts for six weeks and has remained on the *Hot 100* since it was released eight months ago. I know some of the success was due to me unveiling myself as Lyla West. I'm already talking to Vincent about using my real name for whatever comes next. I love Lyla, she's been a part of me for so long that it was hard to accept I needed to say goodbye. She gave me so much, but I have to do this as myself.

"There are few things in the works, but it's time to trade places in the spotlight," I say, looking at Garrett.

His first solo album is set to be announced at the end of the week. We've been writing together whenever we feel like it, which is nearly every day. Writing isn't the same as it was, it's more. The shift isn't only due to Garrett, though, it's great to be able to work with someone who is able to complete my thoughts before I finish them and push me further than I thought possible.

Being able to connect with my fans and the people who listen to my music has added so much to my life. Sure, there are plenty of people still criticizing the way I went about starting my career. As I feared, journalists and bloggers picked apart my connections, looking at my relationships with Fool's Gambit and Avery. At the same time, there have been just as many people coming to my defense saying that as Lyla I proved my talent without leaning on the people in my life publicly. There will always be that push and pull, but having Garrett, my family, and my friends to talk about it more openly than I used to makes it manageable. We're still work-ing through maintaining healthy lines of communication. It's been an active effort to not keep things to myself, but that also means I get to share my wins with them too.

"Speaking of which, Garrett, how are you adjusting back into the industry after your time away?" Walt asks.

Garrett shifts next to me. I smile every time I look at him. I do in general, but yesterday I finally won a chess game and today I'm reaping the reward. He's wearing a shirt that says *I heart my girlfriend*, with the heart drawn out. It matches my shirt that says *Girlfriend*. There's a video recording of the podcast that will be released and I'm not above reminding everyone we're together.

"It's nice to not feel pressured to wear skinny jeans any-more," he says dryly. "Being back has been good, in general. Part of the reason I held off on it was because I thought I'd be doing it alone, instead of with bandmates. Obviously, I'm not alone in it." His eyes jump to mine and hold before returning to the hosts.

"What is it like working together?" Clement takes his turn with this question. "From a listener's perspective, there was this new energy to it all that we got to experience. Give us some insight into behind the scenes. Do you both always agree on creative directions and artistic choices?"

"Always agreeing on things would be so boring," I tell them. "If we always agreed we would never have ended up here in the first place. The first time we ever went out as a couple we went to this berry farm, Barlowe Berry Farm in the Hudson Valley. Really, if you have the chance you have to visit, you should. The owners told us something that's stuck with me: we don't compromise, we collaborate. We both know what we're doing with music, and we communicate the best we can to elevate what we already know."

"That, and I like giving her what she wants," Garrett says.

"That too." I look up at him and when his eyes meet mine it feels like there's no one else in the room.

The interview lasts for another hour between the rest of their questions and a friendly chat after. We would have stayed longer because I got sucked into the conversation as I tend to do, but Garrett reminded me we would be running late.

"I really am looking forward to seeing you in a wig," I tell him as I slide into the passenger seat of my SUV. His truck is at Fletcher's garage, needing a new round of repairs. It will probably last a few more months, so I've been looking for another of the exact make and model but less wear for sale.

"Is there any way you'll forget in the two hours it takes us to get there."

"Absolutely not, I've been holding on to this dream for a year. It's the only reason I've stayed with you." I act aghast, holding my hand to my mouth in exaggerated horror.

"If I hold off then I get to keep you longer?"

"You get to keep me anyway." I reach over and squeeze his thigh. Before I pull my hand away he catches it and keeps it there. "And you get to see me in a wig, too."

We won't be performing this year at the festival, but we want to next year if we can make the proper preparations for security and ensure it won't disrupt the festival itself. Instead, we'll be attending with the help of cheap disguises, Garrett already has his and I ordered myself a blonde wig and massive sunglasses for mine. Since we didn't get to experience it fully last year, I've been thinking about our trip back to Hartsfall nonstop for the last few weeks. Garrett has been able to go back to visit and help with his usual assortment of odd jobs. I had planned on joining him for Christmas, but my flight got canceled.

We talk and listen to music for the rest of the drive until we pull up to a familiar Victorian house on Austen Dr.. It's exactly the same as the last time I saw it with its little white fence, bay windows, and porch that was designed to be relaxed on. For a moment, I feel like I'm dreaming and that this last year never happened. This isn't the first time I've felt like this. There have been nights where I forget what city I'm in because everything feels too good to be true and my body tricks me into thinking I never had any of it. On those nights, I'll roll over to see Garrett there and remember I belong right next to him.

The festival is just as magical as I remember. Blueberry wine stains my tongue as the hours fly by. We get our faces painted with hearts before we slow dance with the other couples enjoying the live music. I almost breeze past the letter writing station, but Garrett pulls me to it.

"I don't need another one," I tell him and it's the truth. He's given me enough for a lifetime. Sometimes we still opt to use calendar invites instead of texts.

> Can you come get the remote, I'm too comfortable: Tuesday, 11 a.m. - 11:10 a.m. @ The Couch

> People watching at The MET: Wednesday, 10 a.m. - 3:30 p.m. @ Meet you downstairs.

> I miss you, that's it. I miss you: Sunday, All Day Event @ Right Here

"So many of our love letters have been heard by the entire world. I'm going to write one just for you," he says as if he hasn't done enough.

After gathering the materials from Haven, who gives me a conspiratorial once over because of the wig, we find spots on opposite sides of the booth. I'm still working to write down every last word that comes to mind when I look up to find that Garrett is already folding his. Several minutes later, I fold mine up and seal it with the wax that Haven has to add a special touch.

"Here," I say, handing my letter to Garrett.

"If I give you yours you have to promise to wait to open it."

"Wait until when?" I question.

"You'll know."

"Okay."

He hands over the letter and I put it in my back pocket. My curiosity over its contents quickly fades. I know how he feels about me. We tell each other in so many ways. It's in the songs we write and the moments when we don't talk at all. I'm comfortable with him in silence or in a crowd.

The streets are nearly empty by eleven. Business owners are packing up and we do our best to help with breaking down the folding tables and decorations. I think we both want the night to stretch as long as possible. I know I do. We're collecting plastic cups with blueberry wine that festival goers have left stranded all over the square.

"Shit," Garrett hisses as he loses his grip on one and it spills down his shirt, dark blue staining the white.

"You did that on purpose," I say.

"And why on earth would I ruin my new favorite shirt?"

I roll my eyes in faux annoyance. There's nothing I can do to hide how elated I am about today.

"Give me the cups you have. I'll toss these and clean up a bit," he says as he extends a hand to stack my cups in his. "You know what I've been wondering?"

"What?"

"If there's still that nest in the gazebo."

"I'll go check," I say as my attention flicks to the structure in question. "Meet you there?"

"Yeah."

I slowly make my way to the gazebo, occasionally bending down to pick up trash and put it into the trash cans that have been brought out for the event. The streetlamps cast a blanket of warm light on the area.

Once inside the gazebo, I tilt my head up and slowly spin. The nest is still there, but of course, the birds we saw last year are gone. There are also no new hatchlings. I guess that's natural. We move on.

"I found a replacement shirt, but I'm not sure how to feel about it," Garrett says, and I turn to face him.

My voice catches as I read the words. "Why's that?"

"I'm not sure if it's accurate. Before you say anything, read the letter. Please."

I've hung on to this paper for weeks waiting to figure out what to say. If this is going to be the first love letter you ever get, I want it to be perfect.

I read the first two lines then pause as I realize this isn't the one he wrote earlier today. My vision starts to swim with tears, but I force them back so I can read the rest.

You're it. I've known it for so long but I don't know how to change who we are to each other. I guess, if you're reading this, I figured out how.

The thing is, when I look at you, I'm speechless. Words don't do you justice, so how can I? Maybe it's the way you try to make everyone laugh with you or that you don't look away when other people would. Then there's the way you sing and make music. You make me understand why sailors believed in sirens that could sing them into oblivion. I would be honored to drown in you.

"I'm sorry I waited so long to give it to you," he says.

I have to swallow the emotions gathering in my throat before I can say, "It aged like fine wine."

"I'd hoped it would."

Garrett gets on one knee in the center of the gazebo and I reread the shirt he's changed into. *I heart my fiancée.*

"Will you marry me?" he asks, and I'm already nodding. There's never been anything I've wanted more to say yes to. I want our forever.

"Only if you have a matching shirt for me." My voice warbles through the press of gathering tears.

"There's one waiting for you on the bed at the house."

"Yes, Garrett Larson. I will marry the shit out of you," I say and seal my words with a kiss.

The clock tower doesn't chime because it is too late for it to be rung. In the morning, we'll share the news and the engagement counter on the welcome sign will go up from 6087 to 6088.

I've tripped right over the edge, and I never want to stop falling.

Acknowledgements

This book taught me more than I could have dreamed of, but also brought me closer to so many people who made Evelyn and Garrett's story possible.

First to my mother, thank you for picking up the phone and always being ready to talk about plot holes and then my subsequent frustrations with those plot holes. I can't fully express how it feels knowing that you talk about my characters like they're real people to our family, though I also hope they never read the piano scene.

Vai and Miah, you have stuck with me through every draft and voice memo. You're the reason I didn't give up. You talked me through scrapping so many drafts, and then celebrated with me as this final iteration came to life. I can't wait to do it all again with the next book.

Courtney, thank you for reading every version of this and cheering me on the entire way. You were a spot of sunshine when I truly needed it.

Brooke and D.J., thank you both for reading the first version of this story and believing in it when I was struggling to make the pieces click.

Elisa, Julia, and Kaily, Evelyn wouldn't be the same without you and the experiences you shared with me about being second generation Americans.

My lovely early readers, Ada, Georgia, Kie, Tori, and Riley, your excitement and feedback fueled me through edits. Your advice gave me the push I needed to make changes I was desperate to avoid. Everyone, thank Ada for "atta girl" and "good boy."

Sabrina, thank you for sharing your expertise as a trauma therapist as I wrote my favorite people pleasers and gave them a happy ending.

Hartsfall would be far less exciting without Jen! Jen, it was an absolute delight to talk to you about the Hudson Valley and New York.

Dear reader, please note that any inaccuracies are my mistakes, not the fault of anyone who was gracious enough to collaborate with me.

About the Author

Marja is an author from Northern New Mexico, and though she doesn't live there now, she'll always claim the mountains as her home. She writes big stories built on a foundation small moments. If she's not writing or reading, she's desperately wishing to nap in the sun.